The
Note

BOOKS BY CARLY SCHABOWSKI

The Ringmaster's Daughter
The Watchmaker of Dachau
The Rainbow

CARLY SCHABOWSKI

The Note

bookouture

Published by Bookouture in 2022

An imprint of Storyfire Ltd.
Carmelite House
50 Victoria Embankment
London EC4Y 0DZ

www.bookouture.com

ISBN: 978-1-80019-958-3
eBook ISBN: 978-1-8001-995-7-6

This book is a work of fiction. Whilst some characters and circumstances
portrayed by the author are based on real people and historical fact, references
to real people, events, establishments, organizations or locales are intended
only to provide a sense of authenticity and are used fictitiously. All other
characters and all incidents and dialogue are drawn from the author's
imagination and are not to be construed as real.

For my sister and my friend Yasmin, whose humor and kindness means more to me than you will ever know.

PROLOGUE

It was as if I had fallen into the depths of hell itself. I looked about me, waiting to see if the devil from a picture book I had read as a child would appear. I prayed to God to lift me up out of here, but I stood, looking at the bodies piled high in the pit, the sun beating down on me as if it were trying to get through my skin and burn me from the inside out.

"I don't want to do this," I said.

"You think you have a choice?" he asked. Then he laughed and looked at the bodies. "You have a choice, yes. What do you choose?"

He aimed his gun at me now. "Do you want to join them?" He nodded at the naked burning corpses.

I shook my head and walked toward the half-dead man, picking up his body to carry into the flames.

I had a choice, and I knew deep down I was a coward and had chosen badly.

ONE

ALICE

It was the evening of my thirteenth birthday in the summer of 1953, and the South Carolina heat was as thick as Gammy's honey. Overweight clouds colluded angrily to create the perfect summer storm, and indoors, ceiling fans swish-swished, flapping at net curtains, pulling strands of hair out of tied-back ponytails, and forced condensation on glasses to drip quicker and quicker toward polished side tables.

I lay on the porch in my blue cotton dress, my skinny arms and legs jutting out like bare sticks, my hair fanned out behind me, and waited for the inevitable storm that would clear the air and give us some respite from the fever that had grasped us all.

"It won't come yet," my older brother, Billy, assured me.

I looked up at him and watched as he climbed onto the porch swing, an iced tea in his hands.

"Where'd you get that?" I asked, sitting up.

"Mom just made some."

"She never shouted for me." I stood now, indignant at being left out.

"That's probably because I'm her favorite." Billy grinned.

I stuck my tongue out at him, a childish gesture for someone who had just turned thirteen, but I had no other comeback and Billy knew it. If I had dared to play-punch him in the arm, or tell on him, he would fight me, tickle me, and then rub my head and say, "You should have been born a boy."

As I walked away, Billy grabbed my arm. "Hey, wait a minute. Come sit with your big bro."

I shook my arm free from his grasp, feeling the sweat from his palm still on my skin. "You need to wash, you're disgusting," I told him, and wiped the dampness from my arm.

"Sit!" he commanded, but he had a smile on his face, like Pops did when he had drunk two beers.

I squeezed in next to him on the porch swing and, with tiptoes, pushed it backwards to get it rocking. Billy, for once, mirrored me, and we sat for a few minutes happily swinging back and forth.

"You're a teenager," he finally said.

"Yup. And so are you."

"I'm almost a man." He nudged me with his shoulder. "I'll be at college next year. You'll miss me."

"I won't." I placed my feet flat on the wooden porch and stopped the swing. "And you're not a man. You still read those stupid comic books. Men don't do that."

I stood and looked at him. His smile had gone, his thin lips pressed together in a straight line, his green catlike eyes on me as if he were waiting for my next move.

"Here," he said, and handed me his iced tea. "Tell Mom I'm going to study at Carl's."

The glass was cold under my fingertips, and I wasn't sure whether he was trying to trick me. But the punch, the chase, or the putdown didn't come. He stood and walked down the porch steps, whistling a song.

I watched as the taillights from Pops' old truck disappeared down the street, sitting alone, still not drinking the iced tea, wondering why he was being nice to me and why I had to ruin it.

After a few minutes, I made my way to the backyard and climbed up the ladder to my treehouse, splinters from the coarse wood that Pops had used to build it biting into my palm. Once at the top, I clambered up, then sat heavily, disturbing the dust so that it lifted into the warm air and swam around me, dancing in the disappearing light. I lit one of the small gas lamps that Gammy had given me, careful not to burn myself with the match. Then I set about pulling out the few splinters of wood in my palm with my teeth, spitting them out one by one.

"You up there, Alice?" Clemmie was climbing up.

"You know I am."

Her round face appeared, red and sweaty, then she hauled herself in so that she lay flat on her belly for a moment before rolling over and staring above her.

Mikey was next; he was quick, agile, and leaped into the treehouse followed by George, whose feet were encased in his slippers.

"I forgot," he said, as he saw me eyeing them.

"More like your mom was putting you to bed before nine." Mikey lit a cigarette as he spoke.

"You shouldn't do that," Clemmie whined. She was sitting now and shuffled back so her spine was against the wall of the treehouse, wafting her hand in front of her face as Mikey smoked.

"No one will know. Don't be such a baby, Clem."

"Where'd you get them?" George asked, eyeing the cigarette like a cat eyes a mouse.

"Pa left them out. I took a couple."

"He'll whip you if he finds out." Clemmie had folded her arms now, reminding me of the school principal who always looked at us with utter disappointment.

"Y'all be quiet now, unless you want my parents up here." I took control. "Besides, it's my birthday, so you gotta be nice."

"It's almost over." Mikey blew out a stream of smoke, then squinted his eyes, which were already watering.

"It's still my birthday," I said, then leaned forward. "You know, this time thirteen years ago, Momma was already in labor with me!"

"You're gross." Mikey play-punched me in my arm.

"Ewww." George shuffled back to sit next to Clemmie, scrunching up his face as if he had had a spoonful of castor oil.

"What's so disgusting? We all came out that way, you know," I retorted.

"You're thirteen. You can't talk like that when you're thirteen," Clemmie said. "Momma says we're ladies now and we gotta act like them."

"I ain't ever gonna be a lady," I said, making sure I spoke like Mikey did, shortening and bludgeoning each word so it sounded like I came from the other side of town.

"You got that right." Mikey smirked at me.

"What did you bring?" I asked.

Mikey dug around in his knapsack and brought out a bottle of lemonade, a slice of cake, and more cigarettes. George followed suit and produced candy, with Clemmie offering up two apples and an orange.

"Why did you bring fruit?" Mikey asked. "It's meant to be a birthday party!"

"Mom says you have to eat fruit. She says that if I eat cake and candy, then my teeth will fall out," Clemmie countered. "I don't want to lose my teeth," she mumbled.

Mikey shook his head at her and, with an act of defiance, took a large bite of the cake, spilling crumbs down his chest.

"You know who's got no teeth?" he asked, his voice muffled with cake.

"Who?" Clemmie was already reaching for the candy bar, the apple next to her forgotten for now.

"That German. You know the one. He lives on Mulberry Street."

"He's got teeth!" George said. "I've seen him."

"When?" Mikey challenged.

"Outside church. He was walking past, and he didn't look like he had no teeth."

"Well, how you gonna know? Did he smile at you? I bet he didn't. It's because he has no teeth," Mikey said.

"You're always saying stuff about him," I said. "You just make it up. Or you say what your pa says."

Mikey ignored me and bit into the cake some more. I didn't want him to talk about the German man again. Since he had arrived a year or so before, he was always telling tales about him, trying to scare us, and as much as I didn't want to admit it to Mikey, it had scared me.

"It's true. All of it. He's a crippled old man, bent at the waist, with skinny fingers that have long yellowing nails. He shuffles when he walks, his long black coat dragging in the dirt. He spits at you if you say hello, and he snarls at babies in their buggies, making them wail in fear."

"You've said hello to him?" Clemmie asked, leaning forward, her eyes wide.

"I sure have. Loads of times."

"You're lying," George said. "I seen him once. He never goes out."

"That's coz he only goes out at night, dummy." Mikey lit another cigarette. He squinted when the smoke got caught in his eyes, then coughed. "He only goes out then so he don't scare everyone."

"Since when do you go out at night alone?" I asked. Mikey was always full of it.

"Always. When I can't sleep. I've seen him in the graveyard

sitting by graves and whispering things to them. Pa says he's trying to raise the dead."

"Well, Pops says that he is a refugee from the war and we should be nice to him." I really wanted Mikey to stop now. If he carried on, I knew I would have nightmares. "You got any more cake?" I tried to steer Mikey away from the German.

Mikey handed over the cake, which was sticky and filled with strawberry jam. "Where'd you get this?" I asked.

Mikey simply grinned at me—I knew it had come from somewhere that it shouldn't. I shook my head at him.

"We need to do some upgrades," he said, his eyes darting about the treehouse.

He was right. The wooden slats that Pops had used left big gaps in between, which on a night as hot as this wasn't a bad thing really, but in winter when we sat playing cards, the wind whistled through and made our fingers turn red, then white.

"Like what?" George was on all fours, his hand reaching toward the last bit of cake, which he eagerly grabbed, then tore in half and handed some to Clem.

"Like cover up all the holes, get a door."

"Ooh!" Clem was excited. "We could get curtains and a rug maybe! Make it all cozy."

"I ain't talking about making it a girly house!" Mikey said. "I saw that Freddie had this new treehouse, and it had a door, and a proper roof—not like that tin thing you got now."

I didn't disagree with him. The tin roof was made from scraps that Pops had salvaged from work, and some had red paint on them, some yellow, and some just ugly gray. And, when it rained, it was like we were under fire—bullets raining down on us—and so we always left the treehouse as we couldn't hear each other talk.

Clem was whispering something to George and he blushed, then saw me looking and moved a little away from her.

"You guys still up there?" Mom's voice sang from the yard.

I stuck my head out. "We're gonna sleep here tonight."

"I've got the porch all made up," she yelled. "Get your butts down here and to somewhere I can keep an eye on you."

It was pointless to argue with her, and I nodded, then dipped back inside.

"She don't trust me, that's what it is," Mikey said.

"It's Pops," I countered. "He says I'm too old to have sleep-overs in here now."

"Yeah, coz of me."

"Why, what does he think you will do?" Clem asked him.

Mikey grinned, then shot out of the door and clambered down the ladder. "Last one inside is a sissy!" he shouted up.

No one wanted to be a sissy, and we followed suit, not caring about the splinters on the ladder anymore, and raced to the porch.

George was last.

"Sissy!" we sang at him as he sat sulking on the swing.

It took a while to bring George round, but with the promise of more cake from Mom and glasses of lemonade with extra sugar, he seemed to brighten and joined in with our talk of what else we could do that summer.

"We gotta do something," Mikey whined. "I mean, playing cards and going round town on our bikes is fun, but school will start back up before we know it and we ain't done shit."

"Don't say shit," Clem admonished.

"Why not? You just did."

"I did not say shit." Clem put her hands on her hips so that she looked like a mini version of her mom. "You said shit, and I said not to say shit."

"You just said it three times!" Mikey rolled about laughing on the floor. "Say it again, Clem, say it again!"

Although Clem was upset she knew, as we did, that Mikey was quicker than us. He was brighter in some ways—not in school ways and learning, but he could outwit a fox if he wanted to. The way he crinkled his eyes when you spoke made you always wonder what he was thinking about and whether you had just fallen into some sort of trap. He had tiny silver scars on his cheeks that you could only see when the light was right, which he had gotten the time his pa had driven drunk and hit a tree, causing the windscreen to fall in onto Mikey. He said the scars made him look tough, but I knew that he really hated them. I'd always liked them though, and wanted to touch them and see what they felt like, but Mikey would never let me.

Everyone at school, including the teachers, were a bit scared of Mikey—wary was the word that Pops used sometimes. He was unpredictable, but what they didn't understand—and what Clem, George, and I did—was that he was only like that when his pa was drunk. And besides, he was always fun with us, and he always made sure that no one bullied George because of his thick glasses and the occasional stutter he got when he was nervous.

"I'm not saying it again," Clem said, and began to unroll the thin mattresses Mom had put out for us to sleep on whilst George fastened shut the fly screens that ran across the length of the porch, something I was supposed to have done sooner.

I smacked a small mosquito just as it tried to suck on my arm, happy to see that once dead it was empty of blood—he hadn't managed to bite anyone yet.

"Remember last summer?" Mikey asked us, holding a cigarette in his hands but not lighting it. "Remember how we went out every day on that raft we built on the lake, and how we made treasure maps and stuff; that was a good summer."

"We could do it again," Clem said authoritatively.

"We could. But we'd have to build another raft because you and George sank the last one."

"I didn't sink it," George said, wafting his hands above his head where a few moths spun madly around the bare bulb, singeing their wings. "It was an accident. Clem was scared, so I tried to get us closer to the bank."

"And you sank it," Mikey concluded.

"It doesn't matter," I said. "We can do it again. Build another one?"

"Yeah, maybe," Mikey said. "I dunno—I just want to do something new this time."

"But you just said that last year was fun." Clem was getting comfortable on her mattress, patting her hair in such a way that I could see exactly what she would be like in forty years' time. "We could go to the church camp," she suggested. "Mom says I can go if I want to."

"Mine too," George agreed, still wafting at the moths so vigorously that he had to stop every few seconds and push his spectacles back up his nose.

"You'd best stop that," I said. "You'll not kill the moth, but you'll break your glasses again."

George looked at me. "You're right," he said, and made his way to his mattress and sat down, taking off his glasses and inspecting the arm that had recently been mended with a bit of old electrical tape. "Mom says she's not buying me new ones for another six months and that I gotta stop dropping them all the time."

"You'd better look after them." Mikey stood up. "Otherwise, you'll be all blind and walking around like this!" Mikey shut his eyes, stretched his arms out in front of him and bashed into the railing, then the swing, then pretended to trip over George and landed on top of him.

"Four eyes, four eyes!" Mikey sang out, whilst George wriggled underneath him.

"Get off me!" he squealed. "I can't breathe! I'll die. You'll see, you'll kill me!"

"If you can't breathe, then how you talking?" Mikey asked, and George immediately shut up.

Clem and I thought it was funny and soon piled on top of Mikey, making a giant sandwich whilst George started to scream and mosquitoes picked at our bare legs.

Finally, we moved off him, and Clem gave him a hug to say sorry, even though we were all still laughing at him.

"Don't worry, George." Mikey lay down on his mattress, folding his arms under his head. "No one's gonna kill you. No one is gonna die tonight."

TWO

ALICE

I fell asleep soon after Clem and George, and could still hear Mikey saying something to me as I drifted further downwards, until I was in a strange dream where I found myself standing on a lonely road. I could only hear the buzzing of mosquitoes in my ears and feel them biting me, but I couldn't see them. I tried to run away from them, further down the dark street, but no matter how far I ran, I never left the road.

Then there were sirens instead of mosquitoes, and I stopped running and looked about me to see if I could find out where they were coming from.

"Al!" Mikey was calling to me.

"Al, wake up!"

Slowly, I felt myself being pulled through that strange membrane between sleep and wakefulness.

"Al!"

I opened my eyes, still feeling as though I were in the dream where the sirens yelled on that strange road.

"I can't get off the road," I said to Mikey, who was pulling at my arm to make me sit up.

It was then that I woke fully. The sirens were real, and

getting closer. Mikey, George, and Clem were fiddling with the
locked porch door, and Pops and Mom had joined them.

"Get up, Al!" Mikey said excitedly. "There's a police
chase!"

Pops mumbled something to Mikey about it not being a
police chase, but that didn't dampen anyone's excitement, and
all of them filed out onto the front lawn to watch as first a police
car shot past our house and then an ambulance.

I anxiously joined them, not feeling thrilled at the sudden
disquiet. Millford, after all, was a town where nothing
happened. It was a community of hardworking dusty mill-
workers and loggers, whose main hobby was going to church
and getting ready to go to church, yet whose real religion was
following the ball games and football season at the high school,
when all the town would congregate to cheer the players to
victory. Indeed, it had worked; whether through their prayers
or their chanting at the games, the school's teams were revered
in this part of the county. The only crime that had occurred in
the recent past was when Mr. Fitzgerald took umbrage at
something that had been said to him in the diner about his
son's behavior at school and his performance at a Friday night
football game. It had ended with a few loose punches thrown
and a night in the cell with Sheriff Howard, and still people
talked about it as if Mr. Fitzgerald had tried to murder
the man.

Another police car brought up the rear and then turned to
follow the others toward Homer's lake.

"What in God's name?" my mother said.

"I'm sure it's nothing." Pops held her hand, trying to assuage
her fear, but I could see that deep crease in his forehead, the one
he only ever got when he was mad or when something was
wrong.

Pops told us to stay put, ran quickly inside and then sat on
the porch dragging on his heavy work boots. Mom followed him

inside, then raced back out, covering her nightshirt with a yellow rain mac.

Other neighbors were already moving toward the sound and the lights as if it were controlling them, beckoning them, and I, too, could feel the draw of the mystery that was unfolding near the lake.

Our neighbor, Larry, was half running down the street, his blue and white striped dressing gown flapping in the wind.

"I hope he's got something on underneath that," Mikey joked.

Another neighbor, a man Pops had gone to school with and whom we had to call Big Jake, stood on his porch with his shotgun in his hands, and I wondered what he thought he might be called to do. Big Jake, whilst as large as his name suggested, both tall and rotund, was as gentle as the stray dog that scrapped about the town's streets, making everyone and no one his owner.

"Stay here," Pops warned us all, and followed Larry with Mom at his heels.

Mikey waited a beat, then ran after them. "Come on!" he yelled back at us. "Come on, you sissies!"

I looked at George and could see my worried reflection in his glasses, then to Clem, who despite being a scaredy-cat was looking eagerly toward the lake.

"Last one there's a sissy!" Mikey called out, his laugh ringing out manically.

In an unspoken agreement, we three started to chase after Mikey like tiny ducklings racing after their mother.

Homer's lake was surrounded by thick pine, sycamore, and chestnut trees, and the only way to reach the water on this side of the lake was down a narrow path, which at night was obscured by the dense foliage. Once or twice I tripped, and both times Mikey pulled me to my feet and held my hand as we ran, Clemmie and George trailing behind us.

We were not the only ones who had heard the sirens and wondered what was happening, and by the time we reached the lake, it seemed like half the town was already there.

The sheriff, Howard, was standing at the shore where bulrushes skimmed the edge of the water, which now seemed to dance with the shimmer of torchlight bouncing off it. Three of his deputies stood with him, all of them staring at something on the ground.

We stood next to Mom and Pops, and Pops looked at me and raised his eyebrow. "I told you to stay put," he said.

But before he could say more, my mother pushed her way through the townsfolk toward the officers, then as she reached them, she stepped back, turned, and looked at us as if she regretted having made her way forward. She walked back toward us, her hand over her mouth.

"It's Nancy," my mother finally said. "Nancy Briggs."

Pops wrapped his arm around her.

"Is she okay?" Mikey asked.

Mom shook her head, then began to cry and leaned into Pops' shoulder.

"Is she...?" Mikey let the question hang in the air, and for a moment, it was as though all sound had disappeared other than the rushing of blood in my ears.

"Home now, all of you," Pops barked at us, breaking the silence and giving us the answer without saying the words. "Go home. Now!"

Mikey pulled at my hand, and I willingly followed him, wanting to leave the lake and Nancy Briggs, the cheerleader with the pretty face and golden hair who was now lying on the ground at the feet of Howard and his deputies.

Others were leaving too, now they had figured out what was happening. Larry pushed past us, wrapping his dressing gown closer to him despite the heat, and joined up with Martha who lived three doors down.

"Terrible," she said, her voice all thick like she was going to cry. "So young."

Larry patted her back awkwardly. "And murder too..." His voice trailed off as they walked away from us.

I looked to Mikey, and he opened his eyes wide and mouthed "murder" at me so that my arms goose-bumped with the thought of it.

I couldn't help but look back though, as if when I did, Nancy would be standing there, a smile on her face, making everyone laugh at the silly joke she had pulled. Yet, she was still on the ground; her parents who had now arrived stood over her wailing, the others looking on, horrified yet guiltily glad it was not their own child. As my eyes scanned the crowd, avoiding that bundle at the feet of the police, avoiding Nancy's mother as she kneeled on the floor and took Nancy's head in her hands, I noticed a figure set back from the others. A lone figure, their face covered by the darkness.

The German.

I stopped, but Mikey pulled me on.

"Wait!" I yelled. "Wait, look!"

"Come on, Al. You heard your pa. You think I want to get on the wrong side of him tonight of all nights?"

"But—"

Mikey wouldn't listen and pulled me away whilst I tried to squint through the darkness at the German who stood to the side, quietly watching the scene unfolding below, barely moving, barely there at all.

When we reached home, we all climbed back up into the treehouse and sat where we had been just a few hours before. No one spoke for a few minutes. Instead, George pulled at the tiny pine needles that had gotten stuck in his slippers, Clemmie smoothed down her hair, Mikey smoked, and I stared out of the tiny treehouse window at the road, waiting to see my parents return, waiting for the night to go back to normal.

As if reading my thoughts, Mikey broke the silence. "Larry said it was murder."

"Murder?" Clemmie asked in a small voice. I could tell that she was near tears, and I was sure that as soon as my parents returned home, she would want to be taken back to her mom.

"Murdered. I think so too," Mikey answered.

"Shut up." I punched him in the arm, not eager for his dramatic take on everything. "Take no notice of what Larry says. He's always saying that he can tell what the weather will do and he's always wrong, and he once thought he saw a bear in his yard, remember? You can't trust what he says. It was probably just an accident, Clem. Maybe she went swimming and got caught in the reeds. You know how thick they can get under the water."

"Swimming, at night?" George asked.

"It's hot," I tried. "Maybe she was so hot, she just couldn't take it no more and thought to have a swim and it went wrong."

"I guess," Clemmie agreed, hardly convinced by my theory.

I had wanted to tell them about the German man that I saw, but now was not the right time. If I said it now, Mikey would jump on it, and go crazy with his murder story until he scared Clemmie to death, George to tears, and gave me nightmares for the rest of the week. So I said nothing and let the quiet settle in once more.

"Y'all hungry?" My mother's voice sailed through the hot thick air up to the treehouse. She was back.

"Mom," I called down.

Within seconds her face appeared at the doorway to the treehouse, her curly brown hair a little mussed from the heat and the run to the lake. She smiled at us, though it didn't quite reach her eyes. "Come on down from there. Come inside now."

She reached out a hand and patted my bare leg. I knew she wanted us close to her and I wanted it too.

Without asking the others, I made my way down the ladder, knowing that they would follow me.

"Where's Billy?" I asked Mom as soon as my feet touched the grass. I knew Billy and Nancy were close and had been friends since kindergarten.

She placed her hand on the top of my head, smoothed my hair, then kissed it.

"He's in his room," she said. "Your pa is talking to him."

"Can I see him?"

She shook her head. "Leave him for now, Al. You can see him in the morning."

"Is she really dead?" I asked. I couldn't help myself. I needed to hear it again.

"Go on now." Mom was grinning madly. She looked at the others who had joined me. "Go on inside, I've got ice cream!"

Clemmie smiled at this news, as did George. Only Mikey looked as serious and worried as me. Nevertheless, he took my hand, plastered on a grin similar to Mom's, and said, "Come on, Al. It's your birthday—ice cream!"

After late-night ice cream, we settled back on the porch, and Pops decided he would sleep over with us too and lay down on the porch swing, his legs dangling off the side.

I was positive that we wouldn't sleep, and as soon as we could hear Pops snoring, we would talk about it all again. But Clem, George, and Mikey fell asleep within seconds, leaving me alone with my thoughts, the hum of mosquitoes, and the police lights that eerily lit up the trees down the street with a blue haze.

All I could think about was Nancy. She had hung around with Billy in their friend group for years—him the jock and she the cheerleader. I would always tease him and say that he loved her, but he never dated her—not that anyone did. She wasn't allowed to date; her father was adamant about it. Yet, it didn't ever stop her from always being surrounded by boys and going to the cinema with them, or hanging out at the diner with them, flinging back her blonde hair and laughing with them all.

Her father knew Pops quite well through their shared love of gardening—where Pops' love was hydrangeas, Mr. Briggs' was roses. He was strict, Mr. Briggs, and Pops would always tell us this when we complained at his punishments; "You should be glad I'm not Mr. Briggs," he'd say, leaving both my brother and me to wonder just how severe Mr. Briggs' punishments were. Mrs. Briggs, on the other hand, looked as though she had never yelled at anyone her entire life. She was a tiny lady, with her blonde-brown hair always tied in a bun at the nape of her neck, her makeup perfect, her clothes the latest fashion. I remembered, suddenly, how last year at the church fair she gave me an extra slice of cake, winked at me, then laughed at her own silliness. I felt a tear track its way down my face as I thought of Mrs. Briggs, and how nice she was and how she didn't have a daughter anymore.

"You okay, peanut?" Pops swung his legs off the porch swing and held his arms out to me.

I climbed up beside him, and he let me rest my head in his lap, stroking my hair whilst I cried and he shushed me to sleep.

THREE

ALICE

The morning broke with the sun streaming onto my makeshift bed on the floor. The others were still asleep at the far end of the porch, out of reach of the early morning rays. I didn't remember getting back into bed, and realized Pops must have placed me there at some stage in the night.

I rolled onto my side and looked through the wooden railings that edged the porch, out into the garden at the blue and pink hydrangeas that Pops tended to daily. Their heads bobbed in the slight breeze that whispered over the town and scattered leaves down the dry sidewalks, making them clitter-clatter like tiny little feet. The finches, wrens, and tits sang out their dawn chorus, as if they hadn't realized that last night someone had died and for now, at least, they should silence themselves.

Nancy was dead. That thought hit me over and over again, making me want to vomit.

Why had Nancy died? She was young; she wasn't meant to die yet. She was meant to finish high school and maybe go to college or get married and have babies. Why had she died?

Suddenly, I heard a cough from the window above me—my brother was awake. I didn't like thinking that my brother was up there alone, maybe crying over his friend, and was desperate to talk to him.

I got up and slowly opened the screen door, not wanting to wake the others just yet, slipped inside and padded my way up the stairs toward Billy's bedroom.

I knocked once, twice, and when he didn't answer, I pressed my face against the door, and in a loud whisper said, "You have to let me in, Billy. You have to."

I knew I should leave him on his own. But something about last night, about Nancy, and seeing the German man at the lake, had made my stomach all wobbly, and I needed to see my brother.

Finally, I heard his bare feet on the wooden floor slapping toward the door.

He opened it wide and looked down at me with tired, red eyes. "You're a pain in the ass. You know that, right?" he asked.

"I know," I said, and pushed past him into his bedroom.

I sat on his chair at his desk and pretended to look at his calculus book.

"Happy second day birthday," he said. There was no joy in the felicitation. It was flat. It was not Billy. Usually, Billy would wake me early on the day after my birthday—he said it was my second day birthday, when we would spend the day together and do the things I really wanted to do. He would normally jump on my bed and sing happy birthday in a silly voice and make me laugh. He'd make me pancakes before our parents got up, then we'd sit on the porch swing together and he'd give me my gift—always the same—a large bar of chocolate and a note that promised to do whatever I wanted for the day. For all the other days of the year when he was mean, or ignored me, he more than made up for it on my birthday.

"No pancakes this year," Billy said quietly. "Sorry, squirt."

"That's okay." I stopped thumbing through the calculus book and finally turned to look at him properly. He was lying down, his head propped up by pillows. His eyes were red from crying; the puffiness of the thin skin underneath them gave it away. But there was more than that—there was something else I hadn't seen in my brother before and I couldn't put my finger on it.

"I'm sorry," I said lamely.

"You know?"

I nodded. "I went to the lake last night—"

Billy shot up. "You were there? What did you see?" His voice was eager, demanding.

"Nothing. Mom and Pops ran down to look, and all the cops were at the lake, and Mom ran over—" I shrugged as if there was nothing else to say.

"Did you see her?" Billy asked. His voice had dropped now. It was like we were playing Chinese whispers.

"Nancy?" I stupidly asked, and saw him wince in pain as I said her name. "No," I said, trying not to think of Nancy's head being cradled by Mrs. Briggs. "No, I didn't see her."

Billy looked at me for a moment, his eyes scanning my face, and I wasn't sure whether he was relieved by my answer or saddened by it.

"So, no pancakes then," I said.

He shook his head. "No. No pancakes."

I stood and walked toward him and, just as Mom had done the night before with me, placed my hand on top of his head, smoothed his hair, then kissed his forehead.

"I'm sorry about your friend," I said, feeling the inadequacy of the words on my tongue.

The usual Billy would have pushed me away, or punched me in the arm, but this Billy didn't. This Billy took my hand, kissed it, gave me a watery smile, then lay down in his bed, facing the wall, and in a muffled half cry said, "Close the door after you."

I did as he said and closed the door, hearing it click into

place. I stood for a moment hearing him cry properly now that I was gone, wanting to cry myself.

By the time I got back out on the porch, Mikey was awake, leaning on the railings and looking out toward Homer's lake.

"Morning," I said.

"Clem and George have gone home," he told me without looking at me.

"Why didn't they say goodbye?"

He shrugged. "I told 'em we'd meet up after breakfast."

"You don't want to go home too? Get changed?" I suggested, even though I already knew the answer.

He looked at me then and grinned, as I eyed his crumpled checked brown shirt and blue shorts from the day before. I could see the tear on the seam of one sleeve and a stain that had splotched itself just under the lapel. His grimy blond hair hung over his blue eyes, and I could see dirt underneath his fingernails. I wished that I could hug him, tell him to live here with us, where my mom would make sure his shirt didn't have stains or tears and where he'd never be hungry and have clean hair and nails.

"You know me." He swaggered over to me and draped an arm round my neck. "I look good in everything—no need to change clothes, I'd still look as handsome!"

I wriggled out from under his arm, then pushed him.

"You love me really," he said, his face splitting with a grin.

I felt my face flame and a burn of annoyance in my stomach, and couldn't rectify the two feelings.

"Go in," I told him. "I'm gonna change."

I showered quickly and dressed myself in denim shorts and a red and white checked shirt, then made my way to the dining room where Mikey was tucking into a pile of scrambled eggs whilst Pops watched intently.

"I just don't know where you put it all," Pops said to Mikey as I sat down.

Mikey shrugged, then reached out and took another piece of toast whilst Mom spooned more eggs on his plate and patted the top of his head like he was an obedient puppy.

"Tell me, could you eat four pieces of toast?" Pops asked Mikey.

Mikey nodded, his mouth too full to answer.

"I bet you couldn't eat the eggs, toast, a whole link of sausage, and some thick bacon," Pops challenged.

"I bet I could." Mikey had emptied his mouth and gulped back some milk, leaving a white mustache on his top lip.

Pops thought for a moment. "I bet"—his eyes twinkled as he spoke—"you couldn't eat twenty hot dogs."

"You mean it? You wanna bet me?" Mikey leaned toward Pops.

"I do indeed. I bet you a dollar you can't."

"Make it two and we have a deal." Mikey held his hand out for Pops to take and seal the deal.

Before he could, Mom came back into the room and gave Pops a light slap on the back of his head. "Leave the poor boy alone!" she admonished. "Challenging him to eat until he'd make himself sick."

Pops looked suitably humbled. "I just haven't seen anything like it, is all. I'd happily pay two bucks to see someone eat twenty hot dogs."

"Don't worry, Mrs. C," Mikey told Mom, "I'd be happy to try. And it wouldn't make me puke."

Mom turned her attention to me as I nibbled at a piece of dry toast, my appetite gone with still feeling so tired after last night.

"What will you get up to today?" she asked me.

"We're gonna go get Clem and George," Mikey answered for me.

"Now don't go hell-raising about town today." Mom waggled her finger at us. "Not today. The town is in mourning, so no hollering and screaming when you're out on those bikes, racing down the street."

I opened my mouth to protest.

"I've seen you all," she warned me, and I closed my mouth.

"And I don't want you cluttering up the house either," she said, leaning back and sipping at her coffee. "I've got the prayer group coming over, and we are going to make some meals for poor Mr. and Mrs. Briggs."

It was then that we realized Billy had joined us. He stood in the doorway, his face pale and eyes red.

Mom pushed herself away from the table and made to stand.

"I'm not hungry anymore," he said.

"I'll bring you something," she told him. "What do you want? I'll make it and bring it to you?"

But Billy was already turning away to make his way upstairs again, confusion plastered on his face as if he couldn't understand why we were sitting eating breakfast and why he had thought it a good idea to join us.

Pops exhaled loudly. "It's gonna take him a while," he said. "He doesn't know which way is up anymore."

Mom nodded, then dabbed at her eyes with a napkin, and Mikey looked at me and tipped his chin back in a way that said, *Let's go?*

I drank back my milk and stood. Mikey followed suit, but not before reaching out and grabbing another slice of toast and putting it in his pocket.

"You be careful today," Mom said quickly, jumping up and giving me an unexpected hug. "I want you all to stay together, and you check in at lunchtime and you're home by four, understood?"

"Why?" I asked. I'd never had to check in before, and 4 p.m. was for babies.

"Just because." She stood straight now and placed her hands

on her hips.

"Do as your mom says," Pops warned.

"It's coz she thinks we'll get murdered," Mikey whispered to me when we got outside, then pretended to stab me with an imaginary knife.

"Stop it!" I shouted at him.

"I was just joking, Al," he said, dropping his arms to his sides.

"I know. Just stop."

Mikey walked sullenly a few steps ahead of me, kicking at a stone.

As we rounded the corner, George and Clem were already walking toward us, their heads close together. As soon as they saw us, it was as though an imaginary person had stepped between them, pushing them apart.

"What we gonna do?" George said, as they reached us. He had a backpack on his shoulders and fussed with the straps.

"What you got in there?" Mikey asked.

"Mom gave me lunch and water, and I got my binoculars and my bird book, and my homework in case we get bored."

"We ain't ever gonna get that bored!" Mikey laughed at him.

Without discussing what we were going to do or where we were going to go, we all started walking together, then suddenly Mikey peeled away from us and began running down the track that led to the lake.

"Come on, you sissies!" he cried out from inside the thick foliage. "I got us a plan!"

I didn't want to go to the lake, and I could see that neither George nor Clem were up for it either, but we all knew that we'd do what Mikey said, and with a shake of my head, I started to follow him.

The sun was already becoming unbearably hot and my shirt was sticking to my back. The thick pine scent and dry dirt clogged my nostrils, and the sticks and brambles scratched their tiny tracks across my bare shins. But then, a minute or two later, the smell in the air changed—a clean smell; the smell of fresh water—and in front of me was the lake. Just below the small outcrop of rocks that we had come to, a scrambly stone-strewn path led to the shore, and we followed Mikey who walked down with ease whilst George, Clem, and I picked our way down carefully.

As soon as we reached the shore, I kicked off my shoes and sat down, putting my feet in the water and letting it lap against my toes.

Mikey stood, hands on hips, scanning the lake. "See there! I knew it. Give me your binoculars, George," he demanded.

George huffily opened his backpack and handed over his prized birdwatching binoculars, mumbling under his breath that they had been a present from his dad and were very expensive.

"There's a boat," Mikey said. "Howard's there, on the shore, and there's a dog too and some other cops.

"See! It is a murder!" he shouted. "Why else would they be looking around?"

Mikey handed me the binoculars, and I stood and looked through them. There was Sheriff Howard, sucking on his pipe, the smoke hanging thick over his head in the warm air. His hat obscured his face, and I couldn't tell what he was looking at. A deputy was crouching on the ground, and Howard bent down to his level. The two men then stood up and looked out at the lake, where a small boat was being rowed by no other than Homer himself, his bloodhound at his side, and another small man, a deputy, in the bow wearing a heavy orange life preserver.

As I scanned the scene, Howard suddenly turned and looked in my direction. I fell to the dry ground and indicated to the others to do the same.

"I think he saw me," I whispered.

"Lemme see." Mikey grabbed the binoculars off me, slithered on his belly toward a rock, and slowly peeked over the edge. "They're putting something in a bag," he told us.

"What is it?" George whispered.

"I don't know, I can't see. Maybe a shirt or something—something material." Mikey slithered back to us.

Mikey leaned his back now against the rock and lit up a cigarette. "You know what I think?" he said, as smoke came out of his nose like dragon's breath. "I think I know what that thing was they were putting in the bag. I think it was that German's scarf. That's what I think."

"You said you thought it was a shirt," I countered.

"Yeah, but I've thought about it now. And you know, the German always wears that green scarf—that thin one. And that's what I think I saw."

Without thinking, the words darted from my mouth. "I saw him last night!"

Mikey, George, and Clem looked at me wide-eyed. "You saw the German?" Mikey said. "Why didn't you say something earlier?"

I shrugged, feeling quite smug at having seen something they hadn't. "I saw him standing in the bushes. He was there, just watching, you know?"

Mikey whistled through his teeth. "Well, that's it then. He murdered her. We know it now."

Suddenly, I felt annoyed with myself for saying anything. Mikey would grab hold of this and make it something it wasn't, just like he did with everything. It was as though he wanted his life to be like the movies—as though reality were not interesting enough.

"I said I saw him standing there. Not that I saw him kill her," I tried. But my reasoning fell on deaf ears.

George's eyes widened. "Wow," he said. "So it was definitely him."

Mikey crinkled up his eyes as he looked toward the lake that the sun now fiercely bounced off. "It is." He nodded sagely. "It's definitely him."

"So, what?" Clem asked. "If it is him, then the sheriff will go arrest him."

"Let me think a minute," Mikey said, leaving us with the simple sounds of the lapping water on the shore and the calls of the bitterns that stood on one leg in the shallows, lethargic from the heat.

As we waited for Mikey to come up with his next theory, I drew in the dirt with my finger, writing my name and wondering if Nancy had ever done this. I didn't believe Mikey—I still maintained it was an accident. I had seen Nancy here before with my brother and their friends. They had jumped off rocks into the lake, looped a rope around a low-hanging branch and swung themselves into the cool lake, shrieking and laughing as each person splashed into the water. I could imagine that she had come here at night, maybe with a few friends, and some-thing had gone wrong. It was an accident; I was sure of it.

"We go to his house." Mikey broke into my thoughts. "We go to his house and we watch him and see if we can find any clues, and then we go tell Howard what we've seen and then they have a parade for us because we got the murderer."

"A parade?" Clem leaned forward. "For us? Really?"

"Sure," Mikey nodded. "Why wouldn't they?"

"Or," I suggested, "we could just go home and have cake and play in the treehouse?"

"Oh, come on, Al." Mikey stood and brushed the dirt off his shorts. "They're baby games. You're thirteen now, and this is a proper game—no, not even a game. It's like our job or some-thing. We have to do it."

"Yeah, come on, Al." Clem took my hand. "Just think of how popular we'll be when we go back to school. Come on. If I'm not scared, then that's saying something, right?"

"I'm not scared." I let go of her hand. "I was just thinking it was boring, is all."

I stood and put my shoes back on. Scared, me? I was nothing like Clem. I was scared of nothing.

"Let's go," I said, and picked my way back up the rocky path with purpose.

I walked quickly out of the brush and trees, hearing just the crackle of twigs underfoot alerting me that the others were following. I hated being called a scaredy-cat. Billy would say it when I didn't want to do something, and I was not going to have wimpy Clem tell me she was braver than me.

By the time I reached the road, the others had caught up. George's face was red and his chubby cheeks had inflated like balloons. He wiped his forehead with the back of his hand, and it was on the tip of my tongue to try one last time and suggest going home for some cool lemonade rather than going to the German's house. But then it would prove to Clem I was scared, and I would never do that.

"Come on." I waved them on. "Mulberry Street."

It wasn't far to the German's house on Mulberry. As per its name, it was lined with mulberry trees, their tiny white fruits almost ready for the hungry birds that waited on the branches, giving some welcome shade as we walked along the sidewalk. The houses on Mulberry were the same as my parents' house; white wood with a gray stone base that had a small opening into a storm cellar. They were well cared for, with tended gardens and roses and hydrangeas in abundance. Mrs. Graham, who taught me in second grade, lived here with her husband and three cats, and she was always in her garden wearing a wide-brimmed summer hat and pink gardening gloves. Today though, she wasn't in her garden—no one was. There was no hum of a lawn mower, no distant music from wireless radios, no laughing children. Not even a dog was barking.

"It's weird," Mikey said, walking beside me now. "Like everyone has gone."

"It's too quiet," I agreed.

Behind me George started whistling to fill in the quiet, and Mikey turned around and told him to stop.

"Why?" George whined.

"For Nancy," Mikey said. "Everyone is mourning her. Be quiet."

I gave Mikey's hand a squeeze. I knew deep down he understood more than most his age, and I was grateful he had realized that our game, whilst an entertainment, was based on something horrible that had happened to someone we all knew.

"It's here," Clem whispered.

We stopped and stared at number 27. The German's house. It was the same as the others, displaying a well-cared-for garden and trimmed lawn, but it was darker here, with an old oak on the driveway spreading itself to take away any sunlight that tried to get through.

The red shutters on the first floor were all closed, making it even gloomier, and there was only one wicker chair on the porch that wrapped its way around the house, as if the German was advertising that he wanted no guests.

"I don't like it here," Clem whispered behind us.

Neither did I. There was something about the place that made the small hairs on my arms stick up and made me want to run all the way home. I looked at Mikey, who wasn't betraying any fear if he felt it.

"Come on." He turned to us. "Round the back."

"We can't do that," George said. "That's trespassing."

"So why'd we come here then?" Mikey waved his arms in the air. "You can't solve a crime without taking a few risks."

"Well, I ain't going." Clem had already taken a few steps back, as if preparing to go home.

"Me neither," George said.

"Fine." Mikey looked at me. "It's just you and me, Al."

I looked once more at the house with the closed shutters and the shadows that enclosed it.

"Not me," I said. "I'll stay here."

Mikey looked at us three and, for a moment, I thought he would give in, but then he grinned, turned, and sprinted away from us up toward the house and around the side, disappearing from sight.

"Shit," George said. "You gotta go get him, Al."

"Me? Why?"

"He got in trouble last week for stealing apples in Mr. Clark's orchard. You know what his pa will do to him if he gets in trouble again."

I opened my mouth to protest that Mikey was on his own with this one, but I knew what George meant. If Mikey got found doing something bad again, his pa would whip him to within an inch of his life.

Taking in a large breath and concentrating on my feet and not the house, I ran up the driveway, following Mikey's path.

The rear yard was made up of a large lawn, its edges mostly just soil as if someone were getting ready to plant, with a few large sunflowers already in bloom that poked their heads up toward the sun. At the very back was a glass greenhouse and Mikey was sitting beside it, staring at the windows on the ground floor of the house.

"Mikey," I whispered, stepping carefully toward him. "We gotta go, this is stupid. You know what your pa will do if he finds out."

"Shhhh." Mikey pulled at my arm to make me crouch down beside him. "He's home. I seen him."

"So what?"

"So, we see what he does. We wait awhile."

"What do you think is going to happen, Mikey? You think

he's gonna come outside with some evidence and hand it to us, or you think he's gonna confess?"

Mikey narrowed his eyes, then stared at the ground and quickly scooped something up.

"Here." He handed me a small pebble.

"What's this for?" I stared at the smooth gray pebble in my hand, feeling the cool weight of it in my palm.

"Throw it," he said, a grin on his face.

"At what?"

"The house. Throw it. It will make a noise, then he'll come out and we can take a proper look at him at least."

"I thought you said you'd seen him before. You know, at night when you go to the graveyard."

"I forgot what he looked like," he said, but he didn't look at me when he spoke.

"I ain't doing it, Mikey." I tried to hand him the pebble back, but he wouldn't take it.

"Fine, come on then." He stood and walked casually away from me.

I started to follow, then stopped as Mikey bent down, turned to me, and smirked once more. Then, he threw whatever was in his hand at the back porch, which bounced off the wooden floor and hit a window, cracking it like a spider's web, and ran toward the street. For a second, I didn't move. Then, just as the porch door started to creak open, I realized where I was, and that the German had heard us, and I started to run, dropping the pebble from my hand as I did.

When I reached the end of the driveway, it was empty. Clem, George, and Mikey were all running down the sidewalk, and I could hear their silly laughs.

Just as I turned to chase them, I saw a figure at the front door, shrouded with the darkness that came from inside. The figure waved at me, then as if he had never been there at all, disappeared into the still of the house.

FOUR

ALICE

That evening I was back on the porch, lying down in my nightshirt after my bath. A cooler air brought the scent of the lake toward me, and the hoot of an owl drifted through the trees. I thought about what Mikey had done—how he had smashed that window and run away, leaving me alone with the pebble in my hand. He never apologized and simply grinned at me when we reached the house, breathless and sweaty, adrenaline coursing through us.

"Ah, come on, Al. It was just a joke." That's all he had said.

I had tried to laugh along with him, and when Mom and Pops had sent them all home, I had busied myself helping Mom and her friends bake bread and cakes for poor Mr. and Mrs. Briggs.

Now though, I was alone with a strange feeling in my stomach that had been growing all day. I knew what it was. I had felt it before when I had stolen a pencil from the store and put it in my pocket. Guilt.

As much as I hadn't thrown the rock that had hit that window, I was there. I should have apologized for Mikey and for myself at being in the German's yard.

What if the German came to the house and told my parents? I sat up. Or what if he told Mikey's pa too? Mikey would be whipped and me too.

I chewed at my lower lip, wondering what to do, then looked to Billy's window which was dark—he would know, but I couldn't ask.

Then, I knew exactly what to do. I raced inside to Pops' office, a place he rarely used for writing or reading but rather a space where he could listen to the radio and smoke his pipe.

I fussed about on his desk until I found a piece of writing paper and a pencil. Quickly, I wrote to the German that I was sorry. That it had been an accident and that I would give him my allowance for however long it took to pay for the window. I was happy with the way it read; it sounded like I was really sorry. I nibbled at the end of the pencil as I decided whether to write my name, and feeling suddenly brave and grown-up, I signed it. There, he knew who I was and I had said I was sorry. There was nothing more I could do.

I waited until morning, when Mom was in the kitchen making breakfast and Pops was reading his newspaper, to sneak out and cycle the mile to Mulberry Street, yelling at them as I closed the door that I was going to see Clem and racing out before they could say anything.

The streets were still eerily quiet, and the only sound came from the squeak of my chain as it dryly rotated the wheels.

On the corner of our street was our church, First Methodist, a gleaming white structure with a bell tower that skimmed the clouds. It had been paid for and built a year before by fundraising events that entailed a lot of baking and car washing, but now it stood proud, and yet the bells were silent.

On the lawn leading to the front door, a few people milled about, flowers in their hands, and I knew it was for Nancy and

Mr. and Mrs. Briggs. They would come and say a prayer and more than likely gossip about what had really happened.

I pulled on my brakes a little to slow myself so that I could see who was there, but they screamed as the brake pads rubbed against the rubber, making a few coiffed heads of the ladies on the lawn look over at me.

So, I pedaled on and turned a sharp right onto Mulberry, once again glad of the shade provided by the trees. I sped up as soon as I was on the street, enjoying the feeling of the air on my neck as my hair fanned out behind me. For a moment, I forgot about my errand and felt a lightness creep over me—that same feeling you get every summer when school is out and you have endless hot days stretching out in front of you. Then, it hit me once more—Nancy was dead, and I was nearing the house where Mikey was sure her killer lived.

I pulled harshly on my brakes, which squealed in protest, and came to a stop just outside the German's house. Discarding my bike on the sidewalk, I felt inside my pocket for the note and held it in my sweaty hands, leaving damp fingerprints on the paper.

What if Mikey was right? I wondered. What if I went to his house and he killed me? Or, what if he hadn't done anything but was really mad at what Mikey had done and told the police?

Billy would tell me I was being stupid; Mikey would tell me I was being a baby. I looked about for the German's mailbox, sure that it would be at the end of the drive, but was surprised to see none. Turning, I scanned the other houses, and sure enough their white, gray or blue mailboxes sat atop a pole at the end of their driveways.

I'd have to go to the house and drop it on the porch.

Standing straight, I ignored the voice in my head that told me to turn around and go home, and marched toward the front door.

The house was as quiet and dark as it had been yesterday, and once again the small hairs on my arms prickled. I stepped onto the porch, the white paint peeling and revealing rotting wood underneath. The floorboards creaked underfoot, and I stupidly shushed them as if they would obey.

Wiping sweat from above my top lip, I bent down and placed the note on the doormat, and slowly began to back away, all the while keeping my eye on the door.

"Hello."

The voice came from my side. I stopped walking backwards.

"Hello," the voice said again.

I turned to my right and there stood the German, a smile on his face and a bunch of sunflowers in his grubby hands.

"Do you like them?" He nodded at the flowers. "I just picked them."

"I..."

"Is that for me?" He walked toward me, his head now nodding at my note on the mat.

"Yes—"

"I don't get many letters. Let me read it," he said, his accent clipping at each letter as if he were trying them out for the first time.

I watched as he placed the sunflowers on the chair and, wiping his hands on his trousers, he slowly bent down to pick up the note.

I knew I should run, I wanted to, but it was like I was in a dream and my head and legs were no longer connected to each other. Instead, I watched as he unfolded the paper, his brown eyes scanning the words I had written.

He wasn't old, the German, not like Mikey had said anyway. He had dark brown hair with a few streaks of gray, and his face was like Pops' with fine lines around his eyes and deeper creases in his forehead.

"Alice," he suddenly said, then cocked his head, considering me for a moment. "Thank you, Alice."

"I didn't mean it," I tried. "It was all a silly game. I'll pay for the damage. I get an allowance, see, and maybe by Christmas I'll have enough and I can pay, and then it will all be okay?"

His head still stayed to the side, just like the robin that visited me in the garden and would sit on a fence post watching me, weighing up whether I was a threat or not.

"I'm Jozef," he said, then held out his hand to shake mine.

I took it, eyeing his nails, seeing whether they were long and scratchy like Mikey had said. I could feel him observing me and felt like he knew exactly what I was doing.

"You don't need to be scared of me," he said quietly and let go of my hand. "I understand that you might be—I am a stranger, after all—but there is no need."

I nodded and stared at my feet.

"Look at me, Alice," he commanded. Despite the fear, the wish to run away, I did as he said.

"You don't have to be afraid of me, okay?"

I don't know whether it was the way he said it, or how his brown eyes that had flecks of green in them held on to mine with such force, but I suddenly felt a bit easier around him.

"Now, the window," he said. "I'll tell you what: go and sit there on my chair, and I will get some lemonade and we will discuss your offer, yes?"

I nodded, not really sure what else to do, and sat in the rocking chair, moving the flowers to the windowsill whilst he disappeared into the dark house.

He was gone a matter of minutes and returned with a glass of homemade lemonade for each of us. He perched on the balustrade across from me and drank deeply. When he had finished, he wiped his mouth with the back of his hand, then looked toward the large oak in his garden, where a pair of crows fought and screeched over a nest.

"I hate crows," he said. "They are so loud, so screechy all the time. Even in the quietest of places you find a crow disturbing the peace. It is as if they do not realize, or perhaps do not care what is happening around them—they just want to be noisy."

"Pops sometimes shoots at them," I said, remembering how last summer a few of them had swooped at Pops whilst he gardened, and he had taken his gun and shattered the air with the pop-pop of gunfire to scare them away.

Jozef shook his head. "I don't care for guns either."

He gave up on his surveillance of the crows and turned to me. "Now, the window. I was thinking that perhaps it will take you some time to save enough to pay for it, and I think I have come up with a solution that will suit us both."

"Please don't tell my parents," I begged.

He held up his hand to quieten me. "I have no intention of doing so. What I propose instead is that you help me in the garden a little, perhaps help me paint this old porch. You are not at school now?"

"Not for six more weeks."

"Well then, plenty of time to work off the debt perhaps? And if you do a good job, then maybe you can actually earn a few dollars here and there too."

"You'd pay me?" I was confused.

He shook his head. "Not at first. First, you work and it pays for the window, and then, maybe a week or so later, there will be some money for helping me."

"I don't know," I said. There was no way my parents would agree—although there was no way I could tell them, as if I did, they'd find out about the window and about Mikey.

"You look concerned," Jozef said. "What are you worried for?"

"My parents," I said.

"You can bring your friend with you if you like? The boy who was with you in my garden."

He had seen Mikey. Had he seen Mikey throw the rock and not me?

"Maybe," I said.

"All right. You think about it. You decide what you want to do. That is what is most important, that you make the decision— do you understand?"

I nodded, even though I wasn't sure what he meant.

"I think I should go." I placed the glass on the windowsill next to the flowers and stood.

He held out his hand to me once more. "It was nice to meet you, Alice."

"It was nice to meet you too, Jozef," I replied. Then, without looking back, I quickly walked to the sidewalk, picked up my rusting bike, and cycled away, feeling a mixture of relief and excitement that I had finally met the German, and Mikey could not have been more wrong.

I frantically pedaled toward town, skirting past the diner that sold the best milkshakes and the handful of stores that lined Main Street. Although there was nothing outstanding about Millford, its townsfolk were proud of it and kept the sidewalks swept, the store signage freshly painted, and the little bells that hung over their doors polished. Everyone knew everyone, so as I raced by, Mr. Johnson who owned the hardware store gave me a wave and told me to slow down, and Mrs. Davis the proprietor of a ladies' clothing shop shouted after me that I should act like a lady.

I waved back at them, not slowing on my mission to get to Mikey's house and tell him what I had seen.

In front of me was the wide town square with a stone statue in the center, dedicated to old General Millford, who had founded the town way back when. I was supposed to know more about him, but as my history teacher could attest, I hated learning about the Civil War, and dates and generals' names went over my head. I skirted round the square and past the sheriff's office, then pulled on my brakes.

Outside, Mr. Briggs stood with Sheriff Howard and a few onlookers had crowded around.

"Do something!" Mr. Briggs was yelling at Howard who, for the first time ever, was flustered. His face was red and sweating, and he alternated between mopping his brow with a dirty napkin that had a steak of ketchup on it and gesturing in the air as he spoke.

"We are. We are," I heard Howard say. "This will take some time."

"I warn you, Howard," Mr. Briggs said, and the sheriff scrunched his eyes with annoyance that his title had been dropped. "You watch yourself, y'hear. You sort this. You find out what happened or else I'm gonna call someone in Columbia!"

"There's no need for that," Howard said, but Mr. Briggs cut him off.

"I know people. Don't think I don't. You want to stay sheriff in this town, then you fix this now."

Mr. Briggs pointed his stubby finger in Howard's chest as he delivered those final few words, then turned his back on him and walked away, the gaggle of people following in his wake.

Howard looked like the fish Pops caught when they had just been dragged from the water—all bulgy-eyed and scared. Then, he saw me, and the look disappeared.

"You go on now," he told me. "And stop riding that thing so fast round here. You think I want to deal with someone knocked off their bike right now?"

I nodded at him and cycled away at a slightly slower speed, but as soon as the sheriff's office was out of sight, I let my legs pump at the pedals to get me to the other side of town.

I was bursting with what I had just seen. Just wait until I

told Mikey—I'd met the German, Jozef, who was nice and nothing like what Mikey had said he'd be like, and I'd seen Mr. Briggs all hopped up with anger, and Howard all cowed by him. Mikey would be so mad he'd missed it.

I crossed the train tracks, my tires bumping along the ridges, and tried not to think about the story Billy would tell me on Halloween—how two young lovers had been run down by the train and would haunt the lines. Despite telling myself I did not believe it, I still shuddered, then looked over my shoulder to check that there were no strange apparitions watching me.

Mikey lived on a ramshackle street of tiny wooden houses with untended yards that held old tires, armchairs, and rusting cars hiked up on breeze blocks—always waiting to be fixed.

Most of the houses were empty now, and their roofs had fallen in on themselves during the last storm. It always reminded me of dominoes, this street, as though one by one the houses would lean into each other and soon flatten themselves on the dusty ground.

A lonesome dog barked at the end of the street, and someone shouted at it, to which it fell silent.

I stopped outside Mikey's. His yard was a little different. Rather than being a junkyard for forgotten things, nature had taken over and four-foot-high grass almost obscured the doorway. Mikey joked about it and said it was his jungle, and that him and his pa were so poor they didn't even have the required junk to fill their yard.

Not for the first time, I wondered what the house had been like when Mikey's mom had lived there—before she ran away with the manager of a bank from a neighboring town. I would imagine that it had been tidy, flowers on the narrow porch and window boxes full. The kitchen window would have always been open, letting the aroma of freshly baked apple pies float out into the still air.

Whether it had been like that or not I didn't know, and Mikey remained tight-lipped about his life when his mom had been there.

I negotiated the grass, stomping through where Mikey and his dad had trampled enough down to make a pathway.

I knocked on the door, hoping that Mikey's pa wasn't home —I never knew what to say to him, even though he was always nice to me and called me "pretty lady."

There was no answer. I tried again, but still there was nothing.

Strange. Mikey was either at my house or at home.

I went round to the side and spat on my hand, then smeared it across the dirty window and peeked in.

All was dark—no sign of Mikey or his pa.

Deflated, I walked back to the sidewalk and wiped my hand on my shorts. I could go and see Clem or George, I thought. I could tell them about what had happened today. But, all of a sudden, I realized I didn't want to tell them about Jozef. Not yet anyway. I quite liked having a secret from them, and the way they had been acting lately—always together, always having a quiet shared joke and not letting me in on it—made me anxious and a little annoyed with them, even though I wasn't entirely sure it was the appropriate feeling.

I picked up my bike and cycled home, this time racing across the train tracks and through town, not caring that Howard would yell at me if he saw me.

That evening I sat in the treehouse alone, trying and failing to concentrate on a book. All I could think about was what Jozef had said and whether it would be right to take him up on his offer. I had my money box next to me, a porcelain pink pig that

Mom had written my name on and presented to me when I was eight. She told me then that if I saved my allowance every week, one day I could travel the world.

Not that I had listened. I rarely saved anything, and as soon as those coins were in my palm on a Saturday morning, I would rush to town with George, Clem, and Mikey and spend it on ice cream and candy.

Outside came the creak of the wood as someone climbed up the ladder. By the way it groaned and moaned, I expected it to be Mom or Pops, but to my surprise, it was my brother's face that appeared in the doorway, his hair disheveled with dark smudges under his eyes.

"Mind if I come up?" he asked.

I nodded and he hauled himself in, then shuffled himself backwards on his butt until he found a spot where the eaves were higher and his whole body could unfurl.

"You're too big for this place," I told him.

"Not quite yet." He managed a small smile. "See, I still fit." He held his arms out.

"What's up?" I asked.

"Nothing." He shrugged. "Just saw the light up here. Wondered what you were doing."

I wanted to tell Billy about the German and the window and my worries about Mikey, but the way he looked told me that now was not the time.

"Just thinking," was all I offered.

"About?" He raised his eyebrow.

"How much does a window cost?"

"A window?" he asked.

"Yeah, you know, like the glass. How much does it cost?"

"Why do you want to know?"

I shrugged and tried to look as nonchalant as possible. "It's for a summer project for school. We gotta find out the prices of things and stuff."

"Sounds like a dumb project."

"It is. So how much?"

"I dunno, Al. Probably like twenty or thirty bucks. Maybe more."

Twenty or thirty dollars? I had thought maybe ten. It would take me over a year to save up my allowance to get that much.

"You sure?" I asked.

"No. Ask Pops. He'd know."

I nodded. Yes, Pops would know. But Pops also knew when I was lying and he would soon find out why I wanted to know.

"You hear about Mikey? Is that why you're up here hiding? He'll be fine, you know," Billy said.

"What about Mikey?" I shot back, thinking that the worst had happened—Jozef had told on Mikey and the window.

"George came over when you were gone this morning— where were you by the way? Anyway." Billy wiped his hand over his face as if using words were making him tired. "George said that Mikey had got caught smoking by his pa, and his pa went crazy and beat him with his belt right on the front porch. Howard ended up coming with two deputies to get him to stop, and took Mikey to his aunt's for a few days and put his pa in a cell to sober up."

"He's okay, though?" I asked in a small voice, trying not to cry.

Billy shuffled toward me, bending his head under the eaves to fit. He put his hand under my chin and made me look at him straight in the eye. "I promise you he's fine. And in a couple of days, I'll drive you over to see him at his aunt's myself. Okay?"

"Okay." I sniffled.

"Good. Now, squirt?" Billy was making his way to the ladder.

"Yes?"

"Be good, okay. Do your homework and read your books. Just be good and safe, okay?"

I nodded that I would, not wanting to say anything out loud as I knew already what I was going to do.

Pops left for work at the mill every morning at seven, and Mom would leave at nine to go and work in the local beauty salon. Pops always said that she didn't need to work, but Mom loved it and was forever telling me that a woman should always have her own money, her own friends, and her own life. "We're not here just for the men," she would say, and look at my father and wink.

It was up to Billy during holidays from school to keep an eye on me, which he rarely did at the best of times, and now at the worst, it was easy to leave the house without Billy even batting an eyelid.

Grabbing my trusty, or rather rusty bike, I shot off as soon as Mom left and followed the same route to Mulberry Street as I had the day before.

When I reached Jozef's house, he was sitting on the porch and waved at me as if he had known all along that I would turn up. I wheeled my bike up his driveway, leaned it against the wall, and joined him on the porch.

Jozef sat in the rocking chair that I had sat in yesterday, and next to him was a smaller wicker chair and a table that now housed the sunflowers in a white vase.

"I thought if I was to have visitors, then there should be somewhere nice for them to sit," he said, then nodded toward the chair for me to take a seat. "You have thought about my proposal?" he asked.

I nodded. "I can help with the yard," I said. "I'm not so sure about the painting as I'm not great at it. One year I tried to help Pops paint the house and I got more on me and the ground than I did on the wood. I had white paint in my hair for weeks."

A sudden bark startled me. Then I realized Jozef had let out a laugh at my story, his whole face lighting up, making him now seem even younger than Pops.

"How old are you?" I suddenly asked, then wished I could take it back.

"How old do you think I am?"

"Fifty, maybe? That's how old Pops is."

"Then maybe I am." He grinned at me.

Oddly, the way he was playing this game, and the way he smiled, made me smile too. "So," I said, "what do you need me to do?"

Within minutes, Jozef had taken me to the backyard, given me a spade, and shown me how to dig to make another border.

"What do you think I should plant?" he asked.

"I'm not so good with plants," I said, trying to concentrate on slicing away a neat edge of the lawn. "I like bright things, colorful stuff. Everyone round here likes roses and hydrangeas; I think coz that's what's in everyone's garden. Mom says they have no imagination."

Jozef laughed again. "Then I shall try and be imaginative."

Jozef didn't hover over me whilst I worked, which I was grateful for. I hated it when Pops or Billy would watch me do things, as I would always make a mistake if there was someone looking at me.

I must have worked an hour or two with the near-midday sun beating down on me, feeling the trickle of sweat track its way down my spine and into my shorts. The whole while I dug, I thought of Mikey, and it kept me going and stopped me from thinking too much about how hot I was.

"Lemonade?" Jozef called from the kitchen.

I dropped the spade and wiped my brow with the back of my hand, then made my way to the front porch and my own little chair.

Jozef handed me the glass, and I drank the lemonade back

in one go. He refilled it for me from a jug on the table and offered me a cookie.

"You work hard," he said.

"I try," I spluttered through a mouthful of crumbs. "Mikey says that girls don't work as hard as boys, but Mom says they do, and we should always show them that we can do what they do."

"Your mother sounds like a very intelligent woman," he said.

"Kinda, I suppose. She works in the beauty salon, so I dunno how intelligent you have to be to work there."

"Where you work is not a measure of intelligence," Jozef said. "A measure of intelligence is what you say, how you say it, and how you think."

"I guess." I shrugged.

"Is Mikey your friend?" he asked.

"Yup. Best friend."

"He was the one in my garden?"

I nodded.

"Why didn't you bring him with you?"

"He's at his aunt's house. It's a way away. Like maybe an hour in the car."

"Why's he there?"

"He got hurt," I said. "His aunt, she's old, but she takes care of him from time to time."

Jozef nodded as if he understood everything—as if he knew about Mikey's dad.

"Do you have a best friend?" I asked.

"I used to, a long time ago."

"How long ago?" I reached for another cookie.

"Well, I am fifty, or so you say I am, so a really long time ago."

"Like when you were my age?"

He nodded.

"But you're not friends anymore?"

"Not anymore."

"What happened?"

"You ask a lot of questions, Alice." Jozef laughed.

I felt my face flame with embarrassment.

"No, no! I like it. No one has spoken to me in a long while; no one seems interested. Which at one time I thought was maybe a good thing, to just have the quiet and my thoughts. But now I see I have missed it. Do you want me to tell you about my friend, Alice?"

"Yes, please," I said, leaning back in my chair now, loving nothing more than someone telling me a story.

"Well then." He made a steeple with his fingertips and rested them against his chin whilst he thought. "Where do I start?"

FIVE

JOZEF

He was my friend from when I was about five years old, or perhaps earlier than that—who can tell where memories start exactly. Perhaps we became friends on those cold winter days when boys would congregate on the streets and pretend to skate on the thin black ice that had covered the roads. Or perhaps we met in the long summer months when I would sit in a field near our house and read. Perhaps he swung down from a tree branch like a monkey and made me laugh, and forced me to put my book away to go on an adventure together.

All I do know is that Bruno became my very best friend, and it seemed to me that he had always been there.

We were different, Bruno and I; where he loved to run, shout, build kites, and take them to the highest hill and watch as the wind picked them up and whipped them into the sky, I preferred to read, to sit quietly and watch butterflies and birds. Yet, despite these differences we complemented each other, and where Bruno would challenge me to run faster, play sword fights, and generally try to make some form of mischief, I would encourage him to read, finding him books I knew he would like, and got him to talk to me, to open up and tell me everything.

In the summer, we would wake early and each of us would take food from our parents' larder and run out toward the one field that a nearby farmer never plowed, leaving it to nature and letting it run riot with wildflowers. We would meet underneath the ancient beech tree that sat in the center of the field, its gnarly thick trunk holding up drooping branches that offered us both shade and a place to hide. We called this spot our home in the summer, and would say to each other in the evening that we would see each other the next day at home.

We would sit underneath those branches, hidden from view, and unwrap our spoils. Bruno was a better thief than I was, and his picnic would always be far superior, consisting of thick slices of chicken, cheese, and warm fresh bread.

He would not sit still on those days and would climb up into the branches, challenging himself to hang upside down, his thin legs wrapped around a tree branch looking as delicate as a spider's. His light brown hair would hang over his face, covering his eyes, leaving just that wide mouth that moved nonstop—sometimes in conversation, but most of the time with laughter.

He knew I would worry about him, hanging upside down like that, but he never heeded my pleas for him to climb down and sit by my side where I knew he would be safe.

"You could break your leg," I would tell him.

"And that would be wonderful," he would reply. "Then I could lie in bed all day, and everyone would have to be nice to me all the time and bring me gifts!"

"Who isn't nice to you?" I asked, indignant that he thought I was a bad friend.

"Not you," was his only reply.

It was only years later that I realized there were people who were not nice to him, and if perhaps that day I had pushed him to answer, there may have been a chance to change his life—to change our histories.

. . .

One memory stands out to me more than the rest—a day that precipitated a change in our friendship, one which I wasn't aware of at the time—but it was a memory I have always returned to when I think of Bruno, and I am sure it was this one incident that changed both him and me.

I was twelve years old in my bedroom in our house on the outskirts of Munich. It had been snowing all night, and I woke that morning to ice on the inside of my window that had designed itself like miniature snowflakes. It was a gloomy day; the clouds were burdened by the weight of snow and the streets were quiet, the snowfall muffling the world outside.

My older sister Elisa was in her bedroom singing. I banged a few times on the wall that separated us, but she did not care for my interruptions, returning the knock on the wall and resuming her singing.

I sighed and pulled on my dressing grown, a hand-me-down of my father's that still hung too big on my frame, the sleeves covering my hands, yet I loved it so much and refused to wear a smaller, better-fitting one.

Traipsing down the stairs, I heard a familiar voice. Bruno.

I took the rest of the steps two at a time, almost tripping on my too-long robe, and raced toward the sound—eager to hear what adventure Bruno would have planned for us on this overcast, icy day.

When I reached our cluttered, book-strewn living room, I saw Bruno sitting on the couch with my mother, who was saying something that was making him smile and laugh.

"Hello!" I excitedly greeted him, yet the happiness soon drained from me when Bruno turned his head to look at me, the left side of his face red and bruised, and a small cut above his eyebrow.

"What happened?" I flew toward him and sat next to him on the blue sofa, staring at his face, which seemed to be swelling in front of my eyes. "Did you fall on the ice?"

Bruno shook his head, then looked to my mother, who had always been wary of him and his family. They were not Jewish, not educated—in short, she thought I could find a better friend.

But now, her face was soft and her brown eyes were watery.

"Jozef, don't worry yourself," she began. "Bruno here has had a difficult morning, and he is going to stay here with us today."

"Today? All day?" I asked. "But it's Friday."

Friday meant that I could not see Bruno in the evening. It was the beginning of Shabbat, and that meant the lighting of the candles, prayers, and a large meal with friends and family.

"I know," she said. "Bruno is going to stay all day with us, even through dinner, and maybe spend the night too."

As excited as I was to hear this news—that I would get my friend for the entire day and possibly night—I knew that the reason for this generosity from my mother was written all over Bruno's face.

My mother left us side by side whilst she went to make us hot tea and toast. I waited for Bruno to speak, to tell me what had happened to his face, but he didn't talk and instead stared at his feet, which he swung one at a time as if kicking an imaginary ball. The carriage clock on the mantle clicked the seconds away loudly, and I began to count along with it, telling myself that in ten seconds he would speak—no, in twenty, thirty perhaps.

Finally, I could not take it anymore. "Tell me," I said.

He shrugged and still looked at his feet, then turned to me and said, "I fell down."

"But why does Mama say you are to stay here? Won't your mama be worried about you?"

Bruno shrugged again.

I thought of Bruno's mother, a tall, thin, beautiful woman whose blonde hair was always coiffed in the latest style, her clothes perfect and jewelry sparkling from her ears and neck.

"She wears it all because she is showing off," my mother would say when I told her about the diamonds the size of my fist that were in her ears. "She doesn't really have anything, so she tries to pretend she does."

I didn't understand the logic my mother presented but readily agreed with her as I wasn't sure what the other side of the argument was.

I was sure, though, that she would want to look after Bruno. Perhaps not his father. His father was a politician and ex-soldier. His father had a mustache the whole time I knew him—bushy and turned up slightly at the edges, as if the mustache itself were trying to smile. But Bruno's father rarely smiled. In fact, I don't think I can ever remember him smiling or laughing, and I didn't like being around him. I never pushed to go to Bruno's house to play, even though their back garden was much bigger than mine.

It was then, thinking about his father, that I wondered whether Bruno had gotten into a fight with someone, and if he went home, he would be scared of what his father might do.

I began to kick my feet in the same rhythm as Bruno, unsure of what to say and think.

Thankfully, my mother broke the silence and brought not only tea, toast, and honey, but a smile and stories of her week that I am sure she embellished in order to make us laugh, but I did not call her out on her stretching of the truth as I was glad of the tales, glad that they made Bruno laugh and smile once more.

That evening Bruno stayed with us for our Friday meal, and his face, illuminated by the candles, seemed to shift, causing me at times not to entirely recognize him.

"I want to do this every week," he told my father afterwards.

My father, a kind, gentle man, put his hand on Bruno's shoulder and told him he was welcome anytime.

"Do you think I can live here with you?" he whispered

sleepily, as we lay top-to-tail in my bed that evening. "Do you think your parents will let me?"

"Why don't you want to go home?" I asked him.

"Do you remember when I said I wanted to break my leg so that people would be nice to me?"

"Yes," I whispered.

"I was wrong. They won't ever be nice to me."

"Your parents?"

"My father," he said, then turned on his side to face the wall, and fell into a fitful sleep, which gave him dreams that made him whimper like a small puppy.

This revelation meant that I did not fall asleep right away. I lay there in that bed, feeling the warmth of my friend's body against me, unsettled at the thought of what had happened that morning with Bruno and his father.

But what I did not know then was that this was just the beginning of a larger change—a change in everything around us and one which would tear our friendship apart.

SIX

ALICE

Jozef stopped talking and looked at the oak tree where the crows that so annoyed him were screeching again, filling the air with angry threats.

"What happened?" I asked.

He appeared not to hear me and kept his eyes trained on the crows, which flapped their black wings at each other, hopping from branch to branch, arguing over nothing.

"What happened?" I asked again.

He looked at me now, confusion knitted onto his brow that furrowed deeply as he considered me.

"I hate those crows, you know. Hate them, but I cannot do anything about it," he said.

Before I could ask once more what had happened to his friendship with Bruno, he stood and checked the time on his watch. "It's time for you to go. You've done enough for today. It's getting too hot."

I wanted to stay and hear more, but by the way he stood, his hand shielding his eyes from the sun as he watched the crows, I knew there was little point in me pushing him.

"Tomorrow then?" I asked.

He nodded in reply and was still looking at those damned crows as I sped away on my bike.

I spent the afternoon doing very little. Clem wasn't at home and neither was George—both had been made to go to a church activity day by their parents. I was glad that whilst Mom and Pops went to church each Sunday, they never made us go to those awful activity days, which mostly revolved around baking in the sun outside whilst reading the Bible and singing hymns. I was a bad singer, I knew that, and I couldn't understand why God would want me to sit all day and sing if I did it badly. Surely, he'd much prefer me to do something I was actually good at?

It turned out that I was very good at sitting on the porch or in my treehouse with a book, and drinking gallons of lemonade and eating whatever I could lay my hands on. I was sure that if Jesus were here he would have joined me on those hot summer days and done exactly the same thing. At least by telling myself that, I assuaged some guilt at not being as wholesome and good as Clem and George.

I missed Mikey. He would have sat with me and lazed about, and wouldn't have felt any need to reason why he did what he did. I wondered if he would be at his aunt's for long, and whether if he came back, things might now be different for him.

With thoughts of Mikey and the soupy summer's heat, I soon drifted off into a strange sleep where I dreamt I was running with Jozef through a field, and Mikey was stuck in a tree and could not get down.

That evening we sat at the dining room table with the French doors wide open to let in a little air, as we ate our way through fried chicken and salad. The ceiling fan swish-swished above our heads, fluttering the paper napkins next to our plates and gently ruffling our hair. Billy pushed at the food on his plate with his fork and soon begged to leave the table, saying that the heat had taken away his appetite.

"It's tomorrow at 10 a.m.," Mom said to Pops, who was ripping apart a drumstick with his teeth. "You think you'll be able to come?"

"The whole town's gonna be there," he said, spraying a few crumbs on the white tablecloth. "I don't think Hank would dare tell any of us we couldn't have a few hours off to attend."

"Everyone's talking about what Howard told Jeanette at the store," she said.

I looked to each parent as they spoke, waiting to see if they would take notice of me and explain what they were talking about.

"It has to be an accident," Pops said. "I can't see that anyone would do anything like that to such a young girl."

"Are you talking about Nancy?" I interrupted.

Both of them looked at me. "I thought you'd left the table?" Mom said.

"That was Billy," I replied.

"Yes, of course." She looked at Pops and he shrugged as if to say that he hadn't realized I was still there either.

"It's the funeral tomorrow," Mom said. "You'll come, as will Billy."

"What did Howard say?" I asked.

"Nothing." Mom pushed herself away from the table and stood, scraping leftovers onto her plate.

"Did he say it wasn't an accident?"

"Just gossip, Al," Pops said and winked at me. "You know what Jeanette is like. Just gossip."

"But if it wasn't an accident—"

"It was. Leave it, Al." Pops clattered his fork onto his plate.

Although the room was stuffy with the end of the day's heat and the scent of fried chicken almost tangible in the air, I felt an icy shiver over my body. It wasn't an accident; I could tell Pops was lying.

I did not sleep well that night. Thoughts of Nancy and what could have happened to her consumed me. I thought of Jozef and couldn't picture him doing anything to anyone. He spoke gently and thoughtfully, and besides the first time I had met him, I didn't feel any fear when I was near him; in fact, I had been looking forward to seeing him again.

If I were to bet on anyone doing something in this town, I would say it would be Mikey's pa. He was a violent drunk and we all knew it, but no one seemed to care too much or try to stop him other than shoving him in a cell now and again to sober up.

Or it could have been an accident, and maybe Jeanette was just gossiping like Pops had said. Once I had decided upon one explanation, another argument would appear in my mind, and around and around I went until falling asleep as the first song-birds woke to the rising sun.

I fell asleep twice at the funeral. And both times Mom gave me a sharp jab of the elbow to my ribs to wake me up. I knew I was going to get in trouble later for being disrespectful, but the priest's voice, lackluster at the best of times, had taken on a lamenting tone that hummed in my ears and beckoned me to sleep.

It was only when Mr. Briggs got up to talk about Nancy that I fully woke up. He spoke quietly, barely looking up from the piece of paper in his hand that shook as he talked. He told us all about Nancy growing up, how she was special and kind, funny and thoughtful, intelligent and athletic. Nancy was everything that any father could want, he said, and I didn't doubt that he was right.

When we left the church, we followed the white casket out into the graveyard where a fresh hole had been dug, soil heaped in neat piles nearby, ready to fill the hole once Nancy was lowered in.

As we stood watching the pallbearers lower her into her final resting place, I felt my hand being taken. I looked over to see that Billy was watching the casket, his eyes dry but his lip trembling. I squeezed my brother's hand, this gesture silently telling him I loved him and that it was all going to be okay.

Moments later, Nancy was gone. The priest murmured about ashes and dust, and Mrs. Briggs let out a wail that made my stomach flip. I looked to Billy, but he was gone. I hadn't felt him let go of my hand.

Behind me he walked away amongst the rows and rows of neat gravestones like a neat set of dentures, his head bowed, with Carl and two of his schoolfriends following.

I knew what would happen. They would go to the lake and drink beer that Carl had taken from his father's fridge. I knew that they did this at the weekends up at the creek, but today would be for Nancy and they would go to the lake and toast to their friend.

Later that afternoon, Pops took me home whilst Mom went to work, and he said he, too, would have to go back for a few hours.

"Behave yourself," he said. "I know Billy's not here, so I'm trusting you. Don't go turning on the oven and burn the damned house down!" He chuckled at me and kissed me on the top of my head, leaving me on the porch with nothing to do and no one to talk to.

Clem and George hadn't been allowed to go to the funeral; instead, they had been shipped off to their grandparents.

"Their parents treat those damned kids like they're babies," my mom had said that morning. "As if they'll break."

I had agreed. Both George's parents and Clem's were the meekest, mildest of people, all of them teachers, all of them wearing brown a lot. I sometimes wondered whether they were all related in some way. I was glad of my mom with her red lipstick and purple high heels that she wore when she was in a good mood—she was interesting at least.

I changed quickly, deciding to go to see Jozef once more, ignoring the little voice in my head that sounded so much like Mikey, which told me it was not safe.

He was waiting for me on the porch—or at least that's what it looked like to me. As I walked up the steps, I could see that Jozef was not alone. At his feet sat a shaggy blond dog, one I knew as a stray that hung around town and accepted pats and food from any generous hand.

"What's he doing here?" I asked, immediately bending down to fuss over him.

"He followed me home," Jozef said. "I think he wants to live here with me."

"You'll keep him?" I grinned. I loved dogs, but Pops always said I wasn't responsible enough to have one.

"I will. I will name him Amos after my father."

Amos seemed to like his new name and licked my face, then looked to his new master who gave him a piece of chicken.

"He likes you," Jozef said. "I cannot believe that he has had no home."

"He did have a home for a bit," I said, standing up then plopping myself in the chair across from them. "He stayed with Mikey for a bit. But then his pa found out and kicked him."

"Kicked who? Your friend or Amos?" he asked.

"Both," I said, and shrugged.

"You said your friend, Mikey, is not here at the moment."

"Nope. He's with his aunt. But he'll come back. It happens a lot."

"It does?" He raised his eyebrow at me.

"Yeah, his pa—" I stopped, unsure of whether I should say anything more.

"Parents are a strange thing," Jozef said. "Sometimes, they can love you too much and sometimes, they don't love you enough. Each set of parents is so different."

"But your parents were nice," I said.

He nodded. "They were. Bruno's, not so much. But here's the thing," he said and leaned forward, "you can still be whoever you want to be. Even if your parents are terrible, even if they smother you with love, they shape you, yes, they shape who you might become, but you can always change that. Mikey will be all right. He won't always be a little boy."

"But there's nothing I can do now to help him, is there?" I asked. "I mean, it's okay if in years to come he's all right, but he's not now."

"There isn't much you can do other than be a good friend. Listen to him. Talk to him. Always be there for him."

"I try," I said. "But Mikey, he doesn't always want to talk to me, you know? He won't tell me about his mom. And he always changes the subject if I ask him about his pa. Sometimes, I just feel stupid. Like I should know what to say, but I don't."

"I understand," Jozef said simply. "You miss him a lot when he's away, don't you?"

"Yeah, he's always around, you know. I don't like it when he's not."

Jozef grinned at me. "I once felt the same way."

"About Bruno?"

"No. Although I did miss him when he wasn't around. It was someone else, a girl. When she wasn't there, I felt as though I were missing a limb."

I understood what he meant—it felt like that when Mikey

wasn't there, as if my arm were gone and I couldn't quite do anything properly without it.

"What was she like, the girl?" I asked, forgetting that I was supposed to be working and paying off my debt.

Amos rested his chin on Jozef's leg, and Jozef leaned back a bit in his chair and looked upwards to find the right words for his memory of her.

SEVEN
JOZEF

1930

This I remember so clearly.

I was fifteen years old sitting in my field, under my tree, as I waited for Bruno to join me. The sky that day was streaked with thin clouds, as if a painter had absentmindedly dragged his brush across the purest of blue. I wondered if I could teach myself to paint the sky one day, then I could look at it always and remember these days of my childhood.

Across the brown stubbled grass of summer, I saw a figure approach. I squinted, realizing that perhaps Mama had been right and I did need glasses, and saw not just Bruno who trailed behind, but a girl wearing a dress the color of sunflowers. She ran ahead of Bruno, now and then turning round and laughing at something he said, then ran quicker and quicker until she was standing in front of me. She stretched out her hand and grinned at me, her cheeks flushed from running, her dark curly hair mussed from the breeze, and said in a singsong voice, "I'm Adeline, pleased to meet you."

I was speechless. Her green eyes bored into mine, and she

laughed at my silence, then stepped closer and grabbed my hand.

Her hand was warm, the skin soft, and I wanted to stroke it, then felt foolish for thinking that thought. As if she had read my mind, she laughed again.

Bruno soon caught up and immediately climbed the tree, hanging upside down to make Adeline smile.

"Come up," Bruno told her. "It's easy, see." He grabbed the branch with his hands so that he was now clinging to it with arms and legs, then released his legs, swung out wide and dropped to the ground.

"I'd rather sit," she said, and took up a position next to me.

Bruno sat next to her. "Adeline, meet Jozef; Jozef, meet Adeline."

"We've already introduced ourselves whilst you were plodding along like my grandmother," Adeline said, then nudged him playfully in the arm, making him blush.

I'd never seen Bruno blush before. He was never shy or embarrassed. If he said the wrong thing, it didn't bother him. He would just shrug and carry on as if nothing had happened.

"She's living next door to me." Bruno looked at me now, pride spreading across his face.

"We just moved here," she said. "Papa has work here."

When she said Papa, her accent changed slightly. She must have noticed my look and said, "Papa is French. Maman is German."

French. Suddenly, to me, Adeline was even more exotic than I first thought her to be.

"She's from Paris," Bruno continued for her. "Imagine, Jozef, Paris! She said that she goes to cafes with her friends, not sitting under trees in a field. I've been telling you that we have to find something else to do."

It was my turn to blush. "I like my tree," I said. "Besides, what else is there to do?"

"I like it here too," Adeline said. "Cafes are boring anyway. What do you do other than talk? We can do that here and it's just the same."

I was glad that she had agreed with me and felt oddly triumphant, but Bruno was clearly put out.

"Sure, talking is fine," Bruno said, "but what about an adventure?"

"What kind of adventure?" Adeline scrunched up her nose and smoothed out her dress.

Bruno picked a large strand of grass and twisted it, then pulled it apart bit by bit as he thought. Finally, he looked at us, that grin of his spreading across his face, his eyes crinkled with delight.

"We'll have a party," he said.

"Just us three?" Adeline asked.

"We can invite others," Bruno said.

"Not much of an adventure." Adeline shrugged.

"That's where you're wrong." Bruno stood and put his hands in his pockets, pacing back and forth in front of us like a teacher who was explaining our next task. "First, it's not a children's party. We won't be playing silly games. It will be a proper party, like my parents have. Ladies come dressed in nice clothes and furs, men wear suits and ties. We play music on the gramophone and drink wine and champagne."

Adeline let out a laugh. "And where do we have this crazy party of yours?"

"At my house, naturally." Bruno nodded at her. "We will smoke cigars and dance a little, perhaps. My parents are away next week, and that's when we shall do it. It will be our last adventure as children and our first as adults."

"Your father will kill you," I said, finally finding my voice.

Bruno didn't seem to hear me, and continued to talk about the music we would play and the dancing we would do. I could see that Adeline was warming to the idea, coming up with names of girls she could invite and what she might wear to such an event.

I wanted to tell Bruno that it was a bad idea. That it would go wrong and that his parents would surely find out and his punishment would be severe, that we should have our usual adventures of going into the city to admire the older girls from the college, with their rouged cheeks and perfect hair. Or taking food from our larders and having a picnic under the tree, or riding our bikes down to the Isar late at night, where we'd sit on the bank of that mighty river, dip our feet into the cold water and smoke a cigarette between us. Our adventures were tame and that's why I liked them—there was little risk involved but just enough that pushed me to do something I would never have done on my own.

Bruno shrugged. "I'll invite some friends from school. Jozef, you invite some too."

I nodded but knew I wouldn't. I had no real friends at my school; a few that I talked to during the school day, but no one I really spent time with. I suddenly realized that Bruno was my only friend.

Adeline squeezed my hand, so briefly that I wondered if I had imagined it. I looked at her and she gave me a little smile, one that told me she had somehow known my thoughts. "It'll be nice, Jozef," she said. "I'll dance with you."

It wasn't until later that evening that I replayed the moment in my mind. Adeline had thought I was worried I would have no one to dance with, and my cheeks burned with shame. I, of course, wanted to dance with her, and the more Bruno had spoken about the party, the more my excitement had grown, especially thinking about Adeline all dressed up, her hair swept back and her hand in mine as we danced. But I didn't want her to feel sorry for me—to feel as though I was so lonely and quiet that no one else would want to be my dance partner.

In that moment, I resolved that I would have a girl on my arm for this party, and Adeline would see I was just as handsome and popular as Bruno. And maybe, just maybe, she would look at me differently—even though I wasn't sure what that meant.

Bruno was as good as his word, and the following weekend was set as the date for our adventure into adulthood.

"They leave on Friday," Bruno told Adeline and me as we sat on a bench in my garden.

Adeline was in charge of inviting people, Bruno said he would be in charge of the drinks and food, and I, apparently, had nothing to do.

"I can help," I said.

"There's nothing more to be done," Bruno said. "Adi and I have got it all sorted. We've been planning it for days."

Adi? When had he started calling her that?

Noticing my confusion, Adeline turned to me. "He called me Adi one day and I like it. You can call me Adi too if you want to?"

I looked at Bruno, who didn't seem pleased that she had invited me to call her by his pet name for her, so I agreed I would call her Adi and felt a little proud of not giving in to Bruno for once.

"When did you plan it?" I asked. "You said you'd been planning it for days."

Bruno shrugged.

"You said you had a lot of studying to do," I accused him.

"I did. Adi helped me. Then she helped me plan the party. What's the big problem, Jozef?" Bruno asked.

"Nothing." I looked at Adi, willing myself to find the words to see if she would spend some time with me, but my mind remained blank and my mouth firmly closed.

"So, we'll say it starts at eight," Bruno continued. "We think there'll be twenty or so, which is enough I think for a party."

I looked at him as he spoke. His eyes were firmly on Adi, and his voice had an authoritative edge to it that I hadn't heard before.

"You sure your parents won't find out?" I asked, hoping to shake his confidence a little.

"They know already."

"They know?"

Bruno nodded. "They said we are allowed to drink the cheap wine but not the expensive stuff."

Adi was visibly impressed. "I wish my parents would trust me like that. Gosh, Papa makes me go to bed at nine each night like I'm still a little girl!"

"So how will you be able to go to the party?" I asked.

"I'll climb out of my window, of course! You don't think I always do what my parents say, do you, Jozef?"

"He always does what his parents say!" Bruno laughed at me.

"Not always. I haven't told them about your party. I haven't told them that your parents won't be home."

"Ah look, my little Jozef is all grown up!" Bruno pinched my cheek and Adi laughed along with him.

I swiped his hand away and stood. "See you at the party," I said.

"You want us to leave?" Bruno asked.

"I'll see you at the party," I repeated, and turned on my heel away from them.

"Don't forget to bring your date," Bruno called out. "Adi and I can't wait to meet her."

I turned back to them, feeling stupid that I had said I had a date only to see what Adi's reaction would be. "And don't forget yours," I told him.

"I already have mine." Bruno nodded toward Adi. "Adi and I will see you there."

I watched them leave, and felt my stomach plummet. She was already his, which meant that she would never be mine.

When I went back inside the house, my mother was sitting at the kitchen table, humming a tune whilst she chopped carrots.

I sat across from her, picked up the green fronds from the tip of a carrot, and ran the soft tendril across my palm.

"Did you ask her?" my mother asked.

I shook my head. I had lied to Bruno. I had told my parents about the party and about Bruno's parents not being home. I couldn't lie to them and for that, they respected and trusted me. I was allowed to go to the party but had to be home by midnight.

"Why not?"

"She's going with Bruno," I said.

"She'll change her mind," she said. "Trust me. I saw the way she looked at you and the way she looked at him. She likes you. Bruno is just a passing love. Yours will be the real thing."

"How can you be so sure?" I asked.

"Do you know why I always tell you to be honest with me, Jozef?" she asked.

"So you can know everything I am doing," I said.

"No," she chuckled. "I do it because I will always be honest with you. If you talk to me, then I can talk to you. You are almost an adult now, and your father and I were brought up in such strict households we never wanted to do that to you and your sister. We wanted you both to always want to talk to us."

"Is that why you don't like it when Oma and Opa visit?" I asked, thinking of my mother's parents, who always visited for

Hanukkah and always shouted at my sister and me for talking too loudly and eating too little.

"Exactly," she said. "So, you know I am being honest with you now about Adeline."

"Adi," I corrected her. "She likes to be called Adi."

"Adi then. A woman and a mother knows these things. She likes you, Jozef."

"So why is she going with Bruno?"

"Because he asked her first." She stood and wiped the blade of her knife on her apron. "Which means that if you want something, you have to go after it, Jozef. You have to get there first."

"It's too late now," I said.

"It's never too late." My mother kissed the top of my head. "You'll take your sister with you to the party."

"No!" I screamed at her. "That will be so embarrassing."

"It won't. She can keep an eye on you all, and besides, there may be a nice man for her to meet."

"Without a chaperone? Papa won't like it," I tried.

"You'll be her chaperone," she said, her face now in a cupboard, her voice all echoey as she searched for whatever foodstuff she needed.

"But, but..." I tried to find the words to win my argument, but nothing was forthcoming.

"She'll help you, you'll see." She turned to look at me now, a bag of flour in her hand and a triumphant look on her face. "Found it," she said. "She'll help you. She'll talk to Adi and tell her how wonderful you are, and Adi will soon be yours, trust me." She kissed the top of my head again, and I put my face in my hands and groaned.

This was going to be the worst night of my life.

EIGHT

JOZEF

The evening of the party was soon upon me, and I stood in my bedroom wearing a suit that was a bit too big for me, the sleeves covering my hands a little, the trousers scuffing the floor.

"Ah! You look so handsome." My mother barged her way in and took me into an embrace. "Just like your father used to look."

"I still look like that now." My father stood in the doorway. "I like to think I am still as handsome as I was when I was young." He winked at her.

"You're getting saggy," she said, then laughed and kissed his cheek. "But I still love you."

I had always loved how different my parents were to other friends' parents. They were warm and loving and teased each other, laughing together just like they were best friends. They were open, honest, and allowed us to discuss things with them that other parents would balk at. I could ask my parents about girls, parties, drinking—anything, and they would never get mad. But in that moment, wearing that too-big suit and knowing I was taking my sister as my date, I wished they would be like other parents and not allow me to go.

It was not to be, however. My sister, Elisa, waltzed into my bedroom wearing a light blue cocktail dress that made her look older than her seventeen years. Her hair was pinned back with tiny pearl clips that caught the light.

"You look lovely!" My mother grasped her now and held her tight. She was going to cry, I knew it.

"Too nice if you ask me," my father, said not looking properly at her but fussing with his pipe, which he was trying to stuff with tobacco.

"Be quiet, Amos!" she admonished him. "She looks just like I did, don't you think?"

"I'm not sure about that dress." He nodded toward her bare shins.

"It's the fashion. Don't you want your daughter to be fashionable?"

"Why did she get a new dress and I had to wear Papa's suit?" I asked. "It's not even her party."

"Hush now." My mother tucked a curl behind Elisa's ear. "No arguing. Go and enjoy the evening, and Jozef, keep an eye out for your sister."

"She's older than me," I whined.

"And you're her chaperone. We are trusting you, Jozef. It's important that you are there with her, and she is not seen to be chatting alone with strange men."

"Then don't let her come," I said, and sat on my bed.

"Don't be such a baby," Elisa said. "It'll be fun, Jozef. I promise I won't ruin your night."

"Fine." I stood, pushed past my parents, and made my way down the stairs. "Hurry up," I called to Elisa, hearing her heels click-clack on the floor after me.

Outside, Elisa took my arm. "Thank you, Jozef."

"For what?"

"For letting me come. Although it was sort of my idea, you know, saying to Mama that I could look out for you and, in turn,

you'd be my chaperone. A friend of mine has a younger brother
—you know him, Saul. He's in your school?"

I knew Saul; he was always in trouble. I hadn't invited him,
and I wondered if Adi had.

"Well, Saul's brother Magnus will be there tonight to watch
him, and we have been trying to see each other for a while."

"Why don't you just ask Papa if he can come over?" I asked,
concerned about my sister's secret.

"You know what it would be like. They would have him
over for dinner, and ask him lots of questions about his family
and marriage and babies, and soon enough it would scare him
and he would run off."

"Why would it scare him?"

"Oh, Jozef! You're too young. You don't understand. Look."
She stopped under a streetlight, her hair all aglow with the
pearl pins. "I did this so I can see him for a while, alone, just to
talk. And it will help you too. I will talk to that Adi girl and get
her to like you."

"You can't make someone like you."

"Just trust me, all right? You'll have the best night!"

She grinned at me, and in that moment, I believed her. I
would have the best night. I crooked my arm for her to take it,
and with a giggle, she linked her arm through mine, and the pair
of us continued on our way to the party, our thoughts full of
what the night could bring.

Bruno did not disappoint. By the time we arrived, his house
was full of guests, many of whom I did not know. The dining
table was covered with fruit, meats, breads, cheeses, and much
more, and in the living room, the furniture had been moved to
allow for a makeshift dance floor where bodies were already
swaying to the deep soulful American jazz singers that called
out from the gramophone.

A funny fluttering in my stomach alerted me to the fact that
I was rather excited to be here. A waiter, who I knew as Bruno's

parents' gardener, offered me a glass of champagne from a silver tray. I took it, as did Elisa, who suddenly spotted Magnus standing idly by a large fern and made her way over, leaving me next to the gardener-cum waiter.

A laugh boomed behind me and I knew it to be Bruno. I turned and saw him in the foyer, laughing with some of his school friends, Adi beside him wearing a silver spangly dress and a little matching cap on her head. As she moved, the light caught the sequins of her dress so that she looked like a dream that was just about to escape. I coughed, trying to force words into my mouth, knocked back the glass of champagne and made my way toward them.

Adi was the first to see me, and she beamed at me, then kissed my cheek. Despite myself, I felt my cheeks burn and looked at my shoes rather than at her face.

"You made it." Bruno wrapped his arm around my shoulders. "Where's your girl?"

Before I could answer him, Elisa let out one of her high-pitched giggles and Bruno's eyes sought out where the sound had come from, finally seeing Elisa merrily talking to an animated Magnus.

"You brought your sister?" he asked.

Around me I heard stifled laughter from his friends and looked to Bruno to see if he was going to make more of this or let it be. He was grinning, almost wanting to laugh, but he must have seen my embarrassment and escorted his friends toward the dining room.

Only Adi did not leave me.

"Do you want to go out on the terrace?" she asked. "Get some fresh air for a few minutes?"

I nodded and felt her take my arm just as Elisa had done on our walk here. She led me to the rear terrace that looked out onto the large grassy expanse of a garden, the flowers hidden by the night.

"You're so quiet all the time," Adi said.

"I'm sorry," I stupidly replied.

"No, no, that's not what I meant. Don't be sorry. I like that you are quiet. It's just nice to be with someone and know you don't have to talk sometimes."

"I have things to say," I said. "But sometimes the words just don't find their way to my mouth, it's like there is a blockage in my brain." I shook my head again, trying to find the words I really wanted to say in front of her. I wanted to be funny, clever, witty even, and instead I'd told her that I had something wrong with my brain.

"I'm the same," she said. "I say things, but then I wonder why I said them and didn't say what I really wanted to."

"Bruno always knows what to say."

She waved her hand as if swatting a fly. "He just says things to hear his own voice, I think. Most of what he says isn't really him anyway. He's always trying to impress everyone."

"He doesn't try to impress me," I told her. "He knows he doesn't need to do that with me."

"Are you joking?" She looked me dead in the eyes. "He does it the most with you!"

"He does?"

"All the time. He's always trying to be funnier when you are there, to make you laugh, or he'll say something extraordinary just to see how you will react. He likes that you look up to him."

I hated what she said. I hated it because it was true and I didn't think anyone else knew. I did look up to Bruno. I wanted to be like him—confident, charming, and daring. If Adi could see it, who else could?

"Oh, I love this song!" Adi suddenly grabbed my hand and placed it on her waist. "Let's dance!"

I took her other hand in mine and slowly shuffled left to right. "I'm not very good," I said. "You'd be better dancing with Bruno."

"I want to dance with you."

"But you came as his date," I said, whilst watching my heavy feet stomp from side to side, trying to find a rhythm.

"Not really," she said quietly, resting her head on my shoulders. "I just said I'd come early to help him set up. I didn't say I would go with him."

I accidentally stepped on Adi's foot. "I'm sorry. I told you I was no good at this."

Adi didn't reply and kept swaying from side to side, her head comfortable on my shoulder.

The song soon ended, and a horn and trumpet changed the tempo to an upbeat tune. Adi pulled away from me and kissed my cheek, then turned and walked back inside.

I stood limply on that terrace for some time, thinking that I could still feel her lips on my cheek and wondering if they had marked me in some way. I touched my cheek, hoping to feel something there that I could carry with me. It was then that I realized, even though I did not know Adi well, I was hopelessly in love with her.

The night progressed with rapid speed. Once I rejoined the party inside, I drank more than I should have, soon feeling a fuzziness in my brain and a thickness on my tongue. I tried to keep an eye on Elisa, but she soon became a blur on the dance floor, and I could no longer discern who was who.

Bruno seemed to be always in my sights, though he couldn't possibly have been. It seemed to me that he was everywhere—talking to the group of girls near the fireplace and at the same time changing the record on the gramophone, then laughing with his friends.

I sought out Adi a few times, always finding her chatting to others, and me and my fuzzy head and thick tongue could never muster up the right words to interrupt them or inject myself into the conversation, so I would stand, swaying slightly with a stupid grin on my face.

I don't know what time Elisa finally found me in the drawing room, where I sat alone on a leather chair, staring at the floor as it dipped then rolled to meet me.

"How much have you drunk?" she asked me, bending down and tipping my chin upwards to look at her.

"Some," I said, then laughed, thinking I was funny.

Magnus was suddenly there. Had he been there the whole time or had Elisa fetched him? I tried to remember and found that time was slipping away, and then I thought about time in general, that maybe all time slips away and we don't ever really remember anything.

I tried to explain my thoughts to Magnus, who said that he understood, but the way he looked at me told me he didn't, so I tried to explain again, but this time I forgot what I was trying to say.

I was soon outside.

"I have to say goodbye to Bruno," I told my sister, who had one arm linked though mine and Magnus who had the other.

"You already did," Elisa said.

"No. I have to say goodbye. He's my best friend, you know. I have to let him know that it was a good party."

Suddenly, the air hit me, and I doubled over and vomited onto the street. How long I was there I do not know, and I don't remember getting home or going to bed.

But I awoke the next morning still dressed in my oversized suit, with the stench of vomit surrounding me.

I cleaned myself and dressed and gingerly made my way downstairs, sure that my parents would be sitting waiting to admonish me. Yet, to my surprise, it was Adi who awaited me, in the sitting room with Elisa, the pair of them chatting happily.

As soon as Adi saw me, she stood and came to me, wrapping me in her arms. "I was worried about you," she said, then with her hands on my shoulders, she held me away from her whilst she surveyed the damage I had done to myself.

"Tut-tut, Jozef," she said, grinning. "Who would have thought that you would have gotten drunk out of everyone there."

"I'm sorry," I said. "The champagne."

Adi nodded. "Could have happened to any of us."

"I've made coffee and breakfast." Elisa stood. "I'll fetch you some."

"What did Papa say?" My voice was small and weak.

"Lucky for you, they were in bed. Magnus helped me get you inside, and they didn't hear a thing!"

I watched my sister walk happily away; I dare say she was happier for herself than for me—she had managed to meet Magnus, he'd even walked her home and been inside the house, and she had gotten away with it too.

Adi sat me on the sofa and held my hand. "Shall we do something today?" she asked.

"Like what?"

"Like anything."

"I don't think I can do much." I shook my head, then winced from the pain.

"We can just sit and talk, and maybe later, when you feel a little better, take a walk?"

"And Bruno?" I asked.

She shrugged. "Let's just have it the two of us today."

And so it was. Just the two of us. Not just that day, but the next and the next, and by the time I realized it, we had spent every day together for a week; reading under my tree, taking a walk, playing cards. It was perfect being with her, as if all the time I had spent before I met her was in vain.

Bruno was strangely quiet. We had called on him a few times and no one had answered the door, but we knew they were home as we saw the curtains twitch at our knocks.

At the end of the week, I found the courage to kiss Adi, and to my utter surprise, she returned it, sealing the fate of our friendship into something much more. But with the good must come the bad, and it was waiting for me on my doorstep when I had walked Adi home. Bruno.

His arm was in a sling, and he stared at the ground right up until I was in front of him, then slowly raised his head with a look on his face that I couldn't decipher.

"What happened to your arm?" I asked.

"Where's Adi?" he said.

"I've walked her home."

"I saw you, you know. Kissing her under our tree. I was there, coming to find you, and I saw you."

I wanted to tell Bruno everything, as I always did, but I could see that he didn't want to listen to my happy tale.

"You're angry at me?" I asked.

"What do you think, Jozef? She was mine, mine. I saw her first!" He stood and pushed me off the bottom step with his good arm.

"It just happened, Bruno," I tried.

"Just happened? You knew I liked her, and this is what you did to me—you were supposed to be my friend!"

"You never said you liked her," I rationalized.

He pushed me again. "Never said! Jozef, are you that stupid? Do you not have eyes in your head?"

"But, but..." I stammered.

"But what, Jozef?"

"But, I love her. She loves me," I said quietly.

Bruno laughed, but it did not reach his eyes. It was a barking, sarcastic laugh that scared me.

"She loves *you*? You think so? Why would she love you, Jozef? A bookworm, a little boy who's scared all the time. You do nothing without me. I make your life interesting and fun. Why do you think she would love you?"

I let the questions hang in the air whilst my brain scrabbled about trying to understand what was happening.

"Forget it, Jozef." Bruno walked past me, then turned. "Forget me too. You're not my friend anymore."

I watched him walk away from me, then disappear around the corner, and only ventured inside when my father opened the front door and told me to come in.

Papa sat me down in his study, a musty place filled with old books, their binding coming away after being read and reread. An old teacup sat on the side table, the stain inside showing it had been there for some time. Papa did not talk; he lit his pipe and puffed at it behind his desk. I stared at my shoes. I wasn't sure what Papa wanted to say, or what he wanted me to say, but I was used to his silences, which meant he was thinking and soon a conversation would start, but not until he was ready.

"He is still your friend," he finally said.

"I don't think so."

"He is. He is just angry now, but it will pass. His feelings are hurt and his pride, but it won't last long."

"He said I am nothing without him," I muttered, feeling anger growing in my stomach.

"He didn't mean it. Often people say things that they consider themselves to be. Perhaps he thinks he is nothing without you, and it hurts him, so he knew that it would hurt you."

I shrugged.

"Jozef, look at me," my father demanded.

I lifted my head and met his gaze, his eyes half-hidden by his bushy, unruly eyebrows.

"You have done nothing wrong. Adi chose you, and that's what is hurting Bruno. Should you have talked to him about it? Perhaps, but you are fifteen years old, and these things happen. You are not an adult yet and not wise enough to know how to handle things, and neither is Bruno. Trust me. He will come back to you; you just need to be patient."

"You said I have done nothing wrong, so why do I feel so guilty?" I asked.

"Because your friend is hurting. That's why. But one day, I promise you that you will look back at this and laugh. You and Bruno, when you are old, married men, will reminisce about this and see how silly it was! He won't want Adi forever. He'll soon move on."

"His arm is broken, I think. It's in a sling."

"I saw. Did he tell you why?"

I shook my head.

"He will."

"Do you know why?" I asked.

Papa didn't answer straight away, but leaned back in his chair and stared at the ceiling. "I have my suspicions. But it isn't for me to say. Let Bruno tell you."

"He won't," I said, willing my father to tell me what he knew.

"He will. Be patient. Let him know that you are still his friend, no matter what he says."

"How?"

"Go to his house. Take him his favorite book to read."

"But what if he doesn't come to the door?"

"It doesn't matter. He will know you are there, and that's all that matters."

I nodded, even though I didn't quite understand how my father's advice would work, and left my father in his study with the pipe smoke hanging in the air.

All summer I tried. I knocked on Bruno's door, with and without Adi. I bought him a new kite. I left his favorite book on the doorstep, but each time the maid would answer the door and tell me he was not home, even though I could see him like a shadow in his bedroom window.

"Do you think he'll ever forgive me?" I asked Adi one late summer's afternoon.

We were sitting under the tree, both of us absorbed in our reading. She placed the book on her lap and turned to me.

"He will. Eventually. But you did nothing wrong, Jozef. If anyone was wrong, it was me."

"Don't say that!" I kissed the tip of her nose. "You never do anything wrong. You're perfect."

"I'm not, Jozef. I'm human."

"Well, you're perfect to me."

"I shouldn't have spent so much time with Bruno, and I shouldn't have encouraged him like I did."

"Why did you?"

"Because I was stupidly trying to make you a little jealous, I suppose. You were so quiet, and you would look at me in such a serious way, and I couldn't decipher whether you liked me or not. So I suppose I let Bruno think more of me than he should have, just so that maybe you would talk to me and maybe you would like me."

I laughed at her perception of me. "I was shy, Adi! That's all. I liked you from the moment I saw you. And I fell in love with you just a week later. I like that you thought I was serious and brooding, though!"

She nudged me gently on the arm with her own shoulder. "Still. It was wrong of me."

I took her hand in mine and kissed her knuckles. "You're still perfect to me."

"Jozef, look." Adi let go of my hand.

A few yards away was Bruno, walking slowly toward us. I moved a few inches away from Adi as if it would make some sort of difference, and waited for Bruno to reach us.

"Bruno, how are you?" Adi was the first to greet him and

stood, kissed him awkwardly on the cheek, then sat back down. "Want to join us?"

Bruno nodded, sat cross-legged and snapped at blades of grass.

"I'm sorry, Bruno—" I started, but he held up his hand to silence me.

"You did nothing wrong," he said, still looking at the grass. "Thanks for the kite and the book," he added.

"We could fly it tomorrow maybe?" I suggested.

"I won't be here tomorrow."

"Why?"

"Father found out about the party," he said.

"But I thought you said they knew about it?" Adi asked.

Bruno raised his head and looked at us, smiling wryly. "I say a lot of things. It turns out, though, that I went too far this time. Father found out and was mad. But oddly, he was more angry that we had drunk all his best champagne. I'm glad we did, though. It was a good party, wasn't it?"

I nodded and waited for him to continue.

"Military school. He thinks I need discipline. I leave tomorrow."

"He can't!" I said. "Surely, your mother won't let him?"

"He might be right, you know. Perhaps I do need discipline. He tried to show me what happens when you're not disciplined —that's what he said, you know, when he grabbed my arm and twisted it until the bone snapped—he said this is what happens. So I was glad I drank his champagne, you know. I don't regret it."

"He broke your arm?" Adi gasped.

I wasn't as shocked. I remembered the day Bruno had come to our house with a bruise and cut on his head.

"It's all right, though. He doesn't really mean it. He told me he just wants to be proud of me. Maybe me going to the school will make him proud of me." He shrugged.

I didn't know what to say. I simply stared at my friend, who seemed different to me now. Broken and distant, like no matter what I said, it wouldn't quite reach him.

Adi knew what to do; she hugged him and told him she was sorry. He told her it was all forgiven and that he wanted to be friends once more.

"We never stopped being friends," I told him.

He gave a slight nod of the head, then stood and dusted off his trousers. "I'd better go. A new adventure is waiting to be had!" His voice forced joviality.

I stood, not sure whether to hug him or not. In the end, Bruno stepped forward and gave me a bear hug, squeezing me tight and making me laugh.

"I'll write you," he shouted over his shoulder as he walked away from us. "Make sure you don't forget me!"

"Never!" I shouted back, feeling a tear track its way down my cheek.

NINE

ALICE

"Did he write you?" I asked Jozef, who had started to stare at the tree with the crows in it again.

"He did. For a long time. He told me all about the school and how he hated it. But then—I don't know why—things changed for him and he started to love it. He wrote about his new friends, the drills, how his father was so proud of him, and soon, perhaps when I was nineteen or so, the letters just stopped."

"So you didn't see him again?"

"Not for some time," Jozef said, but he wasn't really listening to me and his answer seemed false.

"The crows?" I asked.

"What?" He looked at me now.

"The crows. You keep staring at the tree they live in."

He smiled. "You need to get to work, I suppose. I have been keeping you with all my tales."

I shifted in my seat, then Amos came over to me and licked my hand.

"He likes you," he said. "You can help me train him

perhaps, when you come over? We can teach him to hold up his paw, and roll over. I think I'd enjoy that."

"He needs a bath," I said, feeling his matted fur.

"Well, that shall be your job today. I'll get you the garden hose and some shampoo, and you can bathe him."

"I'd like that," I said. Jozef smiled at me, a big happy smile that lit up his eyes. "I'd like it very much."

That evening I spent time in the treehouse with Clem and George, playing a variation of poker that Mikey had taught us. The problem was that we couldn't really remember the rules, and each time Clem yelled out "Poker!" George rolled about laughing.

"That's not how you play it," I said, not seeing the humor.

"It's how *we* play it—me and Clem," George said. "Remember the other day, Clem, how you said poker so loud you scared your mom's cat and he jumped off the table and knocked over that vase?"

Clem grinned, and George grinned back at her in a way that made me uncomfortable.

"When did you play?" I asked them.

They both looked at me and their smiles dropped. "The other day," Clem said, then took up the cards and started to clumsily shuffle them, dropping one every few seconds.

"Yeah, what day?"

"I dunno," Clem said, but she wouldn't look at me.

"How come you didn't invite me?" I picked up a card she had dropped and handed it back to her.

"I dunno," she said again.

"Where were you this afternoon? You went to the funeral, right?" George asked.

"I went," I said, not wanting to tell them about Jozef now, even though I had made my mind up earlier to tell them. If they could hang out without me, then I could hang out with Jozef and not tell them, I decided.

"Did you see her?" George asked, then rubbed at his eye under his glasses.

"See who?"

"Nancy."

"She was in the coffin. How was I meant to see her?"

George shrugged. "Never been to a funeral. I just wondered. Mom said once that she went to her grandmother's funeral and the coffin was open and you could look at her. I thought maybe you could have seen her."

"I don't want to see no dead bodies," Clem said, and dealt the cards.

I took my hand and tried to remember what Mikey had said —which cards were good and which were bad. A queen and a king of hearts—was that good? I chewed on my bottom lip.

"You heard from Mikey?" George asked me.

I shook my head.

"You think he'll be back soon?"

"Oh shit, George!" I suddenly yelled. "Do you ever stop asking questions?"

The pair of them gawped at me.

"Sorry, sorry," I said hurriedly. Where had that come from?

"Wanna do something tomorrow?" I asked now in a more conciliatory tone. "We could ride down to the creek and go fishing? Or we can fix this place up for when Mikey gets back?" I suggested.

"Can't tomorrow," Clem said.

I was about to ask her to elaborate when she smacked her cards down on the dusty floorboards and yelled, "Poker!" to which George rolled about laughing again.

"Shush," I told them. "You hear that?"

They shook their heads, and I peered out of the tiny window. It was a car. But Mom and Pops were home. As the car pulled to a stop, I saw Sheriff Howard illuminated by the porch light.

"What in the hell is he doing here?" I said.

Clem and George looked out too. "Maybe he knows we've been playing poker?" Clem said worriedly.

"Don't be stupid, Clem. We're playing cards."

"It's still gambling," she whined.

"What we gambling for?" I asked her, and swept my hand over the five or six matchsticks we had been using as money. "You think he's gonna arrest us for playing for them?"

Pops was now out on the lawn, shaking Howard's hand, then beckoning him inside.

Was it the window? Had Jozef told the police? Was it Mikey? Was it worse than everyone had said?

My heart racing, I hurried down the ladder from the treehouse and snuck up onto the porch, Clem and George at my heels.

"Be quiet," I whispered to them. "If Mom or Pops see us, we'll be sent to my room, so hush, okay?"

They nodded and crouched down low next to me.

Howard was in the living room, murmuring something about Nancy.

"We just have to ask the questions," I heard Howard say, louder now.

"He's in pieces with grief, for the love of God." Mom was almost yelling. "Can you speak to him another day?"

"It has to be now."

"I'll get him," Pops said, and I heard the tread of his feet as he ascended the stairs.

"I'm sorry," Howard said. "Really I am. It's hard for so many of us right now."

"I still think your timing is lousy," Mom said. "The day of the funeral. You choose today?"

"My hands are tied," Howard said.

More footsteps, then Billy's voice: "Sheriff," he said.

"Billy, I know this is hard. I just need to ask you a few questions."

Someone spoke—Billy?

"Right, so, I just need to know when the last time was that you saw Nancy?"

"The day before—you know," Billy said. "During the day. With Carl and Barbara and Susan."

Howard mumbled something: "—like the others said."

"So that's it then?" Pops asked. "He told you and the others have said the same. What are you trying to insinuate here, Howard?" His tone had taken on an edge that I hadn't heard before.

"Nothing, nothing at all. It's simply routine. Just trying to piece together her last few hours."

"What does it matter?" Mom asked. "It was an accident."

More mumbling from Howard.

"What's he saying?" George whispered.

I held my finger to my lip to shush him.

"—not that easy—not clear just yet—waiting for reports—I understand. Yes. Of course we are all grieving—yes, poor Mr. and Mrs. Briggs." Snippets of the conversation wafted outside to us, and I strained to hear whether he said "murder" or "killed." "No—no more questions—so sorry, Billy—I know your friend—"

Pleasantries were being made, and I quickly turned and motioned for Clem and George to run back to the treehouse.

Once there, we stayed quiet until we heard the scrunch of tires alerting us to Howard's departure. Only then did I feel like I could breathe.

"Billy hasn't done anything wrong." George was the first to break the silence.

"I know," I said.

"But it means it's more serious than an accident," Clem said authoritatively.

"Not so," I countered. "He said it was routine."

Clem shrugged, and I didn't believe myself either—not after seeing how Mr. Briggs confronted the sheriff.

"Al! You up there? Come on in. Say goodbye to your friends," Pops yelled from the backyard in a strained voice that meant there was no point in arguing.

"See you later." Clem gave me a quick hug and climbed slowly down the ladder, followed by George who gave me a weak grin, neither of them really knowing what to say.

I needed Mikey. I needed a friend.

The following day the wind woke me. It whipped at the trees and spindly branches tapped at my window. I rolled onto my side and watched those woody fingers tip-tap, wanting to be let in. I loved it when the wind stirred like this. It would create tiny dust tornadoes that Mikey, Clem, George, and I would try to chase down the street until they settled and disappeared. Dogs would bark at the invisible gusts that rattled porch doors and whistled through gaps, whilst cats chased dust bunnies that ran all over the house.

I wanted to go and see Amos again, and Jozef. Yesterday, it had been fun bathing Amos, who had tried to catch the water in his teeth as it sprayed from the hose, then ran madly around the garden trying to dry himself. Jozef had seemed relaxed and helped bathe him, laughing at Amos' antics, and made me lemonade and cookies for afterwards. He had not told me any more about Adi and Bruno, and as much as I wanted to know more, I oddly knew I couldn't force Jozef to talk. He would when he wanted to, and I was willing to be patient in order to hear the rest of his stories.

"Al, get up!"

I turned to see Clem at my doorway, her face flushed and hair wild from the wind. "Mikey's back."

I dressed quickly, grabbed a couple of dollars from my piggy bank, then told Mom and Pops that we were going to the diner to celebrate Mikey's return.

"George has gone to fetch him," Clem said, as she rode her bike next to me.

I could barely hear her as the wind raced through my ears.

"Did you see him?" I shouted to her.

"Mom did this morning. Howard went to fetch him from his aunt's. He says his dad is sober now."

I knew Mikey's dad would have dried out for a few days in a cell, closely watched by Howard, and I knew that he wouldn't stay sober for long. The only reason Mikey had not been shipped off to live with his aunt full-time was because Howard was Mikey's pa's best friend since high school and he wanted to see him get better. Hell, we all did, but we knew that sooner or later Mikey would turn up with a small bruise, shortly followed by a larger one, until the cops were called again.

We reached the diner in record speed, and I patted my bike as I clambered off it, telling the rusty old thing well done for still being so fast when needed.

The bell that hung over the diner door jingled when we entered, and in a red booth at the rear sat Mikey with George across from him.

I ran over and stood in front of the booth, waiting for Mikey to jump up and hug me, or high-five me, but he sat staring at the table, listening to George, who was excitedly telling him about a kite he had been given and how today was the perfect day to fly it.

"Hey," I said, and slid into the booth next to him.

"Hey," he said, his voice flat.

Clem shoved George up and sat down, all of us looking at Mikey and wondering what to say.

"What can I get you guys?" Frank, the diner owner, stood at

the table, his pad and pencil in hand, his grin showing his white teeth.

"Milkshakes all round," George said.

"Bit early for a milkshake." Frank shook his head. "How 'bout a nice pancake or some eggs?"

"Mikey came home," I told him. "We're celebrating."

Frank looked at Mikey then back at us, his smile faltering for a moment. Then, he plastered it back on. "Milkshakes it is. On the house," he said.

We didn't have to tell him what we wanted. It was always the same. Chocolate for all of us, with extra whipped cream.

"How was it at your aunt's?" Clem ventured.

"Okay. You know what she's like. Always fussing and making me eat loads. It was fine."

"You glad to be home?" George asked, and I gave him a hard stare so he looked at the table.

"Don't answer that," I told Mikey.

"Why?"

"Well, you know, your pa—"

"I'm glad to see you guys." Mikey finally looked at us and gave us a weak smile. I could see a scab on his eyebrow, knitted together with thick black stitches. He saw me looking.

"I'm gonna have a cool scar when this is healed," he said.

Frank placed the giant milkshakes in front of us, and we all eagerly spooned the whipped cream into our mouths, enjoying the natural silence. As we ate, the bell rang, and Howard the sheriff waltzed in and sat at the counter.

"What can I get you?" Frank asked him.

"Usual," Howard said.

He hadn't seen us sitting in our booth, and I was glad he hadn't. I didn't want him to come over, pretend everything was okay and tell Mikey that his dad was a good guy really, he just had problems. I reckoned if Howard did come over, I might end up throwing my milkshake on him, damn the consequences.

"You heard any more 'bout the girl?" Frank poured coffee into Howard's cup.

"I shouldn't say," Howard said, taking a deep drink from his coffee so that Frank had to refill it.

"So, my kite," George started.

"Shhhhh," Mikey warned him. "Listen. They're talking about Nancy."

George, chastised, concentrated on his milkshake whilst Clem, Mikey, and I cocked our ears to hear if Howard would spill.

"If you shouldn't say, sounds to me like you know something," Frank said.

"Ha! Always one to know when I'm hiding something, Frank. Say, you ever thought of joining the force?"

"Not for me, Sheriff. Me, I'd rather just listen to folks talk, make them some food, keep everyone happy."

"I'd like to make everyone happy," Howard said. "But this time it's gonna stir up some bad feelings."

"So what happened?"

"Coroner says she was dead before she went in the water. Something about the water in her lungs. There was semen too."

"Oh Lord!" Frank put his hand to his mouth. "You think she was raped too?"

"No doubt about it. I spoke to her father. He says she wasn't allowed to date. Had no boyfriend. Seems to me that someone took advantage of her."

"What in hell was she doing down at the lake, though?" Frank asked.

"That I don't know."

"Any idea who it might be?" Frank asked.

"We're thinking some drifter. Been a few of them looking for work, some young men too. Thinking maybe one of them got her to go down to the lake with them. But there's nothing solid, not yet."

"I can't imagine anyone round here doing anything like that," Frank said.

"Makes you wonder though, don't it? Maybe it is someone we know. That's what I'm afraid of, you know, telling everyone and then they'll all be panicking and looking at each other. I'm hoping it's a drifter."

"Could be that German, you know the one. Came after the war, a refugee. He's a funny one. Doesn't talk to no one, doesn't go to church."

"He's Jewish, Frank, that's why he doesn't go to church."

"Yeah, but I'm just sayin' he's a funny one."

"He might be, but it don't mean he's a killer. Keep those thoughts to yourself, Frank. Don't be spreading no rumors."

Frank mimed zipping his lips closed. "Not a word, Sheriff, not a word from me."

I thought I saw Frank wink at me, and I looked to Mikey whose face had become animated. As soon as Howard started to tuck into his eggs and bacon, Mikey began talking.

"I knew it! I told you, didn't I? Hell, I should become a sheriff when I'm older. I'd figure out crimes like *that*." Mikey snapped his fingers.

"I don't want to talk about it," George said. "Let's talk about my kite. Let's go fly it."

"Yeah, I agree with George," I said, and took a sip from my milkshake.

Only Clem didn't talk.

"Clem agrees with me, don't you, Clem? That weird German guy killed her and raped her," Mikey said.

"I don't know," Clem said quietly.

"You okay, Clem?" I asked.

She wiped a tear away from her eyes. "It's just so sad." She sniffed. "So sad. I don't want to get excited that maybe we were right about who did it. What does it matter anyway?"

"What does it matter?" Mikey slammed his fist on the table,

making the salt and pepper shakers jump and clatter back down onto the silver tabletop. "What does it matter? It matters because people shouldn't get away with stuff. We can't sit here and pretend it doesn't matter."

"Calm down, Mikey." I placed my hand on his forearm.

He shook me away and stared at his milkshake.

"Look," I said, breaking the tension. "They'll find out who did it. We can't do anything anyway, right? And besides, who knows. It might not be him. He might be a really nice man who saves homeless dogs and is scared of crows and who had a best friend and a girl and things were bad for him, and maybe he is forgiving and a bit lonely and wants friends but is scared to make them."

All three looked at me as if I had gone mad. "I'm just saying, that's all. I'm just saying we don't know, do we?"

"You've some imagination on you, Al." Mikey laughed. The tension had been broken.

"Yeah, like you're gonna say next that Homer has pet bunny rabbits and only pretends to shoot 'em to look tough," George chimed in.

"Or that the principal is a nice guy and loves kids!"

"Yeah!" Mikey agreed. "Or that my pa loves me and really he's a great guy!" Mikey started laughing uncontrollably, and we all fell silent and stared at him, not knowing what to say.

Frank came over and put his hand on Mikey's shoulder. "Say, you busy today, Mikey?"

Mikey stopped laughing and looked at Frank.

"I'm just wonderin' whether you'd like to help me here today. You could earn a few bucks and have all the ice cream you want."

"Can I work here?" George asked eagerly.

"Yeah, me too!" Clem joined in.

"Perhaps I could do with a few more. You want to, Mikey?"

"Yeah. Yeah, that would be good," Mikey said.

"And you, Miss Alice?" Frank looked to me.

I shook my head. "I've got chores to do," I lied.

"Ah, come on, Al. We can all work here and have ice cream all day!" Clem cajoled.

"I can't," I said. "Sorry."

"That's okay," Frank said. "I got me three new employees. That'll do for now. Keep you all busy and out of mischief." He grinned.

The three of them scrambled off behind Frank, who started telling them what duties they would have, Mikey scrunching up his brow like he did when he was concentrating. I was glad Frank had asked him to help out. He needed the distraction, and I didn't know what to say or do that would help him. But I did know one person I could help.

My trusty bike gave up on the turn into Mulberry Street, the chain refusing to go back onto the little wheels of teeth that made it go round.

"You were fine this morning," I told it as I walked with it beside me. "You did great. And now you do this to me. You know, if you're not careful, I'll save my money and buy a new bicycle and you'll be gone!"

The bike squeaked next to me as I walked, and I suddenly felt sorry for it.

"Sorry. You're old. I get it. I won't throw you out."

"Are you talking to your bicycle?" Jozef's head popped up from behind a bush, his pruning shears in his hand.

"Yeah." I blushed.

"It's all right. I talk to things all the time. Sometimes, I imagine that they talk back to me."

"Some people would call you crazy for saying something like that," I said.

"People will always think what they want. If they want to think I am crazy, then that's up to them. Can I take a look at it?"

I let him take the bike away from me, and he wheeled it up

to the side of the house and tipped it upside down. "I can fix this for you. Make it like new."

"Really?"

"Of course. Let's go see Amos and get you some lemonade, and then I'll fix it."

"I thought I was supposed to be doing chores for you?" I asked.

"You will. The wind earlier has made a mess of the lawn out the back. Leaves everywhere. You and Amos can clear it together. I tried earlier, but Amos wanted to play with each leaf as it blew, so we didn't get much done. But now it's dropped a little, he might be a bit more helpful."

I agreed to Jozef's plan, then sat on the porch and played with Amos whilst he fixed lemonade for me.

"You seem different today?" Jozef said, placing the lemonade on the table and giving Amos a quick ruffle on his head.

"Different how?"

"I don't know." He sat and tilted his head to the side. "Sort of a bit sad, I think. Yes. A bit sad."

I sat down across from him and kept stroking Amos. "My friend Mikey has come home."

"And that makes you sad?"

"I dunno. I was excited to see him, but he was different."

"Sad?" he asked.

"Yeah. Maybe sad. But maybe angry too. When his pa has hit him, I can usually cheer him up, but this time it was like he was back, but he wasn't really back, you know?"

Jozef nodded. "I understand. You just need to give him some time. It will be hard for him—he still loves his father, but he's scared and angry too."

"Still loves him?" I almost laughed. "How can he love him? He beats him all the time."

Jozef shook his head gently. "It's not that easy to hate your parent, especially a boy who only has his father left. Deep down, he loves him and wants him to be proud of him and love him back."

"Well," I said, crossing my arms over my body, "if my pa hit me like that, I wouldn't love him anymore."

"It's complicated, Alice. You would. Deep down, you would always love him, even if you hated yourself for feeling that way."

I fell quiet again and concentrated on stroking Amos, who looked at me with his large brown eyes, and now and again licked his lips in satisfaction. Jozef was wrong. There was no way I would love Pops if he hit me like that. No way.

"There's something else too, isn't there?" Jozef said, noticing my reluctance to speak.

I raised my eyebrows at him in question.

"I can tell. What else has upset you?"

"It's just something someone said," I answered reluctantly.

"What did they say?"

"It's stupid really. Just gossip."

"About you? About Mikey?"

I shook my head. "About you."

"And what are people saying about me?"

"It's just gossip," I repeated. "Mom says I shouldn't gossip. But I think you should know, so I think that it's okay for me to tell you. Frank at the diner was talking to the sheriff, Howard. You know Howard?"

Jozef nodded.

"Well, Howard was saying that Nancy—you know, the girl that was found dead—well, he said that she was murdered and maybe raped, and Frank said that no one in town would do anything like that, and then—"

"And then," Jozef cut me off. "He said what about that strange German man who lives in our town?"

"How did you know?" I asked.

"I know that people will always talk about someone they don't know. They fear what they don't know or don't understand. I keep myself to myself, I don't have any friends—it's natural that people should think I am a little strange."

"But not a murderer," I said. "They shouldn't think that."

"When you first met me, you were scared of me, weren't you?" he asked.

"A little, I suppose."

"But now?"

"Now I'm not."

"Do you think I killed that girl?"

"No."

"And why don't you think I did?"

"Because you're nice."

"Because you know me, don't you?"

"Yeah."

"Well, that's all it is with the gossip. They don't know me, so they will just say things and be scared for no reason."

"Why don't you get to know some people?" I asked. "Like maybe if you went to the diner, you could talk to Frank, and he can see you're nice and that he's wrong? I could help you, if you like?"

Jozef smiled and shook his head. "I cannot change what people think of me, Alice. You know, for years, in Germany and all around the world, people thought that Jewish people were bad."

I nodded. I knew. We had done some classes on Hitler and the war at school.

"They thought that for no reason. Or maybe because they wanted to believe it so that they had someone to blame for all their problems. I've learned that I cannot change what people think and what they say. They have always done it and probably will always continue to do it."

"Because you're Jewish?"

"Because I'm different."

"Mom says it's good to be different," I said.

"It is. But it comes with a price."

"What price?"

Jozef stood and went inside, and only came out a few minutes later, stuffing a folded wad of paper into his pocket.

"Do you really want to know? About the war, about why I am here and what price I have paid?" He leaned forward and looked me hard in the eye.

I returned the stare. "I do."

"You're sure?"

"I am."

TEN

JOZEF

1938

Adi and I married in 1935. Despite the madness surrounding us, we hoped for a future—as Adi would say, in the darkness, that is when you need the light the most.

And so it was for us that we tried to find the light, but it was hard to do, especially as the years wore on and the darkness seemed to envelop us completely.

It started slowly, but soon gathered speed. I was studying history at university and hoped to become a professor, whilst Adi worked as a nurse—something she excelled at and loved with all her heart. Before we were married, the changes had started—Jewish professors at the university were fired, many left seeing what was to come of Hitler's power, but some of us thought that it would pass. Indeed, if history taught us anything, it was that things come and go, and this power that the Nazi party had I truly believed would wane. I was naive, of course. Young and naive and in love with Adi, and excited about our future. Even when my own professor left for the United States and warned me to do the same, I remember scoffing at him for being so excitable and decided it was his age that made him afraid, and that we young students would stick it out and show everyone that it would all turn out fine.

I was allowed to stay at the university up until just after our marriage in the summer of '35, and then I found myself and my fellow Jewish students banned from studying, banned from our library and our future.

But I did not give up. I taught instead—private students mostly and sometimes small groups—Adi still nursed, and we still ate and we still seemed to live. The bans on where we could go and what we could own got worse, but again, for some reason, I still believed that it would not last. That changed for me, and for my parents, in the early winter of 1938, when I finally realized with a crashing blow that I had been wrong, stupid, and careless. We were in danger and it was not going to pass.

On November 10, Adi woke early to go to work. It must have been around 5 a.m. She kissed me lightly on the cheek and woke me a little just so that I could tell her I loved her.

I rolled over and fell back to sleep, but just moments later, Adi ran into the room screaming, crying, and telling me to wake up.

"The streets are on fire!" she screamed at me.

I thought for a moment I was still dreaming and shook my head to try and wake up from this nightmare, but Adi was tugging at the curtains, pointing and screaming at me to get up.

I did. I looked out of the window and saw the synagogue on the corner of our street engulfed in flames that licked at the walls and reached up into the sky.

"My God!" I said.

I dressed quickly and followed Adi outside to see the Jewish youth center also on fire, businesses belonging to our friends and neighbors being smashed to pieces, not only by men in frightening uniforms but average everyday people, who threw bricks through the windows and laughed as they shattered.

"Your parents." She looked at me, her eyes wide with fear.

We raced to my parents' home. They had been lucky to still own it given all the restrictions, and had bribed and paid any amount to keep it. Adi's parents were in France, gone two years before back to Paris where they thought the Nazis would not reach them. Her father had said as much when we left them at the train station—"Why would the Germans want France? There's nothing there for them apart from us Jews. That's what they want—us out of their country, so here we are, leaving it."

As soon as we reached my parents' front door, they opened it and dragged us inside. "You shouldn't have come," my mother said, not looking at me but over my shoulder at the wall, as if she could see what was happening outside.

My father was pacing the living room, sucking hard at his pipe so that the smoke billowed out behind him like a steam train.

He saw me and opened his arms. I went to him and let him embrace me, not really wanting to let go.

"We should have had the papers by now," he fretted.

"They'll come soon."

"Your sister and Magnus, they got theirs two months ago. They're already there. Why aren't we?"

"It'll be your turn next, I know it," I said.

"You two need to come too." He pointed at Adi now, who had her arm around my mother's shoulders. "Palestine. It's where we belong. We'll all go. We'll get you some papers."

My father half ran into his study and brought out a messy batch of paper, spreading the pages frantically across the wooden floor.

"They're here somewhere. The applications. I got them for you too. I know you said you didn't want to go, I know. But you have to. Now is the time, do you see it now?" He looked up at us both, his eyes red from lack of sleep and the smoke.

There was a knock at the door. A loud unfriendly knock.

"Go out the back!" my mother whispered harshly to Adi and me. "Go out the back now."

"I'm not leaving you," I told them.

"Don't be stupid, boy. Get out. Now." My father, not one to show any violence in his entire life, gripped my arm with such force that I knew he had bruised it, and dragged me through the house to the rear door that led into the garden. "Get out through the gate at the back. Keep your head down. Go. Now."

Before I could argue with him, he had shoved both Adi and me outside, shut the door and marched toward the front door, where the knocking had turned into hammering and shouting.

Adi was the one who made me move. I could have stood there like that for hours, my mind not catching up with what was really happening.

We were at the rear gate that led into an alleyway and followed it to the corner, when suddenly Adi pulled me aside behind a large bush and told me to be quiet.

I followed where she was looking and saw Gestapo officers loading people into cars, all of them white with fear.

"We should have listened. We should have left years ago," I said. "I should have convinced Father back when my professor told me to leave. I shouldn't have thought that it would be all right." My thoughts were rambling, my speech quick and unclear.

"Now's not the time," Adi said. "We both believed things would get better. We both did. Now is not the time to look at what we should have done."

I saw my father being loaded into the back of a car and driven off by two Gestapo. We waited a few minutes, then a few minutes more to see if my mother would be next, but she wasn't and we raced back down the alleyway, through the gate, and crouched low under the kitchen window, peering inside to see who was there.

It seemed as if no one was home—but where was Mama?

"I'm going to go in," I told Adi.

"Don't," she said. "They may still be there."

"If they were there, then they'd make noise, Adi. They're not going to creep about quietly like mice."

Adi giggled.

"Sorry," she said. "I don't know why I laughed. I'm scared."

"I know."

I slowly turned the doorknob, wincing as it squeaked under my hand. Bit by bit I edged my way inside and looked into each room. When I reached the living room, I found my mother sitting on the floor, her head in her hands and her shoulders heaving.

"Mama." I sat next to her and held her close.

Adi was soon there, and we both held my mother until her sobs came under control. She looked at us with red-rimmed eyes. "They took him. Your father. They took him for questioning because of the books he writes."

"They're about science," I said. "He wrote them years ago. Why now?"

"I don't know!" she screamed. "I don't know, Jozef. Why are they doing any of this? Why did you and your father think it would be all right? You both sitting there in the evenings in front of the fire with all your academic discussions, thinking we are hysterical whilst all around us the world is falling apart, and neither of you would listen until it was too late!"

"I'm sorry," I tried, feeling a knot in my throat. "I'm sorry."

"You saw him!" She pointed to the pile of papers still on the floor. "You saw what he has become these past few months. He realized too late and it's killing him. He doesn't sleep. Doesn't eat. And now—now they've taken him, Jozef."

I couldn't talk. I didn't know what to say. She was right. My father and I had buried our heads in books, theories, and academia, thinking that it would save us—that knowledge would save us. Yet, the knowledge we needed was the reality we lived in, and we had ignored it.

"Come, come with me." Adi helped my mother up from the floor and sat her on the sofa.

"I'm sorry, Jozef," my mother said. "I'm sorry."

I nodded at her and looked at Adi. My beautiful, brave, caring Adi. I knew I had to save them both.

"We need to leave, now," I said.

"What if he comes home? No. I have to wait here in case he comes home," my mother said.

I could hear shouts and screams from outside, and looked out of the window to see a neighbor's house being set alight.

"We need to leave now," I said, trying to thread some authority into my tone.

"Where would we go?" Adi asked.

"Frau Meyer," I said. "She lives an hour away. Her house is in a small town. We go there for a few nights."

"How do you know she will take us in?" my mother asked.

"She was your friend, Mama, for years. She still is. She will take us."

"She might side with them." Adi nodded toward the noise outside.

I shook my head. "She wouldn't. Not ever. We go now."

My mother, tired, weak, and afraid, had no fight left in her. She allowed Adi to pack a small bag for her, and we led her out of the house, down the garden toward the gate, and away from her home.

Frau Meyer opened her door to us a few hours later. She did not speak but held out her arms for my mother to fall into and weep upon her shoulder.

We eventually sat in her tiny sitting room, the coffee table touching our knees. She poured us all hot thick coffee and gave us sweet pastries.

"You need your strength," she told my mother, who pecked at the pastry like a newborn bird. "Eat it. You need to eat."

"Thank you, Frau Meyer," I began.

She held her hand up to stop me. "Ingrid, please. I think you are old enough now to call me by my Christian name."

I nodded. "Ingrid. We didn't know where else to go."

"I assume they have your father?" she asked, leaning back in her rocking chair, looking older than I had ever assumed she was. I knew her to be older than Mama; the pair of them had begun a friendship as next-door neighbors when Ingrid's husband had died and Mama had played cards with her, taken her food, and sat talking to her long into the night. When she had moved, they had seen less of each other, but had always written, sent postcards, and had dinner once a month with each other.

I realized now that Ingrid must be in her late seventies or early eighties and perhaps we should not have imposed upon her—it was too much.

"Your father," she said again. "They have him?"

"They took him for questioning," Mama said.

"They've taken quite a few, from what I hear. You should have left. I thought you had when I hadn't heard from you."

My mother did not answer her friend and looked at me, then back at her pastry.

"It's my fault." I coughed, clearing my throat. "It's my fault. We should have left."

"Bastards, the lot of them," Ingrid suddenly shouted, spraying crumbs from her mouth as she chewed. "Bastards. Stupid, small-minded bastards following that evil little man and his ideas. It goes to show you how stupid so many people are, doesn't it? I blame the parents, you know. They didn't educate their children and now look at what we have got. A bunch of idiots running around smashing things because one man told them to. Bastards."

I smiled despite the seriousness of the day. I liked Ingrid and the way she spoke. I could see a fire and a strength in her that I had never seen before.

"Don't you worry," she said. "I'll help you. Sure, I'll go down there myself and get him out of prison. You watch me. I've money. I know people. You'll see, I'll get him for you."

"No, Ingrid, please." My mother placed her hand on her arm. "We don't want you getting into trouble too."

"No trouble for me. My nephew, he's one of those bastards, but he thinks he'll inherit when I die, so you'll see, I'll get him to get Amos home. Trust me."

And I did trust her. She was defiant and stubborn, and I bet that her nephew, whilst listening to his Führer's orders, was probably more scared of his aunt.

"Tell me, when he comes home, you are going to leave, yes?"

"I hope so," my mother said. "I hope we can go to Palestine."

"And you two?" Ingrid looked at Adi and me.

"Maybe France," Adi said. I shot a look at her.

"We haven't decided," I said.

"My parents are in Paris. We can go there. I can't leave them much longer. Papa is almost blind now—his diabetes. Maman is sick all the time. They need us."

"You don't want to go to Paris?" Ingrid asked me.

"I don't want to be forced to leave my home by anybody," I said.

Ingrid cackled at my response. "Don't be stupid, Jozef. This is not your home now. Your home is wherever you make it. France, Palestine, Britain. Who cares? You have Adi, a wife. Go, make a happy home somewhere."

I nodded. She was right, of course.

"Take me with you." She looked at my mother now. "When

you go to Palestine. Take me with you. I'll convert. I'll be Jewish. Don't leave me here with this lot."

My mother smiled gently at her. "I'm not sure how easy that would be."

"Pah, easy!" Ingrid cackled again. "I have money. Don't you worry. If you say I can come with you, then I'll make sure I get the papers. Money can make a lot of things happen."

"Of course I'd want you to, but—"

"Good," Ingrid cut my mother off. "That's settled then. Better get planning, eh?"

Over the next two days, Ingrid was true to her word. She went continually to the offices in the city and found the prison where my father was being held. She was able to get him his pipe, tobacco, and extra food, and checked on our house to report that the door had been broken down, but it wasn't on fire, and there were no Gestapo around.

"We should go home," my mother said when she heard the news. "We need to go home, find the application papers, and try to get our visas."

"No," I told her. "It's too dangerous. They could come back."

"I agree with your mother, Jozef," Ingrid said. "We go to your house. Find what we need. Any valuables that you can sell or give to someone for safekeeping. Then we can come back here each night. And you two"—she pointed at Adi and me—"need to decide now what it is you are going to do. Talk to each other and figure this out. Now."

I had barely spoken to Adi since we had arrived at Ingrid's. I wasn't mad at her; I was angry at myself for not protecting her and my parents, and for being so stubborn about it all. I felt as if I had let her down and she knew it, and I was scared to talk to her about France, or Palestine, or anything in case she told me what I already knew—I wasn't good enough for her.

Adi touched my hand and I looked at her. She smiled and stood.

I took her hand in mine and allowed her to lead me outside onto the tiny, cobbled street of Ingrid's town, which held nothing more than a church, a cluster of cottages, and a small shop.

As we walked, Adi hummed a tune.

"You're not afraid anymore?" I asked.

"I am. But I have to think positively. I have to think that this will pass and we will be fine."

"We'll go to Paris," I said.

"But you never wanted to."

"Things change. Things have changed. So have I. We can't stay here anymore," I told her. "And I'm so sorry, Adi. So sorry. You have every right to be mad at me. To want to leave without me. I haven't been a very good husband to you."

She stopped walking and held my face in her hands. "Stop it, Jozef. Stop it now. I wanted to believe you that things would change, I wanted to believe not for you, but for me. We were both wrong. But we know now what we need to do. Ingrid is right. We can make our home anywhere we want to. And you'll love Paris. You'll really truly love it. You can go back to university, study and become the great professor you always wanted to be."

"I don't speak very good French," I mumbled.

She laughed. "You'll learn. I'll teach you."

I smiled at her, my lovely, wonderful wife, and kissed her until she squirmed away from me, embarrassed at my public display of love for her.

. . .

The next day we went back to my parents' home, and planned to go to our apartment afterwards. On almost every street we saw gangs vandalizing homes—throwing furniture, clothes, and bedding from broken windows. Adi held on to my arm tightly and my eyes constantly scanned left to right, in front, behind me, checking to see if anyone was looking at us or following us.

Ingrid and my mother walked in front of us, Ingrid telling Mama a story from when she had been a young girl and gone to a dance, and on a dare lifted her skirts and shown her calves.

"It was a big thing back in my day to do that, you know!" Ingrid laughed.

My mother laughed along with her, and I was so glad of Ingrid's company—she desperately wanted to take our minds away from what was happening and more often than not, she succeeded.

Our street looked oddly peaceful. The wind ruffled the leaves, and birds trilled their songs as if nothing had happened and nothing would happen here.

The front steps had shards of glass scattered on them, the front door hanging by its hinges.

Inside, the living room had been turned upside down—pillows knifed open revealing their fluffy contents, the clock on the mantlepiece now a shattered affair on the floor. Pages from books had been torn out, leaving their leather carcasses flat. Dishes in the kitchen were broken, smashed, splintered. Nothing, it seemed, was untouched.

Mama raced upstairs and Ingrid slowly followed. I waited for a scream, a cry, something to indicate what destruction lay in wait, but no exclamation came.

Mama finally descended the stairs. "They didn't touch the bedrooms," she said, relieved. "Go check your apartment, we'll be fine here."

I looked to Adi. I didn't want to leave them here alone.

"We'll go later," Adi asserted. "We have barely anything of value, so it's not like we'll miss much."

"It's still your home," Mama said.

"No. Our home is together. It's just bricks. It doesn't matter," Adi said. "We'll stay here. Tidy a little. Help you get your things together."

For four hours, we swept up broken glass, boarded the windows, hung the front door back on its hinges, and packed our valuables into two cases, which Mama and Ingrid said they could sell and exchange the money into US dollars to hide on their bodies when they left.

Ingrid was already in possession of her visa. Her wily ways with money and contacts had gotten her a new name and passage to Palestine. A bribe to an official, she said, had secured my parents' visas too, which would be ready the following day.

"We can't go without Amos," my mother said later that day, as we sat in the living room on the ripped sofa cushions, still noticing slices of glass that glinted on the hardwood floor.

As with stories in books, it was of course at that moment that my father walked into our home; shaggy, tired, with a bruise over his right eye and a cut on his lip.

My mother made a noise that I had never heard before and one which I think was a mix of pure relief and love. She ran to him and took him in her arms. For the first time in his life, my father looked smaller and more fragile than my mother, and I cried silently as they embraced.

ELEVEN
JOZEF

1938–1942

We left for France soon after my father's release. The day we left, I held my parents close, breathing in their scent so that I could always remember it—my mother's sweet perfume and my father's musky odor that always reminded me of the smell of an old book.

I told him this and he laughed, wiping a tear away from his eyes. "I like that this is what my smell is," he said, "a book. Every time you read or smell a book, you will now think of me."

He kissed me fiercely as if trying to imprint it onto my skin forever, and they stood, waving at us as we walked away.

We had little trouble leaving Germany. I had expected it would be harder, but there were so many people packed onto the platform and the trains that we and our papers became invisible, and the guards barely glanced at them before waving us on our way.

"They want us all to leave," Adi said when we had settled ourselves into our seats. "They don't want us here."

It was a bittersweet journey to Paris, a place I had never

been before. As much as I felt some relief at being able to achieve some form of safety for both Adi and me, I was still leaving my home, my country. As I watched the fields race by in a blur of green, I wondered who I would become now. Would my identity be left behind in my country? Would I be able to take it with me and still feel, in some way, myself?

Adi, I knew, was happy to be returning to Paris, a place that had been her home for more years than Germany had. She often told me that to her, her identity was split right down the middle and she liked it that way. "It means I can be freer than most people—I can be a part of two languages, two cultures, and never feel like I have to be rooted in just one spot."

Indeed, Adi wanted to travel more. She liked the idea of living in London, or traveling around the vast states of America. She even wanted to see Australia and feel that awesome heat on her skin, see a sky that stretched on for days. I didn't share her sense of wanderlust. I liked having roots, having my parents nearby, and seeing familiar faces each day. The thought of not knowing anyone in Paris other than Adi's parents worried me quite a bit, and I wondered if I would ever be able to master the French language that came so easily to Adi, but felt stilted and too exotic on my tongue.

I did not share my worries with Adi. She was excited to see her parents and friends she had not seen in years, and I did not want to dilute that with my childish fears and worry about when I would see my own parents again.

For the first year, Adi and I settled into some sort of routine. We were able to rent a small apartment in Montmartre courtesy of one of Adi's father's friends who owned a restaurant underneath us, which got rowdy and stayed open late into the evenings. I suspected that we were the only ones desperate enough to live there, as it was a never-ending cacophony of music, laughter, shouting, the clinking of glasses, and occasional smash of a plate or dish. Whilst the noise bothered me sometimes, Adi seemed to come alive with it. She adored the constant wheezing of the accordion that an old man called Pierre played each evening, and would dance in our tiny living room and sometimes manage to cajole me into joining her.

However noisy our apartment was, Montmartre itself was a place that quickly grew on me.

Our apartment was on Rue Berthe and basked in the shadows of the Sacré-Coeur basilica. On cloudy days, the whiteness of the basilica gave some lightness to the drab cobblestones and heavy skies, and I would wander the streets, taking in the names of shops, trying out the words on my tongue.

I would force myself to have coffee alone, to make myself speak the language without Adi taking over, and on those days I found that my nervousness at being in a foreign place started to dissipate.

I made a friend. Or rather, a sort-of friend. His name was Albert, a local policeman who spent more time in cafes and bars, reading the newspaper, smoking, and chatting to customers, than he ever did patrolling the streets. He knew Adi's parents; indeed, he knew everyone it seemed, and would join me on my strolls around the quarter, pointing out who was who, where to buy the best wine, and where not to eat.

"You see that restaurant over there?" He pointed toward the red awnings that covered the outside tables on one of our walks. "That is owned by René. He's a beast of a man and thinks his meat is superior to the other places to eat. But really it tastes like car tires and will make you spend an unfortunate time on the toilet!"

I laughed at his description and told him he must review restaurants for a newspaper—his sense of humor would be welcome to read, rather than the constant news of what was happening in the world.

"I'd like that," he said, lighting yet another one of his thin cigarettes. "But then I like this job. Very little is needed of me. The odd robbery, perhaps a fight," he shrugged. "Nothing much happens here."

It turned out that Albert's uncle was someone high up in the gendarmerie and got him the job because he was not fit to do anything else.

"Surely that cannot be true?" I said to him. "Surely you have a passion—a job that you would like to do?"

"Pfff," he said, a noise I had found many Parisians made when they felt bored or indifferent. "It is what it is. My passion is smoking, coffee, wine, food, women! I am a true Frenchman and I don't need to love my job, I just need a job so that it pays for my other passions."

I understood, yet I was getting bored with not having a job yet, and I knew that my French was still too rusty to be able to properly study or teach.

"You'll find something," Albert said when I told him of my boredom. "I tell you what, I'll help you find something. You like history, yes?"

I nodded.

"Well. A friend of mine, he looks after the cemetery. I can see if he needs help with tending to the graves and registering the history of each. He is always complaining about the archives for the graves—always—he even cancels dinner sometimes so that he can get his records in order! Not a real Frenchman if he cancels dinner!"

"A cemetery? I'm not sure that would be good for me," I said, thinking of all the dead bodies underground.

"It's not just a cemetery," he said, raising his arms wide. "It's a city of the dead! They have their own streets, their own little houses. Have you not been yet? You should go. You will see so many famous people there. You know Dumas? The writer?"

"I do."

"He is there! You can visit with him. Give me a few days and I will sort it for you."

That evening I told Adi of Albert's suggestion. "It's macabre," I said.

"I think it's a wonderful idea!" Adi beamed. "I have got a nursing position now, and you can't walk the streets all day. Just think, you can learn about the people buried there, write about them perhaps. Think about the possibilities, Jozef."

So I did. I thought about what I could write about a grave-yard and came up with very little, until I visited it the next day and saw the necropolis that awaited me.

Albert had been right. It was a city of the dead, with mausoleums housing entire families, graves with sculptures, and elaborately carved and engraved headstones all edged by cobbled streets and maple, chestnut, and lime trees.

I spent a whole afternoon wandering each street and found myself lost a few times, yet it did not worry me or make me feel uneasy like most graveyards; it was beautiful, sad, and interest-ing, and I knew what I would write about.

"If Albert can get me the job," I told Adi excitedly that evening, "I am going to write a history of the dead."

"A history of the dead?" She raised her eyebrow at me, and I could tell she was wondering if I had partaken of an afternoon drinking wine with Albert.

"Indeed. Think about it. I can write about the traditions we have with our dead, go back through history and write about this cemetery in particular, who the wealthy families were, their history as well as their traditions. What do you think?"

"I think it sounds like it will keep you busy. And I think it would be good for you to be studying again, researching and writing. It's what you love."

"That is where you are wrong." I jumped up from my armchair and wrapped my arms around her as she stirred a sauce for dinner. "It is you that I love!"

She giggled and turned, allowing me to kiss her, and for the first time in a long time, I felt as though things were going to be all right, after all.

Albert was as good as his word and got me a job with his friend Matisse. We mostly worked tending to the graves, clearing away weeds and litter, making sure that the little streets were clear and as welcoming as they could be. He allowed me to look through the notes and archives that he had and would tell me stories about the people buried there.

"See here, this is Yves. He died in 1876 at just fourteen years old. I like to think of him as a youngster, running through the graveyard and playing hide-and-seek with his friends. Morning, Yves," he said, clearing away a string of ivy that had tried to curl itself around the marble headstone and little stone angel that sat atop it.

"What have you been up to today?" he asked the grave.

At first, Matisse's conversations with the dead unnerved me a little, but as time wore on, I, too, began to talk to the inhabitants, imagining who they had been in life and picturing them sitting next to their own graves, giving me a wave as they saw me coming, happy to have a visitor.

We had other workers who tended parts of the cemetery too, but these men worked quickly and hard a few days a week and did not seem to have the same bond with the necropolis that both Matisse and I shared.

To say I was happy would not be quite true. I missed my parents who had successfully managed to emigrate to Palestine; I missed my friends in Munich, my students, and the life that I had left behind. Yet, I was content with this new life and as happy as I could be.

In 1940, things changed once more. The invasion of Poland sent us all reeling, knowing that Hitler was stronger than we had ever imagined he could be, and as his armies marched both east and west, in France we wondered how long it would be until we would feel the reach of Germany here too.

Scores of people left during the first few months of 1940, gathering up what they could carry and taking to the streets.

In May, a newspaper announcement made Adi and me grow cold once more with fear: "...Tout les ressortissants de l'Empire Allemand et les Dantzigois, Sarrois, Rheinians [sic] de deux sexes de 17 à 55 ans vont être internés..." (All nationals of Germany, Danzig, the Saarland, the Rhineland, male and female, age seventeen to fifty-five are going to be interned.)

Whilst Adi was French, we still did not feel safe. The German army was moving closer to Paris, and although Albert assured me that they would never take France, I knew from past experience not to be complacent.

"We cannot leave," Adi said one evening.

We were sitting in her parents' apartment. Her father, Charles, was almost completely blind now, the diabetes having taken his sight and his confidence. Her mother, Sarah, was also sick with various ailments that no doctor could seem to cure.

"We will be fine," Charles said. "Adi is French, that is enough. You are married to a Frenchwoman. There is nothing to worry about."

I shook my head. We needed to do more.

"But we can't leave," Adi said again. "We need to help Maman and Papa. They cannot manage a journey south."

"And I won't leave my home," Charles stubbornly said. I watched as he poured himself a glass of red wine, refusing any help and slopping the liquid all over the table. He did not seem to notice or care and walked slowly to his chair, bumping twice into the side table that he shouted at and accused Adi of moving.

"Don't move anything in this house," he said. "I know where everything is, and if you move it, I will walk into it."

"I didn't move it," Adi told him.

"You did. Or someone did."

"It doesn't matter, Charles," Sarah scolded him. "Jozef is right. What if they take him anyway? He hasn't been here long, and they could easily decide that he is still German and that is that."

Sarah's commentary made Adi start to cry, and Charles tried to move over to find his daughter and take her in his arms.

"What can we do?" I asked.

"Change your names. New papers," Sarah suggested. "Change your religion too. Change it all, be someone else."

"Maman!" Adi said.

"What?"

"How can you think it all right to change who you are and what you believe?"

"Don't be naive, Adi. They will come for us eventually—they started in Germany and they will keep going, and your father and I cannot leave. We are too sick, too old. Do it. Change your surname, change your religion on your papers. You'll need to pay, of course."

Adi stared at me in disbelief, and I understood how she felt. We had already left our home and our country, and now we had to change what we believed in; our faith, who we were.

The discussions between Adi and me went on until the Germans marched into Paris that summer and it sealed our fate. We would change what we could, we would pay what we could, and we would hope and pray that we had not been too late.

"How do we do it?" Adi asked me early on a Tuesday morning.

"I'm going to ask Albert," I said.

"You trust him?"

"I do. He's my friend, he's in the police. He can get us new papers, new identification, and we will be all right."

I kissed her forehead and took her in my arms, squeezing

her tight to let her know that it would be okay, whilst inside my stomach churned with what I was about to do.

Albert met me for coffee at our favorite cafe and had already ordered sweet pastries to accompany the bitter black coffee he so favored.

"The thing with coffee," he said, lighting a cigarette then taking a sip, "is that you have to find flavors that complement each other. This tobacco, for example, is sweet but has a hint of dark chocolate, so with the coffee and the sugary pastry it gives the mouth a mixture of flavors."

"Albert," I said, trying to inject a seriousness into my tone. "I need your help."

He stopped his ruminating about the flavors in front of him and leaned forward. "I'm listening," he said.

I outlined my request, but he did not answer, smoking quickly until he flicked the end onto the street where a pigeon stumbled over thinking it was food.

"I can do this," he said finally. "I cannot do a lot, mind you. I can get you a new ID, but I cannot find your original documents and make them disappear, which could be a problem down the road. I have heard of others doing the same, so you are not alone, but they had contacts to get new birth certificates, even diplomas from school and university to back up their new identity. All I can do is register your name and religion. Would that be enough?"

"If that's all you can do, then yes," I said, relieved that something could be done.

"It will cost, mind you. I will have to pay a few others to get the correct documents."

"Of course," I said. "I am willing to pay."

"Good. All right then. What surname would you like?"

I did not want to give up my surname. I could not imagine being anyone but Jozef Ruben. "Is it really necessary to give up my name?"

"Of course. You are already registered here as Jozef Ruben. If anything happens, then they would look for Jozef Ruben but not find him there. We'll change your name, and you need to change your address too."

"My address?"

"Ah, come now, Jozef. You have to do this properly. I tell you what, I know of an apartment, it is where my aunt lives and closer to the cemetery—why, you can even see it through the living room window. It will cost a little more, but at least you won't have all that noise from the restaurant each evening."

I had become accustomed to the noise and the wheezing accordion, but Albert was right.

"If I may," he said, "let me suggest a name for you. How about a good French surname of Monet."

"Like the painter," I said.

"You know his works! Ah, you will be a true Frenchman yet. Jozef Monet. It is good, no?"

"I suppose."

"Good. It will be done. Leave it with me."

We moved one street away a week later, our new names, religion, and address noted at the police station and on new ID cards that Albert had gotten. They looked slightly different from the ones we already held—the color of the card and the typeface was a little off.

"They are forgeries, of course, but good enough ones," Albert said, as I handed over a wad of francs that would mean Adi and I could eat little for the next month or so. "Make sure Adi changes her job, eh. Somewhere new with her new name."

I returned to our new apartment, which was a little larger than our previous one and had a small balcony, which Adi and I could sit on and look out across the cemetery and beyond. That evening, we shared the last few mouthfuls of a bottle of burgundy in celebration of our new security. We could see the cafes and restaurants fill with the new German arrivals, who seemed less concerned with destroying the city or fighting for their Führer than they did with wanting to experience the delights that Paris could offer them.

Women with short dresses and faces full of makeup flirted with the soldiers, who invited them for a glass of wine and cigarettes.

Before we could even begin to discuss our thoughts, a siren wailed across the darkening sky. We looked at each other, our eyes wide, not sure what to do.

A neighbor shouted from below to come downstairs, and without hesitation we did, following the other neighbors down the staircase to the basement.

I expected the atmosphere to be tense, some fear seeping through the residents. But it was a strangely jovial mood. A neighbor from above us called Thomas had brought three bottles of wine with him, "My babies," he had said when I looked at them. Another had rescued her small dog, who kept us laughing at his running around and attention seeking. A portly woman who still wore her kitchen apron had brought food, scared that she may be without it for some time, and all shared what they had, each of us swigging from the wine and picking at the ham, chicken, and cheese.

Once the sirens quietened and we were allowed back upstairs, Adi and I resolved that if it happened again, we would grab any food, wine, or books we had close by so that we had something to share with our neighbors.

The German occupation of Paris was not as I thought it would be. Jews had to wear the yellow Star of David, but I did not, and I felt confident that our new identities had duped the authorities. We fell into a routine once more and got used to seeing

uniforms everywhere, the changing names of cafes and restaurants to German ones, the swastika flag adorning most buildings, air raids, and planes flying low overhead, but little fighting
happened.

The biggest change was the quiet in the city. Many had fled
during the summer of 1940 and, together with the restrictions
and curfews, left the city looking unkempt. I wandered in the
Jardin des Tuileries where the lawns, which were usually so
well shorn with trimmed edges, now resembled a summer
meadow with long stalks of grass and wildflowers poking
through. The pond near the Louvre, where so many would sail
tiny boats, where children would laugh and run and feed the
swans, was now still, reflecting the sky and the damned planes
that droned constantly.

It was on July 15 at a belated birthday dinner for Adi's
father that our world was shattered, and this time there was
nothing I could do to save both Adi and me.

That evening, Charles was in a good mood. He had
managed to procure a few bottles of his favorite merlot and was
generous with his pouring.

"You've got better at that." I noted the lack of spillage on the
tabletop.

"I am the master of myself," he said, his words slurry around
the edges. "Just because my eyes no longer see, I can still make
my body obey my brain."

Only Sarah was quiet, and she would stare at the wall or
outside at the evening sky, not really noticing what we were
talking about.

When Charles began to sing, Sarah admonished him,
reminding him of the curfew that both Adi and I were already
breaking by being there, and of the trouble we could all find
ourselves in if someone came to the door.

"Let them come!" Charles raised his glass high, spilling it
onto the rug, but what he could not see, he did not care about.

"Hush, Charles," Sarah said. "You have no idea, do you?"

"I'm not listening to all those gossipers that you are friends with, Sarah," he said. "You need to stop listening to them—we will be fine."

"What gossip?" Adi asked.

"The women! They always gossip," Charles shouted. "All the time saying the world will end."

"They're not saying that," Sarah said. "There have been rumors that there will be a roundup of Jews in the coming days."

"They've been saying that since they arrived," Charles said. "Honestly, you women. Stop with all the gossip. It's my birthday!"

Sarah stared at her husband for a moment or two, then drank her wine in silence. Even Adi's cajoling could not stir her to talk anymore.

When we had scurried home, only a street away, Adi changed for bed and turned to me, her hair hanging around her shoulders, her face as pale as the nightdress she wore. "Do you think Maman is right?" she asked. "Do you think it will happen?"

I held her tightly. "Even if it does, we are safe. We are, and we have the paperwork to back it up."

"Only that ID card Albert gave us," she whispered. "And you could see it was fake from the start."

"They won't come for us, Adi. They won't."

I was wrong.

The following morning the first roundups began. I went for coffee before beginning work and saw gendarmes leading scared-looking families onto waiting buses. I drank my coffee back in one go and raced home.

"We won't go to work today," I told Adi, when I breathlessly got to the top of the stairs and opened the front door. "Let's stay."

"You said we are safe, though?" Adi looked at me, her voice wobbly.

"We are. I'm sure we are."

"Won't they come here, to our home?"

I shook my head. "We're safer here, surely. If you are at work and someone says something..." I knew a few of Adi's colleagues knew of her deception, as they had known her since she was young.

Adi nodded slowly.

We spent that day in our apartment, keeping the curtains drawn, sitting quietly and jumping at every slam of a door or every knock.

We got through that day, though. Until 6 a.m. the following morning, when there was a loud bang on the door.

"Don't open it," Adi said, scrambling into a summer dress.

Still in my pajamas, I agreed with her until the banging became incessant. "It's better to open it. To show them our ID. It might be nothing, Adi, it might be Matisse—maybe he is wondering why I didn't come to work?"

I padded across the hallway and opened the door.

"Albert!" I almost threw my arms around my friend, who stood in front of me in his police uniform, my racing heart starting to slow with relief.

"Jozef," he said. His voice was different, quieter.

"What is it?" I asked.

"I don't know how to say this," he said.

In my mind I thought he was going to tell me that Charles or Sarah had died, and as my friend he had come to give us the news himself. "Come in," I said, ushering him inside and letting him sit down in my armchair. "What's happened, Albert?"

He stared at his shoes as he spoke. "I'm here to take you away," he said. "I'm so sorry, Jozef. So sorry. They knew I had been giving out fake identity cards."

I shook my head. "No, no," I said quickly, "no, they couldn't know."

"I had to tell them the truth." He looked at me now, his eyes bloodshot. "There had been questions and they didn't know who had been doing it, you know. I couldn't say it was me. I just had to tell them who everyone really was. They're not stupid, these Germans, not stupid at all."

"No!" I cried again, not knowing what else to say.

"I'm sorry, Jozef. I thought it was better if I come rather than someone else. If you had been French, perhaps you would have been spared this—they are only wanting foreign Jews and refugees."

"But Adi is French," I said.

"And German."

"She does not need to be taken," I said. "She is a French citizen."

Albert shrugged. "She's your wife, though. And she's still German too. Technically, she is foreign."

"How? How is she foreign, Albert?"

He shrugged again as if he did not care, and I could see the truth now and who my friend really was. "How did they find out, Albert?" I shouted at him now. "Did you give us up? Did you take payment? What could they have offered you to make you do this?"

He looked at his shoes again and would not answer the question.

"You did, didn't you! You bastard!" I went for him then and tried to hit him, but he stood quickly and pushed me to the floor.

I heard Adi cry out, then footsteps as another gendarme entered the apartment.

"I'm trying to make it easy for you, Jozef. Really I am."

I stood, trying to retain my dignity. There had been no point in getting the IDs; there had been no point in trying to pretend to be someone we weren't. They had always been coming for us and now it was time to go.

"I'll go," I said. "Please, Albert, let Adi stay."

He shook his head. "They know you lied. They know you got fake documents. She has to go too."

"But we got them from you! Are you coming with us?" I asked, sarcasm dripping from each word. The other gendarme looked at Albert, who ignored me completely and lit a cigarette.

"Where are we going?" I asked him. "Where are you taking us?"

"I'm not taking you anywhere, Jozef. The Germans are. I'm just doing my job. A courtesy for a friend to tell him gently to just get dressed, and pack a few things in a suitcase. That's all I can say."

In a daze, I got changed. Adi and I packed in silence, her hands trembling as she placed summer dresses, winter coats, and shoes into a valise.

We were then led out of our apartment, down to the street, and herded onto a bus where frightened faces greeted us. We sat next to each other, clutching our bags, and only realized it was really happening once the bus spurted into life and drove away from our home. Toward where—we did not know.

TWELVE

JOZEF

1942

The bus seemed to stop every street or so, picking up more and more people until we were all tightly packed in. Babies wailed, children repeatedly asked their parents where they were going, and the rest of us stared blankly out of the grimy windows, trying to guess where it was we might stop.

Adi scanned each face as they got on, waiting to see if her parents would be next, but their faces never appeared.

"I am sure they are fine," I told her.

"You think?" she asked hopefully.

"I know it," I lied, all my hope drained out of me.

I thought of Albert on that bus ride. I thought of how he had betrayed me and how many others he had scammed and then given up in order to get a promotion, or better pay. How could he do it? How could he be my friend for almost three years and turn me over without a second thought? I hoped deep down (a feeling I would never share with Adi as it frightened me so) that Albert would have an untimely death, one that was beset with pain and anguish. I hoped as he lay dying he would remember what he had done and realize that his death meant little in this world.

The bus soon slowed as we passed the Eiffel Tower, then came to a stop outside the Vélodrome d'Hiver, a winter sports stadium that up until now I had never noticed nor had any interest in.

Again, we were herded like animals off the bus, and told to line up as one by one we were taken inside the vast stadium that seemed almost full up already of mirror images of us—scared faces, wide eyes, each person as bewildered as the next.

We found a place to sit, and I could not speak to Adi. She talked constantly, trying to work out how to convince the gendarmes she was French, that her husband was French. A French Jew was okay, we could stay. A foreign Jew was not. She was not foreign, she repeated over and over again, until I feared that she would soon lose her mind.

"Hush, Adi, hush." I wrapped an arm around her shoulder and pulled her close. "Let me think. Let me think for just a moment."

My thoughts, though, were as useless as Adi's repetitions. No matter that Adi was French; Albert had told the authorities that our IDs were fake, thus this was Adi's punishment. The only solace I could give Adi was that her parents would probably be safe.

"For now," she said.

She was right. For now. We had lived with that for years— we were fine for now when the restrictions began, we were fine when business were closed, we were fine when we had to leave our home. And we had stayed fine in Paris. Until now.

The air in the velodrome soon became syrupy with heat. Each breath in felt as though I were eating soup, making me cough and breathe in harder each time as if the next breath would be cleaner and fuller. The stands were packed with bodies, all looking as bewildered as I felt. I held onto Adi, my arm around her shoulders and looked to the exits, trying to figure out a way to escape.

"They're green," she said. "Look, everyone looks green."

I thought that the heat had gotten to her and she was delusional, but as I looked about me, I could see that she was right—the faces around me had a green hue, making me feel as though I were in a dream and no one was truly real.

Above me the glass roof, once giving a view of the sky above, was painted blue. I suspected that this had been done to shield any eyes in the sky from what was happening below. That blue was making the velodrome take on the green hue, and it was keeping the heat trapped inside.

I wiped my face with my handkerchief, seeing the grubby stain of my skin smear against the white.

"I need water," Adi said, licking her dry lips. "I can't see anywhere. Where do we go for water, Jozef? Where do we go?"

Her voice had taken on a high-pitched plea, and I stood, kissed the top of her head, and told her not to move. "I will find us some water. Do not move, Adi, please do not move from this very spot."

"I won't," she said.

I looked to my left and right. To the left was an old man who had managed to bring along his battered violin case, and to my right was a woman with a baby clamped to her breast. I took their images in my mind in order to anchor Adi's position so that I would not lose her and as I walked, I repeated to myself, *man with violin, woman with baby*, a mantra that kept me from thinking about where I really was and what was really happening.

I picked my way through those who had decamped on the velodrome floor. Above me, the stands were packed, tiered to the top, full of green faces and hunched shoulders.

There was a queue of people seemingly a mile long that waited at the one tap for drinking water, and to the side another queue to the lavatory. I took my place behind an old couple who shuffled from side to side as they waited for their turn at the tap, their gnarled hands clasping each other's so hard that their knuckles were turning white.

I looked behind me constantly, afraid that Adi would move or be moved, and as I did, I saw more people being ushered into the velodrome by policemen with guns in their hands and blank faces.

"They can't possibly get any more in here," the old woman in front of me told her husband. "What are they doing to us? Will they cram us all in until there is no air left at all?"

"Hush now," the husband soothed her. "It will be all right. We will be fine."

The old woman's watery eyes looked at me, then rapidly scanned the people around her—she knew that things were not going to be as her husband said. Nothing about this was going to turn out right.

I stood in that line for hours, shuffling forward bit by bit. It was only when it was my turn at that one rusting tap jutting out of the wall mockingly that I realized I did not have anything to put the water into.

I felt tears sting my eyes. Exasperated, I turned around and the others in the queue looked at my empty hands, then at the tap that dripped each precious drop onto the dusty floor.

"Drink from it," someone in the line said. "Put your head under and drink from it."

"But my wife—"

Suddenly, I felt someone at my side. It was the old woman who had been in front of me. She handed me a chipped mug. "Take this," she said.

I shook my head. I couldn't take it from her.

"Take it. I will share with my husband. We have another. Take it."

Humbled at her generosity, I took the mug and filled it from

the weak stream that flowed. Then I stuck my head under the
tap and took a few gulps for myself. The water in the mug was
just for Adi.

Making my way back, I heard a pop-pop, then a scream.

I looked to the exit and a body lay on the floor, a woman
standing over it, wailing, her screams filling the dome. It seemed
as if everyone fell silent; even the babies ceased their crying.
The woman was dragged away from the body by another
woman, and the body was dragged outside by the police.

The noise soon came back—as awful as the sight was, no
one could be silent for long. We were all wondering if we would
be next.

Thankfully, I found my way back to Adi who had clearly
been crying whilst I was gone.

"They shot someone," she said quietly. "I saw him trying to
sneak past the police guards. He was only young, Jozef. Why
would they do that?"

I didn't know how to answer her and kissed her forehead,
then pressed the mug of lukewarm water into her hands.

She looked at the water then back at me. I nodded, a silent
conversation between us. Yes, this was all there was. This is all
there is.

I cannot describe the following days in all their horror. We
were there for four days in total, each day longer than the last.
The heat increased each day and the air became even thicker
than before; I was sure that we would soon all die from lack of
oxygen.

We were told nothing. We did not know where we were
going, or if in fact we would ever leave this place.

The toilets stopped working altogether, and the stench that
came not only from the drains but from the defecation that we
all had to do on the floor of that velodrome was so intense that I
felt myself grow dizzy and almost pass out many times.

A few people high up on the stands threw themselves off,

killing themselves—perhaps knowing that where they were going after this would be even worse. One woman killed her own son with a glass bottle and went mad—screaming and clutching at her clothes as she wailed over his bloody, battered body, wondering if she had done the right thing. If someone were to ask me now if she had done the right thing, I would tell you that she had—what awaited him was worse, much worse than this.

Adi was so quiet during those four days that I became louder, funnier, and sillier as each hour passed. The more she looked at the ground, lost in nightmarish thoughts, I would think of a song to sing, a joke to tell, or a story that would make her smile and take her mind away from itself.

The man with the battered violin I found out was called Levi. Levi had been a musician in his younger years, and was now retired. His family had managed to get south at the outbreak of war, he said, but he had refused to leave.

"It is my home," he told me. "For seventy years, it has been my home. My wife died here. My children were born here. I would not leave."

"Do you regret not leaving now?" I asked him.

He shook his head slowly. "I am old. They will do what they will to me. I cannot stop them and I understand that now. I am too old to run and hide. Let them have me and let their souls rot for what they will do."

I understood him. Oddly, both Adi and I had thought we were safe here. We should have fled south too, or to England—anywhere. But we had, like so many others, thought that we had survived so far, and that the end of the war could not be that far away.

Levi would play his violin, taking requests from others, his bow scratching away on the strings, trying once more to take our minds away from where we were.

On day four, things changed again.

We were herded out of the velodrome and packed into trucks and buses. Again, we were not told where we were going or why.

"Maybe they are taking us home?" Adi said quietly, staring out of the window at the daily life of Paris just beyond the thin glass, where cafe awnings flapped, pigeons strutted along the pavements and people walked, heads held high, on their way to the market, to a friend's house, to work.

The bus lurched forward into traffic and took us just outside of the city center, through a barbed wire fence that was controlled by guards with fierce-looking guns and dark eyes that regarded us on the bus much like stock that was arriving to a warehouse.

It stopped inside the barbed wire fence and the gate was closed firmly behind us. In front of us was a large three- or four-story apartment complex in a U shape.

"Is this where we are going to live now?" Adi turned to me, her eyes wide with fear.

"I don't know," I said, feeling foolish for not having the words that she needed to hear.

Once more, we were ushered off the bus and into the courtyard where we stood for hours on end, waiting, always waiting to find out what would happen to us next.

By the time the sky had patterned itself with a carpet of stars, we heard the rumble of wheels on tracks and a spotlight was lit overhead. We looked to the spotlight and then to the billow of steam that chugged into the night.

"Quick, quick, move!" the guards told us, pushing us toward the billowing train and the spotlight that was too bright. I held tightly on to Adi's hand, all the while looking about to see whether we could escape this madness. But there were too many people, all tightly packed together, moving as a tide toward the cattle cars of the train, an inevitability to it that we could not drag ourselves away from.

Babies cried, dogs barked, men shouted, women yelled out; a cacophony of sounds that bewildered me. Adi was talking to me, saying something, perhaps crying herself, but with the spotlight and the noise, I could not form a thought or concentrate on just one sound.

It was only when the door of the wooden slatted cattle cart slid shut, blocking out all light, and the train's wheels screamed as if in protest at having to drag away its cargo, slowly picking up pace, that I could think a clear thought.

"Jozef." Adi was holding on to my arm. "Come, we need to sit."

She was right. Everyone else had found a spot, and through the murky darkness of huddled shadows, we found a spot and held tightly on to each other, not knowing what to say.

To tell you about those days on the train would be harder than trying to explain the days in the velodrome. The stench on the train was worse, if you can imagine it. We had a bucket in which to relive ourselves, which soon became full, and we had no way to empty it. We all sweated in the heat, our body odor mixing with our excrement, so that no one scent was distinguishable other than the fact that it burned in our nostrils and made us breathe through our mouths to avoid the smell.

To tell you that we were thirsty and hungry would be an understatement. I never knew before what real thirst was until we were in that cattle truck. My lips dried, peeled, and bled. I became distinctly aware of my tongue, which seemed to have grown twice as big and stuck to the roof of my mouth. Every time I swallowed, I imagined I could hear my Adam's apple click in my throat.

I was sure we would die on that train. I was sure that this was the end.

At some stations, we were given some bread, some water, but not much—nowhere near enough.

Adi slept. I envied her. I watched her sleep, her eyelashes

fluttering as she dreamt. I hoped that she was dreaming happy dreams, and I hoped that if we were to die, she would go in her sleep, away from this.

I talked to a man whose wife was severely ill. He told me we were going to a camp—he knew of them and some of his family had already gone there. He did not know what the camp would be like, but he had an optimistic view that it would be better than this.

He stroked his wife's head as she slept, gave her his food and water when he had any. But by the time the train stopped at our final destination, she was dead, her head in his lap, and he had never stopped stroking her hair.

I could tell you more about those days on the train, but I won't. To try to put into words the fear we felt, the hunger and thirst, the stench, the dreams of a quick death, is not possible. I am not even sure I can put the next part into words either. But I will try...

As soon as the door slid open, we realized we were on a new train platform. This one was dotted with German guards, guns, and barking German Shepherds that strained at their chain leashes.

Again, we were told to be quick. "Get out, *schnell*, quickly, come on!" they shouted at us, once again the mixture of sounds making my thoughts fuzzy.

Men wearing striped pajamas walked amongst us, dragging a cart and telling us to put our belongings in them. Adi let her small valise fall into the cart—a wedding gift from my parents— and I watched it as it disappeared beneath the piles of strangers' belongings.

Guards were now separating people in front of us—men in one line, women in another, some of them still clutching their children's hands. Some children had been separated from their parents and called out to them—"Mama! Papa!" Their parents called back and told them it was going to be all right. To be strong and that they would be together again soon.

Older people, those crippled or ill, were separated once more into another group and led away.

"Where are they going?" Adi asked. Her hand was gripping mine so tightly now that I could feel her fingernails digging into my palm.

"Here! Here!" A guard pulled Adi toward the line of women. "Here! Now!" he yelled.

"Jozef!" she screamed. I watched as she was pulled from me, her not letting go of my hand until the last possible second.

"It's all right," I told her. "It's all right. We'll be okay. We'll be back together soon."

I repeated those words to her, just like the parents to their scared children, not knowing what else I was supposed to do.

She disappeared into the line of women who were taken away, leaving us men altogether, all of us feeling as though the ground had been ripped from beneath our feet.

It was our turn to be led away from the train platform now. I saw a small teddy bear on the gray cement, its owner made to leave it, or perhaps they had dropped it in the fray. I ached to pick it up and keep it, hoping to give it back to the child, and just as I steeled myself to quickly bend down and grab it, a soldier kicked it onto the tracks.

I cried then. Silent tears. Tears that marked my face and the fear I felt and could not properly comprehend, let alone express. I felt no shame in crying—other men were doing the same, all of them wiping their tears away with a childlike scrunched-up fist, fighting the urge to break down and weep forever.

Again, we were not told where we were, or why we were there. Just like the days before, we were pushed and shoved by those men with guns, all of them looking alike to me, and told to undress. Once naked, our heads were shaved and our pubic hair. We were deloused with a white powder that stung our eyes and given striped overalls, like the men from the train tracks. Finally, we were tattooed with a number and our photograph was taken.

Within the space of a few hours only, we had been stripped of our belongings, our family, our hair, our clothes, and our names. We were now all the same—only distinguishable by the inked numbers on our forearms.

We were given a blanket, a bowl, spoon, and tin cup, and shown to a large bunkhouse with tiered wooden bunks and thin mattresses that, on close inspection, revealed they were full of wood shavings, and told that this was where we were to stay.

I chose a top bunk at the rear and lay down, exhaustion overcoming me, and I soon fell into a deep sleep.

THIRTEEN

ALICE

Jozef stopped and stared at me, blinking once, twice, three times —it was as though he could not see me at all.

I leaned forward and placed my hand gently on his knee. "Jozef," I said quietly.

He flinched under the touch of my hand and quickly stood. "That's enough for today," he said, collecting the empty glasses on the table. "You can go now."

"But the leaves," I said stupidly. "I haven't cleared them."

He looked at the glasses in his hands and scrunched up his brow as if he wasn't sure what to do with them now. He placed them back on the table and said, "The leaves can wait."

His abrupt change in mood worried me. All the other times he had spoken about his life he had been a little odd, sure, but this time it was as if he wasn't himself and couldn't look at me properly.

"I can stay awhile if you like," I suggested, thinking of Gammy when she had one of her turns and needed someone to watch her in case she decided to cook something on the stove and then forgot about it, burning down the house.

He shook his head, then patted his pocket where I had seen

him place some papers earlier. Noticing they were gone, he swiveled his head left and right, panic in his eyes.

"Here." I stood and bent down to where they had fallen in their tightly folded square next to his chair. "They fell out of your pocket."

He snatched them from me, looked at the papers then at me. "I haven't read them," I said.

He shoved them back into his pocket and his face relaxed. "I'm just tired, Alice. You can go now. Please. We'll talk again soon."

I nodded. There was no use asking him whether he was still going to fix my bike for me, not today anyway, so I wheeled my bike home and decided I would bug Billy to do it, even though he was still refusing to come out of his room for longer than a few minutes at a time.

Dinner that evening was Pops grilling in the backyard whilst Mom yelled at him that he was burning the meat. Billy sat at the table with me in the yard, his eyes like Jozef's—seeing but not seeing at the same time.

I played the game that he always played, where I spread my hand out on the tablecloth and with my fork jabbed in between the gaps, first slowly then picking up speed. Just as I was getting into a rhythm, he reached over and grabbed the fork out of my hand.

"Stop it," he said.

"I'm just playing," I retorted, and tried to grab my fork off him.

Mom placed a large bowl of salad on the table. "Stop it, you two," she said, but she was looking at Pops and watching as the smoke from a burger that was being singed rose above his head.

She left us and marched toward him. I heard her say something, then Pops laughed and put his arm around her shoulder.

"Why don't you like playing games anymore?" I asked Billy.

"It's stupid, is all."

"You're no fun anymore," I cajoled him. I had tried to be nice; I had tried to talk to him, but nothing would work. Pops had said to be patient, that he had lost his friend and I should think about what I would be like if one of my friends died. But my patience was wearing thin with Billy, and it was making me anxious, watching him every day like a ghost wander about and bump into things—seeing but not seeing.

"I can't be fun all the time," he said, and reached over for a bread roll and held it in his hands.

"You gonna eat it or look at it?" I asked.

He looked at me then, and tore into the bread, a little smile appearing on his face.

I grinned back at him. "Say, you know tomorrow, you reckon you could fix my bike? The chain's come off."

"Again?"

"Yup."

"You need a new one."

I shrugged. "I kinda like it still."

"Maybe," he said.

I reached for some bread and chewed on it for a while, thinking of Jozef and the things he had told me that day, trying to imagine France, what it felt like, the smells, the sounds. Then I tried to think of the train he took, and it made me shudder. I stopped thinking when my thoughts reached the camp he'd told me about.

"What you thinking about?" Billy asked.

"Just stuff."

"What kind of stuff?"

Normally, I wouldn't tell him, but I was glad he was talking to me, so I decided to go for it. "I was thinking about the war."

"The war? Why?"

"I dunno. We did some stuff about it at school and Pops talks about it sometimes."

"He wasn't really in the war," Billy said. "He was a bad chef at one of the bases."

I looked to Pops who was still burning the meat, and felt sorry for all those soldiers who had had to eat his food for two years.

"Not the stuff Pops says. Like the other stuff. You know, the camps and what they did to the Jewish people."

"Don't think about that, Al," he told me. "That kind of stuff will give you nightmares."

"But we should think about it, don't you think? Like Gammy says, just because you don't say something, or acknowledge something, it doesn't mean it's not there or didn't happen."

"Ha!" Billy laughed. "Gammy's mad, Al. She burns her kitchen down and walks around talking to her plants all day."

I remembered that I had talked to my bike earlier that day and wondered now if I was turning into Gammy. "Anyway," I said. "I'm gonna think about it. I'm gonna read some books and stuff. I want to know what happened. And maybe one day I'll go there, to France and Poland and Germany, and I'll see it for myself."

"You won't see anything, Al. It's not happening anymore."

"I know that!" I said, exasperated. "I mean I can imagine it better if I see where it happened."

Billy scrunched up his eyes at me, then shook his head like he was tired of me now. "I'm going to go help Pops." He pushed his chair out. "Otherwise, we'll never eat."

I went to bed early without any persuading from my parents. The day's events of Mikey, Jozef's stories, and the worry over Billy filled my head so much that I yawned throughout dinner and couldn't wait to close my eyes to make it all go away for a moment.

I was in a deep sleep when I heard the ping-ping of tiny taps at my window. At first, I couldn't seem to wake up properly and felt as though I were trying to swim through treacle to reach the surface.

Finally, I opened my eyes and waited for the noise again. It was there, and I knew who it was.

I didn't bother dressing and padded quietly outside in my nightdress to find Mikey on the porch, a few stones still in his hand. "I thought you were never gonna wake up!" he half whispered. "I was thinking I was gonna have to try and climb up and knock on your window properly, but then I thought it might scare you and you'd scream and I'd fall," he rambled.

"You all right?" I asked.

"Can't sleep," he said.

"You wanna stay on the porch for a bit?"

"Nah. Let's go for a walk," he suggested.

It was not unusual for me to now and again accompany Mikey on one of his nighttime walks. We usually just walked until one of us yawned and then went home our separate ways, but tonight I could see something different in Mikey, and I wasn't sure I wanted to walk with him when no one knew where I was.

"We can just sit," I suggested again, pointing at the porch swing.

"Nah, come on, Al. I need to walk."

I looked at the bruise on Mikey's head. I couldn't deny him. I grabbed my sandals, strapped them on, and followed Mikey out into the night.

He didn't talk at all, just walked a little in front of me, and I couldn't understand why he wanted me there as he wasn't interested in me.

Suddenly, he picked up pace, then disappeared down the

track that led to Homer's lake, the one we had chased my
parents down.

"Mikey!" I called out and didn't follow. "Mikey, come out!
I'm not going in there!"

I stood listening to my breathing for some sign that Mikey
was coming back, but there was nothing. I didn't want to follow
him, but there was something wrong with Mikey. This time, the
beating by his pa had done something to him, and I was worried
for him and a little scared of him all at once. I thought of Nancy,
of what happened to her down there, and I knew I couldn't
leave Mikey alone.

Taking in a deep breath, I told myself not to be scared and
to run quickly, find Mikey and go home.

The branches whipped at my face as I ran. I couldn't see
the track properly, but I knew where I was going and wasn't
afraid that I would get lost. A tree root stubbed my ankle and
my brain screamed out that someone was trying to grab my foot
from the undergrowth. I yelled for Mikey, then ran on, sweat
now collecting on my face and little cuts letting warm blood
ooze from my skin.

When I reached the edge of the lake, I could see the silhouette of Mikey standing by the water's edge, the quarter moon
reflected on it.

I walked toward him and touched his arm.

"You took your time," he said.

"Let's go, Mikey. Why we even here?"

"You think she was under the water or on top of it?" he
asked.

"What?"

"Nancy. I keep trying to picture what it was like for her, you
know. I mean, I know Howard said she was dead before she was
in the water, so like, was she under it? Was she on top of it?"

"I dunno," I said, wanting the conversation to stop.

"Let's go in," he said. "Let's go for a swim!"

I looked at his face in the moonlight, and although he was smiling, it was manic.

"I don't want to," I told him.

"Come on, Al."

"No. You can't even swim that good."

"So?" he shrugged. "Maybe I'll drown and then that will be all right, won't it? My pa would be happy."

"Don't say that, Mikey!" I grabbed his arm hard now. "Come on, please, let's go."

He shook me off and ran into the water.

"Mikey! Come out, please! You're bad at swimming! Please!"

He kept wading out further and further, the black water edging up his body like tar, and soon all I could see was his head.

"Mikey!" I yelled. I looked behind me and wondered if I should run and get Pops. If I did though, I would get spanked.

Chewing my bottom lip, I made the decision and ran into the water, which splashed up against my legs until it reached my waist and I dived in and swam toward Mikey.

He was floating on his back, his eyes open. "I can float," was all he said.

"Come back now," I tried.

"Go on, lie on your back, look at the sky, Al. Do it and I promise I will come back."

Treading water and feeling my nightshirt lift up and billow around me, I turned my body and allowed myself to float, stretching my arms out and gently rippling the water through my fingers.

"Can we go now?" I asked.

"You think she was definitely dead before she went in the water? Or do you think she saw this before she died?" he asked.

I looked up at the night sky pinpricked with stars. I hoped she had seen this.

"Al!" I heard my brother's voice and stopped floating, almost going under with shock at hearing Billy's voice. "Al!" he screamed again.

I saw him now, running into the water, then launching himself in, his strong arms pushing against the flow to get to me.

Once there, he grabbed my arm under the water. "What the hell are you doing?" he yelled.

"We were just floating," Mikey said, still lying on his back, seemingly immune to my brother. "Just seeing what it would be like to be Nancy."

Suddenly, my brother went for him, grabbing him and pulling him underwater.

I screamed out for them to stop, but then realized Billy was half swimming back to the shore with Mikey under his arm.

I swam after them, finally reaching dry ground, and sat next to Billy. He was patting Mikey on the back, who was coughing and spluttering.

"You trying to kill me?" Mikey yelled at Billy.

"You're not to see Al anymore." Billy stood, yanked at my arm, and started to drag me away.

"We can't leave him here," I pleaded with Billy.

"If he wants to kill himself, let him," he snarled. Then he stopped, turned, and seemed to change his mind. He let go of my arm, picked up Mikey, threw him like a bag of flour over his shoulder, and carried him.

Mikey did not protest. He let Billy carry him away from the lake to our house and deposit him on the porch.

"Go to bed, Al," Billy told me.

"But, Mikey," I said, looking at my friend who was now pale and frightened.

"Me and Mikey are gonna have a talk. Go to bed."

"He's my friend." I was indignant.

"And if you let me talk to him, then maybe he'll still be your friend tomorrow."

I looked to Mikey who nodded, then at my brother, whose face was a mixture of fear and anger. I turned away from them and went to my bedroom, hearing the quiet drip-drip of my sodden nightshirt splotching on the hardwood floor.

I quickly changed and opened my window wide, leaning out to try and hear what Billy was saying.

"You can talk to me, you know," Billy said. "I understand."

"You can't understand," Mikey said, his voice low but still hard and angry.

"Nancy's pop hit her, you know."

Mikey didn't answer and I held my breath, scared that they would hear me and stop.

"Hit her for talking to guys," Billy continued.

"You sure?"

"Yeah. All her friends knew. You wouldn't think it, though, right? Nice Mr. Briggs, a bit stern but a good father? Nancy once said that he hit her mom too."

"And look what happened to her," Mikey said.

I couldn't hear what Billy said, but then Mikey responded with a weak, "I'm sorry."

"You need to move to your aunt's if you can. Or maybe talk with Howard," Billy advised.

"Can't. Aunt Milly is old. Howard's pa's friend."

"There'll be a way. I promise you. It won't be like this forever," Billy said.

Suddenly, Mikey began to cry, and I pulled away from the window. I had never heard or seen Mikey cry, and it made me afraid to know that he could get that upset.

Billy's voice became soothing, and I could hear the creak of the porch swing. Soon, my eyelids began to droop. I'd close them, just for a minute, I decided. Then I'd go back down and find out what was happening.

Before I knew it, it was morning, and I found myself on my window bench, curled up like a cat.

My neck hurt from sleeping in an odd position, and I could feel the sting of the tiny cuts from the branches on my arms and legs.

Mikey. Billy.

I jumped up and ran to Billy's room, pushing open the door without knocking.

He was asleep and I jumped on him to wake him.

"Where's Mikey?" I asked, as soon as he opened his eyes.

"At home," he said. "I took him home."

"What did you say to him?"

"We just talked."

"About what?"

"Oh, Al," he groaned, pushing himself up to sit and look at me properly. "He's not good right now."

"I know," I said. "His pa scared him this time, I think."

"It's more than that, Al. He's not right at the moment. He knows it too. He says he's gonna go spend more time at Frank's and help at the diner for a bit."

"I'll go see him," I said, hoping Billy would tell me not to. After last night, after the fear of thinking he was going to drown and then the talk about Nancy, I wasn't really sure I wanted to see him.

"Leave him for now, Al," Billy said. "Just leave him awhile. I think it's best."

I nodded and pulled at a loose thread on Billy's pillow.

"You all right?" he asked.

"Yep," I said, but I could feel that lump in my throat that came whenever I was about to cry.

"Why don't you go see Clem today?" he suggested. "Go do something. Here." He rolled onto his side and reached for his wallet on his side table. "Take this." He handed me five dollars. "Go to the cinema or go buy something nice, okay?"

"Okay," I said, crumpling the money in my hand.

"Now scram," he said, lying down once more and pulling the blanket over his head. "I've got some sleeping to do."

I left Billy alone, went to my room and cried for a while. I wasn't sure what I was crying about, and just felt tired and achy and unsure of everything.

When I had cried enough and my sobs turned to hiccups, I thought of Billy's suggestion to go see Clem. Most of the time I found Clem a bit boring. All she liked to do was bake with her mom, or do drawings or watch TV. I was jealous that she had a TV set before us, but it became boring to me, and I always fidgeted when we would watch show after show.

But today, Clem was just what I needed. I needed someone quiet and uncomplicated who would teach me to bake a cake or cookies, and we would eat them whilst watching her favorite TV show.

Feeling lighter, I changed and ate breakfast, telling my parents where I was going, and happy that I had another friend I could spend time with and talk to.

My bike, still unchained, meant I had to walk to Clem's. I enjoyed the warmth of the sun on my back and the birdsong for about two blocks, until the heat got too much and I could feel my shirt sticking to my back. I decided that when I was older, I would live in a colder state—somewhere where the air was thinner and the sun didn't burn through every day.

Clem lived on Archer Avenue, a street of just six houses, all built years ago with pillars out the front holding up second-floor balconies that no one ever sat on. Although Clem's parents were both teachers, her mom came from money—her grandma had married a man who had something to do with oil, and when her grandparents moved away, they gave their giant mansion house to Clem's parents.

Clem always wanted to remind everyone that they weren't rich, even though they had a full-time maid and a gardener. And her parents were the same, always wanting to make sure everyone knew that they were teachers, that they had their own lives and that they weren't part of the giant oil family, even though we all knew they were.

I didn't understand it myself. I thought that if my parents lived in a big house and had oil money, I'd not pretend we didn't have it. I'd just live in that big house and be happy I lived there instead of always pretending it was some sort of burden pressed upon me.

I reached their house, walked up the front path to the lacquered black door, and grabbed the giant lion's head knocker, enjoying it as it made a loud thud against the wood.

Their maid, Regina, opened the door, looked at me with disdain as she always did, and told me that Clem was in the kitchen.

I nodded my thanks and grimaced as my sneakers made a squeak on their checkered marble floor. I imagined that Regina was standing behind me, shaking her head at the dusty footprints I was leaving behind.

Clem was on her own in the kitchen making chocolate milk, stirring in the granules with gusto.

"Hey," I said.

"Hey, Al! You want some?"

I nodded, and she grabbed a new glass and began furiously stirring chocolate powder into the creamy milk. I sat at the kitchen table that they always used for dinner, never using the giant dining room as Clem said that her mom thought it was pretentious. I'd had to look the word up in a dictionary when she'd said it. I still thought their dining room was nice; a large polished walnut dining table that sat twenty people, with bay windows that looked out onto their manicured gardens. I didn't think it was pretentious. I'd sit there and eat my meals if I was them.

Clem soon joined me, plopping the glass down so that a little milk spilled out onto the wood. She didn't clear it up.

"You wanna do something today?" I asked. "We could go to the store and get candy." I pulled Billy's five dollars from my pocket.

"I can't," Clem said, and slurped her milk through a red and white striped straw.

"Why?"

She shrugged.

"Clem, come on. Why not?" I asked again.

"Okay. Well. If I tell you, you gotta be nice and not laugh."

"Okay," I said, wondering what on earth I would laugh about.

"I've got a date," she said.

"A date? You're thirteen! Your mom lets you date?" I couldn't imagine my mom letting me date.

"It's a secret," she said, her face turning red.

"Who is it?"

"George."

"George!" I laughed. "You mean you and George!"

"I told you not to laugh!" she shouted at me, her eyes filling.

"Sorry, sorry." I placed my hand on her arm and gave it a squeeze. "I'm sorry. Tell me."

"There's nothing much to tell," she said. "He just asked me to go to the cinema and I said yes."

"That doesn't mean it's a date," I said. "Mikey asks me to go places all the time, but it's not a date."

"It is," she insisted. "It's a date."

"It isn't," I said. "I'll come with you guys."

"You can't, Al!" she pleaded. "It's a date. I know it is. He said so."

"He said it was a date?"

"Yes." She was insistent. "It is."

"Can you not do it another day?" I stirred the milkshake with my straw. "I could really do with spending some time with you today."

"Why?" she asked.

I shrugged.

"Go see Mikey. He's probably at the diner helping Frank. Go see him."

"Not today," I said.

"Tomorrow," she said. "We'll do something tomorrow, I promise. Just you and me. We'll bake something!" She was excited now. "We'll bake with Mom and watch TV."

"Can't we do it today?" I tried one last time.

"I can't, Al, really I can't."

"Okay." I put the five dollars back in my pocket.

"Sorry," she said.

"Nothing to be sorry about." I smiled at her, feeling empty in my stomach.

We talked for a while, Clem and I. Not about Mikey or George, but about baking and school and clothes. I was soon bored with it and could see she was itching to get ready for her date with George, so I left her to it and wandered away, wondering what to do with my day.

It was odd, thinking of Clem and George on their own. Every summer we had always been together the four of us, and now Mikey was being weird, Clem and George were maybe dating, and I was on my own.

I kicked at a stone and felt sorry for myself. Was this what it was going to be like now? Billy always said that things change when you get older, and I had been so excited to turn thirteen, but now I wished I could go back in time and let it be the way it always was.

At the end of Clem's street, I wondered if I should go and see Jozef, but he too had been strange yesterday with his staring and quietness, and I wasn't sure I wanted to be there either.

Without really thinking about it, my feet took me toward the lake, and I was surprised to see the cool clean water in front of me and wondered if I was going mad like Gammy and had forgotten how I had got there.

I sat on a rock and stared at the lake for some time, watching as dragonflies bobbed and hummed over the water and at small bubbles that appeared on the surface as fish searched for food.

I didn't know what to think about Mikey, or about Jozef, or Nancy. My head was humming like the dragonflies, and I couldn't make proper sense of my thoughts.

Suddenly, I jumped with surprise at the feel of something wet on my arm and looked to see Amos, his tail wagging and eyes alight with glee that he had found a friend. I hugged him to me, letting him lick my face and laughing at him as he ran, grabbed a stick, and walked back proudly to me, his head held high with triumph.

"A stick! You brought me a stick, good boy," I told him, then tried to wrestle it away from him. "What are you doing here, silly? You run away?"

Amos of course didn't answer, but rubbed his whole body against me, then saw a bird swoop at a fish in the water and decided to chase it. Clumsily, he ran into the water and tried to swim, then realized he wasn't so sure about his skills and came back to me, shaking himself, making drops of water fly all over me.

"There he is!" A breathless Jozef stood next to me. He bent over and placed his hands on his knees as he breathed in deeply.

"He can run, that dog! I thought he would follow me, but he smelled something in the air and took off!"

"Perhaps it was me." I rubbed the top of Amos' head, then wiped my wet hand on my shorts.

Jozef sat down next to me, watching Amos as he ran about, chasing dust and leaves.

"He's really happy now," I said, remembering the straggly dog that whined for food and always hung his head with sadness.

"It doesn't take much to make him happy. Some love, some food, and some attention. It's the same with people too. It doesn't take much," he said.

I picked up a stone and threw it into the lake, not even bothering to try and skim it along the water, where it sank with a satisfying plop.

A family of geese honked above in a V, finally lowering themselves and landing on the water near some reeds and bushes. I watched them as they took in their new surroundings, seemingly happy with the tiny skater bugs and flies that skipped on top of the lake.

"You're very quiet today," Jozef observed. "Usually you are full of energy. But today, not so much."

I didn't respond and kept my eyes on the lake.

"This is where she died," he said.

I looked at him. "You were there that night, I saw you."

"I was. I heard sirens and followed the trail of people."

"Did you know her?"

"Nancy?" he asked. "No. I only know you. I don't really speak to anyone else."

"So why did you come down here if you don't know anyone or care? I mean, why did you care that time?" I didn't know why, but frustration was seeping into my voice, and I oddly felt that lump in my throat again as if I were ready to cry.

"I didn't say I didn't care," he said quietly. "I do care. If someone needs my help, I'll help them. I'm just not very good at talking to people, and when I first came here, I didn't want to talk to anyone, I just wanted to be alone with my thoughts."

"You talk to me," I said.

"I do now. Maybe I don't want to be alone with my thoughts anymore."

"I don't either," I said, and threw another stone into the water.

"What are you thinking about? Your friend again?"

I nodded. "I don't know what's happening to him." Suddenly, the lump in my throat wouldn't be swallowed away and tears ran from my eyes. "I'm scared of him. He's acting so strange, and then Clem, she's with George now, they're dating, and I'm on my own and my brother is quiet all the time, and I don't know what to do and what to say to make it all better again —to make it like before."

"Tell me, what was it like before," Jozef said.

"I dunno." I rubbed at my eyes.

"Go on. Tell me."

"It was just us," I said. "Just us four. And we did everything together all the time. But now Clem and George, they do things without me, and Mikey too even."

"Maybe right now, they have to do things without you."

"You mean they don't want me to be their friend anymore?"

"No. I'm just saying that maybe for Mikey, he has to change something in his life because of all the things that have been happening to him. Maybe if he changes something, some good will come out of it."

"Nothing bad has happened to Clem and George," I said.

Jozef laughed a little, a gentle laugh. "Sometimes, Alice, people still have things happening to them—maybe not huge problems like Mikey, but small problems all the same, and it changes them. And sometimes, they just grow up a little and want new, bigger things. Can you really say that everything in your life is perfect and you wouldn't change something if you could?"

I thought of Billy, of the police visiting, and told Jozef about it, and how it worried me.

"See! And your friends don't know how much it has upset you, do they?"

I shrugged.

"So you are dealing with it on your own. And maybe you

will change a little because of everything that's happening. There's nothing wrong with that, Alice."

"I don't want to change," I said stubbornly.

Jozef simply laughed.

But then, thinking about it, I realized I was changing. I was keeping secrets from Mikey and my friends. I was even lying to my parents, so I could sneak off and see Jozef. But that wasn't a good change, was it?

Jozef patted my head like he did with Amos, and didn't say anything for a while—neither of us did and I was glad of it.

"Do you know why I have been telling you about what happened to me?" he asked.

I looked up at him. "Because I keep asking you questions?" I suggested.

He laughed and shook his head. "It's because I have to. I haven't told anyone before now, and it's important to get it outside of me so that it's not swirling all the time in my brain. Sometimes, just talking about things makes them better. You can't change what has happened, but you can learn from the past and things can be different."

"I want things to be better," I said.

"Sometimes, change is better."

"I was thinking about the camp you told me about, where Adi was taken and you were scared. And I think that I shouldn't be upset about Mikey and Clem and my brother because you had to go there and everyone was horrid to you, and it's not fair that they were. I keep thinking that if you can be okay now, then I can be okay. Does that make sense?" I rambled, the words tumbling out one after the other.

"It does. But you know, it's okay that you are worried and scared sometimes. Everyone can have those feelings."

I was quiet a while longer, and my thoughts drifted to imagining Jozef lying on that bunk in the camp, Adi gone, and his home, his family, all gone or taken away.

"What was it like, in the camp?" I asked. "How did you get out and get here?"

"I'm not sure it is the right thing to tell you more," he said.

"But you said it was good for you to tell someone what happened, so you can tell me."

"I know. But the camp, what happened there..." He fell silent. "It will haunt your dreams," he said.

"I know about what happened," I said. "My teacher told us. That you had no food and that people died."

"It was much more than that, Alice, much more."

"Then tell me," I demanded.

Jozef turned his gaze away from me, and I thought that he wasn't going to tell me anything. Then, just as a breeze blew through the trees, their branches scraping along the water, he began.

FOURTEEN
JOZEF

1943

The days and months that followed my arrival at what I now knew was Auschwitz in Poland were monotonous. We were woken before dawn, given a small ladle of coffee into our tin mug and a slice of bread, and told to wash quickly. My mug, bowl, and spoon quickly became my prized assets, as if you lost them, you did not get your ladle of coffee, or the watery soup that was given to us in the evenings. One of my campmates lost his spoon, so he was forced to eat with his hands or tip the bowl back into his mouth to drink his soup. You would think that it would not matter, but as I found out, as hungry as you were, you wanted the meager portion of food we did get to last as long as possible. Perhaps it was about fooling your stomach that you were eating much more than you actually were. I would spoon the tiniest drops of soup into my mouth, scared that it would disappear too quickly. In short, I did not want to drink it back, thus I did not lose my spoon.

The guards were always telling us to do things quickly—wash quickly, get in line quickly, dig quickly, faster, *schnell*. I wondered whether they realized that if they wanted us to do things quickly, they should give us more food and water— perhaps then our tired and withering bodies would be able to keep up with their demands.

Of course I thought of Adi. I thought of where she was and what she was doing. I tried not to listen to the gossip in the bunkhouse, where some would tell tales of the pits that dead bodies were thrown into and of a gas chamber. I tried not to listen as I did not want to think of Adi there, or that little child who had dropped their teddy bear on the tracks the day we had arrived. I preferred to live in my imagination and pretend that they had escaped and were living in the countryside some-where, in a small cottage with plenty of food and water.

It was foolish, I know that. But it was the only way during those first few months that I could survive. I didn't talk to the others in my bunkhouse, or those I worked with digging trenches—endless stretches of trenches, and we were never told what they would be used for. I could not talk to others as I was scared to hear what they had seen, or perhaps hear their own stories and their own fears.

Now, you would say that I compartmentalized. That I shut my brain down to think of the bare minimum, and utilized my ignorance and imagination to think of something else. To think every day of what was happening around me—the beatings, the death, the hunger—was too much for me. I could not do it.

It was then, at the beginning of winter, that something changed and I came out of the fugue state I had been in; a place that was going to send me mad and make sure I didn't survive. That day the clouds were low, blotting out the landscape and any hope of light. My breath hung in front of me as I dug into the hardened iced ground, once more digging a trench under the watchful eye of three guards, who shuffled from foot to foot to keep warm.

"You're Jozef," a voice next to me said.

I looked at the speaker. It was a man from my own bunkhouse, his name was Ezra; a middle-aged man with large hands and a loud voice. He often held court in the evenings, telling anyone who would listen what he had seen, what would happen to us, and when the war might be won. He was the complete opposite of me—where I wanted to pretend that nothing was happening, he seemed to relish in the details of each brutal beating and every punishment. For him, survival meant knowing your enemy and being prepared for anything.

Before I answered, I looked at the guards again, who were now smoking and talking about an American actress who they all seemed to like with a passion.

"I am," I said, turning back to my spade and that damned frozen ground.

"I am worried for you," he said. "You don't speak to anyone; you don't even look at others. It is as though you are a ghost and you silently flit between us all, as if you are immune from this place."

I wasn't sure whether Ezra was criticizing me or complimenting me.

"You don't need to be worried," I told him.

"I have seen men like you before, and they do not survive. You are fighting against the reality that you are in, my friend, and the only way to survive it is to face it head on."

"I disagree," I said, and dug hard into the soil.

"Listen. I am trying to help you. Tomorrow, I am going on a different work detail. I am a mechanic by trade, you know—and the idiots here have finally seen that I may be of use. I am working in the garage tomorrow, and they said I could bring one other with me. Someone who works hard. I want to bring you."

"Why me?" I asked. "I'm not even a mechanic."

"They don't know that." He cocked his head toward the guards. "They don't care."

"But why me?" I asked again.

"Because it will help you. Get you out of this place. Some others have been reassigned to the pits, and you were on that list. I didn't think you would be able to survive seeing that horror."

I had heard about the work detail at the pits—about the bodies, young, old, that were flung into large graves and then set alight. An image of Adi flooded my mind and I shook it quickly away.

"Are you sure?"

"Certainly," Ezra said. "You need this and you need a friend too. Let me help you."

I nodded at him, grateful to him and yet scared that he was opening my eyes when I wanted to keep them firmly closed.

The following morning, Ezra and I were taken to the camp's garage where trucks, cars, and motorcycles were parked up in front of a large shed. The scent of diesel was strong, but it made for something new to smell, and the sounds of a revving engine that came from inside the shed comforted me in an odd sort of way, perhaps as if I were simply in Paris now, taking the car for a tune-up myself.

Ezra was full of energy that morning, and I could suddenly see the man he used to be—a man with four children and a loving wife, the owner of a large garage near Berlin. He would have had a rotund stomach back then, I guessed, and I could imagine him patting it whilst chatting to customers, grinning happily at his daily life and all that awaited him when he got home each evening.

He saw me staring at him. "Have I something on my face?" he asked, then smirked at me, giving me that tiny glimpse of the man I imagined Ezra used to be.

"Go in." The guard who had escorted us pointed in the direction of the garage. "The Rottenführer will be with you in a moment."

I entered the garage behind Ezra and looked about me.

Another campmate was sitting in the cab of a truck, revving its engine whilst black smoke chugged out of the exhaust.

"Damn it!" he said, then clambered down, ignoring us, and kneeled next to the exhaust.

Ezra joined him and both talked about the exhaust, the types of trucks and cars, and what could possibly be wrong with this one.

For Ezra, this was giving him some sort of normalcy, but it was making me nervous. I knew nothing about engines. My whole childhood I had spent with my nose in a book, never learning about mechanics, but more interested in what had come before me—history, sociology, and religion. Even after I married Adi, I never gave a thought to learning how to fix things; instead, I assumed we would always have money, at least enough of it, to get a professional to do it for us.

Ezra had chosen wrong. I was not the man for this place, and it would soon become apparent just how inept I was.

Heavy footsteps interrupted my train of thought, and I looked to the rear of the garage where there was a doorway. From it walked a guard, his arm in a sling, his eyes on the ground. As he came closer, my heart felt as though it had stopped beating in my chest. My fingers became tingly and a cold shock rippled over my skin.

Those eyes, that face with the tiny scar on the forehead. The hair was now shorter and tucked under a cap, but I knew that face—Bruno.

He barely looked at me when he reached us; instead, he tucked his hand into his pocket and produced a packet of cigarettes. He shook it until the tip of one peeped out, placed it between his lips, then foraged once more for his lighter. The performance was nuanced due to his right arm in a sling, and I could see that hours of dropping cigarettes onto the floor had perfected this routine.

Once the cigarette was lit, he breathed the smoke in deeply, then eyed Ezra and the other man who were still looking at the exhaust.

"You figure it out yet, Stanislaw?" Bruno said.

Stanislaw stood and wiped his stained face on an equally grubby piece of cloth that he had tucked into his waistband. "Not yet." He shook his head. "This is Ezra, he's good. I think he will be able to help."

Bruno nodded through the smoke that he had just exhaled, seemingly bored already by the exchange.

"I'll be in the back if you need me," he said, then turned on his heel and went back toward the door, slamming it shut behind him.

"He used your name." Ezra stood, his eyes wide, disbelieving.

Stanislaw smiled. "He's not too bad, you know. I don't think he wants to be here, and he doesn't do any work. Just lets us get on with it. If anyone comes, then he acts up a bit, you know, calls us names, laughs about us, and says that he has punished us by not giving us food. But it's all for show. Just go along with it and you'll get on fine here."

"Where did the others go?" Ezra asked, looking about him.

"Gone," was all Stanislaw said.

"You all right?" Ezra noticed me now. "You look like you've seen a ghost."

I was thinking quickly now. Should I tell them that the man, the guard that oversaw us, was my childhood friend? I looked to the door he had gone through. No. If I told them, they might think I was still friends with him, and I had heard how much the others hated anyone who helped any guard, particularly the kapos.

"Just the fumes," I said, and made a show of wafting my hand in front of my face.

Ezra narrowed his eyes—I could see that he didn't believe me, but he didn't challenge me. "This is Jozef. He knows

nothing about cars, trucks, machines in general—eh, Jozef?"
Ezra chuckled.

"That's right, I know nothing." I shrugged at Stanislaw.

"So we teach him a few things," Stanislaw simply said. He
tucked his cloth back into his waistband and beckoned for me to
follow him to the front of the truck, where he showed me the
engine and began to explain its inner workings.

I did not have time to think of Bruno again that morning, yet
my ear was attuned to the door opening and closing and any
footsteps that may come our way. They didn't, however—Bruno
preferred to stay away and hide in whatever was at the rear.

Lunch was measurably better in the garage than in the
camp. We had huge chunks of bread, butter, and a small slice of
cheese with thick coffee to wash it down.

"He gets us a few things," Stanislaw told us, as Ezra
marveled at the amount of food. "It's not much. He leaves a loaf
of bread out and cheese, sometimes meat, sometimes potatoes.
Never says anything about it. Never says they are for us. He just
puts them under that workbench over there"—Stanislaw
pointed toward it—"then covers it up a bit, has a cigarette, then
tells us to get on with work and disappears into his office."

"Still a pig though, if you ask me," Ezra said.

"Of course he is!" Stanislaw sprayed crumbs out. "I'm
pretty sure he could have saved the other two that were here
before you, but whether he tried or not, I don't know. They
disappeared and now you are here. But here's the thing: we do
our job, keep out of his way, don't try to escape or anything
stupid, and he gives us food, lets us have a heater, and doesn't
beat us. It isn't much, but I'll take it."

As I chewed the bread and left Ezra and Stanislaw to
discuss the various workings of each vehicle in the yard, I
wondered if Bruno had recognized me. His demeanor told me
he hadn't, but if I had recognized him, why hadn't he me?

It was then that I caught my reflection in the shining

hubcap that was leaning against the wall. Although my features were distorted and strange from the curve of the surface, I could see the hollows of my cheeks and darkened eyes.

I ran my hand over my face and my fingertips did not recognize what they were touching either. I realized that I didn't even recognize myself. I was thin, too thin, with no hair, and wearing a uniform meant to make us all look the same. The old Jozef was gone and in his place was this aging man, a sliver left of who he used to be.

I did not see Bruno again that day, or even the following one. By then I had convinced myself that I was wrong—that it could not possibly be him, and the madness of the camp had finally infiltrated my brain and I was now seeing things that were not there. I honestly hoped that I was going mad, and that one day my mind would take flight completely, no longer connected to my body, and I would finally be free of this place.

On the third day of working in the garage, where my daily tasks were now driving the cars into the shed, tidying up after Ezra and Stanislaw, and generally being their assistant, getting them whatever they required, the man who I thought was Bruno summoned me into his office.

He stood at the door, leaning on the frame with his good arm, looked at me and said, "You. Come here."

I looked to Ezra and Stanislaw, wondering what I had done wrong, but they seemed as perplexed as I was.

Pushing myself up to stand from where I had been kneeling, clearing up an oil spill from a leaking jeep, I followed him through the door into a small office, a desk, chair, and heater filling the space.

He sat behind the desk, which was a muddle of paperwork, and leaned back in his chair. There was nowhere for me to sit, so I stood, my hands behind my back, eyes on the floor, and waited.

I wanted to lift my head and look at his face for the resemblance I had seen a few days ago. But to look a guard in the eye, to stare at him openly, could mean a beating, and I was not sure of who this man was and what he would do.

A clock somewhere ticked the seconds away, and it took me back to the day that Bruno had come to our house with a black eye. I wanted to speak to break the silence. Instead, I coughed; not that I needed to, I just wanted a noise other than that clock.

"You're not a mechanic," he finally said.

I shook my head. That voice—could it be Bruno? It was gravelly, but then I was sure my own voice had changed through the years too.

"Jozef," he said, quieter now. I knew that voice. "Look at me, Jozef."

I raised my eyes, finally meeting his, and I could see my friend in those tired eyes. The smile, the twinkle that had been in them all those years ago, had not yet completely disappeared. Despite where I was, despite who he was, I felt myself smile.

"Jozef," he said again, a smile pulling at his own lips. "I didn't recognize you."

"I don't recognize myself," I said. My voice was flat, even though I felt a small ball of excitement in my stomach at seeing my friend again.

"We've changed, haven't we?"

I nodded, not sure what he wanted me to say. All I wondered was why he had changed so much to be in a place like this, to be a part of this nightmare.

"If I remember right, you were always smarter than me. Better with words, writing, numbers even. I was thinking that perhaps you could help me with all of this." He nodded toward the mess of papers. "I'm still terrible at it."

His voice was formal, not betraying the Bruno I used to

know. I wanted to cajole him, get the real Bruno to appear—the boy who made me laugh and pledged to be my best friend forever. Although, it occurred to me now that perhaps the real Bruno was the man in the dark uniform in front of me.

"Do you think you could help me, Jozef?" he asked.

"I can," I said. "Of course I can."

"Good!" He slapped his good hand on his desk. "We start tomorrow. I'll get you a chair and you can sit just outside the door and work. I'm afraid I can't have you in the office with me."

"Of course," I said.

"If I could, I would. But if someone were to see..." He let the sentence dangle and stared hard into my eyes. "I would if I could."

I nodded.

"Tomorrow then?" He smiled at me now, a hopeful Bruno smile that spoke of adventures.

"Tomorrow," I agreed, leaving the office and making my way to tell Ezra and Stanislaw that I could no longer be their dogsbody.

That night I could not sleep, which was not entirely unusual. The cold seeped in through every crack and whistled along, making each of the men shiver and curl up tighter into balls. I wore all the clothing I had, including the thin jacket we had been given that kept out little of the winter chill.

It was not the cold that kept me occupied that night, though; nor, for the first time in months, was it Adi. It was Bruno who swirled through my brain. I remembered the letters he'd sent from military school that soon dwindled in number before disappearing altogether. I had thought that the letters had stopped because he was still angry at me that Adi had chosen me and not him, and perhaps we had simply drifted apart. Was it possible that he had stopped writing because he had started to believe the lies? I shook the thought away. Bruno, my Bruno, would never believe in the propaganda. He knew me. He knew my family. We had been like brothers.

I turned onto my back and stared into the blackness, waiting for Adi's face to appear in my mind. I would have pretend conversations with her in my head about Bruno. I would imagine her laugh at the absurdity of it and hear her tell me I was lucky to have my friend watching over me.

The following morning, I found a small desk and chair positioned just outside Bruno's office door. As soon as I arrived, he beckoned me into his lair and sat once more behind his desk.

"I have to explain to you what I need you to do," he said. He then went through the orders, ledgers, and reports for each vehicle. It was straightforward, and I imagined that he was more than capable of doing it himself.

When he had finished explaining, he looked at me, let out a sigh, and wiped his good hand over his face. "Jozef," he said. "I am so sorry."

His voice was gentler now, but his eyes could not settle on me for too long and flitted about the room, as if he would find the words in the air that eluded him so.

"I don't know where to start, what to say. I could always talk to you and I thought that this would be easy—to be like we were —to talk."

"We are not who we were," I said, and opened my arms for a moment so he could see me in all my striped glory covering my thin frame and dry, sallow skin.

He shook his head and looked away, his eyes finally settling on the wall just behind my shoulder.

"I am not who you think I am," he whispered. "I don't want to be here. I don't want to be a part of this."

Emboldened, I said, "Then don't be. You have a choice."

He nodded, once, twice, three times. "I know. I know. But

it's not that simple. I am not brave, Jozef. I am not anything. My father won't let me leave."

"Your father?"

"I was in the army, Jozef. That was all. Which is bad enough. I know this. Then I was injured, and do you know why I got injured?"

I shook my head.

"Because I was a coward and tried to flee from the enemy. I thought I was a soldier, but I couldn't do it, so I ran, and then I was shot as I ran away. I wasn't injured for being brave. I was injured as I ran away, trying to get home."

"What does your father have to do with anything?"

"Don't you know, Jozef? Don't you know who he is now?"

I shook my head. All I knew of his father was that he had worked all the time and didn't seem to care much for his son or his wife.

"He's high up now in the SS. Higher than he should be. But then this suits him, doesn't it? This violence. I am not trying to make excuses, Jozef, truly I'm not—"

He shook his head again and slammed his fist onto the desk, frustrated that the words were not coming out correctly.

"I could have been court-martialed," he said. "Father got me out of it. Sent me here instead and told me that this would be the making of me—thought that I would do well here. Can you imagine?"

I felt a sliver of sympathy for him, even though I still felt he could leave and run away from this place. "I'm sorry, Bruno," I said. Saying his name for the first time in years sounded strange to my ears.

"No, Jozef, don't ever say you are sorry for me. I am the one who is sorry. I am sorry that this has happened to you."

I nodded, and like a dam opening I felt tears loosen in my eyes. "Everything has been taken from me. Everything." My voice cracked.

"Adi?" Bruno sat up straight.

"She was brought here," I said. "I don't know what has happened to her. I pretend to myself that she has escaped and is safe."

Bruno sat quietly chewing on his lower lip, letting the clock once more destroy the silence with its ticking.

"Right!" He stood, a renewed energy about him. "I can help, can't I, Jozef?" He spoke as if he were a child again, asking me if he was a good boy, if he was clever or funny. "I can, can't I, Jozef?"

"If you want to," I said, unsure where his train of thought was leading him.

"That's it, Jozef. I can make things right. I can do something to help. I'll find Adi, Jozef. I'll find her and I'll keep you both safe."

Suddenly, he walked toward me and wrapped me up into his arms. I held him back and could smell tobacco on him, and a strong scent of whiskey.

He let me go and smiled at me; it reached all the way to his eyes, where the twinkle began to shine once more. He was ready for an adventure, yet he did not seem to grasp that we were no longer children and this was certainly not a game.

"I'll find her, Jozef. I'll find her for you. Trust me."

FIFTEEN

JOZEF

That evening the camp was unusually quiet. My shoes, although soaked through, made a pleasant scrunching sound as I walked through the newly fallen snow. For the first time since this had all started, I felt a little more like myself, and I knew it was because I had the hope that Bruno would find Adi for me.

Ezra had a cigarette that Stanislaw had given him, and when we were near our block, he lit the cigarette, the end glowing in the dark.

"You seem different." Ezra turned to me and offered me the cigarette.

I took it from him, remembering that the last time I had smoked had been months ago when I had been at home, drinking strong black coffee on the balcony whilst Adi sang in the kitchen as she prepared breakfast.

"I am, a little, perhaps," I said.

"You were talking to our Rottenführer a lot today." He raised his eyebrow at me as I handed him back the cigarette.

I wanted to tell him the truth about Bruno, but I couldn't risk anything—not now that Adi might be found.

So I shrugged. "Just discussing the papers."

"He seems to like you, though. I mean, I know he's not the worst of them, but when he found out you couldn't fit a light-bulb, let alone fix an engine, I expected that he would send you to a different work detail."

"He's no good at numbers," I said. "He asked me if I was good. I said yes, so that's all."

I could feel Ezra looking at me.

"It's strange, isn't it, when it snows how the sky is lighter." I looked toward the navy sky, hoping to distract Ezra from his train of thought.

"I suppose," he said, then finished his cigarette and ground it into the snow.

As I climbed onto my bunk, I knew I would have to be careful around Ezra. It wasn't that I didn't like him—I did—but I wasn't sure that I could trust him just yet. And if I told him, and he told the others, it would spell disaster for me and for Bruno.

Bruno. His face flooded my thoughts again. Did I trust him now? He was one of them—one of those who wore ominous uniforms, who beat us, starved us, and killed us. Yet, our friend-ship from years before was what was guiding me, and I knew it was foolish. People change; Bruno had that moment he was sent away to military school by his father. He had listened to the others, to their politics and views, and he had become absorbed by it. Why did I think he had forgotten that? But then, why did I think he had forgotten who he used to be—my friend?

The questions rolled around in my brain, and I could not find one answer that gave me comfort.

What should I do, Adi? I asked silently.

Surprisingly, my imaginary Adi did not answer, but instead a memory assaulted me. I was maybe eleven or twelve and walking home from school. Two boys stood on the street corner and at first, I paid them very little attention; instead, I thought of the model plane Bruno and I had been building, wondering when we might get it finished so we could play with it properly.

"You!" I heard one of the boys shout, but I didn't turn around.

"You! Jew!" they shouted again.

This time I turned.

"What have you got in there?" the bigger one asked. He was fifteen, maybe, with a shock of red hair and freckles almost obscuring his pale skin. He pointed at my satchel.

"My books," I said simply, still not understanding the danger.

"What else? Money?"

I shook my head.

"I bet you do. I bet you have money in there."

"Turn him upside down," the smaller one cajoled, his voice not yet quiet broken, so it alternated between squeaks and growls.

"Good idea," the big one said.

Within seconds, they had knocked me to the ground and grabbed hold of my ankles, holding me upside down and shaking me as if they thought sweets and money would simply fall out of me.

Getting bored and annoyed at the lack of interesting things about my person, they decided it would be fun to drop me on my head.

"No! No!" I screamed out. "No, please!"

"Let him go!" a voice yelled out.

I knew that voice: Bruno.

"Let him go. Now."

"Who are you? Another Jew? Or just a Jew lover?" the squeaky boy said.

"Put him down."

They laughed at Bruno, but then the laughter stopped

though I couldn't see why. Then slowly they lowered me to the ground, gently laying me down.

When I looked up, I saw Bruno, a gun in his hands. The two boys held their hands up in surrender, then ran away from us.

Bruno, a large grin on his face, put the gun in his pocket and held out a hand to pull me to my feet.

"Are you all right?" he asked.

I dusted down my jacket, still too stunned and shocked to fully realize what had happened.

"It's not real." He grinned at me. "Well, it is. But it doesn't work. Father gave it to me to play with."

I didn't know what to say to him and walked by his side all the way home, listening to him whistle a song. When we reached my house, I turned to him and hugged him to me.

He hugged me back briefly, then barked out a laugh. "I'll walk you home from now on, okay?"

I agreed, thinking he was joking. But every day from then on, Bruno walked me to and from school, making himself late each morning, but not caring about the punishment he received from both his teacher and his father.

Lying on my bunk, I felt relieved at the memory. It had reminded me of who I knew Bruno to really be, and I would hold that close to ward off any more thoughts that he was one of them—one of those who wanted me dead.

Just before the final bell sounded which meant that we had to go to sleep, much like a parent telling their children that whispering stories in the dark now had to stop, a young man entered the bunkhouse. He was thin, clean-shaven, and had rosy cheeks —a new inmate. He had a large P sewn into his shirt and walked along the bunks soon to reach me. Up until this point, I had managed to sleep alone, whilst many of the others had to double up on their thin mattresses with a new arrival. Ezra, for example, had had over three bunkmates in less than a year. I didn't ask where each of them had gone to.

The young Pole stopped at my bunk and looked at me with large, frightened eyes. I simply nodded at him, and he climbed up into the bunk beside me. He did not speak to me, and I respected his wish to remain silent for now, and allowed him to curl up and sleep, at least getting some warmth from his body.

It seemed that he was not the only one to arrive that night. By morning, all the bunks were filled with two bodies apiece, and as we queued for our ration of bread and coffee, I saw at least three Greeks, two Italians, and a handful of Hungarians. It interested me a little as to who they were and what their lives had been like before. I felt Ezra nudge me as I stared at them. "Don't try to get to know too many of them," he told me. "A few, yes. But not too many. It hurts too much when they disappear."

I wanted to ask Ezra how many people he had known before they disappeared, but I knew he wouldn't want to tell me —at least not this early in the day, when our brains were still adjusting to where we were once more.

After roll call, Ezra and I made our way to the garages. Above us the sky was a clear blue, but I heard no birdsong other than the black crows that squawked and circled the ground, eyeing up any bodies that had been put out during the night ready to be buried the next morning. Indeed, Ezra reminded me that he had seen no fewer than twenty bodies with their eyes pecked out, leaving bloody holes in their faces.

"We just have to make it to spring," Ezra said. "If we can get to spring and some warmth, then there is one less thing for us to think about. One less enemy."

I agreed with him. The ever-present hunger was unbearable, the long hours of work, the beatings, the fear, and the violence. But the cold kept us occupied now, and the conversations in the evenings revolved around how to keep from getting frostbite on your toes and fingers, and how to steal an extra shirt from the laundry.

The garages were quiet when we entered, and Stanislaw sat, relaxed on a stool, smoking a cigarette and drinking coffee as if it were his own place of work. He smiled at us cheerily and waved us over.

"He's gone out," he said, and pointed us toward the coffee pot. "He left this for us this morning."

I poured myself a cup of the coffee and drank it back too quickly, the heat burning my tongue and catching at the back of my throat. But I didn't care. I just needed the warmth of the coffee, the richness. When I had finished, Stanislaw poured me another cup, and from behind his back, he produced some bread. "He left this too."

Ezra and I wolfed down the bread, drank more coffee, and a smug smile appeared on all our faces simultaneously, making us laugh at our good fortune. "Always eat and drink whatever is here as quickly as you can," Stanislaw said, offering me a cigarette. "Just in case another guard pokes his head in. You don't want our little secret to get out, trust me."

I nodded. I didn't think I could savor food or drink anymore, even though I tried my best in the evenings with the soup. Instead, breakfast disappeared so quickly that I often questioned myself as to whether I had eaten it at all.

"He's left us here with no one," Ezra said, looking around to see if a hidden guard would suddenly jump out behind the pile of tires.

"We could escape," Stanislaw said, then laughed at his own joke.

"We could," Ezra said quietly. "I mean, not now. But if we planned it, we might be able to."

As soon as he said that word, escape, I felt my mouth go dry and my memory drag me back in time to soon after I had first arrived. I didn't want to access this memory; indeed I had tried at the time to disassociate myself from everything that was happening around me, so I hoped this one remembrance had faded away into the recesses of my mind, never to return.

But it was here. It was still warm that day. We had been told to line up for an extra roll call, which wasn't entirely unusual, and no one seemed to think much of it until we saw the ten inmates, their heads bowed, lined up in front of us, as if they were about to start putting on a play.

There was an SS officer in front of them. Not the usual brutes of our everyday misery, but someone more senior who spent his time ordering the others and having very little to do with our existence. You could tell he didn't come here often just by looking at his boots, which shone so brightly you would swear that they had been bought just that morning. The other guards, whilst they polished their boots, always left a few scuffs, and by the end of the day they would be covered in dust or mud.

The officer did not wait to explain why he had had to come here that morning. He was displeased that he had been drawn out of a meeting and that we had effectively ruined his day.

"A prisoner tried to escape this morning," he told us.

As much as we tried to remain silent, there was a collective murmur amongst us, all of us wondering the same thing—who was it and how far had he got?

"He did not succeed," the officer said. "And I want to remind you what happens if just one of you tries to escape. Whether you succeed or fail, it is of no consequence to me."

He didn't wait a beat. He turned to the men lined up behind him and shot each one in the head in quick succession.

The bodies dropped to the floor, their blood pooling in the dirt.

"For every one of you that even tries to escape, ten inmates will be shot. Is that understood?"

Quietly everyone said yes, they understood, whilst our eyes remained focused on the bodies.

They didn't remove the bodies that day or the next. They let them lie there with fat sluggish flies landing on them, reminding us at each roll call what fate awaited us if we tried to escape.

"You all right?" Ezra shook me out of my memory, back to the garage.

"You remember what happened in the summer," I said. "Don't even joke about it."

"It wasn't a joke," Ezra said. "I meant it. We could escape."

Before I could reprimand him once more, the roar of an engine entering the forecourt to the garage made us jump up and look busy quickly.

Two guards got out of a jeep—one of them Bruno.

They walked toward us, and both Ezra and Stanislaw worked quickly and quietly whilst I stupidly stood there watching Bruno approach.

The other guard was taller than Bruno, thinner, with a wisp of a mustache on his top lip, and I wondered why he bothered as it was so thin you could think he had some food or fluff stuck there and immediately want to wipe it away for him.

"You forget how to work?" he asked me, sneering.

"I—" I began, but before I could say anything more, he hit me on the side of my head, knocking me down to the grimy floor.

I tried to stand. My ear was ringing from where he had landed the punch, but I managed to get onto all fours. A mistake. He kicked me hard under my ribs, making me cough and vomit up the coffee I had recently drunk.

"I'll take care of him later," I heard Bruno say.

The tall thin man laughed and followed Bruno into his office, leaving me retching on the floor.

SIXTEEN
JOZEF

That afternoon I kept away from my little desk near Bruno's office, returning to my duties as helper for Stanislaw and Ezra. Not that I was of much use. My ribs ached from the kick and I wondered if they were broken.

"Not that it would matter," Ezra had said. "Bruised, broken, it doesn't matter, you just have to live with it."

Stanislaw was more sympathetic, and gave me a job where I could sit on a small stool and clean pieces of the engine that they were taking apart with a dirty rag.

I took to my task with gusto. I don't know why exactly, but the repetitive movements of pushing that rag back and forth, checking that the oil and smears of grease had been cleaned away, gave me a calm feeling and allowed my thoughts to simply float about in my brain without taking anchor on one subject.

Stanislaw suddenly coughed, a hacking sound, and I looked up. Bruno's door was opening.

I stood, afraid to be found sitting by the thin man, and stood a little behind Ezra and the pile of tires, hoping like a child to be hidden from the bully. It worked. The thin man had no more interest in us; he hopped back into his jeep and drove away.

"Jozef," Bruno's voice came from the office. I followed it to find him sitting behind his desk, flexing his right hand.

"It's stiff since I've stopped using the sling," he said. "The doctor told me to keep the fingers moving, but I don't think it is working.

"Here," he suddenly said, picking up a piece of paper and handing it to me. "Read it," he said, still clenching and unclenching his hand, his eyes concentrated on the movement.

I looked down at the paper, and when I did, I saw handwriting. Handwriting that I knew. Adi.

Just as I'd eaten the bread that morning, I devoured the letter, once, twice, then had to slow myself to read it a third time to properly take in all that she was saying.

Dearest Jozef,

I write this to you as quickly as my hand will allow. I am well. What I mean to say is that I am alive. Bruno is standing in front of me as I write, looking about at anyone who might see, and he is telling me to be quick, but there is so much to say and I find I don't know what to write.

I cannot believe that Bruno is here. Why have I written that? Why haven't I written of how much I miss you and love you? Because I do, you know that, don't you?

Maybe because he once loved me, I now can't understand how he is one of them. Is it really him? I mean, I know it is, but like I said, I cannot believe it.

Are you well? Bruno says he is keeping you safe and he will keep me safe too. Can that be true? Will we really have a chance of surviving this place?

There is so much death, Jozef, so much. I try to help those who are sick, who are old, and those who are besieged with grief over family that they will never see again. I tell them stories, I wipe their wounds, and I try to make it easier for them. But it isn't easy, is it? I am lying to them to appease their fears. I shouldn't lie, but how can I not?

I am sorry. I am rambling. My thoughts are tumbling over themselves, fighting to get out, and my heart—oh, my heart—I feel it beating with joy at knowing that you are alive!

Bruno is telling me to be quick again. He tells me I must stop now.

I love you, Jozef. We will be together again, I know it.

Your wife,

Adi.

I did not know I was crying until Bruno handed me his handkerchief, a light blue letter B embroidered on the corner—a memento, it seemed, from his childhood.

"I told you I would do it," he said.

I looked at him—he had that triumphant glow on his face like he had when he was a child and had outwitted someone, or taken a risk and it had paid off.

"Thank you," I said.

"Don't thank me, Jozef. I don't deserve your thanks, or forgiveness. And I'm never going to ask for it. I can try and do something here. I can try and keep you and Adi safe, and maybe others."

"What was she like?" I asked.

"Still Adi." He grinned. "Still trying to help people and being strong."

"Is she well?"

"She is thinner. I told her I would try to get her more food, and she asked if I could get a few medical supplies so she can help the other women and I said I would."

I didn't know what to say. I thought of Adi, thin like me,

hungry and cold, and felt so useless that a ball of rage in my stomach turned and grew.

"Write her back," Bruno said, handing me a blank sheet of paper. "Write her back now, and I will get the letter to her tomorrow and she will write you again."

I took the paper and a pen from Bruno and set about writing to my wife who I knew was now alive, realizing that all this time, I had thought, truthfully thought, she was dead.

My darling,

I cannot express how happy I was to hear that you are alive! All this time I have been pretending that you had escaped to take my brain away from the horrible possibility that you may not have survived. But now, I see how wrong I was and if anything, you would be the one to survive rather than me.

I, too, find myself not sure of what to tell you, as this life we lead is not normal in any way. It is not as though I am spending my days researching and writing, drinking a strong cup of coffee at a cafe and chatting with friends. It is not as though anything about this life is something that I really want to relay to anyone.

So, my Adi, what I will talk about with you is our past and perhaps our hopes for the future, as that at least is happy and it is not this place.

I have a friend, Ezra, and perhaps I could count Stanislaw as a friend too. We work together and, sometimes, we talk of what our lives will be like once we are free again. At first, I did not join in with this make-believe, feeling as though it was foolish child's play and hope was the worst thing to feel in a place like this. But they wore me down with their talk of opening a garage together one day where they would mend cars, and in the evenings they would go to the local tavern and toast a beer to their hard day's work. Ezra believes that his wife and children are safe as they were taken in by Christian neighbors and hidden, and he believes that they will be waiting for him on his return home.

Stanislaw does not have any family; hence Ezra has suggested Stanislaw join his and share in Ezra's hopes for the future, and Stanislaw seems happy to accept.

My future, though, is harder to see. I wonder whether we will return to France or Germany. Or will we go to my parents? I know that you have always said it doesn't matter where we are as long as we have each other, and that is all I can think for my future—that you and I are together.

In my mind's eye, we have a cottage that stands alone in a field with wildflowers. There is a stream at the rear of the garden and a small bench under a tree, where we sit and read and listen to the water as it babbles over the stones.

I don't know where the cottage is, exactly, and it doesn't seem to matter to me much. We have a dog and a cat and they are friends, not enemies. They run around the garden and chase each other, and you and I sit on our bench and laugh at them!

At times, I have tried to picture children, but at the moment I cannot. Every time I think of children, I think of those that were on the platform the day we arrived here, of how they screamed with fear as they were ripped from their parents, and for some reason I cannot resolve a happy picture of a child, even an imaginary one, with the reality of seeing those children.

Can you picture our children, Adi? Can you? If you can, tell me about them, tell me what you see and help me to see that part of my future too.

I want to write more, Adi, but the siren has gone alerting us all to the end of our work, and I must return to my bunkhouse and eat whatever meager food we are given this evening. But I will enjoy getting into bed tonight, your letter with me, a piece of you now with me, and I think I shall sleep soundly.

I will write again.

All my love,

Jozef.

I passed the letter to Bruno, who nodded at me. I knew he would get it to Adi.

After dinner—a soup of cabbage and carrot which tasted worse than it looked—we all sat in the bunkhouse, all of us tired yet not willing to go to sleep until the siren rang out to tell us to. These moments together we could pretend, to some extent, to be normal, or at least to be in charge of ourselves once more.

As I had rarely participated in any group conversations, I was much ignored, and happily spent my time perched on the edge of Ezra's bed as a few men held court.

One such man was David, who worked in the laundry and had the reputation of being the best thief. He had, he told us that evening, managed to procure a chisel, had hidden it in the laundry and would sell it to the highest bidder.

This type of transaction was not unusual. All manner of things were bartered for food, and no questions were asked as to why someone would want, for example, a tin of paint, or indeed a chisel.

Two hands shot up and both eagerly wanted said chisel from David.

"Extra soup," said one man, Elias, who worked in the kitchens and could easily get his hands on extra bits of food.

"Only soup?" David scoffed. "For a chisel?"

"What will he do with a chisel anyway?" I asked Ezra, who watched the bidding with great interest, a small grin on his lips.

"Probably try to break out."

"With a chisel?" I shook my head.

The other man, whose name I did not know, though I knew him to be a Pole who did not speak German, was not getting on well in his transaction with David, who was German born.

Finally, someone helped out the Pole and said, "He's offering a coat."

"A coat, you say." David stroked his chin, where I imagine he once had the most illustrious of beards. He nodded, and started to raise his arm to accept the proposal, when Elias suddenly shouted, "Four potatoes and extra bread for a week."

There was a general cry from the spectators as they appreciated how high the stakes had now become.

Ezra was almost falling off the bed with excitement. "Take the food!" he yelled. "Take the food!"

I thought about it and decided I would probably take the coat, and told Ezra as much.

"Don't be stupid," he told me. "If they find you with an extra coat, then that's it for you." He dragged a finger across his neck. "Take the food. Always take the food. It's obvious."

A cold wind rattled at the door as we waited for either of the men to raise their bids, but the Pole had nothing else to barter and Elias knew it.

"Four potatoes, extra bread, soup, and any scraps I can find!" Elias shouted.

More men shouted their opinions at David—"You don't need the coat! You work in the laundry! Take the food, you madman!"

David, enjoying his moment, finally looked at the Pole. "I'll take the coat," he said.

A collective groan filled the bunkhouse. *Take the food. Always take the food.*

Elias looked utterly defeated and shuffled off to bed, where he turned his back on the rest of us.

As I got into my own bed, I thought about the Pole and the coat and what he may do with the chisel. Would he keep it with him at all times? Would he try to kill a guard or himself? What could you do with a chisel in here anyway?

I thought David had been right to take the coat, and I wished for extra layers every time I moved. It was as though the cold air could now get through my thin skin and touch my bones, and as much as I wanted more food, it would be a bitter, quick win of a little bit extra for a while, only to then go back to having less once again. I would still feel the cold, gnawing away at my insides.

Ezra was in a chipper mood the next morning, as he had heard from someone who had heard from someone else that the weather reports said there would be no more snow.

"Spring is on its way," he said. "One less thing to think about."

"When we are warm, we can just concentrate on being hungry," I said.

"Always the optimistic, aren't we, Jozef?" He smirked.

"How can you keep this humor all the time?" I asked. "Nothing seems to bother you."

"That's where you're wrong." He stuck his hands in his pockets. "You couldn't be more wrong. Just because I try to be positive, just because I try to see a way out, it doesn't mean that I don't see what is around me, or worry constantly about my wife and children."

Suddenly, he stopped walking and looked at me. "I worry so much, Jozef, that I think it is killing me. I can feel it, in here." He pointed to his stomach. "It's killing me bit by bit, I know it."

His tone scared me, and I wished I could take back what I'd

said and let Ezra keep his chirpier mood about the warmer weather.

He did not talk for the rest of the walk to the garage, and went straight over to Stanislaw to see what needed to be done.

I sat at my desk and totaled up some invoices, then tried to decipher a note written in a messy hand by a guard who had sent in a car whose chauffeur said it kept stalling.

"Jozef." Bruno was at my shoulder. "I have to take a car to the front gates to be picked up. Come with me and you can carry back a few parts that were delivered this morning. It will save someone a trip."

I was aware that it was unusual to be riding in a car with my overseer and felt as though it was a trick of sorts. But I needn't have worried as I wasn't actually allowed to ride in the car; I had to jog by the side of it whilst Bruno drove it slowly to the gates, the wrought-iron *Arbeit Macht Frei* hanging above them.

Once Bruno had delivered the car, he pointed toward some boxes and told me to carry them. I was already so exhausted from jogging alongside the car that my muscles screamed with pain as I tried to lift them. Bruno bent down to help me.

"Don't," I told him.

He looked to the gate where a guard watched us closely, then stood straight, his face a picture of helplessness.

We walked slowly back, Bruno matching my shuffled gait. Once we got clear of the main gates and the watchtower, he told me to set the boxes down and rest a moment.

"It's safe here," he said.

I sat on a piece of damp grass as he stood and smoked and looked about him.

"Do you remember when I wanted to live with you?" he suddenly said.

I looked up at him. "Yes."

"I often wonder what would have happened if your parents had taken me in."

"You'd be sitting next to me on the grass right now, wearing the same outfit as me."

"Maybe," he said, lighting a cigarette and blowing out a stream of smoke. "Or maybe I could have saved you. You and Adi and your parents."

"My parents are safe," I said.

"And Elisa?" he asked.

"She's fine," I said. "Managed to leave before it all fell apart."

"I wish I had left," he said, looking away, over the barbed wire-topped fences toward the trees that bowed gently in the breeze.

"Where would you have gone?" I asked.

"America," he said with glee. "America. And I would have become a film star!"

I laughed at him.

"And you would have come with me," he said.

"I don't think I would've been a great actor."

"Not so, Jozef, not so. Don't you remember when we were little? Really little? Your sister had those puppets and we would put on shows."

All of a sudden, I was there in my parents' parlor, a plump Bruno at my side, moving puppets that danced awkwardly on their strings, singing a made-up song and reciting the script we had written for them.

"Sabine and Hans," I said.

"Hans was a grumpy old man," Bruno started.

"And Sabine was a dancer with one leg!" we said together.

"Why did we make her have one leg?" I asked through my laughter.

Bruno shook his head. "All I know is that it seemed like a good idea at the time, to remove a leg. Like it would make our show even more interesting!"

"Elisa wasn't happy," I said. Then Bruno bent double with

laughter, remembering how Elisa had stormed out of the room and gone in search of the leg, and when she had found it, waved it in front of our childish faces and yelled, "Tell me! Which one of you made my puppet a one-legged spinster?"

Soon we stopped laughing and regained control. "I'm sorry," Bruno said quietly.

"If I remember correctly, I think it was me who removed the leg," I said.

"No, I'm sorry. I'm sorry about all of this."

I looked at him. He wiped his hand across his face. "I am. I can't say it enough."

"Stop, Bruno. You don't have to keep saying it."

"I do." He crouched down now and leaned in close. "I am sorry, Jozef. I am sorry for all those years we lost too. You were, are, my best friend and I stopped writing you."

"We grew apart," I said. "We grew up."

Bruno shook his head. "I stopped writing you at school because I was ashamed, Jozef," he said. "I knew what everyone thought about Jews and about Hitler's plans, and I'll admit that I went along with it for a while. Mostly for my father. I wanted to make him proud, you see, and it was the only way. I see now that it wasn't worth it. That my father was never worth anything. But you can understand, can't you, that I had to play along?"

"I can try and understand," I said. "I find it hard sometimes; I won't lie to you. But I know you, Bruno. I just hope I am not wrong."

Bruno nodded and did not look at me. "You're not. You'll see how I am not like these men, how I am different, how I am still who you thought I was. You'll see."

SEVENTEEN
JOZEF

David, it seemed, had gotten his coat from the Pole, and spent the evening in the bunkhouse wearing it and proclaiming to all how warm he was.

"You'd better watch it," Ezra warned him. "If you're found with it, it is going to hurt."

David waved away the warning and continued to say how warm he was, and that he now had a broom in his possession and wondered who would bid for it.

A man called Otto, usually loud and opinionated, was exceptionally quiet that evening. Ezra tried to get him to bid for the broom, if for nothing more than a bit of entertainment, but he steadfastly refused.

"Just leave me alone!" he screamed at Ezra, his face puce.

Ezra stood back, his hands clenched into balls. I thought he was going to punch him, and I grabbed Ezra's sleeve and pulled him away.

"What's wrong with you?" Ezra shouted back at him.

"What's wrong with me? I'm on the list! Me. Tonight is my last. You know who else is on it? Your friend, Stanislaw. I bet he doesn't know and I wish I didn't."

"List?" I asked.

Ezra turned to me, his face pale. "There's a prisoner, Nikolay. He can sometimes get access to the list of people who are next for the wall or for the chamber. He's obviously told Otto."

"Stanislaw," I said.

"He might not know." Ezra looked to Otto, who was rocking back and forth now, crying, whilst others tried to comfort him, but there wasn't much anyone could say.

"We should tell him," I said. "We should try to get word to him."

"And say what? Tonight is your last? It's better he does not know, Jozef. Look at Otto."

I did. I looked at Otto, who seemed to be unraveling before my very eyes. My stomach, which usually groaned with hunger, was silent and felt as though it had sunk in my body. I cannot quite find the words to describe that feeling. A hopelessness beyond anything I have ever known, and a fear that it could so easily be me made my head ache.

I wanted to say something, but my mouth was dry and I didn't have the right words. I thought of what Adi would say but again, nothing came to me. Then I thought of my father and as soon as I did, I knew what to do.

I pushed my way through toward Otto and sat on the floor. Then slowly, quietly, I began to pray.

At first, Otto seemed indifferent to my prayers, but soon he began to speak the words along with me and gave me his hands. We sat that way, Otto and I, until dawn, whispering prayers in the dark, asking God to save our souls.

Otto was not taken at roll call, and as I watched him walk off with his work detail, shovels in hand, an image assaulted me of him digging his own grave. I turned to Ezra to tell him what I had thought, when my number was called—my work duty had been changed.

I was ushered along to Block 11, along with five others who all walked slowly. I knew of Block 11 and the torture that was meted out there, and I knew, too, of the wall where prisoners were lined up and shot, their bodies falling onto the ground in heaps, one after another. I thought quickly—what had I done? Had I been seen or heard talking to Bruno and was now to meet my punishment?

I could feel Adi's letter in my pocket and wondered if they would search me, and on seeing Adi's name find some form of punishment for her too. Just meters away, through barbed wire fences, I could see the outside world—the trees bowing in the wind, the sky blue and speckled with thin white clouds. It was just there, just within my reach, yet there was no way I would be able to get free.

Outside Block 11 a pile of bodies were already on the ground.

"Move them," was all we were told.

A part of me breathed a sigh of relief—it was an actual work detail and I was not one who would be tortured, kept in a tiny cell where I could only stand, starved and beaten in that red-bricked building.

But then I realized my task—moving bodies. The other prisoners had done this before and set about their task, heaving the bodies onto a wooden cart. When it was full, it would be wheeled to the ovens, where the Sonderkommando would burn the bodies and tip the ashes into a nearby river.

"It's better than the pits," a Pole next to me said in broken French. "I heard you speaking French one day, but you're German, aren't you?"

I nodded, unable to speak.

"I'm Aleksy, but everyone calls me Alek."

"Jozef," I managed.

"So, all we need to do is move the bodies and that's it. Try not to look at their faces. It sounds cold, I know, but trust me, you don't want to look at their faces because they will haunt you and you will never be able to get rid of them."

I followed Alek to the pile.

"They were busy this morning. Needed room quickly for some new arrivals. Quickest way, up against the wall. I hope I get the wall when it's my turn. I know someone in the Sonderkommando, he works mostly at the pits, and he says they have to undress the bodies after the gas gets them. Says the gas takes at least six minutes. So I think I'd rather get a bullet."

Alek talked the whole time he worked, separating each body from the other, entwined with their legs and arms, and dragged out the body toward the cart where another prisoner helped him to lift it.

I bent down and tried not to look at their faces, but it was impossible. Their features were frozen in a grimace of fear and horror, their eyes open, staring at me.

I lifted an arm and recoiled as the skin of their hand touched me, as if they were reaching out to be helped.

"Come on," Alek said. "You have to work."

I tried again, this time reaching for the back of someone, hoping to drag them to the cart without having to see their face. It was only as I got the body free that I realized how light it was and how small. I looked down to see in my arms a child of ten or less. A boy or girl, I did not know. I dropped the body, turned from the scene and vomited, my hand on the brick wall, where I could feel the stickiness of blood underneath my fingertips.

Suddenly, my number was called out yet again and a guard walked toward me. "You're to return to the garage," he said.

Alek nodded his goodbye to me as I walked away, and I hoped to God that I would never have to see that again and that Alek would never be one of those bodies on the ground.

As soon as I reached the garage, I could hear Ezra and Stanislaw inside, arguing over the best way to fix a carburetor.

"Stanislaw!" Forgetting myself, I went to him and pulled him into a hug, a bewildered look on his face.

Ezra shook his head at me—he had had a reprieve, it seemed, and I was to say nothing.

"Jozef." Bruno stood looking at me, relief in his face. "Please, come. We need to talk about the accounts," he said.

I followed him into his office and he closed the door, and for the first time gave me a chair to sit on whilst he perched on the desk. He handed me a flask. "Drink," he said.

I did, feeling the burn of whiskey on the back of my throat.

"I am so sorry," he said. "They changed your work detail, and I didn't know until this morning when Ezra said. I made sure you came back, though—I told them that you were one of the best and I could not work without you."

"And Stanislaw?" I asked.

"Ezra told me of him too this morning. I have made sure that he will be safe for now."

I could not say any more for some time. My hands shook and my stomach grumbled at the alcohol I drank to make my head cloudy. I didn't want to think of the child, but the feel of their body in my arms was still there. I looked to my hands to check, and saw only dirt and the rust color of dried blood.

"They're still here," I said eventually.

"Who's still here?" Bruno asked.

"The child. They are still here; I can feel them."

Bruno placed his hand on my forehead. "No fever," he said.

"I'm not ill," I told him. "There was a child at that wall. A child!"

"Hush, hush." Bruno kneeled in front of me. "Drink some more," he encouraged.

"Can you imagine, Bruno? A child." I looked at him, trying to see if he really understood the complete horror of this place. "They shot a child. They were probably hanging onto their parents' clothes, scared, crying, wondering what was going to happen."

"I know," he said softly. "I know."

"How can anyone kill a child?"

"I don't know," he said, and would not meet my eye. He stood and perched himself on the edge of his desk once more.

"I don't think I can do it, Bruno. I don't think I can watch this happen and do nothing."

"There is nothing you or I can do to stop this," he said. "All you can do is stay alive, and I will help and I will keep Adi alive."

"I need to do more," I said.

The minutes ticked by, and I kept drinking until there was nothing left in the flask.

"I know what you can do," Bruno said. "Write it all down. All of it. Your story, how you got here, what happened to you here. I will keep the pages safe for you, each and every one, and I will get your story out."

"To whom? Who would want to read it?"

"The Americans, British—someone. I'll let people know what is happening here. Write it down, Jozef. You have to be a witness to this. You have to tell your story."

"I don't want to think about it," I said, my words slurry with whiskey. "I don't want to think of that child."

"But you must, Jozef." Bruno came close to me now and held my shoulders so that I had to look at him. "You must."

EIGHTEEN
ALICE

"Did you?" I asked, when Jozef fell silent. "Did you write it down?"

"I did," he said.

"And did Bruno give it to us or the British?" I asked.

"No, he did not," he said.

"Why?"

Jozef shook his head, then picked up a twig on the ground and threw it in the general direction of Amos, who was sniffing at a bush.

"Why?" I asked again.

"I don't think I want to talk about it anymore today, Alice," he said quietly. "It is hard to think of it all, of the child. I can't talk anymore today, I'm sorry."

"You don't have to be sorry," I told him.

Jozef stood and dusted off his trousers, and whistled for Amos to follow him. I watched him walk away, his gait slow and steady, his eyes on his feet as they negotiated the brambles and stones, and wished I wasn't such a child and knew the right thing to do or say.

I stayed at the lake for an hour or so more, thinking about

what Jozef had told me and wondering if it had been a good idea for him to do so. My brain, which had been full of Nancy and Mikey and Billy, was now full of images of bodies and a little child crying for their mother as someone pointed a gun at them.

I couldn't understand, just as Jozef couldn't, how anyone could be so cruel, and whilst I understood why no one really talked about what happened in the war, I felt that we should— surely we should all be talking about it and make sure that this could never happen again?

On my walk home, I decided that I would do what Jozef had done. I would write down things that I learned, from him and from talking to Pops and maybe others who went to war. I would write it all down and show it to everyone so that in some way, I was helping.

I set about my task that evening, quietly sitting in my tree-house, covering pages and pages in my notebook until my parents got worried about me and told me I had to come inside.

I woke early the next morning and over breakfast read back what I had written the night before. My writing was childish and my descriptions of what Jozef had told me about the camp were not good enough, real enough. But would they ever be? I had never experienced it and was trying to reimagine a life I had never lived.

I spread more butter on my last piece of toast and stuffed it into my mouth, feeling the melted grease escape from my lips and drip down my chin.

"You'll choke yourself," my mother reprimanded me, and I just nodded at her, my mouth too full to say anything.

As I washed it down with cold milk, I remembered what Jozef had said about being hungry and how he savored every-thing he ate. I looked at the boiled egg Mom had just given me and decided to eat slower, taste everything, and enjoy it.

After breakfast, I shoved my writings into a backpack and ran outside.

"It's fixed." Billy's voice stopped me short.

I turned to see him on the porch swing, his face drawn, thinner somehow.

"Thanks," I said, and walked toward him.

"Only took a minute," he said, but he would not look at me. "Where are you going?"

"Just out," I said.

"Mom and Pops said I have to watch you better. They said I can't stay in my room all day."

I jostled from foot to foot, eager to get away, to get to Jozef's so I could find out more for my writing. I was counting on Billy to stay in his room and leave me be, but then I felt guilty for thinking that. It was good Billy was out of his room.

"I'm just going to see Clem," I lied.

"You could stay here," he said, looking at me now. "You could stay and I'll make you pancakes like I was supposed to for your birthday."

"I already ate," I said. "I really have to see Clem. It's for this summer project for school."

"Oh yeah, the one about how much window glass costs?"

For a second, I forgot I had asked him about the window costs, then recovering myself I nodded eagerly. "Yeah, you know, having to do a budget or something for when you have your own house. We have to say how much we'd need to live on in a year." The lies rolled easily off my tongue, and I knew if Mikey were here, he would be proud.

"Maybe later then?" he asked.

"Yeah, later, definitely." I raced away from him toward my bike before he could ask me anything more.

"Hey, squirt," he yelled after me. "Stay away from the lake, okay?"

"Sure!" I called back to him as I turned onto the sidewalk, my legs pumping at the pedals.

I'd not spend long at Jozef's, I decided. I'd see if he would talk a little more, and then I'd go and see if Billy wanted to take the five dollars he gave me and go to a movie, or maybe go to Frank's and get a milkshake. He never wanted to spend time with me if he really didn't have to, and I didn't want to pass up the opportunity to get a milkshake, nor did I want to leave him alone for too long. His face had scared me—drawn, pale, his eyes still red from lack of sleep and crying. I had to try and make him better, I decided. I'd be quick at Jozef's, then I'd make my brother better.

The house on Mulberry was quiet when I arrived. I'd expected to be greeted by an excited Amos, or perhaps Jozef would be sitting on the porch, but I soon found out that no one was home.

I peered through the kitchen window, just in case he had not heard my incessant knocking at the front door, and saw the kitchen table with the chairs neatly pushed under it and a vase of sunflowers in the middle.

I looked about the backyard, at the new border I had dug, and realized I had done very little since I had been coming here. I marched my way with purpose to the tiny shed at the rear of the yard, and found a broom, a rake, and some shears and set about tidying the lawn, raking any fallen leaves into neat little piles, then moving them to the compost heap, where I was sure that Amos would end up jumping in and disturbing my work.

I wiped the sweat off my forehead and surveyed the neat lawn, then examined the straggly bushes and shrubs. I didn't know what they were and I wasn't sure whether you were even supposed to cut them back, but their branches and misshapen edges were ruining the view of the orderly lawn and, taking a deep breath, I began hacking at them with the shears, hoping that I was doing it right.

After an hour or so, I stopped and cleared away the debris and saw that I had made a mess of the pruning. The bushes, which I had been aiming to shape into boxes like the ones Mr. Briggs had in his garden, were blob-like, and the few shrubs I had trimmed now resembled tall skinny fingers. I was pretty sure they weren't meant to look like that.

"It looks good."

I turned to see Jozef at the kitchen door, a grin on his face, and Amos struggling to squeeze through the gap between his leg and the doorframe in order to get to me.

"I think I've ruined it," I said, cocking my head to the side to see if the bushes looked better that way.

He walked over to me with Amos, who reached me first, jumped up, and gave me a huge lick on the face.

"I like it," he said. "It looks like art."

"It isn't right. The bushes are meant to be boxes and they're not."

"Well, I like them. I don't want my garden to be like anyone else's. At least I have an original garden!"

I knew he was humoring me and I was mad at myself for doing such a bad job, when in my head the vision I had had been so perfect.

"Come on inside," Jozef said. "I've been to the store, and I think you might be interested to see what I bought."

Sulkily I followed him inside, plopped myself in a chair at the kitchen table, and watched as he took out some items from two brown paper bags. Eggs, bread, milk—so far nothing interested me, and I kept looking out of the window at my handiwork, cringing with embarrassment.

"Here!" he said, and with a flourish handed me a stick of Mamba fruit chews.

"What are these?" I asked.

"New candy!" he said. "When I got to the store, they had a promotion for them—brand-new candy, all fruit flavors—and I thought to myself, I know a young girl who would appreciate these!"

Without even saying thank you, I unwrapped the candy and popped one into my mouth, biting into the sticky chew, tasting strawberry on my tongue.

Jozef took one too. "I have orange," he said through his chewing. "What do you have?"

"Strawberry," I mumbled.

We both tried another each, then another.

Amos soon realized that food was to be had and pushed his wet nose onto the tabletop, sniffing out what was there, then sticking his tongue out to try and reach a sweet.

"Silly boy." I pushed his nose away. "Not for you."

"This is for you." Jozef took a bone off the counter and threw it in Amos' general direction. "I got it today for him from the butcher. I couldn't leave him out, could I?" He winked at me.

Amos grabbed the bone and ran into the other room. "Outside!" Jozef shouted after him.

"I'll get him," I offered, and before Jozef could say anything, I raced after Amos, seeing my chance to investigate the insides of Jozef's quiet dark house.

Amos had run into the living room and was sprawled out on a green sofa that had gold tassels at the bottom. As soon as he saw me, he turned his head to hide the bone and to pretend he hadn't seen me, so that he didn't have to remove himself from the sofa.

I was disappointed with the room, although I wasn't sure what I expected to see. It had hardwood floors, and a patterned rug in the center that had a low coffee table atop it. There was an armchair that matched the sofa and a book on a side table.

I looked instead at the walls, which had a few oil paintings, and on a sideboard I struck gold—photographs.

Letting Amos sit for another moment, I went to the sideboard and looked at the photos that were in silver frames. There was an old woman on her own, looking sadly at the camera, a man and woman on their wedding day, and a baby. I looked closely at the man, but it wasn't Jozef. Who was the woman?

"They're not mine."

I jumped; Jozef was next to me, having entered the room silently, it seemed.

"Sorry," I said, backing away.

"No need to be sorry. Sit, sit down." He nodded toward the couch.

I pushed an irritable Amos to the floor and sat. Jozef picked up the photo of the old woman and sat in the armchair, looking at the wrinkly face.

"Who is she?" I asked.

"She's the aunt of a rabbi I know," he said. "This is her house."

I remembered then that an old woman had lived here years ago.

"She lives in New Jersey now, with her son," he said by way of explanation.

"Why do you keep the photographs?"

He shrugged, then placed the frame carefully on the side table so that the picture was facing him. "It makes me feel less alone," he said.

I wasn't sure what to say. I hadn't ever felt lonely, apart from the time Mikey had gone to his aunt's a year ago, and Clem and George were on vacation. But even then I still had Mom, Pops, and Billy.

"Where's Adi?" I quietly asked. "Do you not have a photograph of her?"

He gently shook his head.

"Did she die in the camp?"

"No." He looked properly at me now. "No, she didn't die in

the camp. She died when she reached America. Ironic, isn't it, that when she was finally free, she died."

"I wanted to tell you something," I said. "I mean, I wanted to show you. It's in my backpack. I've been writing about the war and about the things you told me, and I wanted to know if you would tell me some more—tell me how you got out, and more about Adi and what happened to Bruno."

"You're writing it down?" he asked.

I nodded. "You said that you had written it down too, and I thought I could write about what you told me and maybe find other people, like Pops and some of the others who were in the army, and write about what it was like for them too. To do what Bruno said—write it down to show people."

He smiled a strange smile at me, and I wasn't sure whether he was mad at me.

"I suppose," he said, "that if you are going to write it down, then you need to hear the last part."

"Is that about when the war ended?" I asked.

"No. It's about when I escaped from Auschwitz."

NINETEEN
JOZEF

1943

As much as I didn't want to, I did as Bruno had suggested and began to write my story. The more I wrote, the more I saw that others in the camp were doing the same—they wanted to document what was happening to them. It made me feel as though we were a part of something much larger, and that perhaps what we were doing would in fact change something in the future.

Spring arrived and soon gave way to summer. Ezra now complained of the heat instead of the cold. I had not heard from Adi again, as Bruno said that she had been working in the women's infirmary and he had only been able to get my letter to her.

"But she's alive?" I'd ask him, each time he would come back after trying to see her.

"She is. I saw her with my own eyes, but I could not find a way, an excuse to get her away from her work without causing someone to question it. You have to remember that it is odd for a

Rottenführer from the car garage to be talking to a female inmate."

I nodded. I didn't care too much. All I cared about was that she was alive, and I would have to make do with that until she was able to write me again.

One evening we sat outside our bunkhouse, smoking and talking and enjoying the cooler air that arrived with the end of the day.

David sat with Ezra and me, and talked at length about how he was aiming to get his hands on a mop.

"What are you going to do with that?" Ezra asked.

I wondered the same—I couldn't see anyone bidding for a mop.

"It's not for us." He nodded toward the fence. "It's for them."

"Them who?" Ezra asked.

"People out there. Normal people. There's been some selling of things now and then to the villagers, and they pay a pretty price. I sold two brooms last week for a packet of cigarettes and a loaf of bread!"

I grinned at his ingenuity and knew of others who would easily join in.

"What do they need?" Ezra asked.

"Anything—depends on what you can get. You have to get it to me, you see; I hide it in the laundry and someone else takes care of the transactions. You name your lowest price—we always ask for more, so don't worry—but at least you'd get something."

"What are you thinking, Ezra?" I asked.

"We've got tools. Fuel even."

"I can't get fuel out!" David half laughed. "Smaller is better. Or something we use every day so that no eyebrows are raised if they see a prisoner with a broom or a mop."

"I'll think about it. There will be something."

I wanted no part in it. I was oddly content with the way things were. I felt safe—as safe as I could feel—under the watchful eye of Bruno. We had extra to eat and drink; we had a good enough job that kept us from digging ditches, building more barracks, or much worse. There was no way I was going to risk it.

We sat in companionable silence for a while, until David raised his head and seemed to sniff at the air.

"Can you smell it?" he asked us.

I inhaled deeply through my nose and could smell burning.

"The crematorium is working then," David said.

I knew of the change. No longer were bodies flung into pits, but a new set of buildings had sprung up to accommodate large ovens that burned the bodies quickly.

It was the first time I had smelled the smoke from those bodies. Whether it was because the air was still that night, I do not know, but the smell was something I will never forget and is indescribable to someone who has never before smelled it. It had a sickly quality to it and was thicker and more rancid than normal smoke from a fire. It stayed in your nostrils, clinging to the tiny hairs so that when I tried to sleep that evening, I could still smell their burning flesh.

The following evening, I found myself once more sitting outside with Ezra and David. Ezra was quiet—too quiet. He had been grumbly all day, shouting at Stanislaw and kicking things that seemingly got in his way.

"What's wrong?" David asked him. "Did something happen today?"

"Something happens every day," he said.

I offered Ezra one of my cigarettes, and he took it and inhaled deeply. "Can you hear them? Can you? I swear to God they are driving me insane! I hear them when I sleep, when I eat. I hear them all the time."

I looked to David, who looked as concerned as I was and

placed his hand gently on Ezra's arm. "What are you talking about?"

"The crows! For God's sake, the crows! They squawk all the time. No songbirds—oh no—just that maddening death screech. They know, you know, the birds. All the nice little birds that sit on their branches and sing a song have flown away. They don't want to be here—they know what is happening. It's just the crows that stay. They don't care, you see. They'll take an eyeball right out of your head."

As worried as I was about Ezra and his mad ramblings, I knew what he meant and now he had pointed it out to me, I, too, found that all I could hear day in and day out was that awful screech and flap of wings in the trees, as they fought over whatever morsel of food they had found. I hated them—all of them—and wished never to hear a crow again in my life.

The summer heat was intense that month, and we found ourselves for a third night sitting once more outside, but this time a Pole joined us—a new prisoner who still had some weight on his bones and looked at our skinny frames with utter horror. He spoke some German, and we managed well enough to get along in conversation to find out that he had been sent here along with his whole family, his father and brother taken at the train station and led away.

"Where have they gone?" he asked. "I have asked everyone if they have seen them."

David shook his head. "They've gone for a shower," he said.

"A shower?" the Pole asked.

"Don't tell him," Ezra said, his eyes on the trees where the crows lived.

"He'll know sooner or later," David said.

"Know what?"

As gently as he could, David described what he knew. He knew that people were led to a shower block and told to undress. He knew that certain prisoners, Sonderkommando, were made to sift through their belongings and pile them on carts to be taken away. He knew that instead of water coming from the shower, a type of poison was released in the form of a gas. He knew that it took a while for them to die, and that their bodies were then taken to the crematorium, where any gold teeth were taken from their mouths, their hair was collected, and then they were placed inside an oven.

The Pole did not believe David, and began to scream and shout at him in Polish. David tried to calm him, but the Pole was running now, toward the wire fence, yelling in his language for his father and brother.

"I told you not to tell him." Ezra stood and was about to run after the boy, but David pulled him back.

Just as the boy reached the fence to the outside world, a quick pop-pop of gunfire silenced him, his body a heap on the ground.

Others who were outside did not bat an eyelid. It had happened many times before and would happen again. Mostly it occurred when someone wanted it to—they ran at the fence knowing what their fate would be.

Ezra sat back down and resumed his staring at the trees. "I told you not to tell him," he said again quietly.

I sat for some time, staring at the young boy's body, and strangely I felt jealous. He was gone now, free of this and what was to come had he stayed alive. There was a part of me, every day, that wanted to find the courage to end my life. I had even asked the other Pole, who had bought the chisel from David, if I could have it the day after I had seen that child's dead body, thinking it might be sharp enough to drag across my wrists. But he had sold it on, he had said—he had no use for a chisel.

Yet, there was a resolve inside me to try and survive this place. There was talk, always talk, about when the war would be over, and everyone assumed that the Americans would provide the force needed to finally end it. But it hadn't happened yet.

I thought of Adi to give me strength and knew that if she were here, sitting by my side now, she would tell me to be strong, to pray, to help others. I almost scoffed at myself when I thought of praying. I hadn't prayed since I was with Otto, and he was now gone, as were so many others. I wasn't sure that God could hear me in a place like this and told Ezra as much.

"It's the crows," he said again, his face pale and eyes rimmed red. "He can't hear you over the crows."

I didn't know the extent of Ezra's illness until a week later, when at work, he tried to steal some keys from Stanislaw and said that he was going to escape.

Both Stanislaw and I wrestled him to the ground, where he curled up into a ball and wept like a child.

Bruno came from his office and saw what had happened. He told us to place Ezra in the office away from prying eyes, and allowed me to sit with him and give him sips of Bruno's own whiskey to try and calm his nerves.

Once the madness had passed, I asked him, "What were you thinking?"

"I have to get out," he said, his hands shaking. "I just can't do it anymore, Jozef. I have to go home. I want to go home." He cried and cried, and I didn't know how to settle him.

Bruno came into the office and told me to take Ezra to the infirmary and tell them he was sick with a fever, but not to say anything about his mental state. I knew that if they thought he had gone mad, he would soon find himself in the shower block.

After leaving Ezra in the infirmary, I had to make my way back to the garage. I had wanted to stay with him so that at least I could explain away his ramblings. I felt bereft at losing my friend, but tried to tell myself that he would soon be back at work and would find his humor once more, even though I wasn't sure I believed it.

"Jozef." Bruno nodded toward his office when I returned.

Before I could tell him about Ezra, he said, "Adi is sick."

Then, I felt all of my insides plummet and a cold shiver overtook my body. "How sick?"

"I'm not sure," he said. "I saw her yesterday and she is wasting away, Jozef. All the food I give her she gives to others. I asked her if she had a letter for you, and she said that she had nothing to say anymore. I think she has given up."

I understood, of course I did. A part of me had given up that day I had moved a dead child onto a cart laden with bodies. It haunted me day in and day out, and the smell of the crematorium, the crows, the pop-pop of gunfire, all of it was taking a piece of my sanity and soul each day.

"I have to see her," I said. "I have to. She'll be okay if I can see her and tell her to be strong."

Bruno shook his head. "Impossible," he said.

"Please, Bruno. Think of something. Please. I have never asked anything of you. Never. You have helped me and for that I am grateful, but this is what I need from you now. Please."

Bruno looked at me for a few moments, then gently nodded his head. "I'll see what I can do."

TWENTY

JOZEF

It took two weeks for Bruno to organize a time and place for Adi and me to see each other, and the awfulness of it was that it was between two of the crematorium blocks.

"It's the only way," Bruno said. "You will be able to see her. I have bribed a few female guards, so they will be looking away when she leaves her barracks. You have to be quick, and if anyone asks, you are working."

"At the crematorium?" I asked, aghast.

"Not *really* working. There is a truck there; I noted to its driver that the exhaust looked as though it was going to come away and said I would send my best mechanic to check it out. I'll be nearby and keep people away. But you have to be quick, Jozef."

"When?"

"Today," he said, and grinned at me. "You get to see Adi today."

The excitement I felt at knowing I was to see Adi that day consumed me and I could not concentrate on the ledgers, the numbers jumping about on the page, refusing to sit still and be calculated.

At midday, Bruno asked me to go with him, and together we made our way to the newer, larger camp where I had disembarked from that train months ago.

It was a sprawling mass of barracks, seemingly full, and I am ashamed to admit it, but when I saw small children clinging to their mothers' hands as we walked by them, I had to look away. I could not bear to see what this place had done to someone so young, and knew if I saw their faces it would be instantly imprinted in my mind and I would forever see them.

The truck that sat between crematoria two and three had a red cross painted on the side. I was confused—had they allowed the Red Cross to come inside and help? Perhaps bring food, clothing?

"It's not what you think," Bruno whispered to me. "Don't look inside."

I made a show of looking at the exhaust whilst Bruno and the guard chatted. Bruno then asked if he wanted a smoke and the two of them walked away, leaving me with the truck and no one else about.

I did what I was told not to do—of course I did—and looked inside the truck. It was filled with small tins of Zyklon B. I picked one up to see a skull and crossbones on it, denoting its toxicity and a warning that it was poison.

I dropped the can and wiped my hand on my trouser leg, then stepped back from it. I looked at the two buildings that I stood in between, their chimneys reaching into the sky above. I wanted to leave then. I wanted to run. I could feel the ghosts of those who had died in there all around me, and I could sense their fear and hear their screams.

"Jozef."

I turned. It was Adi.

All the ghosts went silent, and I did not see where I was anymore. All I could see was Adi—my Adi.

I took the few steps toward her and folded her into my arms.

We kissed like teenagers, our teeth butting against each other's so that we had to stop and stood there laughing at each other, staring at each other.

She ran her hand over my face, her fingers resting in the hollows of my cheeks. "You're so different," she said, and began to cry.

I held her to me, kissing the top of her head, shushing her and telling her how much I loved her.

"I can't do this, Jozef." She finally pulled away from me and looked at me. Her face was as thin as mine, her cheekbones pushing against the skin as if they were trying to escape. Her eyes looked bigger in her face, the whites of her eyes veined red, and her lips were cracked and dry.

"I know. I feel that too, Adi. But we can survive this, we can."

"I can't, Jozef. Please, I can't."

She began to sob again when I heard Bruno's loud laugh—he was on his way back.

"Go now," I told her. "Go. I promise you I will get us out of here. I promise."

"You can't get us out, Jozef."

"I can." I turned now to see Bruno nearing us. "I can."

She reluctantly walked away from me, and I ached to run after her, to follow her and hold her more.

"Is it fixed?" Bruno asked. The other guard seemed disinterested in me and kicked his boot against the crematorium wall to dislodge some dirt.

"It is," I said.

"See, I told you it would only take a moment," Bruno told the guard, who shook his hand with thanks and walked toward his truck with an exhaust that worked exactly as it had done just a few minutes before.

"You saw her?" Bruno asked me, when we were back in the safety of his office.

"You were right—she is not well. She won't survive this. I have to get her out, Bruno."

Bruno laughed, a dry laugh that made me shiver.

"Have you lost your mind as well as Ezra? Get out? And how do you propose to do that?"

I stayed silent and looked at my feet.

"Jozef," Bruno said quietly. "I will help you, you know I will."

"I know," I said.

"But to escape—" He let the word hang in the air.

I nodded and turned to go back to my desk, to get lost in numbers and paperwork.

"Jozef, I will do all I can," Bruno said to my turned back.

I didn't doubt that he would, but I knew he could not help me get out of this place and save Adi too. I knew that no one could save me, not even my best friend.

Ezra came back to the barracks two nights later. He was quieter but no longer raging about the crows, and sat quietly outside with David and me, letting David take center stage and tell us about his latest sales.

"You two are a pair," David suddenly said. "I was going to ask you, Ezra, to cheer Jozef up, but you are as bad as him."

David stood, annoyed with our lackluster conversation, and wandered around to find a more jovial audience.

"What happened?" Ezra asked me.

"I saw Adi."

"You saw her?" Suddenly, Ezra's face was animated and some light was back in his eyes. "How? When?"

"At the crematorium a few days ago," I said. "It was by chance," I lied.

"But you saw her! By God, Jozef, you are lucky. If I could

just have one minute with my wife or children, I would give my right arm for it."

"It makes it worse," I said. "Seeing her has made it worse. It reminds you of what you can't have."

"Perhaps," Ezra said. "But at least you saw her."

"She has to get out, Ezra, she just has to."

"You're talking about escape? I thought you were against that idea?"

"I was until I saw her. But there has to be a way."

Ezra went quiet again. "I thought this idea would excite you," I said. "I'd hoped you would come up with some crazy idea to help me."

"You were right to question it when I mentioned it. Those who have escaped were stronger than you or I. Have you looked at us lately? We are like walking, talking ghosts. Have you noticed how long it takes you to do the paperwork now? I have. You can't concentrate, you can barely keep your head up, and I am the same. I have nothing, Jozef. No energy, no will, no bravery. It's all gone. They've taken it all."

I did not like Ezra talking this way—it wasn't really him—but I knew better than to try and continue my train of thought about an escape. I could not risk Ezra losing his mind again.

Instead, I changed the subject to David, to his business, and made Ezra laugh at the thought of David when we were all free one day.

"He'll be the best businessman the world has ever seen!" Ezra said, then lit a cigarette and began to concentrate on the trees and the crows once more.

It was mid-August. The heat was becoming unbearable inside the garage, and we drank back any water that Bruno gave us.

A new car had been brought into the garage—black and chrome, the tiny little flags with the insignia of the swastika bold against the red and white. Both Ezra and Stanislaw loved that car. They enjoyed looking at the engine and peering at the leather seats inside, both guessing how fast you could drive it.

It was an odd car as it came with no paperwork, thus we did not know to whom it belonged.

"If it's Hitler's, then I say we put a bomb in it," Stanislaw pondered one morning.

"Why would he send his car here?" Ezra said. "I bet it's the Commandant's."

"No. It's not his. I've seen his."

"What's wrong with it?" I joined in.

"Nothing!" Stanislaw said. "Absolutely nothing! That's what makes it all the more interesting."

I agreed that it was. The guards, the whole German regime, were fastidious about paperwork. Absolutely everything was recorded, kept, filed in meticulous detail, and I wondered why they would need all this paperwork and where they put it all. Was there a huge warehouse somewhere, the size of a small country, full of useless paperwork that no one would ever look at again?

As Stanislaw and Ezra debated the owner of the car and its reason for being parked at the garage, I sat at my desk, ignoring the ledgers, and instead continued to write about the camp as Bruno had told me to do.

As I wrote, my hand shook a little. I dropped the pen and flexed my fingers, but they wouldn't stop.

It was then that I felt a pain rip through my chest, traveling up toward my head, where it exploded in a ball of color.

I don't remember screaming out in pain, but I must have, as when I came to, I was lying on the floor, Ezra kneeling over me, his hand on my forehead.

"You're sick," he said. "You're burning up."

"There's a pain," I said. "My chest, my head."

"How long has he been sick?" Stanislaw asked Ezra.

"I don't know."

"It must have been a while for him to get like this so quickly."

Through my delirium I thought back over the past few days; the aches, the dizziness, and the chills that I had attributed to everyday life here I now realized to be the first symptoms of whatever it was that was ailing me.

"We need to get him to the infirmary," Ezra said.

"No." Bruno stood over me now. "Leave him here for now. Put him in the office, get him some water."

I felt hands underneath me, lifting me gently, and Bruno's voice soothing me, telling me that everything was going to be all right.

TWENTY-ONE

JOZEF

"Jozef, wake up."

I tried to open my eyes and felt a searing pain in my head. I closed them again and once more I heard Bruno's voice above me, telling me to wake up.

This time I managed to get my eyes all the way open, the light from the bulb above burning them so that I wanted to cry out.

"We have to go, now," he said. "You have to get up."

I thought I was dreaming and tried to bat away the light above my eyes, then the shadow of Bruno's face as it came closer to my own. "I am helping you to escape, Jozef. You, Adi, and me. We are leaving now."

Those words sobered up my addled brain, and I willed myself to focus on him.

"We have to leave now," he said again.

I tried to sit up on my own but found that my body would not comply. Bruno placed his hands under my armpits and helped me to sit, resting my back against the wall.

"I have all your writings here." He waved pieces of paper in front of my face. "I knew where you were hiding them—under the old tires. We'll take this—we'll show everyone what is happening here."

I wanted to laugh, but I couldn't. I was sure that when someone saw the state I was in, no explanation would be needed for what the camp was doing to people.

"You have to get changed now," he said gently and began to undress me, peeling off the striped uniform and helping my arms and legs into a uniform.

"What is this?" I asked, looking in horror at the SS uniform, black against the white of my skin.

"It's to get you out of here. Adi has one too. I left it for her, hidden. She will be waiting for us so we need to be quick."

My mouth was dry and my thoughts were still jumbled; I couldn't understand properly what Bruno was trying to tell me.

I let him finish dressing me, placing a cap on my head that was too big and fell down a little over my eyes so that I could not see.

"It's better that they can't see your face," he said, then hauled me up to a standing position and walked me to the black car that had sat on the driveway for days.

He placed me in the front seat and climbed in behind the wheel.

"My father's." He looked at me and grinned. "I told him it needed fixing."

I did laugh then. I laughed because it was funny and because I was scared. I laughed because it was as if we were children again and going on an adventure, and because of my fever, I thought it was the best thing I had ever heard.

Bruno told me to be quiet and not to speak. He drove quickly, reaching the gates where he was waved through without a second glance.

I dared not look out of the window in case someone saw me, my gaunt face giving the game away. He turned left, pulling up against a stretch of barbed wire that ran along the larger camp where the train would pull in and all those frightened souls would be taken away.

It was then that I saw Adi.

She pushed her way through a small hole cut into the fence, and ran toward the car, grabbing the door handle and launching herself inside. Before she had even closed the door, Bruno sped off, his eyes flicking to the rearview mirror.

"It went perfectly," Bruno said.

"Jozef," Adi said. I could feel her arms wrapped around me from where she sat in the backseat.

I could barely answer her. The fever, the adrenaline, the feeling that we might be free was too much and I cried quietly, happy to simply feel her arms on my skin.

I don't remember falling asleep, but when I woke, I was in the backseat of the car with my head on Adi's lap.

Adi and Bruno spoke in hushed tones about the escape and how well it had gone.

"It cost a lot," Bruno said. "To get those at the watchtower to be busy for a few moments. To get you that uniform."

"Won't they tell?" Adi asked.

"I doubt it," he said. "I paid a friend of mine to start a small fire and take their gaze away from the fence for a moment. He won't talk, trust me. I was just worried that you might not remember the instructions I gave you, or wouldn't be able to stay later at the infirmary. All day I was wondering if it was going to work."

"Won't they notice that Jozef wasn't at roll call?" she asked.

"That's the beauty of it. As soon as I saw that Jozef was sick, I knew this was perfect. He would be marked as going to the infirmary and that would be that!"

"Where are we?" I asked, sitting up and realizing that we were not in the same car as we had been before. A lightness in the sky told me that dawn was reaching us, and I looked about me at the racing green of the landscape, disorientated.

"Just coming out of Vienna." Bruno grinned at me in the rearview mirror. "We swapped cars a few hours ago. We tried to wake you, but we couldn't."

I was still wearing the uniform that Bruno had dressed me in and looked at Adi, who resembled a shrunken guard from the camp.

"Adi," I said, and let her place my head back in her lap, where she soothed me by stroking my stubbled head, telling me about what our new life would look like now we were free.

We reached Sicily in two days. Bruno drove as fast as he could, napping whilst Adi took the wheel. I had never seen Adi drive before, and didn't know she could.

"Neither did I!" she laughed, as she raced the car down winding roads. Bruno helped her, telling her when she was going too fast or too slow, but nothing dimmed her excitement and she sang as she drove, pointing out trees and flowers along the roadside as if she had never seen them before.

Bruno, true to his training, was organized and prepared for everything. He had thought about what car we would take, stealing his father's and having another hidden miles away where we could swap. He had suitcases packed with clothes for us, food, water, extra cans of fuel so that we did not need to stop. He had papers for Adi and me, and knew where to take us.

"The Americans and British are in Sicily," he said. "That's where we need to be."

"Can I get out of this?" I pulled at the uniform, which was uncomfortable against my skin.

"Not yet. Soon. If we are stopped, we will be safe in the uniforms. As soon as we can, we change."

My fever and delirium had left me in those two days. I slept a lot, spoke little, and ate what was offered to me. It was only when we stopped the car and changed into new clothes, feeling the Mediterranean heat prickle at my skin, that I fully came to life.

Then, parked on a clifftop that looked out to the sea, smelling the salty breeze and hearing songbirds call out from cypress and olive trees, I felt hope. I held Adi to me whilst Bruno sat on the bonnet of the car, and I told her how much I loved her and how we would never be parted again.

TWENTY-TWO

ALICE

"But you were, weren't you?" I asked. "Parted."

Jozef was staring at his lap. "We were. Bruno got us as close to the Allies as he could, then said he would go to France—he knew of a way to get some papers for himself and said that one day we would see each other again in America and become movie stars.

"We showed the Allies our papers. They listened to our story and gave us somewhere safe to stay. The Americans offered us passage to New York on a boat that was taking evacuees, and we took it. But the illness I had consumed Adi on the voyage, and her weak body could not take it. By the time we docked, she was almost dead, and a few days later, in a hospital that tried to help her live, she died in my arms."

"And that's when you came here?"

He nodded. "A rabbi let me stay with him in his apartment for a few months. I hated New York. I hated the noise and the constant reminder that this was where Adi had died. He said he knew of a place I could live—here, in his aunt's house. So this is where I came and this is where I will stay."

"What happened to Bruno?" I asked.

He shrugged. "He never made it to America, that I know. I like to imagine that he stayed in Italy and found a wife and lived by the sea, and he is happy."

I was itching to know more. There was something missing from his story, which had been so detailed and was now curtailed without much description of his last days with Adi, or what really happened to Bruno.

I could see that Jozef was not telling me something as he picked at the side of his fingernails, pulling at the skin, not meeting my gaze.

"You should go now, Alice." His mood had changed, as it always did when he had talked for some time. His memories overwhelmed him, I supposed, and perhaps he did not want to remember those last few days with his wife; perhaps it was too much for him to bear.

I stood and patted Amos' head, then went to Jozef and gave him a brief hug, feeling him stiffen under my touch.

"Thank you for telling me about everything," I said. "I'm sorry about Adi."

"I'm sorry too," he said, and offered me a watery smile.

"I'll see you tomorrow?" I tried. "I'll see if I can fix those bushes so that they don't look like blobs of marshmallow!"

He chuckled at my attempt. "I quite like the marshmallow look," he said. "But yes, I will see you tomorrow."

I rode home and thought of Bruno. I wondered if he was now living near the sea and I wasn't sure what I felt about it. He'd helped Jozef, but he had been in that camp. Could he not have saved more people? Was it okay for him to now be just living his life?

I would have to talk to Billy about it, or Pops. Not now, but eventually. They'd be able to tell me what the right way was to think about it.

When I reached home, Billy was back in his room, and I was sort of glad that I had some time to myself, to write more of what Jozef had told me. That evening Mom and Pops were going out to a dinner party, and I would be left to my own devices as Billy wouldn't even come down for dinner.

"Just leave him for now," Mom told me. "He needs a break from all this."

"I just don't think letting him go is a good idea," Pops said, as he straightened his crooked tie.

"Go where?" I asked.

Pops looked over at me, then mouthed "sorry" to Mom as she shook her head at him.

"He wants to go stay with Aunt Sarah in California for a while."

"I want to go," I said. I had only been to Aunt Sarah's once and loved it. "Please. Can we not all go?"

Mom shook her head. "He needs to get away, Al. I've spoken to Aunt Sarah, and she's going to see if he can do his final year at a school out there."

"He'll be gone for a year?" I felt my heart plummet.

"We'll see him at Christmas and we'll visit him as much as we can." She stroked the top of my head and kissed it. "Now be good, okay?"

She turned from me and took my father's arm. He blew me a kiss that I half-heartedly caught and plonked myself into an armchair.

I was sick of all this change. Of everything being bad and all the bad stuff that had happened to Jozef too. I used to think that everything was great—life was fun, full of camping trips and friends and cookouts. But now all my brain could think about was how cruel everything was and how cruel people could be.

A loud bang above me disturbed my thoughts, and I looked to the ceiling, half expecting to see something come through it.

"Billy!" I yelled.

There was no answer.

Something wasn't right. The hairs on my arms stood up

even though it was humid in the house, and I raced up the stairs to Billy's room, almost crying with a fear that I couldn't articulate.

"Billy!" I yelled again, and opened his door.

His suitcase was on the floor and he had pulled it out from his wardrobe, hence the crash. I watched as he threw clothes in, not looking up at me.

"Billy," I said again.

Now he looked at me, and I saw that my brother's face had been replaced with someone else's. His eyes were bright red, his eyebrows knitted together, his lips moving, muttering to himself but not loud enough for me to hear.

"Billy," I said, quieter now, walking slowly toward him as if trying to tame a scared animal. "It's me. It's Al."

"I have to go," he said, his voice a wail. "I have to go, Al. I have to!"

He suddenly crouched on the floor and pulled at his hair. "I have to tell them. I have to tell them, then I have to go!" he cried.

I could feel tears on my face, unaware of when I had started to cry too. I edged closer and closer to him, saying his name over and over again.

Finally, I reached him and crouched next to him, placing my hand on his arm. "Billy," I said. "Billy, look at me."

He stopped pulling at his hair and slumped onto the floor, stretching his legs out in front of him. I sat next to him and held his hand.

"I did it, Al," he said quietly.

"Did what?"

"I killed her. I killed Nancy."

It was as though all the air in the room had momentarily been sucked out, and all I could hear was my own scratchy throat trying to breathe.

"No, no," I said. "No."

"I did it, Al." He leaned closer to me. I could smell Pops' bourbon on his breath.

"You're just drunk." I tried to laugh. "Pops is going to be so mad!"

He shook his head. "I did it, Al. It was an accident, but I lied, and now I have to tell the truth, don't I?"

"I don't understand." I let go of his hand. "I'll go get Mom and Pops. I'll ride my bike over there and I'll go get them for you, okay?"

I jumped up and made my way to the door, but Billy was quicker.

"No!" He slammed the door shut. "No, Al. You have to listen to me, okay. I know what I have to do. You can't get them. Not yet. Please."

The way he stared at me and the way he stood in front of the door blocking my exit scared me, so I backed away from him and sat on the edge of his bed, trying to count my breaths—in-out, in-out, like we had been taught to do in gym when we had cross-country running.

"It was an accident, I swear it was, Al. But they won't believe me, will they? They think she was raped. I didn't rape her, Al. I didn't. They're all down there every day, Mr. Briggs, telling Howard to find out who did this to his daughter. They'll know, right, Al? They'll come for me."

He looked wildly about the room, grasping at words and thoughts that jumbled themselves out of his mouth. "We were in love, Al. Her father said she couldn't date. Wanted her to be perfect. You know how strict he was?"

I nodded. Pops had told us he was.

"It was worse than just being strict, though. He beat her, did you know that too?

I shook my head, even though I knew from when he had told Mikey.

"He beat her with his belt if she was late home, or if he

thought she was seeing boys. She showed me the marks on her legs and back."

I kept looking at the door, wishing he would move a little so I could run out and go get Pops.

He saw me looking and stepped back so his whole body was against it.

"I'm not going to hurt you, Al! Oh God! Is that what you think? Do you think I'm going to hurt you?"

"No, I just want to go get Pops," I cried at him, the tears spilling out now, hiccups coming over me too. "Please, Billy."

"No. Not yet. You have to listen, Al. You have to listen. We went to the lake, you see—that's where we'd meet. We'd see each other all the time there. She was my girlfriend. I was going to ask her to marry me, and we'd get out of this shitty town and run away together. That night, oh God, that night." He swallowed deeply, then drew in a large breath. "That night we made love, Al. I know you don't understand it yet, but we did and that was that. Afterwards, she was so happy and was messing about on the rocks, just being silly, but she fell, Al, she fell and hit her head. It wasn't bad, Al. Not at first. She was kinda stunned like a fish when Pops catches them, and she lay down next to me, and I looked at her head and it was just a little cut and a bump. Nothing major. We were like that a little while, Al. Not long. Just a little while, then I realized she wasn't breathing. She was just staring up at the sky, at the stars and the moon, and she wasn't breathing.

"I tried to put air back into her. I tried to get her heart going again, but it didn't work, Al, it didn't work!" He screamed the last few words out so loud and at such a pitch that the next-door neighbor's dog began to bark.

"I didn't know what to do! I know what I should have done, I know. I should have run and got help. But I wasn't thinking straight, you know? We'd been drinking and we'd had sex, and I knew her father would blame me. I didn't know what to do,

Al!" He broke down then and dropped to all fours and heaved with fear, crying with an anguish I had never seen before or since.

I went to him, sat on the floor and took his head so he would lay down and put it in my lap. I stroked his hair and told him it was going to be okay, even though I knew nothing would be okay again.

Soon his crying stopped, and he sat up and pushed his back against the door, wiping his face with the back of his hand.

"I put her in the water. I figured everyone would just think it was an accident, and I called the cops from the phone at the diner, then I came home. I shouldn't have done that, Al. I know that. I have to tell the truth."

I looked at his half-packed suitcase. "I was gonna write a letter, you know, saying what I'd done, then scarper."

"To Aunt Sarah's?" I asked.

He shook his head. "I almost told Mom today what had happened. But I couldn't get the words out. I just said I had to get away, and she said I should go to see Aunt Sarah for a bit."

"But they'll find you," I said quietly. "What happens if they find you?"

"Prison," he said, then suddenly started crying again. "Or I'll just kill myself, Al. I'll just end it. I can't go to prison, Al, but they will, won't they, they'll find me?"

It took another half hour before he calmed down again, and he waved for me to fetch the half bottle of bourbon that was on his bedside table.

I handed it to him and watched him slug it back like it was soda.

Soon, his words were slurred and his eyelids heavy. I sat patiently waiting, not really hearing my own thoughts, just staring at him and waiting for him to pass out.

As soon as he slumped forward, I laid him down on the floor, put a pillow under his head and a blanket on top of him, and stepped carefully over him to open the door enough for me to be able to get out of the room.

I ran down the stairs and outside to my bike. I knew where I was going and I knew who would know the right thing to do.

As soon as he opened the door, I fell into his arms and sobbed. He held me tightly and slowly edged me inside, closing the door behind me.

He sat me on the sofa and listened to my mad ramblings, then left me alone for a moment and came back with hot sweet tea.

"Drink this," he said.

I took the cup from him, my hands shaking, so I had to hold it with both hands. I drank back the tea, feeling the hit of sugar wake me a little from my stupor.

"Sugar helps when you have had a shock."

I looked to Jozef, who sat on the edge of the coffee table.

"I didn't know where else to go," I said.

"You did the right thing. Now. Tell me again what happened."

I nodded, drank back some more tea, and told him what Billy had said. "I don't want him to go to prison," I said at the end of my tale. "I can't—" The crying overcame me once more.

"Hush, hush." Jozef stroked my hair. "He won't. Go home now, and do not let him out of your sight, okay? You watch him all night if you have to. Don't let him write a letter, don't let him speak to your parents."

"But what then? What about when he wakes up in the morning?"

"By then, it will all be fine. Trust me, Alice. By the morning it will all be fine. You trust me, don't you, Alice?"

I nodded.

"Then whatever happens, you must let it happen."

"I don't understand," I said.

"Remember when I first met you? You asked me how old I was. Well, I am much older than Billy—he has his whole life ahead of him, all wonderful things that can happen for him, and for you too. I don't have that. All I have is my past and there are regrets there, Alice—big terrible regrets."

I shook my head. "I still don't understand."

Jozef gently smiled at me, then reached out and took my hand in his. "You'll understand one day, Alice. You will. But promise me, whatever happens, let it be. It was meant to happen and it is what I want."

"I promise," I said, not understanding what he was trying to tell me.

I gave him back the empty teacup, and he stood and looked about the room as if searching for something. Then his eyes settled on Amos.

"Take Amos with you tonight," he said. "He will keep you company whilst you keep watch over your brother."

"My parents will be mad if they see him," I said.

"Just keep him with you in your brother's room, and you can bring him back in the morning. If your parents see him, just say you felt sorry for him and do a bit of crying, and I am sure they will be understanding." He smiled at me.

I liked the thought of having some company, and took the lead that Jozef gave me and clipped it onto Amos' collar.

"You can do this," he said as he opened the front door. "Everything will be fine in the morning."

I don't know why I believed him, but I did. I didn't know what he was going to do to make it okay, and I didn't think to ask. I was tired and scared, and I was simply glad that someone had taken charge and told me what I needed to do.

I got on my bike and looped Amos' lead over the handlebar, who was jumping about to be taken on an adventure.

As I cycled off, I waved quickly at Jozef who waved back, a silhouette against the lamps from inside his house.

I did as Jozef told me, and got home and made myself comfortable on Billy's floor right next to the door. Billy had woken and stumbled into bed, his whole body splayed out, exhausted.

Amos snuggled in next to me, and I knew that if I fell asleep and Billy tried to leave, Amos would bark, or move, and it would wake me up.

I heard Mom and Pops come home—they clattered up the stairs, shushing each other and giggling about making noise. They were tipsy, and I was glad. When they were like this, they'd go straight to bed and not bother checking on us, as they never wanted us to see them drunk.

I fell asleep at 3 a.m. I remember because I looked at the clock as my eyelids started to droop, feeling the weight of my shoulders lessen and my jaw that had been almost locked together become slack.

It was the sirens that woke me.

At first, I didn't know if I was still dreaming. Then, recalling all that had happened the night before, I jumped up. *Sirens. Police. Billy.*

Billy was still splayed out on his bed, impervious to the wee-waa that echoed through the dawn sky.

I grabbed Amos by his collar and led him downstairs. Outside the sirens were lessening, and I stood by the front door, almost scared to open it.

Finally, the sirens had disappeared altogether, and I breathed a sigh of relief. Amos whined and scratched at the door, and I let him outside to go do his business in the front yard.

As he circled about trying to find the right spot, I felt the first drop of water on my arm and looked above to see angry storm clouds gathering. A gust of wind rustled along the sidewalk and made Amos bark.

"Come here," I shouted at him, but he ignored me and pointed his nose in the air, then sensing something, took off down the street.

"Amos!" I yelled, then quickly shut up, scared to wake my parents or Billy.

Annoyed, I grabbed my bike and took off after him, the streets still nighttime quiet, drapes still drawn.

Amos knew where he was going—home—and he did not stop once on his quest to get there. I pedaled furiously after him, feeling a few more drops of water fall from the sky. It was going to be a big storm, and I needed to get home before it broke.

"Amos!" I shouted again and again, but he wouldn't look back at me.

Finally, he slowed a little when he reached Mulberry, and I was glad of the respite. I pedaled slower, taking in great lungfuls of air, tasting the difference in it now that it was going to rain. I suddenly remembered how Billy and I would stick out our tongues when it rained in the summer, and I wondered if he had done the same thing with Nancy.

Shaking away the thought, I continued on, suddenly coming to a dead stop before Jozef's house where a police car sat out front, the lights flashing silently.

Amos had not run all the way up to the house either and sat on the sidewalk whining, looking at the house then back at me.

I got off my bike. There was a rush of blood making my ears ring so that all the sounds seemed so very far away.

I felt a hand on my shoulder—Mrs. Graham, my old teacher.

"Come away," she said, pulling me back a little. Amos came to me now and sat by my side.

I knew what was happening, but I couldn't in that

moment actually believe it. Even when Jozef was led out of his house, his hands cuffed behind his back, I still did not believe it.

"Come on now, Alice. This is not for a child to see," Mrs. Graham said.

I shrugged her hand off my shoulder and walked toward Jozef, who was now near the car.

"Take care of Amos for me," he said.

"What in the hell are you doing here?" Howard yelled at me, as his deputy closed the car door on Jozef. "Go on home now, before I tell your parents."

I couldn't move, though. I stood there and watched them drive away with Jozef in the backseat.

"Come with me," Mrs. Graham said.

But I shook my head and grabbed my bike, walking home with Amos by my side as the clouds suddenly broke and began to cry heavy tears, soaking me through.

When I got home, no one was up. In a daze I changed, then sat on my bed, Amos curled up on the bottom of it.

There was a light knock at my door and Billy entered. He tried to smile at me, but soon lost the desire.

"Hey, squirt," he said.

"Hey."

"Can I talk to you?"

I nodded.

"I'm gonna go to Aunt Sarah's. I think it's a good idea, you know. Get my head straight."

"They took him," I said.

"Who?"

"Jozef."

"Who's Jozef?"

"The German. They arrested him."

Billy's face slackened. "It could be for anything, Al."

I shook my head. "I told him. I told him what you said and

he said it was going to be okay. This is how he is making it okay."

Billy was confused, and so I told him about Jozef, about our friendship. "He's doing this to save you," I told him. "And me too."

"You don't know that, Al," Billy said, his voice lacking conviction. "Shit, what do I do?"

I knew what he should do. He should tell the truth. But I was a kid, a stupid kid, and so was he, and we both knew that he wasn't going to tell the cops the truth, and we both knew that if he did, it would mean prison, and Billy wouldn't be able to handle it.

"What do I do, Al?"

Over the next few days and weeks, Billy and I pondered the question of what he should do. Some days he said he would tell the truth, and others he said he couldn't. I eventually convinced him that he could not tell the truth—that Jozef had said it was what he wanted, even though neither of us could comprehend why.

After it became common knowledge that the strange German refugee had given himself up for the murder of Nancy Briggs, everyone murmured that they had always known it was him, that he was cruel and that something should have been done about him sooner.

Only I knew who Jozef really was, and I wrote letter after letter to him at the county jail, only ever receiving one back.

Dearest Alice,

I know you cannot understand why I have done this, but one day, maybe you will be able to.

Please do not write again. I will not reply.

I am writing you now to tell you to live your life and to tell your brother to do the same. Nothing that he or you can say can change what will happen. I will make sure of it.

Take care of Amos for me, Alice.

Your friend,

Jozef.

I read and reread that letter many times over the next few years, always searching for some hidden meaning in the words and finding none. I wrote him still, even though I knew he would not write back. I told him that my parents had let me keep Amos, that my brother had gone to California, eventually joining the army. I told him that I would free him one day, I just needed to figure out how without hurting Billy or my parents. I told him I was sorry. I told him that he always had a friend and I was always here.

When he was sentenced to the death penalty, I wrote more, hoping that my letters of nonsense and everyday life would cheer him whilst the guilt gnawed away at me bit by bit, a hatred building up inside me for my brother who had done this, until finally I had to escape too.

TWENTY-THREE

ALICE

1963

I had swapped my rural hometown for the glitter of New York when it had come to me choosing to go to college. My father had been against the idea—not just of me moving, but of me getting an education at all. But my mother was my saving grace. The woman knew how to convince my father of anything, and she was the one who suggested I go away to school in the first instance.

I never asked her at the time, but I do think that she wanted me to leave to live the life that she had never been able to, and on the day that I got my acceptance letter to study history she was frenzied with the news, and immediately pulled out a bottle of champagne and insisted we all toast to my future.

That was five years ago now, and I hadn't been home in all that time. Indeed, my life before New York seemed like it never really existed at all. But returning home was on the cards one snowy February morning when I received a letter, my name neatly written on the front and a stamp of the South Carolina penitentiary on the reverse.

Jozef.

I sat by the window that looked out onto the gray misty morning of the city, the tips of skyscrapers hidden beneath low clouds, the steam from grates in the street billowing up and making pedestrians look hazy and misshapen. How long had it been since Jozef had seen the sky? I wondered. How long had it been since he had given himself, his life up for my brother?

Ten years.

I thought of my brother, who had disappeared into the army —a means of penance, he had said, for what he had done—and married a woman I had never met, preferring to stay in California, away from home and what happened that summer.

I didn't blame him in the least. I had done the same.

Slowly, I tucked a fingernail underneath the seal of the envelope and peeled it away, then pulled out a thin sheet of paper. Taking one last look outside at the yellow taxis through the mist and the sleet that seemed ghostlike, I took a deep breath and read.

Dear Alice,

I sit here waiting, day in and day out, for death to come. It has taken them ten years, but they have finally made up their minds that it is my turn next. I welcomed the news. I was tired of waiting.

And that is why I write to you, Alice. All those years ago, you were the only friend I had, and I like to think that you are my friend still. I would like to see you before my time comes. I do not expect you to watch the process—indeed, I hope you do not. But I must impress upon you the need to see you beforehand. I have been given two hours to talk with a friend or family, and you know I have only one of those—you.

I understand that this is a lot to take in given my silence over the years. I received all of your letters to me and I treasured them, but I could not respond to you as what I needed to say wasn't yet fully formed in my mind. It has taken all these years for me to know how to say what I need to, and I realize that now is the time; indeed, it is the only time, and you are now old enough to know my whole story.

Yes, Alice, there is more to me. I told you about my life before meeting you, about the horrors I witnessed and the wife I lost. But Alice, there is more. And I need to tell you. I need you to understand, and perhaps when I have finished my tale, it will give you some peace.

The date and times I have written below. You are to contact the persons listed to secure your hours with me.

Until then, my friend, I wish you well and I look forward to seeing the wonderful woman that you have grown up to be —the one I always knew you would become.

Yours,

J.

I began to cry as soon as I finished reading. I had tried to forget about Jozef and had stopped writing to him the past two years, trying to push away what had happened and focus instead on my future. But now I knew I couldn't ignore it anymore—it was in front of me, begging me to revisit that awful night when Jozef was led away in handcuffs, and the following months when he was found guilty of murder and sentenced to death.

I thought of calling Billy to tell him that now was the time to come clean, that perhaps after all these years he wouldn't get into trouble, but I knew that it wouldn't matter—Jozef had made it clear that he would deny anything Billy or I said, and his silence all these years had shown me that he was not willing to speak about anything. But now he was. Now he wanted to talk and I wanted answers.

A week later, I was driving home in Pops' old station wagon, which he had given me when I first left for New York. I would get there the afternoon before I had made arrangements to see Jozef, and I had telephoned my parents to let them know that I was finally returning.

My mother cried on the telephone, awakening a deep guilt in me that although I had wanted to start afresh in New York, I had abandoned my past, including them. Pops shouted in the background that he would barbecue, which started an argument with my mother, who told him it was too cold to cook outside and that nobody liked his burned meats anyway.

"You like them, don't you, Al?" he shouted down the phone.

"He's trying to get the phone from me!" my mother squealed.

A few mumbles later, my father had won the struggle for the telephone and said again, "You like my cooking, don't you?"

"I do," I answered, laughing at him and feeling a little excited to see him.

"Well, that's all I need to know. I'll make you a feast—you'll see!"

My mother came back on the line. "You should have told him you hated it, Al. He's forever grilling steaks and burning them. For God's sake, someone has to tell him to stop!"

"It's fine, Mom. I don't mind, honestly, whatever makes him happy."

"It's all right for you to say. You don't have to chew your way through rubbery meat each week."

"At least he tries."

"So what's going on?" she suddenly asked, quieter now so Pops couldn't hear.

"Nothing, why?"

"Well, sweetheart, you haven't been home in years and now all of a sudden we're getting you for a night. Are you sure you can only stay one night? How about a week?"

"I can't," I said. "I have to get back for work."

"So why are you coming?"

"To see you!"

"I don't buy it. Something's going on. I'd bet a hundred dollars that something is going on."

"Mom, really, there's nothing going on. I just had a day or two free and I felt a bit homesick so I thought, why not?"

"It's an awful long drive for a day, Al."

"Mom. Please. Stop," I said.

"Fine, fine. But you'll tell me sooner or later, I know you will."

I enjoyed the drive home, seeing the landscape change from gray high-rises and thick traffic to open landscape, fields covered with freshly fallen snow, not yet turned to slush.

I listened to the radio, and sang along to Buddy Holly and crooned with Elvis, even though I wasn't a huge fan, but his voice always took me back in time and reminded me of when Pops would play his records and sing along the best he could, making Mom and me laugh.

I stopped a few times to fill up the tank and grab a quick bite and a cup of coffee to keep me going, arriving back in my hometown at three in the afternoon. I noted the lack of snowfall here; instead, I was met by low-slung clouds and a pitter-patter of icy cold rain.

Frank's diner lit up the sky with its red neon, blinking at me and asking me to stop. I pulled into the parking lot and stared at the shiny chrome diner, feeling as though I had traveled back in time.

I stepped out, my foot landing in a puddle, and shook the water off my boot before going inside.

Frank was not behind the counter, and I knew he wouldn't be. I wasn't here to see him.

"Hey," I said to the back of a white shirt, the wearer of which was brewing coffee.

He turned, surprise on his face, which then broke into a grin. He ran around the counter and took me into a bear hug.

"Hey, Mikey," I said into his neck.

"When did you get home?" he asked, pushing me away from him but keeping his hands on my shoulders so he could take a good look at me.

"Just now."

"And I'm the first person you come to see?"

"Of course!"

"I'll grab you a coffee—go sit, I'll be with you in a minute."

I sat in our booth and pulled at a napkin from the dispenser, twisting it and turning it, trying not to think about the reason I felt so nervous.

Mikey was soon back and slid into the seat opposite, handing me a coffee.

He looked the same, pretty much. He still had the flop of dirty blond hair, still the cheeky grin. But his face was harder than I remembered, something about the way he set his jaw or the way his eyes could not stay completely still, as if he were on edge.

"I can't believe you're here," he said, reaching across the table to take my hand. "It's been too long."

"I'm sorry I haven't been in touch much."

He waved the comment away. "You have a life now in the ole Big Apple—tell me about it!"

I told him about university, about my job at a library that paid little but allowed me to research to my heart's content.

"It's not that exciting," I told him.

"More exciting than this place, I bet."

"So Frank gave you the diner, after all?"

"He did. He's retired now, he says, but he still comes in every day to check I'm doing everything the way he used to!"

I nodded and smiled at him.

"You can ask, you know," he said.

"Ask what?"

"I know you, Al. I can tell you want to ask. Go ahead."

"How was it? Prison, I mean. Sorry, that came out wrong." I felt my face flame with shame.

"It was shit. But good in a way, you know. It got me away from my father and made me think twice about committing a crime like that again."

I chewed on my bottom lip. I remembered the day that Mikey was arrested, his senior year when he was about to finish high school and leave this place. And then he decided to steal a car, and another, and another. I remembered watching him being led away in handcuffs, it hitting me hard, making me think of the image of Jozef being led away too.

"I wanted to be better, you know, writing more to you," I said, feeling that my words were inadequate.

"You wrote plenty."

"I never visited you, though," I said.

"I wouldn't have wanted you to!" He laughed. "It's not a great place for having a nice ole catch-up. I much prefer that you waited. How long you back for?"

"Just a night," I said. "I have to go to Columbia tomorrow."

"Why you want to go there?" he asked. "I went once. Nothing much to see."

I grinned at him. "It's our state's capital," I said. "I'm pretty sure there was stuff there."

He shrugged. "Nothing that interested me anyhow. So what's there for you?"

"Research," I lied. "For work."

"You gonna come back afterwards?"

I shook my head.

"Ah, so a real short visit then?"

"I'll come back again. There's the wedding," I said.

"Oh yes, the wedding! God, if I hear one more thing about that damned wedding, I'm gonna puke!" He laughed.

"Clem annoying you then?" I asked.

"Clem? No! George! He's worse than her. He says that because I'm best man, I have to do a speech. Comes in here every morning for breakfast and asks me what I'm going to say. As if he doesn't trust me." He winked at me.

"I'll be back for the wedding," I promised.

"And will you have a date?"

I squirmed in my seat and would not look at him. "Doubt it."

"Well, that's good news for me. Perhaps you can be my date."

I looked at Mikey properly now. The boy I once knew was long gone, I knew that, but there was still something I was drawn to in Mikey. "Maybe," I said.

Before he could offer anything else to make me blush, the bell above the door jangled and a hungry bunch of construction workers walked in, all clamoring to be fed.

"Hell, we've been awake since 4 a.m. Definitely time for supper now!" one big-armed man yelled at the waitress, who was saying that the dinner specials weren't quite ready yet.

Mikey rolled his eyes. "Back to the grindstone," he said and stood, then quickly bent down and kissed my cheek. "Don't be a stranger, Al," he said quietly, and I felt an unfamiliar turn of my stomach.

As much as I wanted to talk more to Mikey, I knew that this was not the time and that my parents would be eagerly awaiting my arrival. I waved him a goodbye as he poured coffee for the rowdy workers, and set about on the mile or so journey back home.

Pops was in great spirits when I arrived, rushing out of the house in the rain in his slippers to grab my overnight bag and usher me inside like an elderly guest.

Mom was not much better and hugged me for too long, which made her cry, and fussed about me, feeding me, offering me food, a blanket, a cardigan.

"Mom, you saw me at Christmas, in New York, remember?" I admonished her as she threw another log on the fire, insisting that I was cold.

"That was months ago," she said.

"Two, to be exact."

"See," she said. "Months. Besides, it's different. I like coming to see you, but I like it when you are home, Al. It makes it better. Like we are all together again."

"Leave her be, woman." My father handed me a beer and clinked his own bottle against mine in cheers.

"We're not all together, though," I said. "Billy's not here."

"He'll come home when he's not so busy. He's doing well, you know? Getting a higher rank, it seems, each year and his wife, she's so lovely, Alice. You need to go and see them."

I was still annoyed with Billy at getting married and telling us all after the fact. My mother said it hadn't bothered her, but I knew that deep down she was hurt to have missed it. It was as though he was cutting us all out of his life completely lest he remember what he did. I wanted to tell him that it didn't matter if he came home, or if he saw more of us; it would always be there—the guilt—and that was something he had to learn to live with.

"I saw Mikey," I said.

"Such a good boy," Mom said, settling herself on the sofa next to Pops.

"Ha!" I laughed. "That's not what you said back in high school."

"That was ages ago. And look at him now—look at what he's done for himself. Working in that diner day and night, got himself a nice house too. All he needs now is a good woman." Mom stared hard at me.

"Leave her alone!" Pops admonished Mom again. "This is why she doesn't want to come home—you drive her mad!"

Mom ignored him and went to the kitchen to fuss over dinner, and Pops soon joined her, insisting that he was going to light the grill even though it was raining outside.

I sat, warm, next to the fire and enjoyed listening to them argue. They would laugh at each other, call each other names, and it was all in good fun. An image of Mikey and me doing the same suddenly jumped into my brain and I pushed it away, telling myself that once tomorrow was over, perhaps I'd let thoughts of Mikey come back.

TWENTY-FOUR
ALICE

They didn't let me go without a fight.

Each of them begged me to stay; the rain was too heavy to drive all the way to the city, there were muggers and murderers on all the streets, I wouldn't be safe.

I tried to tell them that New York was much worse, then shut up, realizing that wouldn't help me get away any faster.

Finally, they let me go with a bag full of food, a new blanket and pillows, insisting that New York was colder and I needed more warmth.

Where I was headed made my head spin, so I tried not to think about it and instead, listened to the radio again, this time not feeling like joining in with the singers.

I quickly checked into a cheap motel not far from the prison and left my car in the parking lot, deciding to walk the streets for a little while to clear my head before seeing Jozef.

The walk did little to settle my thoughts, and I kept telling myself to put one foot in front of the other, not to think about what was going to happen that evening, not to think about what I was going to witness.

When I had arranged the visit, I was asked, in an eerily

polite manner, whether I would be staying for the execution. The question had taken me aback and I wasn't sure how to answer.

"You're his only visitor," the woman had told me. "You're his family. We need to know whether you want to be there until the end."

Choking back tears, I had agreed, thinking it was the right thing to do. But now, walking the rain-streaked streets, I wished I had said no. Could I just turn around and say no now? Did Jozef know I was going to be there? Did he want me to be?

At three thirty, I found myself outside the prison complex, and went through a security protocol that kept my thoughts at bay.

It wasn't until I was led into a small room with a table and two chairs, a prison guard outside, that I fully appreciated where I was and who I was about to see. I told myself to breathe, to keep breathing, that this day was the worst day of his life and the least I could do was to try and be brave and not cry.

All of those thoughts disappeared as soon as Jozef was led into the room.

He was smaller somehow, but I wasn't sure whether it was the manacles on his feet and hands or the thick chain that kept them together that made him so.

His hair was white, pure white, and he had thick creases in his forehead and around his lips.

The guard took off his chain so he could walk easier and closed the door, reminding Jozef that he had two hours.

As soon as the door closed, I went to him and hugged him to me, but he stayed stiff in my arms. Confused, I stepped back and let him make his way to the chair across from me, where he sat down and fumbled in his pocket for a packet of cigarettes and a small box of matches.

He lit the cigarette and sat waiting for me to take my seat opposite him.

"You came," he finally said.

"You wrote me to come."

"I know. I just wasn't sure that you would."

His voice was different, gravelly, and his eyes were harder than I remembered them. If I didn't know him, I would look at him and think that he had committed an awful crime. I wondered if he had always looked like that or whether prison had turned him into a criminal.

"I'm staying," I said. "You know, later on." I skirted past the word "execution."

"You don't have to," he said.

"I do. You need someone there."

"I have something for you." He placed the cigarette in a small tinfoil ashtray that I hadn't noticed up until now and dug about in his pocket, producing a wad of folded-up paper.

He placed it on the table between us. "It's the story I told you when you were young."

"Your story." I placed my hand over the paper, remembering now how it had fallen from his pocket that day on his porch.

"Not mine." He sucked on the cigarette and blew out a stream of smoke.

"Whose?" I asked.

"Jozef's."

I shook my head, confused. "So it's your story then."

"No," he said again. This time his voice was quieter, softer, reminding me of the Jozef I once knew.

"I'm not Jozef," he said.

"I'm not sure I understand."

"It's all true, what I told you, about Jozef and the camp. It's all there in those pages. That night I was arrested, I took them with me and the powers that be decided that I could keep them. They're yours now."

"I'm not following."

"Alice," he said. "I'm Bruno."

I don't know how long I didn't speak for. I stared at him, waiting for him to laugh and say that this was some sort of strange joke. But he didn't laugh, he barely looked at me. He finished his cigarette and immediately lit another.

"I didn't want to tell it to you like this, you know. In my head I had rehearsed what I was going to say a thousand times, and I wanted it to come out better than this." He shook his head, then let out a little sigh.

"If you are Bruno, where is Jozef?" I asked.

"Dead," he said.

"And Adi?"

"She's actually alive. That bit, obviously, about the escape, it changed a little. I had to change it."

"So the story of Jozef and Adi on that clifftop in Sicily..." I said slowly, measuring my words. "It never happened."

He shook his head. "I wished it had. I told you of what I wished it had been. I wished it had been different and you have to believe that, Alice."

"I don't have to believe anything," I said, scraping my chair back.

"Please, wait, don't leave!" His voice oozed desperation now.

Despite the rage I was feeling inside, despite the confusion and fear, and the tiredness that consumed me, I did not move, I let him speak.

"Don't you understand, Alice, why I did what I did that night for you and your brother? It was my atonement for my sins. I deserved to be here, Alice, to be locked up, to be killed. I could not live with myself anymore, pretending to be my friend, pretending I hadn't been a part of that camp and what they did to people. I was culpable, Alice. I still am. Every day I feel guilty to be alive. I wonder every day about those people, about Jozef, and wonder if they were still alive what their lives would be like now. Would they have a nice home? Children?

"I feel guilty when I drink water. When I eat. When I used to sit outside and watch the trees blow in the wind. I felt guilty having you as a friend, of having a dog that liked me, who let me pat him and who trusted me with his life.

"I don't want you to feel sorry for me. I deserve the guilt and the feeling that my soul could not settle, could not be at peace. It was a punishment, but it still wasn't enough. I needed more. I needed to atone for my sins."

"And have you?" I asked.

"No. No, it still isn't enough. Even death won't be enough," he said weakly.

"What happened to Jozef and Adi?"

He looked at the clock that hung on the gray breeze-block wall, counting away each precious second.

"I tried to save them. I tried to do the right thing."

TWENTY-FIVE

BRUNO

The day I arrived at Auschwitz, I was accompanied by my father. He was some high-ranking official in the SS, and when he heard that I had been injured, he decided to get me a safer job—or so he put it to me.

It wasn't until I arrived that I realized it was a punishment for me. He knew, you see, about me running away during battle. He was ashamed of me, always had been, and thought of me as weak. This was my punishment then, to be somewhere and witness things that he knew would ruin me—a final punishment from father to son.

It was summer when I arrived, and he took me around the barracks, pointing out what went where, who did what, and proudly led me toward the edge of a forested area where smoke rose into the sky.

My father had a strange grin on his lips as we walked, and soon I saw why.

Down the embankment, a large hole had been dug into the dried-up earth. Around the hole, SS guards sat, their trousers rolled up, their shirts off, looking as though they were sunbathing in the midday heat. Some men stood around the hole too, holding rifles in their arms.

I told my eyes not to look into the hole and instead scanned the SS men, the countryside. Then finally, without me meaning to, they rested in the pit. In the hole were bodies; the dead and the dying mixed together, children with their arms wrapped around their mothers for a last embrace. I watched a soldier shoot an old woman in the face as she held her hand in the air. After the soldier shot her, he turned to his comrade and continued his conversation. The soldiers laughed at something, and another pop-pop-pop of shots rang out.

I looked again to the old woman who had just been shot. Perhaps I was imagining it all. Perhaps the baby's head that I now saw—just visible under the body of the old woman—wasn't really there.

I could feel the sweat dripping down the nape of my neck, my breathing becoming heavy. I felt a pounding in my skull and despite the heat, I was cold.

Prisoners wearing striped outfits poured fuel into the pit, which soon caught alight from the cinder underneath. The bodies were quickly consumed with flames, and I could hear muffled screams coming from below.

My father seemed unperturbed by the sight, and I looked to him, my mouth wide, but no words came out.

"You shouldn't have been such a coward," he said to me and smiled.

I had an urge to push him into the pit. I wanted to see him burn. I wanted him to scream out for me to help him and watch powerless as I did nothing.

"This is him?" A man stood by my father now, his jacket open, his shirt buttons revealing his vest underneath.

"This is him."

"We'll get him in line," the man said. He wiped sweat away

from his brow with a handkerchief, then shouted to a nearby guard to come over.

"Teach him what he needs to know," he said. "Get him to follow orders, and if he doesn't, then you know what to do. If he does, then show him to his new job at the garage."

"Yes, Herr Commandant." The guard saluted him.

My father grinned at me, then walked away with the Commandant, disappearing through the thick foliage.

"Some more on their way, you'll just have to wait."

Within minutes, some more bodies arrived piled high on a cart, and prisoners began to throw them in, one by one.

"Help them," the guard told me. "Help that one." He pointed to a man who had blood spattered over his naked body, but his chest was rising and falling.

"Help him," he said again.

It was as if I had fallen into the depths of hell itself. I looked about me, waiting to see if the devil from a picture book that I had read as a child would appear. I prayed to God to lift me up out of here, but I stood, looking at the bodies piled high in the pit, the sun beating down on me as if it were trying to get through my skin and burn me from the inside out.

"I don't want to do this," I said.

"You think you have a choice?" he asked. Then he laughed and looked at the bodies. "You have a choice, yes. What do you choose?"

He aimed his gun at me now. "Do you want to join them?" He nodded at the naked burning corpses.

I shook my head and walked toward the half-dead man, picking up his body to carry into the flames.

I had a choice, and I knew deep down I was a coward and had chosen badly.

. . .

The next few weeks, I drank heavily and was barely awake even during daylight hours. The wound in my shoulder from when I had been injured began to hurt once more, and I put my arm in a sling, mostly so I had an excuse not to do any work.

I didn't hear from my father again, and for that I was grateful. Any time I was awake, I sat thinking of ways to kill him—to make him suffer the way he was making me suffer.

He had told me once, at the start of everything, that being friends with Jozef would ruin me, and he had certainly made sure that I was ruined, inside and out.

When Jozef appeared that day in the garage, I recognized him immediately, but he thought that I didn't. I just couldn't speak, I couldn't tell him how relieved I was to see my friend once more, knowing the uniform I was in and what I had done. It took all my resolve not to drink much after that so I could talk to him once more, foolishly hoping that he would forgive me perhaps, or that we could pick up our friendship where it had ended.

It was stupid, I know, to think that way. To think that I could so easily be forgiven and bring a past friendship into the present that we now found ourselves in. But I wanted to believe that it was possible, that I wasn't without redemption, that if Jozef could see me, the real me, once more, somehow I could find peace.

I helped him as much as I could, and when I saw Adi, I knew I could help her too. I tried to keep him safe and I planned the escape for us—again foolishly hoping that we three friends from our childhood could drive away from the horror and everything would be all right again.

Of course, it wasn't to be.

The night that I had planned to leave, Jozef was ill. He was sicker than I had originally thought and his breaths came in quick, rattled gasps. He wanted to write to Adi, and I helped him to.

"Save her for me, Bruno," he told me. "Save her. Get her to safety. Please promise me you will do this for me."

"I promise," I told him, cradling his thin body like a child on the floor of that office, feeling him get heavier in my arms as his breathing stopped and his body relaxed.

I left quickly after that, leaving my friend on the floor all alone, knowing that I had a small window of opportunity to get Adi out safely.

As soon as she got into the car I sped away, not answering her questions about Jozef's whereabouts until we were clear of the camp. "Here." I handed her the letter that he wrote her.

She howled then, an animalistic noise that sent shivers through my whole body. She screamed and raged and punched me, the car, herself. It was as though she could not contain the grief and it was seeking a way out.

I let her rage. I let her scream for the both of us. We had been so close, so very close, and fate had taken a final swift blow.

She calmed the further away we got. We changed cars and kept driving, neither of us talking, neither of us really knowing what to say.

When we reached Italy, Adi got sick. I had assumed that her silence was grief, or perhaps it was, and the illness that so ailed her was a part of that grief—I do not know. But I could not get her to speak, or eat, and she would only accept small mouthfuls of water when I tipped her head back and let it seep into her mouth.

"Adi, please," I begged her. "Please, you need to eat."

But every time I placed bread, or meat, or cheese near her lips, she moved her head to the side violently.

She sweated and shivered, and I didn't know whether to add blankets to her or take them off.

I had to dress her in civilian clothes as we neared the Allies, staying in a small hotel that charged an exorbitant amount, and it was there that we waited three days until I saw American troops enter the village.

At once, I sprang into action and ran to the soldiers, telling them about Adi, how she was sick, how we needed to get away.

Was this when I told them I was Jozef? Yes. This was when the lie began. At first, it was so I could stay close to her and not give anything about myself away. But when one of the Americans said that for a price he could get us onto a ship to America, I realized it was my chance to get away too—to leave behind everything I had known and never return.

Adi was still in a delirium throughout the voyage, but a doctor on board gave her some medicine that seemed to calm her, and she allowed me to feed her and care for her, even though she would never really look at me properly.

As she grew in strength, I began to think, foolishly once more, that maybe Adi and I could forge some sort of life together, and I whiled away the hours imagining what kind of life we might be able to have.

Stupidly, I told her about my fantasies. I told her I loved her and asked whether one day she might love me too.

"Bruno," she said quietly. "You have saved me, you helped Jozef, but I cannot love you like that, I cannot learn to love you like that."

"It might take some time," I began.

"No," she said, and took my hands in hers.

We sat like that for a while, her holding my hands and neither of us speaking, and I felt a huge hole open inside me. I had lost my best friend. I would lose Adi.

"We can be friends," she said.

But I couldn't be friends with her. I wanted to—oh God, I wanted to—but looking at her, being near her, not only made me want to be with her, it reminded me of Jozef too. Then I would feel searing guilt at thinking this way about his wife.

"Maybe," I told her. "Maybe one day," and I truly hoped it would happen.

But as we neared New York, we decided that it would be best for us to part ways. For her too, looking at me reminded her of Jozef, of the camp, and she said she wanted to disappear, to try to forget, even though we both knew that this would be impossible.

Adi was taken from the ship by the doctor, placed in a waiting ambulance and driven away. The doctor told me where she would be taken, and I pretend to take notice of his instructions even though I knew I was not going to seek her out. I would leave her now, to find a new life, and whatever awaited me, I would go ahead alone.

The rabbi did help me, of course thinking that I was Jozef, and his kindness and generosity pierced me daily like small needles being slowly pushed into the skin until they were hidden underneath, always there to remind me of who I was.

He did not know about Adi, and I did not say anything. In fact, the less I said, the better it seemed for me as they assumed I was in shock, traumatized, and would leave me to my silences. When I said that I despaired of the city and the noise and the rabbi came up with a solution for me to leave it behind, I did not look back and took the train away from the faceless city to find some quiet, and perhaps some peace for my soul. And what I found, too late, perhaps, was a friend who helped me, who brought me back to life.

TWENTY-SIX

ALICE

"I am not asking for your forgiveness, Alice. I am not asking that of anyone. I do not deserve it. I thought that by being Jozef, I could do some good—I could help you and your brother and your friend Mikey. I thought that it was enough, at first, that I could change things for everyone and stop bad things happening, and maybe, just maybe, things would be different. Can you understand that? That by being Jozef, by living the life he would have lived, and by doing the things he would have done, I was letting him live on and making amends for what I had done."

"But it didn't work," I said.

He shook his head, then wiped his eyes with the back of his hand. "No, it didn't work," he said, his voice cracked with emotion. "I felt more guilt. Jozef wouldn't lie like I had. Jozef would tell the truth. But I was never brave like him, Alice. He used to think I was, but I was really the coward and he was stronger than me—he always knew the right thing to do. So that day, with your brother and how the town was braying for blood, I saw my chance at redemption."

The clock on the wall was annoying me, ticking away the minutes, reminding me of what was to come, and not allowing me the time I needed to process what I had heard.

"It's all there." He pointed at the papers again. "It's all true. Right up until that last night. He was trying to write still, trying to keep it all documented. You can see that I have told you the truth."

"Parts of it," I said.

He nodded.

"What I did..." He spread his palms wide. "I am getting what I deserve, Alice. I just hope what I did for you and your brother will allow me some atonement for my sins, and that perhaps God will let my soul rest."

"I don't know what to say," I told him.

He nodded sadly and took his last cigarette from the packet, lit it and then screwed the packet up into a ball.

"I wasn't always the man that Jozef saw at the camp. I was once a boy who loved kites and spending time with his best friend. Can you see who I used to be?"

"I can," I said, then thought of how he had saved Jozef from the bullies, how he had walked him to and from school, how he had risked his life in an impossible situation to try and help his friend in the camp. "You're not a coward," I told him. "You are just as brave as Jozef."

He gave me a watery smile and opened his palm for me to take his hand in mine. I did, feeling the warmth and the roughness of his skin on mine, and felt a huge wave of sadness roll from within my stomach all the way to my head, making the blood pound behind my eye sockets.

"There are people now, you know, writing about Hitler, about how one man could stir up a nation into hate. People now are trying to understand it, and I wish I could add something that would give it a bit more clarity. But for me, it was slow,

Alice. I didn't hate anyone, other than my father, of course, but I was young and stupid and at the military school I was surrounded by opinions, by voices that encouraged me to be like them. Could I have kept true to myself? Yes, I could have. But the better I did at the school, the more my father was kind to me, proud of me even... I can't explain what that did to me. It made me want to impress him, and I forgot about what I thought, what I believed in, and joined in with the rest, because it was easier for me, do you see? It was easier for me."

"You regret it," I said.

"I do. If I could go back in time, I would be braver, Alice. I would have let them condemn me, kill me, even."

"You did what you thought was right," I said, feeling my lip tremble as I spoke. "You saved Adi. You saved me and my brother, and now—" My voice broke.

"Hush. Don't cry. Look at me, Alice, please look at me."

I raised my eyes to meet his.

"This is what I want, Alice. Don't cry for me. This is my atonement. This is what I want."

"But—" I pulled my hand away from his and waved my arms in the air hysterically. "It's all so wrong. It's all so wrong! You can't die, you just can't."

He leaned back in his chair. "I can, Alice. And I will. Death is not always the worst thing that can happen. I have seen the worst, and now I welcome the end."

"Five minutes." The prison guard stuck his head through a crack in the door and warned us.

I searched my mind for the right words to say, but nothing would come forth. I thought of all those days I had spent with Bruno in the summer of '53, and how I had run to him when my brother had told me the truth of what happened with Nancy. I could not align that man with what he had told me—with the person who participated in all those deaths—and yet he had taken care of his friends and others, and tried to save them. He had saved Billy.

"Alice," he said, "please look at me."

I did as he asked, meeting his gaze once more.

"You do not have to stay to watch me die. I came into the world alone and I will leave it alone."

"Time!" The guard came into the room and Bruno stood, allowing him to shackle him once more.

"I'll be there," I said, standing too. "I'll be there tonight," I said hurriedly.

He stood in front of me for a moment, and I leaned into him and held him to me, not wanting to let go.

"Thank you, Alice," he said once I let him go.

"For what?" I asked, wiping tears from my eyes.

"For being my friend."

I stood there, chewing my bottom lip as he shuffled away, an overwhelming sadness washing over me, making me physically ache.

I wanted to race out of that prison and never look back, but the bureaucratic nonsense to get me out was as bad as it was when I came in. Sign here, initial there. Metal detector. More signatures.

When at last I got outside, I stood for a moment in the drizzle and took deep breaths, holding on to a railing for support.

I had to come back at eleven that evening, to a different building where the execution would take place, and I made my feet move forward toward the street, finding relief in the hustle and bustle of the city crowds.

I don't know how long I walked for, but I only stopped when I realized how wet my feet were and how cold I was.

Searching the streets for my bearings, I asked a passerby the direction of the motel I was staying at and hurried off, thankful to get into my warm, cramped room.

As I removed my jacket, I felt a lump in the pocket. I took out the wad of papers—Jozef's writings—and placed them next to the small TV.

I couldn't remember putting them in my pocket, but I must have. I stared at them for a moment, feeling Jozef's story in my hand, taking me back to that week in the summer of '53, when I wrote the note that had changed so many lives, wishing, like Bruno, I could go back in time and change everything.

Numbly I watched TV, not taking in anything that was happening, drank a soda that Mom had put in my bag, and nibbled on a tuna fish sandwich that she had made. The tuna tasted like iron, and the bread felt too stodgy against the roof of my mouth, so I spat it out into the trash can and sipped at the soda instead.

Soon, it was time to leave. I grabbed my coat and switched off the light, the bundle of papers a shadow next to the TV.

I didn't need to go through with this. I knew that. I knew that it would be awful and would haunt me for the rest of my life, but there was something that was urging me to go, to see this through until the end, as if by seeing the death, it would release something in me.

I realized, as I walked, that I didn't want him to die. I had assumed that as my thoughts rearranged themselves, they would come to the conclusion that this was what he deserved—that although not by his own hand, he had been a part of killing millions of people. By doing nothing, by simply being there, he was a part of it. But then there was the man I had known. The man who had saved Billy.

I soon found myself outside the entry to the prison where the execution would be held. A handful of people stood outside the barbed wire gate and small security hut, waving placards against the death penalty. I steeled myself as I walked past them, ignoring their cries, their questions of who I was.

As the security gate inched ever so slightly open, I could see a reporter amongst the protestors, and his eyes were on me, trying to decide whether I was Nancy's friend, her sister perhaps? Both her parents had died, Mom had said through heartbreak, although Mikey had once said her father drank himself to death and Mrs. Briggs had an accidental death due to a bottle of prescription pills. So who was I? I could see the reporter moving closer and wished the security guard would hurry and let me through.

Finally signed in, I scurried inside the building—more signatures, more initials—and then I was shown to a room, a pane of glass covered with a black curtain in front of me as if I were at a tiny cinema and at any moment the show would begin.

I sat at the rear, noting that there were a few people in front who could be relatives of Nancy's. I didn't want to engage them in any type of conversation.

A priest sat behind them, and a rabbi, both of them talking to each other, and I wondered who had been the one to see Bruno in his final hour. The Catholic or the Jew? For all they knew, Bruno was Jozef, and would he not want a rabbi to pray with him?

I let my mind focus on this religious dilemma rather than thinking about where I was and what was about to happen.

Just before the door closed, shutting out the strip lighting from the corridor outside, a woman slipped in and sat a few seats away from me, a scarf wrapped around her hair, and faced forward, not taking in anyone else in the room.

A man with a fat stomach stood in front of us and told us he was the warden, and that today we would see justice done. And as the hands on the clock ticked to just after midnight, the curtains opened to reveal Bruno, sitting on a chair, wires protruding from his body, his eyes closed.

His charge of murder was read aloud to him. The date and time of his execution were given, as if it would make any difference to a man who was strapped to a wooden chair with thousands of volts of electricity just moments away.

Finally, he was asked if he had any last words.

He opened his eyes and sought out my face. "I'm sorry," he said. Then he closed his eyes once more.

Everything from that summer, all the memories of bathing Amos in the garden, of drinking lemonade, of sharing our thoughts and worries, assaulted me and I began to cry. In my memories, that was a summer I spent with Jozef and Bruno. He told me about his life, through Jozef's story.

Suddenly, the lights dimmed, and a hum came from the scene below. Within seconds, Bruno's body began to buck in the seat, his head thrown back, his hands that gripped the armrests of the chair white as they strained against the flow of electricity that pumped through his body.

I couldn't look. I hid my face in my hands and could hear the humming intensify. I closed my eyes and put my hands over my ears, rocking back and forth, whispering, "Please stop," under my breath.

I felt a tap on my shoulder and opened my eyes. It was the rabbi. "It's over," he said.

I looked to the window, which was shrouded once more with the curtain. "It's over," he said again. He held out his hand for me to take and led me out into the corridor, where he told me to sit on an orange plastic chair whilst he went to get me some water.

I couldn't sit, though. I had to get out. I could feel my heart pumping in my chest and thought at any moment it would explode. I had to get out.

Through glazed eyes I signed my name and muddled my

way toward the exit, free of the neon strip lighting and the squeaky corridor floors.

I half ran toward the security gate, only stopping a few yards from it, where I turned and vomited into a neatly trimmed shrub styled in a perfect box shape.

TWENTY-SEVEN

ALICE

The rain fell pitifully when I stood away from the pool of vomit on the soil. They were slow fat drops that splodged onto my coat and would soon wash away my insides, which I had left next to the neatly trimmed shrub.

The harsh spotlights from the prison illuminated the water as it fell, and I felt as if I was not in my own body but seeing this scene from above, or like a movie scene. Either way, reality had somehow suspended itself, and I felt lost, alone, and confused.

I walked the path that led to the tiny security checkpoint, where the guard made me sign out, then pressed a button that slowly opened the barbed wire gate to release me into the free world. I wanted to talk to the security man and tell him what had just happened, that I was stupid to have come alone, and I wanted to ask him if he had known Bruno and what he felt knowing that a man had just been executed a few yards away from him where he sat, dry, drinking coffee, and opening and closing that gate.

I didn't say anything, though. I just wrapped my coat tighter around my body, grimacing as the rain hit my neck and dripped down my spine.

Finally, the gate was open, and I stepped out onto the sidewalk, looking left and right, noticing that the protestors had gone home, the reporter too, as if the show had truly, finally ended. I crossed to the other side, where a line of parked cars sat awaiting their owners, and I wondered whether the other spectators were still inside, celebrating perhaps, that another criminal was now gone and justice had been served.

In front of me, a woman stood under a streetlight. She had her arms wrapped around her waist and stared at me as I approached. I thought at first that she was waiting for a bus, and was about to tell her that the stop was still a few feet away from her. It was then that I realized I had seen her face before. She had been the woman sitting at the back, two seats away from me, alone and staring at Bruno as he died without a hint of hatred or sorrow—a face like a blank canvas.

She still held my stare as I got closer, then suddenly reached out and grabbed my arm.

"You were there," she said.

I nodded; my mouth was dry and I couldn't seem to say anything.

"I saw you. You were there. He looked at you the whole time. You knew him, didn't you?"

Her voice was unmistakable. A mixture of accents, French and German. The face too—the large green eyes.

"Adi?" I asked.

"I haven't heard anyone call me that for some time."

"But you are, you're Adi. Jozef's Adi."

She looked away from me, out onto the silent road where rain steadily fell, a blur in the spotlights that still shone brightly from the prison.

"Why did you come?" I asked her.

"I had to." She looked back at me now, her eyes watery.

"Why?"

"Technically, he was my husband, you know. Bruno was

Jozef. You know that though, don't you? I know you do. I could see it in the way you looked at him. He told you the truth," she said quickly. "Who are you?"

"Let's go somewhere," I suggested. "Let's go somewhere and talk. There's a coffee shop just around the corner." I pointed down the street, and she followed my gesture.

"Around the corner," she repeated.

"Yes. Two minutes. We can get out of the rain and talk."

She shook her head. "No. No, there's nothing to talk about." Yet, despite her protestations, she began to walk, and I hurried alongside her.

"Around the corner," she said. "That's what you said. Where is it?"

I gently touched her elbow to guide her, but she flinched away from me as if scalded.

"Here," I said, pointing at the flashing blue sign that advertised itself as an all-night diner, one which I had stupidly noted to myself as a place to come and eat—as if I would have been hungry after what I had just seen.

She walked inside in front of me and scanned the empty diner, choosing a booth that allowed her to sit and be able to see the street through the steamed-up windows.

I sat opposite her and unbuttoned my coat, shaking it free from my arms and stuffing it in the corner.

A waitress with a name badge proclaiming herself to be Cindy came to the table. She had the tired eyes of someone who had been there all night already, and as she asked for our orders I could see a smear of red lipstick on her teeth.

We both accepted coffee, and I told Cindy that we would let her know if we wanted to eat. She didn't care and went back behind the counter, where she sat and picked up a magazine that had been sitting next to a steaming cup of coffee and an overflowing ashtray.

"Who are you?" Adi asked me again.

"I am a friend—I mean, I was a friend of Bruno's."

"So you know who he is?"

I nodded. "But when I was his friend, I didn't know."

"But you still came, even though you do know. Did he kill that girl?"

I shook my head. "He said he did for me, for my brother. It was an accident, the whole thing—my brother, he was Nancy's boyfriend and she hit her head."

"So why didn't your brother just say that?" Adi asked.

"I don't really know. He was scared, I think. Scared because of her father—he was a mean man and would have thought it was Billy's fault perhaps. And then, when he didn't tell the truth, it got worse. People talked, wanted answers, wanted someone to blame. By then, he couldn't tell the truth—or he could, but he would most likely have ended up in prison."

"So Bruno," Adi started, "he helped you."

Without realizing it, I was crying. Adi handed me a napkin, and I wiped my face. "He was my friend—Bruno, Jozef. He was my friend and talked to me like I was an adult, and we played with his dog, Amos, and it was nice and made me feel safe," I rambled. "I'm sorry. I'm not making much sense."

Adi smiled then. "It makes sense to me. He was my friend too, you know. My first friend when I moved to Germany. He loved me."

"I know," I hiccupped.

"I helped him, you know. I could have given his secret away when we got to America, but I didn't. I didn't say a thing. I never spoke to him again after I arrived. It was too hard." She had a napkin in her hands now and twisted it between her fingers. "He reminded me of Jozef. Of our childhood. Happy memories, but at the time, happy memories were painful for me. And, of course, I knew he wanted to be with me, to love me as he always had done. But I couldn't do that to him—lie, pretend —and I couldn't do it to Jozef. Instead, I built a new life."

"You got married?" I asked.

Adi shook her head. "I couldn't. I tried for a while to go for dinners with men, to talk to them, but all I could see when they spoke was Jozef's face, smiling at me the way he used to, and I realized that my future was supposed to be with him, and if it couldn't be with him, then I would forge on alone."

I smiled at her. "That's a brave thing to do."

"Is it? I thought you might think it rather sad. It hasn't been sad, you know. Not one bit. I have friends—oh so many friends —and each of them has become a part of my family, even their children. And I went to university, became a professor in Jewish resettlement. So I have that too."

"You could still find someone—if you wanted to, that is?"

She shrugged. "I could. Maybe I will. Who knows what is around the corner?"

"How long have you known about him being in prison?" I asked.

"Not long." She took a sip of the coffee, then grimaced with distaste. "A few months only. I saw it in a newspaper when I was visiting a friend here. I didn't believe it at first and thought it must be someone else. But it is him—was him. I made sure that I was able to come and see him—I had to see him, you see, I had to see the end of it."

I nodded. I understood. "I didn't want to come tonight," I said. "But I had to. Just like you, I had to see the end of it. I owed him this much at least, for what he did for my brother."

She reached a hand out and took mine in hers. "You did what you thought was right. Tell me about him, about when you knew him, right from the very start."

I told her everything, from the day of Nancy being found, to the rock that Mikey threw, and all the things Bruno had told me about Jozef's life.

When I finished, I could see that she was crying, and I made to stand so that I could go to her and hug her to me.

"No, no, sit," she said, and waved me away. "I'm crying tears of joy. That story you told, of me and Jozef and our life, it's all true. Every word."

"I have the papers at my motel," I said. "You could come there with me, and I will give them to you."

She shook her head. "I'm staying with my friend; they'll be wondering where I am."

She rustled about in her purse and found a pen and a scrap of paper; on it she wrote her address—California.

"Send me them, when you have time," she said. "I'd like to read them for myself."

I promised her that I would do it.

"Are you still writing?" she asked me. "You said you were writing when you were younger, everything that happened. Do you still write?"

"Not for a long time," I said.

"You should. You should write it down. It's important that you do it. Bruno was right about that at least."

"Can I ask you something?"

"Of course."

"Do you hate him, Bruno? I mean, did you hate him for all these years?"

"No," she said quietly. "I still remember the boy that he was. I still remember that he was my first friend when we moved to Munich, and he was generous and funny and kind. When I saw him in the camp, when he came to me and tried to help, I had to remind myself of the boy I once knew and not the man that stood before me in that ghastly uniform. Even when he helped me escape, I had to remind myself of this. Bruno wasn't a bad man—he had made a choice and it was the wrong one."

"I feel as though my head is in a vise," I told her. "Like I am trying to understand who he truly was, what he was really like, and the choices he made, and I keep asking myself whether I would have done the same thing."

Adi shrugged. "You can ask yourself that question if you want to, but it won't help you. You will never be able to answer it because you were not there, you did not see what was done."

"I feel like I know Jozef, though," I said. "I still feel like I spent that summer with him. Hearing about you and your life. He really loved you."

Adi smiled and it reached her eyes, lighting up her whole face. "He did. And I loved him too."

We sat a moment or two without saying anything, then Adi reached into her purse again and looked in her wallet. She drew out a folded piece of paper and opened it on the tabletop.

"This was his last letter to me. He wrote it as he lay dying. He told me of his love for me and to trust Bruno. He even told me to forgive him. Jozef always had a kind heart, and I know that deep down, he still loved Bruno like a brother."

I looked at the note, the ink faded a little, all of it written in German. I shivered, thinking about when this had been written as Jozef lay dying in Bruno's arms.

"It is cold, isn't it?" Adi noted my reaction.

I looked to her, and smiled broadly. "I'm just tired," I said.

She nodded, carefully folded up the note, and placed it back in her wallet, keeping Jozef's last words with her always.

I grabbed my coat and paid Cindy, who looked at the few dollars and then back at her magazine.

Outside, Adi and I embraced. "You'll send me his writings?" she said.

"I will," I said.

"Be a good girl." She kissed my cheek. "And forgive him—he made a mistake, that is all. You knew who he really was and so did I."

I watched as she walked a little way down the street, then stuck out her arm to hail a cab. She waved again before she

climbed in, and I watched as it pulled awa
the dark night.

I stood on the sidewalk for some time
of cold rain soak me through. I thought
and Bruno. I thought of that summer. I t
and how I had run away to New York, ...
somewhere else, my past would not find me. But it had. Just as it
found Bruno in the end.

I wanted to go home—but where was home?

Then, I knew. I turned and walked back into the diner, and
asked Cindy where the payphone was.

Barely acknowledging me, she nodded her head toward the
bathroom, and I followed the direction to see the phone
attached to the wall.

I dialed the number, knowing it off by heart from when
Mom had given it to me. He was the only person I could speak
to, and I desperately wanted to hear his voice—I needed to
know that everything was going to be okay and that I wasn't
alone.

He picked up on the third ring, his voice thick with sleep.

"Mikey, it's me," I said, quietly crying into the phone. "I'm
coming home."

A LETTER FROM CARLY

Thank you so much for reading *The Note*. If you'd like to keep up to date with all my latest releases, you can sign up at the following link. Your email address will never be shared, and you can unsubscribe at any time.

www.bookouture.com/carly-schabowski

This story came to me one evening when I was reading a book with the central theme of friendship. It got me thinking about friendships—how they are made, how they are broken, and what would happen if someone you loved, someone you considered a friend, was suddenly on the opposite side to you—ultimately your enemy.

The research I completed showed a handful of testimonies about concentration camp guards who had helped Jews from the inside—risking their own lives for others—even if they were wearing the wrong uniform, even though they were the enemy. I wondered then if I could present a story about friendship through the harshest of times, showing that somewhere deep inside there was still humanity, still love. Of course, this is but fiction as so many suffered at the hands of the Nazis and in no way do I want to diminish their testimonies, nor do I wish to posit that Nazi camp guards were misunderstood—as the vast majority were not and they duly deserved to be punished for their crimes.

One story amongst the handful, however, stood out to me:

that of Karl Plagge, who was a Nazi commanding officer of HKP unit 562 (vehicle workshop). It was here that he managed to save the lives of many Jews and their families, and in 2004 Yad Vashem recognized Karl Plagge as a Righteous Among the Nations. Through trying to reimagine what it would have been like for him, my character Bruno came to life, and I began to think about what he might do if one day his friend from childhood walked into his garage as an inmate, and what might happen after the war—who would Bruno be?

I hope that I have shown through Alice, Bruno, and Jozef, and through Alice's friends, that friendship can be a strong bond—one not diminished by time or circumstance, and that we should cultivate and value our friendships as we don't know when we will need them the most.

 twitter.com/@carlyschab11

BIBLIOGRAPHY

Auschwitz Museum online. http://auschwitz.org/en/museum/news/words-in-the-service-of-hatred,1022.html

"Concentration Camp Survivors Share Their Stories." IWM. https://www.iwm.org.uk/history/concentration-camp-survivors-share-their-stories

Edelheit, Abraham J., and Hershel Edelheit. "Legislation, Anti-Jewish." *History of the Holocaust: A Handbook and Dictionary,* 299–331. Boulder, CO: Westview Press, 1994.

Friedländer, Saul. *Memory, History, and the Extermination of the Jews of Europe.* Indiana: Indiana University Press, 1993.

_____. "History, Memory, and the Historian: Dilemmas and Responsibilities." *New German Critique,* 80 (2000), 3–15.

_____. *Nazi Germany and the Jews.* New York: HarperCollins, 1997.

"Karl Plagge, Germany." Yad Vashem: The World Holocaust Remembrance Center. https://www.yadvashem.org/righteous/stories/plagge.html

Khaleeli, Homa. "I Escaped from Auschwitz," *Guardian*, 11 April 2011. https://www.theguardian.com/world/2011/apr/11/i-escaped-from-auschwitz

Levi, Primo. *If This is a Man/The Truce*. London: Abacus, 1987.

Neumann, Birgit. "Fictions of Memory." *Literatur in Wissenschaft und Unterricht*, 37 (2004), 333–360.

Nyiszli, Miklós. *I Was Doctor Mengele's Assistant*. Oswiecim, Poland, 2001.

Parkinson, David. "Night Will Fall: The Story of File Number F3080." BFI (2018). https://www.bfi.org.uk/news-opinion/news-bfi/features/night-will-fall-story-file-number-f3080

Roth, Philip. Interview with Primo Levi: "A Man Saved by his Skills." *New York Times*, 12 October 1986. https://www.nytimes.com/1986/10/12/books/a-man-saved-by-his-skills.html

Sands, Phillipe. "Primo Levi's If This is a Man at 70." *Guardian*, 22 April 2017. https://www.theguardian.com/books/2017/apr/22/primo-levi-auschwitz-if-this-is-a-man-memoir-70-years

_____. *East West Street: On the Origins of Genocide and Crimes Against Humanity*. London: Weidenfeld & Nicolson, 2017.

Schleunes, Karl A. *The Twisted Road to Auschwitz: Nazi Policy Toward German Jews, 1933–1939*. Urbana and Chicago: University of Illinois Press, 1970.

Trouillard, Stéphanie. "The Vél d'Hiv Roundup: 75 Years on, a Survivor Remembers." *France 24*, 15 July 2017. https://www.france24.com/en/20170712-vel-dhiv-roundup-holocaust-france-survivor-remembers-world-war

Walker, Janet. "The Traumatic Paradox: Documentary Films, Historical Fictions, and Cataclysmic Past Events." *Signs*, 22:4. (Summer, 1997) 803–825 http://www.jstor.org/stable/3175221

Zapruder, Alexander, ed. *Salvaged Pages: Young Writers' Diaries of the Holocaust*. New Haven: Yale University Press, 2002.

ACKNOWLEDGMENTS

I would like to thank first and foremost my agent Jo Bell, who believes in my ideas even when they are tiny nuggets and need fleshing out much more before they become an actual story!

Also, a huge thank you to Christina Demosthenous and Celine Kelly for their great editorial advice and keen eye! And of course, to my editor Kathryn, who loved the idea when I pitched it to her and trusted that I would bring this story alive.

Finally, a huge thank you to my family and friends, who are so wonderful that I can honestly say I could not have done this without your support.

Made in United States
Orlando, FL
24 June 2022

19110464R00174

Redis

for dummies®
A Wiley Brand

Redis

Limited Edition

by Steve Suehring

A Wiley Brand

Redis For Dummies®, Limited Edition

Published by
John Wiley & Sons, Inc.
111 River St.
Hoboken, NJ 07030-5774
www.wiley.com

For general information on our other products and services, or how to create a custom *For Dummies* book for your business or organization, please contact our Business Development Department in the U.S. at 877-409-4177, contact info@dummies.biz, or visit www.wiley.com/go/custompub. For information about licensing the *For Dummies* brand for products or services, contact Branded Rights&Licenses@Wiley.com.

ISBN 978-1-119-52080-1 (pbk); ISBN 978-1-119-52083-2 (ebk)

Manufactured in the United States of America

C10007218_122818

Publisher's Acknowledgments

Some of the people who helped bring this book to market include the following:

Development Editor: Elizabeth Kuball

Copy Editor: Elizabeth Kuball

Executive Editor: Steve Hayes

Editorial Manager: Rev Mengle

Business Development Representative: Karen Hattan

Production Editor: Siddique Shaik

Table of Contents

Redis For Dummies, Limited Edition

Introduction

NoSQL is a modern data storage paradigm that provides data persistence for environments where high performance is a primary requirement. Within NoSQL, data is stored in such a way that both writing and reading are fast, even under heavy load.

Redis is a market-leading multi-model database that brings NoSQL to organizations both big and small. Redis is open source, and Redis Enterprise adds several enhancements that are important to the enterprise deployments.

About This Book

This book provides a starting point for those new to Redis and those who have heard about Redis but want to see how it can be used in their organizations.

The book serves multiple audiences, with subject matter for managers and developers alike. You certainly can read the book from cover to cover, but I don't assume that you will. Instead, you can comfortably read chapters out of order based on your interest in a particular chapter.

Foolish Assumptions

In writing this book, I assumed that you're familiar with databases, at least at a basic level. If you're a developer, you should have a development environment available on which you can install things. In later chapters, I show examples using Redis that also utilize Docker and Github, so having a development environment available will be helpful.

It's worth noting that Chapters 6 and 7 are written in such a way that you can follow along with what's going on even if you don't run the examples yourself.

Icons Used in This Book

Throughout this book, I use the following icons to call your attention to details that are important:

REMEMBER

The Remember icon focuses your attention on an important detail that you may have otherwise missed.

TECHNICAL STUFF

The Technical Stuff icon marks some extended information that may not be of interest to all readers. Only the technical need read the stuff located near these icons.

TIP

A helpful little bit of information is all you'll find marked by the Tip icon — possibly something that will make your life a little easier.

WARNING

Stay away from whatever the Warning icon is warning you against. When you see the Warning icon, you'll know that there might be some danger around.

Where to Go from Here

Redis and Redis Enterprise are quite complex, and this book only covers the tip of the iceberg. For more information, head to www.redislabs.com.

Chapter **1**
What Is Redis?

This chapter gives an overview of NoSQL, including a look at types of NoSQL databases such as key/value, document, column, and graph. The chapter continues with a comparison of NoSQL to methods for traditional data persistence.

The chapter also introduces Redis, a popular multi-model database server. Redis goes beyond NoSQL database to provide several advanced capabilities needed by modern applications.

Introducing NoSQL

The term *NoSQL* is used to describe a set of technologies for data storage. In this section, I explain what NoSQL is, outline the major types of NoSQL databases, and compare NoSQL to relational databases.

Defining NoSQL

NoSQL describes technologies for data storage, but what exactly does that mean? Is NoSQL an abbreviation for something? I answer these and other pressing questions in this section.

Depending on whom you ask, *NoSQL* may stand for "not only SQL" or it may not stand for anything at all. Regardless of any disagreement over what *NoSQL* stands for, everyone agrees that NoSQL is a robust set of technologies that enable data persistence with the high performance necessary for today's Internet-scale applications.

SQL is an abbreviation for Standard Query Language, a standard language for manipulating data within a relational database.

Identifying types of NoSQL databases

There are four major types of NoSQL databases — key/value, column, document, and graph — and each has a particular use case for which it's most suited.

The following sections go into greater detail on the four types of NoSQL.

Key/value

With a key/value storage format, data uses *keys*, which are identifiers that are similar to a primary key in a relational database. The data element itself is then the value that corresponds to the key.

An example of a key/value pair looks like this:

```
"id": 12319054
```

In this example, "id" is the key while 12319054 is the value that corresponds to that key.

Column

With a column-oriented data store, data is arranged by column rather than by row. The effect of this architectural design is that it makes aggregate queries over large amounts of data much faster to process.

Document

Document data storage in NoSQL uses a key as the basis for item retrieval. The key then corresponds to a more complex data structure, called a *document*, which contains the data elements for a given collection of data.

Graph

Graph databases use graph theory to store data relations in a series of vertices with edges, making queries that work with data in such a manner much faster.

Comparing NoSQL and relational databases

Regardless of the type of NoSQL database, the patterns and tools that you use to work with data is different from the patterns and tools that you typically find with a relational database. As you just saw, the paradigm for storage and arrangement of the data typically requires a rethink of how applications are created.

Relational databases connect data elements through relations between tables. These relations become quite complex for many applications, and the resulting queries against the data become equally complex. The inherent complexity leads to performance issues for queries.

Many traditional databases include query tools and software to directly manipulate data. With NoSQL, most access will be programmatic only, through applications that you write using the tools and application programming interfaces (APIs) for the NoSQL database.

Relational databases have somewhat less flexibility than a multi-model database such as Redis. Whereas a relational database thrives when data is consistent and well structured, Redis and NoSQL thrive on the unstructured data that is found in today's modern applications while also providing the flexibility to structure data as needed.

Seeing Where Redis Fits

Redis is a NoSQL database and yet much more. Redis is a multi-model database enabling search, messaging, streaming, graph, and other capabilities beyond that of a simple data store.

Multi-model databases

Multi-model databases provide a way to interact with data regardless of its underlying data model.

Redis provides full multi-model functionality through Redis Modules. The use of Redis as a multi-model database enables greater flexibility for application developers within an organization.

Data storage

Redis keeps data in memory for fast access and persists data to storage, as well as replication of in-memory contents for high-availability production scenarios.

TECHNICAL
STUFF

When discussing data storage, the concept of durability becomes important. *Durability* is the ability to ensure that data is available in the event of a failure of a database component.

Redis supports multiple modes for ensuring durability, accommodating most data structures and environment-specific requirements

Data structure storage

Redis supports several data structures. In fact, it may be helpful to think of Redis as a data structures store rather than a simple key/value NoSQL store.

Supported data structures include

» Strings
» Lists
» Sets
» Sorted sets
» Hashes
» Bit arrays
» Streams
» HyperLogLogs

Each data structure has a different use case or scenario for which it is best suited. Beyond these data structures, Redis also supports the Publish/Subscribe (PubSub) pattern and additional patterns that make Redis suitable for modern data-intensive applications.

Chapter **2**
What Is Redis Used For?

This chapter begins an in-depth examination of Redis. Included in the chapter is a look at the various Redis components and how those components can help you. The chapter concludes with an example of how Redis is used for production applications.

Understanding the Components of Redis

Like other server software, Redis has several components working together to provide robust solutions. Understanding these components and the overall architecture of Redis is the focus of this section.

The server and the command-line interface

Redis runs as server-side software, primarily on the Unix-based operating systems like Linux and macOS and also as a Docker container on Microsoft Windows. Redis server is downloaded and installed in just a few steps and then is ready for use.

TIP

The installation process for Redis is fully documented in the Quick Start guide available at https://redis.io/topics/quickstart.

The server listens for connections from clients — either programmatically or through the command-line interface (CLI). Like the CLI for other database servers, the CLI for Redis enables direct interaction with the data on the server.

The client and drivers

Numerous client libraries are available supporting many programming languages. It is through these clients and drivers that you interact programmatically with data found on a Redis server.

For example, if your organization uses Python for its programming language of choice, you'll probably integrate with Redis through the redis-py package, though you have the opportunity to use more than a dozen other Python-related packages for Redis integration, too.

TECHNICAL STUFF

The clients and drivers are typically shared under an open-source license, though the license varies by project. See https://redis.io/clients for more information.

I won't list all 200 or so supported languages, but featured client libraries for several popular languages include the following:

>> **Java:** Three popular clients include Jedis, Lettuce, and Redisson, all of which serve slightly different needs.

>> **Node.js:** The recommended client for Node.js is node_redis.

>> **C#:** Two popular clients include ServiceStack.Redis and StackExchange.Redis.

>> **PHP:** PHP has several clients with PHP, but Predis is recommended.

>> **C:** hiredis is the official Redis client for the C language. Also see hiredis-vip for cluster-related C language support.

Databases, memory, and persistence

There is no formal database creation step with Redis. Like database creation, there isn't a formal table creation step necessary with Redis either. The SET command is used to create data within the current database.

CREATING AND QUERYING DATA

The SET command adds a key to the database in Redis. For example, to create a key for various pieces of furniture in your living room, you might do this:

```
SET furniture:couch:color green

SET furniture:recliner:color brown

SET furniture:chair:color: tan
```

Alternatively, you could retrieve all keys with the KEYS command:

```
KEYS furniture*
```

Note: The KEYS command used in the preceding example is not typically recommended for production usage. Use it for debugging only.

Those familiar with formalized database creation and definition may be uncomfortable with the seemingly informal process of database creation and data handling. However, it's through this flexibility that the true power of Redis is found.

Data is stored in random access memory (RAM) on the Redis server. This means that as data is added, additional RAM is used. Redis on Flash (see Chapter 4) provides a method for supplementing RAM with flash-based memory. Redis writes the contents of the database to disk at varying (and configurable) intervals depending on the amount of data that changes during the interval. Persisting data to disk ensures durability in the event of a software or hardware failure that renders the server unavailable. Other means for providing durability, such as clustering for high availability, are common with Redis in a production environment.

Identifying How Redis Can Help You

This section examines a few popular use cases for Redis. Redis has the necessary capabilities to meet user expectations for performance and features. For example, benchmarks show that Redis Enterprise in an ACID configuration is able to perform more than

500,000 operations per second with sub-millisecond latency and can also achieve 50 million operations per second with the same performance on only 26 compute nodes. The performance of Redis coupled with search features like autocomplete and result highlighting makes the entire user experience better.

Personalization with session management

A session is loaded when a user logs in or when he's using the application in order to track his activity. By nature, session-related data needs to be readily available, with low latency to meet performance requirements that users expect.

Redis is a great fit for such applications because data is available in-memory and data is structured based on its use in the application.

Social apps

End users expect real-time or near-real-time performance from social apps. From chat to follows to comments to games, social apps present a challenge for disk-based data stores. An in-memory data store gives the performance necessary for these applications.

Several features of Redis make implementation of social app features possible:

>> Intelligent caching

>> Pub/sub pattern for incoming data

>> Job and queue management

>> Built-in analytics

>> Native JSON-handling

TECHNICAL STUFF

JavaScript Object Notation (JSON) is a structured data format. By being native JavaScript, JSON-formatted data can be used directly in an app without needing to be transformed into another format.

Search

Allowing users to search data is challenging. Allowing users to search data while providing high performance is even more difficult. With other, slower data stores, secondary indexes frequently need to be added in order to provide adequate performance.

Redis in the Real World

This section looks at some common use cases for Redis related to e-commerce. For example, many e-commerce sites provide search capabilities and need to do so in a high-performance environment using autocomplete. Although this certainly isn't an exhaustive list, it does highlight several popular ways to use Redis.

Caching

Providing fast response time is more important than ever. However, responding quickly, even under high demand, can be resource intensive. This is often solved with caching.

Redis can be used as a means to cache data between the application and the backend data store, such as another relational or NoSQL database. Doing so frees up the database for other operations while also enabling user-friendly fast response.

Large datasets

REMEMBER

Redis handles caching well because of its native data types and its efficient use of memory.

The performance of Redis means that recommendations and customer analytics can be done in real time.

The use of Redis on Flash makes large dataset analysis cost-effective. In this use case, Redis Enterprise Flash is used to extend RAM.

Full-text search

The RediSearch module is used to extend the capabilities of Redis. RediSearch can work up to 500 percent faster than stand-alone search engine products and includes features like scoring, filtering, and query expansion.

Automatic suggestions based on the search are provided with RediSearch, too. All of this is done with the performance that you would expect from Redis.

RediSearch stores data in RAM and can be scaled onto multiple Redis instances.

Geospatial and time-series data

Redis, with its native geo, sorted set, and hash and streams data types is an excellent choice for geospatial and time series data. These data types might be used for location-based recommendations and promotions.

Another geospatial and time-series use case is collection of data from Internet of Things (IoT) devices. These devices and related sensors are constantly generating data and doing so in a manner where their location matters. For example, a traffic sensor noting that the flow of traffic has slowed might be able to relay the message to open additional lanes or that there is another issue that needs attention.

Messaging/queuing

A related use of Redis is handling fast-moving data. In the preceding example, if you have data being generated by thousands and millions of sensors, that needs to be analyzed and processed. It can be collected, streamed, and ingested by Redis using its native publish/subscribe mechanism.

Chapter **3**

Using Multi-Model Redis: Data Models, Structures, and Modules

ata models represent how the data is stored within a database. An implication of choosing a data model is that your application will then be tied to that model.

In the past, relational models didn't reflect the application or problem domain very well. Instead, relational models emphasize other aspects of data storage. With the rise of NoSQL technologies like Redis, the data model can be a reflection of the application itself.

A multi-model database like Redis enables the data to be represented for multiple use cases simultaneously. This means that the data can be used in the manner most appropriate for the application.

Understanding the Redis Data Models

Using a data store of any kind requires making decisions about how to represent the data within the data store. This model then controls how data is added to the database and how it's retrieved.

Data is stored in Redis using keys. Keys can be just about anything because they're binary safe. For example, you could use an image as a key. Most keys are simple strings, though.

Redis has a variety of commands for working with data of different types. A couple notable commands are encountered in this section, including SET and GET. The SET command creates or changes a value that corresponds to a given key. The GET command retrieves the value associated with the given key.

It's worth mentioning that values are overwritten with the SET command. That means if you call SET twice for the same key, the last value will be the one that is stored and retrieved.

The values that correspond to a given key can be formatted in many ways to create a data model specific to the needs of the organization. This section examines the primary data models in Redis.

Strings and bitmaps

The simplest value type in Redis is a *string*. A value can be added to the database with the SET command. When using the SET command, a key and a value are the minimum requirements in order to create the entry. For example, to create a key called user with a value of steve, you simply need to execute this command from the Redis CLI:

```
> SET user steve
```

TIP

Even though double quotes were used for this string value, they aren't strictly necessary when the value is a single word. With that, a simple string value of steve has been stored in the database and can then be retrieved with the GET command:

```
> GET user
```

Doing so retrieves the following value:

```
"steve"
```

There are numerous other commands that can be executed, and some make sense in a certain context. For example, a common way to use simple string values is as a counter. In these cases, commands like INCR (short for *increment*) can be used. Consider this example:

```
SET logincount 1
```

In the command, a new key called logincount is created and set to the value of 1. Then you call INCR on that key:

```
INCR logincount
```

When INCR is executed, the new value is returned immediately:

```
(integer) 2
```

Of course, you can always retrieve the value with the GET command:

```
GET logincount
```

Doing so returns the following:

```
"2"
```

TIP

There are numerous other commands to manipulate and work with string and stringlike data in Redis, though you can't use commands intended for numeric data on string data.

Closely related to strings are bitmaps, which are a form of string storage. Using a bitmap, you can represent many data elements that are simply on (1) or off (0). This is useful for operations where you only need to know those two possible values, such as whether a user is active or inactive. Because it can be only one of two values, you can represent that data efficiently.

TECHNICAL
STUFF

The largest size for a single string value is 512MB. This means that you can store 2^{32} possible values inside of one string value in Redis. This size limit will be increasing and may have already increased by the time you're reading this. Check the latest Redis documentation for the current size limit for string values.

There are commands specific to working with bitmaps available in Redis. These commands include SETBIT and GETBIT, which are used to create or change a value and retrieve a value, respectively. Other commands include BITOP and BITFIELD.

Lists

Lists are a way to store related data. In some contexts, lists are called arrays but in Redis, a list is a linked list, which means operations to write to the list are very fast. However, depending on where in the list the item is located, its performance is not as fast for read operations. Although not always appropriate because of repeated values, a set (discussed later) can sometimes be used when read speed is crucial.

Lists use one key holding several ordered values, and values are stored as strings. You can add values to the head or tail (called "left" and "right" in Redis) of a list and you retrieve values by their index. Values within a list can repeat, meaning you may have the same value at a different index within the list.

Pushing a value onto a list is accomplished with the LPUSH and RPUSH commands. These commands place values onto a list either on the left (or head) or to the right (or tail) of the list. For example, creating a two-item list looks like this:

```
LPUSH users steve bob
```

The list now contains two items, indexed beginning at 0. An individual item can be retrieved using the LINDEX command. For example, retrieving the first item in the list looks like this:

```
LINDEX users 0
```

Retrieving the second item looks like this:

```
LINDEX users 1
```

TIP

If you try to retrieve an index that doesn't exist, you'll receive (nil) as output.

All items or just a slice of items can be retrieved with the LRANGE command. The LRANGE command expects to receive the first and last indexes to retrieve, by number. If you want to retrieve all items in the users list, it looks like this:

```
LRANGE users 0 -1
```

Note the use of the -1 as the second value. The -1 means "to the end of the list."

The output from the LRANGE command for the users table is as follows:

```
1) "bob"
2) "steve"
```

Also notably, because LPUSH was used, the last item, bob, becomes the top of the list, or item 1. If this list had been created with RPUSH, then bob would be the bottom of the list, or item 2.

Sets

From an application standpoint, sets are somewhat like lists, in that you use a single key to store multiple values. Unlike lists, though, sets are not retrieved by index number and are not sorted. Instead, you query to see if a member exists in the set. Also unlike lists, sets cannot have repeating members within the same key.

Redis manages the internal storage for sets. The result is that you don't work with set values in the same way that you do lists. For example, you can't push and pop to the front and back of a set like you can with a list.

Adding a value to a set is done with the SADD command:

```
SADD fruit apple
```

Listing all members of a set is done with the SMEMBERS command:

```
SMEMBERS fruit
```

Given that the key called fruit exists, the command returns a list of all members in that set. In this case, the only item returned is as follows:

```
1) "apple"
```

You can determine if a given value exists in a set with the SISMEMBER command. For example, to see if a value called "apple" exists in the `fruit` key, the command is as follows:

```
SISMEMBER fruit apple
```

When the member exists in the set, an integer 1 is returned. If the member does not exist, an integer 0 is returned.

Hashes

Hashes are used to store collections of key/value pairs. Contrast a hash with a simple string data type where there is one value corresponding to one key. A hash has one key, but then within that structure are more fields and values.

You might use a hash to store the current state of an object in an application. For example, when storing information about a house for sale, a logical structure might look like this:

```
houseID: 5150
numBedrooms: 3
squareFeet: 2700
hvac: forced air
```

Representing this with a Redis hash looks like this:

```
HSET house:5150 numBedrooms 3 squareFeet 2700 hvac
    "forced air"
```

Individual fields within the overall house:5150 hash are retrieved with the HGET command. To retrieve the numBedrooms field value looks like this:

```
HGET house:5150 numBedrooms
```

The result is as follows:

```
"3"
```

Sorted sets

Sorted sets are used to store data that needs to be ranked, such as a leaderboard. Like a hash, a single key stores several members. The score for each of the members is a number. For example, if you were tracking the number of followers for a group of users, the data might look like this:

User Followers:

steve: 31

owen: 2

jakob: 13

Within Redis, this data can be re-created as a sorted set with the following command:

```
ZADD userFollowers 31 steve 2 owen 13 jakob
```

The ZRANGE command is used to retrieve the resulting sorted set. Like the LRANGE command, which is used to retrieve values from a list, the ZRANGE command accepts the beginning and ending number for retrieval. For example, to retrieve all members of a sorted set looks like this:

```
ZRANGE userFollowers 0 -1
```

When that command is executed, the members are retrieved but not the corresponding scores. To retrieve both the member names and their scores, add the WITHSCORES argument to the command:

```
ZRANGE userFollowers 0 -1 WITHSCORES
```

When that command is executed against the previously entered data set, the result is:

```
1) "owen"
2) "2"
3) "jakob"
4) "13"
5) "steve"
6) "31"
```

As you can see from the output of ZRANGE, the members and their scores are ranked by score value, lowest to highest. You can also retrieve the members and their scores in reverse order (that is, highest to lowest) with the ZREVRANGE command:

```
ZREVRANGE userFollowers 0 -1 WITHSCORES
```

The score for an individual member can be incremented by any valid number with the ZINCRBY command. For example, to increment the username jakob by 20, the command is as follows:

```
ZINCRBY userFollowers 20 jakob
```

The resulting score is returned, so in this case the returned value represents the original 13 followers plus 20 more:

```
"33"
```

The result of the ZRANGE or ZREVRANGE will reflect the change to the number of followers, too.

Another way of working with data in a sorted set is to use the ZRANK command to determine where within the sorted set a given member resides.

HyperLogLog

HyperLogLog is a specialized but highly useful data type in Redis. A HyperLogLog is used to keep an estimated count of unique items. You might use the HyperLogLog data type for tracking an overall count of unique visitors to a website.

The HyperLogLog data type maintains an internal hash to determine whether it has seen the value already. If it has, then the value is not entered into the database.

The PFADD command is used to both create a key and add items to a HyperLogLog key:

```
PFADD visitors 127.0.0.1
```

If this is the first time that the value 127.0.0.1 has been seen in the visitors key, then an integer value of 1 is returned to indicate a successful addition to that database. A 0 is returned if the value already exists.

The PFCOUNT command is used to provide an estimate of the number of unique items within a HyperLogLog.

Patterns and Data Structures

I've introduced the basic data types in Redis. But there are also common ways to use Redis, incorporating the data types that you've already seen. I examine some of these patterns in this section.

Pub/sub

Redis can also act as a fast and efficient means to exchange messages in a publisher/subscriber (pub/sub) pattern. When used in such a way, a publisher creates a key/value pair and zero or more clients subscribe to receive messages.

Creation of the channel to which clients will subscribe is as simple as using the PUBLISH command to create a value. For example, the following command creates or publishes to a channel called weather with a message of temp:85f:

```
PUBLISH weather temp:85f
```

The message is published to the channel called weather regardless of whether there are any clients subscribed. If there is a client subscribed, the client will receive a message like the following:

```
1) "message"
2) "weather"
3) "temp:85f"
```

TIP

Clients subscribe to a channel with the SUBSCRIBE command. It's assumed that the client would know the format of messages and be able to parse the messages received correctly. Messages are opaque to Redis.

Like other data types in Redis, pub/sub publisher channels can be split to create a hierarchical structure by convention. For example, creating a weather channel by zip code might look like this:

```
PUBLISH weather:54481 temp:85f
```

Clients can then subscribe to the specific zip code for weather updates. Clients can also subscribe in a wildcard pattern to all weather sub-keys, with the PSUBSCRIBE command:

```
PSUBSCRIBE weather:*
```

Geospatial

Geospatial indexing is a common pattern used for encoding data that relies on latitude and longitude. This pattern and resultant data makes working with spatial data very easy and very fast. After it's added to the data set, you can calculate things like the distance between two data points using built-in functions.

Creating a data set of locations of radio towers might look like this:

```
GEOADD towers -89.500 44.500 tower1
GEOADD towers -88.000 44.500 tower2
```

You can then calculate the distance between those two towers using the GEODIST command:

```
GEODIST towers tower1 tower2
```

The GEODIST command returns values in meters by default, but this can be changed to other measures, such as miles:

```
GEODIST towers tower1 tower2 mi
```

Streams

Streams are best thought of as similar to the pub/sub pattern, but with even more power. With pub/sub, data that is published is never stored by the publisher.

Stream consumers create a unique name or identifier for themselves. Because stream publishers store past messages, new consumers can request to receive all available messages. Additionally, messages can be marked as acknowledged by a given client subscriber.

Streams are created through the XADD command, with other commands similar to that of sorted sets such as an XRANGE command. You can also view pending messages and perform other powerful operations on streams.

Modules

Redis also has several modules available that further enhance the capability of Redis. This section examines three such modules: Redis Graph, RediSearch, and Redis Time Series.

REMEMBER

Redis Labs offers numerous official modules other than the modules discussed in this section. Some of the official modules include ReJSON, ReBloom, and Redis-ML. Redis has a healthy ecosystem of third-party modules available as well.

Redis Graph

Redis Graph is a module that implements a graph database within Redis. Graph databases provide a method for implementation of graph theory through data. A common example when discussing graph database use cases revolves around identifying relationships between social media users.

With a graph database, each endpoint or node can have zero or more properties. Nodes are then connected to each other through an edge. Like nodes, edges can also have properties of their own.

RediSearch

Another highly useful module is RediSearch. RediSearch is a full-text search engine that features document storage within Redis while enabling high-performance search capabilities.

The RediSearch module enables weighted search results, the use of Boolean logic, autocomplete functionality, and several other common features.

RediSearch can also perform concurrent queries and concurrent indexing. This further enhances performance.

Redis TimeSeries

Storing time-series data is another common task for a database and is also common for NoSQL databases. The Redis TimeSeries module is a high-performance way to store and work with data that is ordered by time.

Data stored with the TimeSeries module can be best thought of like a list but with the added bonus of having a timestamp associated with the data. Time-series-based data facilitates easy metadata retrieval and summarized data queries (such as finding the minimum or maximum timestamp, counting, and so on).

Chapter **4**

Redis Architecture and Topology

This chapter focuses on Redis in a production environment, including those elements that organizations need in order to run a highly available enterprise–grade database.

The chapter begins with a look at clustering capabilities of Redis and Redis Enterprise before looking at high availability. Finally, the chapter wraps up with a discussion of transactions and durability in Redis.

Much of the chapter highlights the features that Redis Enterprise brings to a production deployment.

Understanding Clustering and High Availability

A production environment typically requires a certain level of performance and redundancy. Database performance is fulfilled through a number of means, including clustering and sharding.

TECHNICAL STUFF

A database shard is a portion of a larger database. Pieces of a dataset are split among multiple servers, with each server responsible for a subset of the data. Doing so splits the load among the servers.

Redis Enterprise cluster architecture

Redis Enterprise has clustering capabilities built in. With a Redis cluster, portions of a database are shared throughout a set of servers. Each server within a cluster is responsible only for its own set of data.

Cluster management is performed at a different layer of the Redis cluster architecture. This means that requests can be served as quickly as they would be if the server was not running in a cluster.

Within a Redis cluster, a given server is referred to as a node. Each node can be a primary (master) or a secondary (slave) node.

The Redis Enterprise cluster consists of several components:

» **Open Source/Data Layer:** Data is stored and managed at this layer and is the same core as a single instance of open-source Redis.

» **Cluster Manager:** The Cluster Manager is responsible for management of overall cluster health and monitoring, including rebalancing, resharding, provisioning, and de-provisioning nodes, and so on.

» **REST API:** The secure REST API is used for management of the cluster.

» **Zero-Latency Proxy:** Each node of the cluster uses a proxy to provide stateless and multi-threaded communication between client and node.

High availability

Providing high availability in the case of network splits involves running three replicas of the same data simultaneously. In the event of a network failure, the two remaining nodes that can communicate become authoritative.

Organizations using open-source Redis to achieve high availability find the expense of RAM makes doing so costlier and overall more complex. Redis Enterprise provides high availability without needing a third live replica — instead, it uses a third, much smaller server for quorum resolution in the case of network splits. Providing high availability in this way avoids the need for expensive RAM, which, in any scenario, means direct cost savings.

Redis Enterprise uses in-memory replication between the master and slave. Replication with Redis Enterprise is optimized even more than the open-source Redis. Benchmarks show that Redis Enterprise replication is 37 percent faster than the standard open-source Redis.

Behind the scenes, Redis Enterprise monitors both at the node level and at the cluster level. Node monitoring ensures that processes related to node performance are working correctly. If a node becomes unavailable or unresponsive, the node watchdog begins the shard failover process.

Cluster monitoring with Redis Enterprise watches the health of nodes from an overall view and monitors for network health as well.

TIP

Redis Enterprise also supports multi-AZ (availability zone) deployments.

Running Redis at scale

From an architectural perspective, there are several characteristics found in a fully scaled and production-level Redis deployment. The key to running Redis at scale is using Redis Enterprise. Redis Enterprise makes enterprise-level deployments easy by providing many of the components needed for such an architecture.

Redis Enterprise supports both scaling vertically and scaling horizontally, and the choice is not mutually exclusive. Production environments use scaling to share the load or increase compute capability based on demand.

TECHNICAL
STUFF

Scaling up is used when there is available capacity within a server or cluster while scaling out deploys more servers or compute resources and shards the data onto those newly deployed servers.

Redis Enterprise can also scale proxies when necessary. This typically isn't required because proxies are deployed in a redundant configuration and are highly performant on their own. However, when extra capacity at the proxy level is required, Redis Enterprise can do so.

Redis Enterprise also allows for read replicas using a feature called replica-of. The replica-of feature creates another database that can then also be sharded and configured differently than the original.

Redis on Flash

Redis on Flash, available with Redis Enterprise, enables the database to be stored not only in RAM but also on dedicated flash memory such as a solid-state drive (SSD). With Redis on Flash, keys are maintained in RAM while certain values are placed in flash. Specifically, hot values are maintained in RAM and warm values in flash. Redis intelligently chooses which values to place in flash with the implementation of a least-recently-used (LRU) algorithm.

Examining Transactions and Durability

Having the ability to undo a data write in the event of a problem is key to providing reliable data. This section examines durability and transaction support in Redis.

ACID

Atomicity, consistency, isolation, and durability (ACID) describes overall architectural properties of transactional systems, as typically seen with databases, including NoSQL.

Redis supports all capabilities required to be ACID-compliant. This support is accomplished through various methods:

>> **Atomicity:** Redis provides transaction-related commands, including WATCH, MULTI, and EXEC. These commands ensure that operations on the database are indivisible and irreducible.

>> **Consistency:** Only permitted writes are allowed to be performed through the validation provided by Redis.

>> **Isolation:** Being single-threaded, each single command or transaction using MULTI/EXEC is thereby isolated.

>> **Durability:** Redis can be configured to respond to a client write to confirm that a write operation has been written to disk.

A LOOK AT ACID

ACID is a concept that stretches back many years across multiple iterations of database architectures. ACID describes fundamental characteristics that are needed for enterprise database systems:

- **Atomicity:** The ability to ensure that a write or change to data is either fully written to the database or is not committed at all. In other words, no partial writes that could lead to inconsistencies in the data.

- **Consistency:** The data is correct both before and after a transaction occurs.

- **Isolation:** Helps to ensure consistency by requiring concurrent transactions to be separate from each other.

- **Durability:** Data persistence that ensures that when a transaction is complete, it can be retrieved in the event of a system failure.

TIP

Using Redis with the confirmation for writes can affect performance. The next section discusses durability in more detail.

Durability

There are two methods for providing data persistence in Redis:

» **Append-Only File (AOF):** AOF was described in the preceding section. With AOF and the "every-write" setting, Redis replies to the client after the "write" operation has been successfully written to disk, guaranteeing durability.

AOF applies to every shard of the database and can be configured to write to the database file every second or on every write. The obvious consequence of writing to the disk on every database write operation is slower performance. The benefit is ensuring durability.

Redis Enterprise handles AOF different than the open-source version of Redis. With Redis Enterprise, AOF is optimized to increase performance. One of the ways this is done is by configuring AOF only from the slave replica, which means the master sees unhindered high performance.

>> **Snapshot:** Snapshots are a point-in-time copy of the database. Snapshots apply to all shards within a database and are used primarily for the aforementioned durability rather than as a backup.

Both AOF and snapshot, along with the enhancements available to each through Redis Enterprise, help to ensure that transactions and, indeed, the data remain durable and available at all times.

TIP

Another method for providing a level of durability is through in-memory persistence, which can be both safer and faster.

Chapter **5**
Using Redis Enterprise Cloud and Software

R edis Enterprise provides an enhanced, enterprise-ready implementation of Redis. This chapter explains Redis Enterprise and the enhancements that make it appealing for so many production workloads today.

Understanding Redis Enterprise

In a modern enterprise environment, performance and reliability are requirements of all applications. Redis Enterprise is the overall name for the enhanced versions of Redis that are focused on the needs of enterprise users.

There are two primary means to deploy Redis Enterprise:

» Redis Enterprise software can be deployed locally within your data center or cloud provider.

» Redis Enterprise can be used as a fully managed and hosted service, Redis Cloud, available in all major cloud providers (even inside virtual private clouds, or VPCs).

» Redis Enterprise can be deployed in a multi-cloud or hybrid on-premises/cloud architecture.

Both methods for deployment result in a high-performance implementation of Redis. The difference between the two is whether you manage the underlying platform or the platform is managed by Redis Labs.

Regardless of how Redis Enterprise is deployed, you receive the same benefits:

>> Seamless scaling

>> Always-on availability with instant automatic failover

>> Multi-model functionality through modules such as RediSearch, ReJSON, ReBloom, and others

>> Full durability and snapshots

>> Stellar performance

Redis Enterprise also implements geographical distribution in an active–active manner.

CAP THEOREM, ACTIVE-ACTIVE, AND CRDT

CAP Theorem states that it is impossible for a network-based service (such as a server or data shared across a network) to simultaneously provide more than two out of the following three guarantees: consistency, availability, and partition tolerance. Ideally, you would be able to provide consistency and availability of data in a way that was tolerant of network partitions, but in reality, doing so means making trade-offs between the three properties.

Redis Enterprise works with CAP Theorem properties. To ensure availability, Redis Enterprise replicates or copies data across multiple data centers so that an incoming request can be handled by any of the data centers.

Redis Enterprise must also be able to maintain consistency while keeping data available. Redis Enterprise uses conflict-free replicated data types (CRDTs) to maintain consistency and availability of data. Because CRDTs are available across data centers, data within Redis Enterprise is able to handle *network partitions,* or divisions within the network that might otherwise make some or all of the data inaccessible.

Active-active refers to a replication or application model that distributes requests across multiple data centers. Requests can be serviced by any data center, and conflict resolution is used for both simple and complex data types.

Redis Enterprise Software on Docker

Docker makes it easy to develop, test, and deploy an application by placing applications into distinct containers from which they can be deployed and tested.

Redis Enterprise can be run inside a Docker container. To do so, you must first install Docker. After Docker has been installed, executing a simple command will run Redis Enterprise within a container. For example, on a Linux system, here's the command to run Redis Enterprise in a container:

```
$ docker run -d --cap-add sys_resource --name rp
   -p 8443:8443 -p 12000:12000 redislabs/redis
```

Docker will then download the necessary components and begin running Redis inside of the container.

Though using Docker is beyond the scope of what I cover in this book, it's worth noting that the command shown launches Docker with its run subcommand. The run subcommand accepts several options, a few of which are used here to make Docker go into the background (-d), add Linux capabilities (--cap-add), and then execute a container named rp (--name), exposing two ports: 8443 and 12000 (-p).

Redis Cloud

Redis Cloud is a hosted and managed version of Redis in the cloud. With Redis Cloud, you choose the cloud provider from a list of supported providers like Amazon Web Services (AWS), Google Cloud, and Microsoft Azure. Redis is then deployed and managed for you, so that you can focus on development. It's also available in VPC environments of major cloud providers.

Redis Cloud features high availability, seamless scaling without any downtime, and high performance with linearly scaling performance. It's fully monitored, and there is even a free tier.

Redis Cloud's minimal startup cost and effort make it an excellent solution for development environments. It's also ideal for production environments, thanks primarily to its low monthly cost, high availability, and high performance.

Getting Started with Redis Enterprise

Getting started with Redis Enterprise means selecting a platform, either hosted through Redis Cloud or downloadable software. This section looks at those first steps to begin using Redis Enterprise.

Regardless of which method you choose to get started, you need to sign up at Redis Labs. You can do so at https://redislabs.com.

Prerequisites

After you have an account at Redis Labs, you can choose which method you'll use for installing Redis Enterprise: using the cloud or locally. If you're looking to test Redis Enterprise through Redis Cloud, you'll still want to install the command-line interface (CLI) so that you can access the instance after it has been deployed.

For downloadable software, you should have at least 2GB of random access memory (RAM) and 10GB of hard-disk space available for a non-production deployment.

Installing Redis Enterprise locally means selecting one of the supported platforms for Redis Enterprise. The choices include the following:

>> Ubuntu

>> Red Hat

>> Oracle Linux

>> AWS AMI

>> Docker on Mac or Windows

After you've downloaded it, you'll be able to install Redis Enterprise on the chosen platform.

Connecting

Connecting to an instance typically means using the CLI in order to test the connectivity, create an initial database, and so on. The CLI is accessed through the `redis-cli` command that is installed with the server. The CLI provides a set of commands that enable you to work with a Redis server. Similar to a CLI that you might encounter in Terminal on macOS or Linux or the Command Prompt in Windows, the Redis CLI is the work environment that is used for executing commands when not working programmatically.

If you're accessing a cloud-based instance, you'll need to install a CLI to access Redis Enterprise.

When connecting to a *remote instance* (an instance that isn't located on the same server as the CLI), the command looks like this:

```
redis-cli -h <hostname> -p <port>
```

The `<hostname>` is the name of the host to which you're connecting, and the `<port>` parameter is the port number of the instance.

Chapter **6**
A Simple Redis Application

n this chapter, you take a look at a basic application created to run on Node.js and demonstrating basic create-read-update-delete (CRUD) operations. The application is not meant to show everything that is possible with Redis; instead, it demonstrates the foundations to help kickstart your development.

Getting Started

This section looks at what you need to begin building a Redis application in Node.js. If you don't want to set up your own development environment, you can build this application using the free plan available with Redis Cloud.

Prerequisites

A simple Redis application has been coded and made available on GitHub. The application stores information about cars as an example and is meant to show how CRUD operations can be achieved with Redis as a storage engine. The application is built in Node.js. Follow the instructions in the GitHub repo at `https://github.com/RedisLabs/redis-for-dummies/` to set up the application.

Front-end application code

The primary location for the front-end code is the file called `index.js`. This file sets up the application for our use. The `index.js` file uses a Node.js HTTP server that has routes backed by Redis calls.

The remaining code in `index.js` is used to route or direct clients to the proper location.

Even though the file is `index.js`, there is no default web page for this application.

TIP

Creating a CRUD App

This section looks at usage for three of the common Redis data types: sets, lists, and hashes. As you work through this section, you might use `MONITOR` from the Redis command-line interface (CLI) in order to see what's happening.

Within the code repository, you'll find a shell script called `sample.sh`. The `sample.sh` script creates sample data that will be used in this section. To execute `sample.sh`, you need to have the Redis server and the Node.js application running.

When you run the script, it will generate sample data records by running `curl` commands against the Node.js server. You'll receive output like the following, though the values for the `id` field in the car descriptions may be different:

```
Adding cars
----------
Added a ford-explorer
Added a toyota im
Added a saab 93 aero
Added a family truckster
Done adding cars.

Adding car descriptions
-----------------------
{"id":"cjhvatfuc00005mfj2zycewid"} <-- Added SUV
```

```
{"id":"cjhvatfv500015mfj8nzqk34c"} <-- Added
    Hatchback
{"id":"cjhvatfvo00025mfjyfxuyp6o"} <-- Added Sedan
{"id":"cjhvatfw700035mfjaupal85f"} <-- Added
    Station Wagon
Done Adding car descriptions.

Adding features
---------------
Added power-steering
Added climate-control
Added car-play
Added disc-brakes
Done adding features.
```

With the sample data created, you can look at how to query each data type with `curl`.

I describe the script throughout the rest of the chapter. In general terms, the application maps verbs from REST calls to Redis commands.

You can add your own sample data or use data from another source for these examples, too.

Cars (sets)

The sample data script added a few cars to the Redis instance. These were added as a set.

REMEMBER

Sets are unsorted collections of unique members. To access them, you query to see if a given value exists.

Retrieving the members of a set through the Node application is accomplished by sending a GET HTTP request to the cars URL. This results in an SMEMBERS call to the car set. Here's an example:

```
curl http://localhost:3000/cars/
```

The SMEMBERS command is executed by the server when you make that request. Then you receive the following response:

```
["family-truckster","saab-93-aero","toyota-
    im","ford-explorer"]
```

Other operations are possible, too. For example, an HTTP PUT method (executing a SADD Redis command) was used to create the original data (in the sample.sh script). You can also execute an HTTP DELETE method (executing an SREM Redis command) to remove a member from the set.

Features (lists)

Another collection of data added by the sample script was features — that is, features you might find in a car. The features were added as a list. Reading data using the application means sending a GET request. In this case, retrieving all features looks like this:

```
curl http://localhost:3000/features/
```

Behind the scenes, the LRANGE command is executed with 0 and −1 for the indices, thereby retrieving all values. So, the Redis command is

```
LRANGE features 0 -1
```

Because lists are numerically indexed, you can retrieve based on position within the list. The application supports both start and end index, beginning with 0 for the first item in the list. For example, retrieving all the items beginning with the third item looks like this:

```
curl http://localhost:3000/features/2
```

As before, the LRANGE command is executed on the server. Instead of beginning with the 0 index, this time the command begins with index 2 and continues to the end of the list, with the Redis command being:

```
LRANGE features 2 -1
```

You can also set an end index. Retrieving only the third item looks like this:

```
curl http://localhost:3000/features/2/2
```

This time, LRANGE is executed with the same beginning and ending index (2). The full Redis command is

```
LRANGE features 2 2
```

Create, read, update, and delete operations are supported for lists in this application. To create, send a POST request (using LPUSH); to update, send a PUT request (LSET); and to delete, use the DELETE method (LREM).

Car descriptions (hashes)

The sample script added data to the hash data structure in the Redis instance. When the data was added, the first argument in the ZSCORE/HGETALL is the key, containing the unique ID. Working with hash data means creating and requesting that unique ID.

Retrieving the details of a car by its ID looks like this:

```
curl http://localhost:3000/cardescriptions/
    cjhvatfuc00005mfj2zycewid
```

REMEMBER

The unique ID will be different for your database.

When an ID is used in this manner, the ZSCORE command is executed by the server against cardescriptions:collection. This is followed by the HGETALL command. In all, it looks like this:

```
ZSCORE cardescriptions:collection
    cjhvatfuc00005mfj2zycewid
HGETALL cardescriptions:details:cjhvatfuc00005mfj2
    zycewid
```

TIP

The keys used in this chapter are very large. Large keys work well in heavily used applications in order to help avoid overlapping keys. However, you can use more compact unique IDs in your application.

You can see all unique IDs by sending this request:

```
curl http://localhost:3000/cardescriptions/
```

Behind the scenes, the ZREVRANGEBYSCORE command is executed when the call to /cardescriptions/ is made, so this will show all the items in the sorted set. The entire command is

```
ZREVRANGEBYSCORE cardescriptions +inf -inf
```

Like other data types in this application, you can also create (ZADD/HMSET), patch (HMSET), and delete data (UNLINK/ZREM) stored in hashes.

Chapter 7

Developing an Active-Active/Conflict-Free Replicated Data Type Application

In this chapter, you develop an application using the Active-Active mode of Redis Enterprise implemented via conflict-free-replicated data types (CRDT). I start by defining CRDTs and how they differ from other replication methods.

Getting Acquainted with Conflict-Free Replicated Data Types

This section provides some background on CRDTs. I start by defining them. Then I explain how CRDTs differ from other replication methods. Finally, I offer some thoughts on where and when you'll use CRDTs.

Defining conflict-free replicated data types

CRDTs are a special data structure that enables multiple copies of data to be stored across multiple locations in such a way that each copy can be updated independently. The conflict-free part is due to the fact that this data type can resolve any inconsistencies without intervention.

Looking at how they're different

CRDTs differ from other replication methods in that there doesn't need to be extensive communication between copies — or nodes — involved in a CRDT. When a conflict between two nodes occurs, the condition for choosing which data to use is not based on the wall clock; instead, it's based on a mathematically derived set of rules.

Conflicts are resolved at the database level with CRDTs and are consensus free. This resolution is done without user intervention.

The end result is that CRDTs are faster and provide fault tolerance. Application development is also easier, making the process quicker.

Understanding why and where you need them

CRDTs are valuable for high-volume data that requires a shared state. Additionally, CRDTs can use geographically dispersed servers in order to reduce latency.

The geographic dispersal, also called *geolocal servers*, enables high availability even during network or regional network failures. Disaster recovery also occurs in real time.

TIP

Several data types can be used as CRDTs in Redis, including hashes, strings, strings-as-counters, sets, sorted sets, and lists.

Working with Conflict-Free Replicated Data Types

In this section, you begin to build the application. You install pre-requisites in this section and have a good understanding of where you're headed with the application.

Getting an overview of the application

To set up a demonstration in a reasonable amount of time and with a reasonable amount of effort, you'll be creating an environment that simulates a much larger architecture. The overall premise is to use Docker containers for the simulation.

The application being demonstrated runs as a single node and also works great with CRDTs. The end result shows how CRDT-based data converges.

The application simulates a geo-replicated topology to reduce latency. It's worth noting that replication occurs across clusters and not across individual shards or nodes.

Considering the prerequisites

The application uses Docker to make it easy to see the active-active nature of the application and of Redis itself. You need to install Docker before continuing.

TIP

The installation of Docker is beyond the scope of this chapter, but you can find instructions at https://docs.docker.com/install.

The application discussed in this chapter also requires the use of multiple Redis Enterprise instances, each of which runs in a Docker container. The application requires more resources than those required for the preceding chapter. For example, the application in this chapter requires 8GB of RAM for each instance of Redis Enterprise.

The example application also uses Node.js. You may have already installed Node.js as part of Chapter 6, but if not, you can get more information on installing Node.js at https://node.js.org.

Finally, the files for the application itself are contained on GitHub and can be found at https://github.com/RedisLabs/redis-for-dummies. Within that repository, the directory /crdt-application/ contains the files for the application in this chapter.

Starting the containers

To start Docker and the Redis Enterprise containers, run create_redis_enterprise_clusters.sh.

TIP

You may need to make the script executable, depending on your platform. This typically entails running chmod 700 <scriptname.sh> from a command prompt or terminal window.

Running the script creates two network (one for each cluster) and two clusters:

>> **172.18.0.2:** Runs Redis on port 12000 and an administrative port of 9443. The administrative port is forwarded to port 8443 on your local development environment.

>> **172.19.0.2:** Runs Redis on port 12002 and an administrative port of 9445. The administrative port for this cluster is forwarded to port 8445 on your local development environment.

The create_redis_enterprise_clusters.sh script also connects the two networks so that they can communicate.

The creation script takes a few minutes to execute, depending largely on the amount of resources such as CPU and RAM available and whether Docker needs to download the image. You can test whether the instances are up and running by pointing a web browser to http://localhost:8443 and http://localhost:8445. If you see a setup prompt, the instances are working.

WARNING

Do *not* follow the prompt. You'll set up the clusters automatically using a script.

Although there is a user interface for creating the clusters, you'll do so automatically via the command line. To do so, run setup_redis_enterprise_clusters.sh.

This script will configure two clusters in each Docker container. The clusters have the sample username of r@r.com and a password of test.

WARNING

Do not use these clusters in a production environment or in an environment that may be otherwise compromised. The clusters should be used for testing only and have very little security hardening.

The final step to get the clusters configured is to run `join_redis_enterprise_clusters_crdb.sh`. You may need to change the permissions on this script, just as with the previous scripts executed in this section. See the tip earlier in this section for more details.

The `join_redis_enterprise_clusters_crdb.sh` script accesses the Redis API to join the clusters. This same task could be accomplished through the user interface, too, but using the API makes it easy.

The final outcome of the script will be to join the two clusters in a conflict-free replicated database spanning both clusters.

Testing the conflict-free replicated data type

The first step in testing the CRDB is to connect to each cluster. Execute the following command to connect to the first cluster:

```
redis-cli -p 12000
```

This command invokes the Redis command-line interface (CLI) and attempts to connect using port 12000.

If you receive a > prompt, you're connected and you can execute the following commands within the CLI:

```
SET test hi
EXIT
```

Now connect to the second cluster. To do so, use the `redis-cli` command, but this time use port 12002, like so:

```
redis-cli -p 12002
```

As before, if you're connected, you'll see a > prompt.

TIP

When you're done within the CLI, type **EXIT** to end your CLI session. This command was included in the previous example but is not shown in subsequent examples.

Retrieve the previously set test key and then change the test key by running the following commands:

```
GET test
"hi"
SET test howdy
```

Finally, connect back to the first cluster and retrieve the test key:

```
redis-cli -p 12000
```

At the prompt, retrieve the test key:

```
GET test
"howdy"
EXIT
```

If these tests are successful, the clusters are communicating properly.

Watching Conflict-Free Replicated Data Types at Work

The code example illustrates a simulated Internet of Things (IoT) configuration that tracks cars as they enter a monitored street. In the configuration, multiple sensors are simulated in order to report cars passing by to track which roads they're on and which position marker on the road they've passed.

In the simulation, each sensor can be connected to the geographically closest cluster to achieve the lowest latency.

TECHNICAL
STUFF

As simulated cars pass a marker, they're idempotently added to a set using the SADD command and then added to a hash that contains an incrementing counter (HINCRBY) to indicate how many markers have been passed.

Setting up the examine code environment

The sample code requires its own environment installed through Node.js. It's worth noting that the example code shows just one way to use CRDTs. There are numerous others, and the example commands can usually be executed whether in cluster mode or when using them on a single cluster or even in a single instance.

TIP

The instructions here give the most common example command. See the README file within the example code for specific details, updates, and notes about the example code.

From within the /cdrt-application/ directory, execute the following:

```
npm install
```

Viewing the example with a healthy network

Behind the scenes, several Redis commands are executed by the code. These commands add a set and perform other related commands in order to achieve the desired result.

The example code runs the following commands:

```
SADD all-roads {passed road from command line}
MULTI
SADD roads:{passed road from command line} {passed
    plate}
HINCRBY road-marker:{passed road from command
    line} {passed plate} 1
EXEC
```

TIP

You can view the commands in real time on the first cluster by executing the following from within another window:

```
redis-cli -p 12000
> MONITOR
```

Connect to the second cluster by changing the port to 12002 instead of 12000 in order to see the commands being executed on the second cluster.

The client can be connected to either cluster. On the first cluster, execute the following:

```
node car.js marker  91street --plate 1234
  --connection ./rp2.json
{
  "entered": "91street",
  "onRoadPreviously": false,
  "marker": 1
}
```

On the second cluster, execute the following:

```
node car.js marker  91street --plate 1234
  --connection ./rp1.json
{
  "entered": "91street",
  "onRoadPreviously": true,
  "marker": 2
}
```

Note how the incremented value is coordinated across the clusters.

Now add another car:

```
node car.js marker 118avenue --plate 4567
  --connection ./rp2.json
node car.js marker 118avenue --plate 4567
  --connection ./rp1.json
```

Viewing the roads on either cluster shows synchronization in action. To view the roads, run the following command:

```
node car.js viewroads --connection ./rp1.json
{
  "118avenue": {
    "4567": "2"
  },
  "91street": {
    "1234": "2"
  }
}
```

```
node car.js viewroads --connection ./rp2.json
{
  "118avenue": {
    "4567": "2"
  },
  "91street": {
    "1234": "2"
  }
}
```

As you can see from the results, both clusters are the same and, thus, synchronized. Behind the scenes, the `viewroads` command executes the following:

```
SMEMBERS all-roads
```

Then it executes the following for each member of the road set:

```
HGETALL road-marker:{a member from the previous
    set}
```

Breaking the network connection between clusters

In this section, you use Docker to simulate a break in the network connection. Execute the following script, after making it executable if necessary:

```
split_network.sh
```

After that command has been executed, the client software from the example code is still communicating with each cluster but the clusters themselves are no longer communicating with each other.

Viewing the example in a split network

Now you'll execute commands to demonstrate how the example operates in a split network configuration.

Run the following:

```
node car.js marker 118avenue --plate 4567
   --connection ./rp1.json
node car.js marker  91street --plate 1234
   --connection ../rp2.json
```

Then run viewroads:

```
node car.js viewroads --connection ./rp1.json
{
  "118avenue": {
    "4567": "3"
  },
  "91street": {
    "1234": "2"
  }
}
node car.js viewroads --connection ./rp2.json
{
  "118avenue": {
    "4567": "2"
  },
  "91street": {
    "1234": "3"
  }
}
```

Now that the two networks are split, the clusters no longer maintain synchronization with each other. Updates can continue on each cluster while the network is split. However, the clusters can rejoin at any time and no updates will be lost when the clusters rejoin.

Rejoining the network

Reconnect the networks with the rejoin_network.sh script, making it executable if necessary:

```
rejoin_network.sh
```

It will take a few seconds for the clusters to discover that they are reconnected, after which time the clusters will reconnect and synchronize without any intervention. All data will be converged using CRDT semantics, and no data will be lost.

Looking at the example in a rejoined network

Now let's look at the example in a network that has been reconnected after a split.

Execute the following:

```
node car.js viewroads --connection ./rp2.json
{
  "118avenue": {
    "4567": "3"
  },
  "91street": {
    "1234": "3"
  }
}
node car.js viewroads --connection ./rp1.json
{
  "118avenue": {
    "4567": "3"
  },
  "91street": {
    "1234": "3"
  }
}
```

Now pass a marker on each road to see how the data is synchronized again:

```
node car.js marker  91street --plate 1234
  --connection ./rp2.json
{
  "entered": "91street",
  "onRoadPreviously": true,
  "marker": 4
}
```

```
node car.js marker  91street --plate 1234
  --connection ./rp1.json
{
  "entered": "91street",
  "onRoadPreviously": true,
  "marker": 5
}
```

As previously stated, the example shown in this chapter is just one of many ways that a CRDT can be used. The underlying and essential elements of Redis are the same when using them stand-alone or with a single cluster.

Chapter 8
Ten Things You Can Do with Redis

This whole book is about what Redis can do for you. This chapter lists ten things you can do with Redis.

TIP

A single Redis cluster can be used to do any of these ten things, regardless of whether it's a transactional or analytical workload.

>> **Use it as your primary database.** Redis is not just a NoSQL database. It goes well beyond NoSQL to implement numerous features for today's enterprise customers. Redis is more than simple key/value storage — it provides multiple data models and multiple methods to access data.

Redis can be utilized by the entire application stack within an organization.

>> **Cache most frequently used pieces of data.** Load data from slower data sources into Redis and provide near-instant response times. Redis keeps data in random access memory (RAM) to make retrieval fast.

>> **Use it for session storage.** Session storage requires very fast response times, both for writing data as users progress through an application and for reading that information back.

Redis is an excellent fit for session storage due to its native data-type storage that mirrors the kind of storage needed for storing session data.

» **Decouple services.** Redis streams and the publish/subscribe pattern enable service decoupling. Services can write to and read from Redis streams or can publish and subscribe send messages using Redis as the facilitator of the pub/sub pattern.

» **Provide rate limiting.** Redis can be used to rate-limit users and endpoints. The high-performance, real-time nature of Redis means that tracking can be done in real time along with the users and endpoints.

» **Ingest data quickly.** Redis is known for its capability to work with large amounts of data at speed. Consuming or taking in data in large quantities and then processing it or handing it off for further processing makes Redis a great choice for data ingest.

» **Build real-time leaderboards.** Native data types that promote sorting and counting operations enable Redis to be used as the back end for real-time leaderboards.

» **Build a store finder.** Redis includes GEO-based data types that natively handle geospatial data like latitude and longitude calculations. A store finder is another use case where Redis is the compelling solution.

» **Perform analytics efficiently.** Data that needs to be processed can be stored in Redis in a compact manner. Data that may take terabytes in another storage medium can be processed in such a way that it requires significantly less resources when you use Redis. For example, probabilistic data structures can be used that then help to maintain counts, frequencies, and percentiles very efficiently.

» **Index large amounts of data.** Redis handles large amounts of data well. As an organization and its application portfolio grow, so does the amount of data. Redis has the flexibility and extensibility (through modules) to store data for multiple consumers and the performance and efficiency to store large amounts of data for established and new organizations alike.